Hurst John Fletcher

Life and Literature in the Fatherland

Hurst John Fletcher

Life and Literature in the Fatherland

ISBN/EAN: 9783337149932

Printed in Europe, USA, Canada, Australia, Japan

Cover: Foto ©Andreas Hilbeck / pixelio.de

More available books at **www.hansebooks.com**

IN

THE FATHERLAND.

By JOHN F. HURST.

NEW YORK:

NELSON & PHILLIPS.

CINCINNATI: HITCHCOCK & WALDEN.

1875.

CONTENTS.

IV. GERMANY IN FIGHTING MOOD.

V. KNAPSACK AND ALPENSTOCK.

I.

THE HOME.—TASTES AND USAGES.

THE GERMAN'S FATHERLAND

Where is the German's Fatherland?
Is't Prussia? Swabia? Is't the strand
Where grows the vine, where flows the Rhine?
Is't where the gull skims Baltic brine?
No! yet more great and far more grand
Must be the German's Fatherland.

     *   *   *   *   *

Where, therefore, lies the German's land?
Name, now, at last, that mighty land!
Where'er resounds the German tongue—
Where German hymns to God are sung—
There, gallant brother, take thy stand;
That is the German's Fatherland.

     *   *   *   *   *

That is his land, the land of lands,
Where vows bind less than claspéd hands;
Where valor lights the flashing eye;
Where love and truth in deep hearts lie,
. And zeal enkindles freedom's brand;
That is the German's Fatherland.

That is the German's Fatherland!
Great God, look down and bless that land!
And give her noble children souls,
To cherish, while existence rolls,
And love with heart, and aid with hand,
Their universal FATHERLAND.

                           ERNST MORITZ ARNDT.

LIFE IN THE FATHERLAND.

CHAPTER I.

ENCOTTAGED IN BREMEN.—THE FAULENSTRASSE.

M Y first arrival in Germany was late in August, after
a long voyage in a superannuated wooden steamer.
How long this venerable structure had been tempting the
destructive wrath of Neptune was known to few, but in
the only stiff breeze we had, which was when we were
drawing within the jaws of the English Channel, she
creaked and stretched and yawned with each new wave,
as if every bolt and brace were in a state of outright re-
bellion. To my remark to a gray Jack Salt, who leaned
most complacently against the gunwale and smoked his
grimy clay pipe, that the very deck-seams widened now
and then with the strain, there came the philosophical
response, that all good vessels are like baskets—they must
bend and give, or they are good for nothing. And, in
very sooth, that ancient craft did bend and give most bas-
ket-like. Years afterward, so I have learned, her name
was changed, quite harmoniously with our American wont
in cases of ante-mortem maritime canonization, and she

1*

was transferred to the Central American trade.   Later—
thus runneth the legend—she rounded the Horn, and did
duty on the Pacific coast in the region of San Francisco.
For aught I know, she may now be in the Chinese or Japa-
nese traffic, and never wanting for fresh paint, like a persistent old *danseuse*, to hide the wrinkles of her many
years.   Sweet be her sleep, on whatever bottom her bones
lie down to rest !

Just ten years after my first view of the flat banks, trim
gardens, thatched cottages, and quaint and leisurely wind-
mills of the unpretentious Weser, I arrived a second time
in Bremen, after a delightful passage in the " America," a
beautiful iron ship of great strength and speed.   But the
August sun was not shining this time   The welcome was
chilly enough.   Madame de Stael says, " The first impressions that are received on arriving in the north of Germany, above all in the middle of the winter, are extremely
gloomy. . . . The frontier of the Rhine has something
solemn in it." *   This is every traveler's experience, even
the cockney's, with his beard dripping with London mists.
I reached there late in the autumn ; and a German November, especially within reach of the breath of the North
Sea, means furious winds, driving rains, now and then a
gust of snow, thick furs and gay woolen wrappings, and
great patches of frosted dahlias and fuchsias.   My first
impulse was to run off with the first train to greet Herr
Registratur Sack, on the Wilhelmsplatz in mediæval and
still moated Brunswick, to congratulate him on his new
book on Chimneys, to look at the red Waterloo ribbon in

* Germany, vol. i, p. 93.   New York : 1861.

his button-hole, to get close beside his great porcelain stove, to go over the good old days when we lingered among the books of Wolfenbüttel and climbed the Brocken, to gaze out of his window upon the bronze lion which brave crusading Henry IV. put in position seven centuries ago, and then to bury myself in work, as a decade agone, in a little third-story room in Frau Müller's house, in muddy, crooked, placid, learned Halle.

But there was now a different path ahead. I was to be domesticated this time in Bremen, and passing the former half of my time in that city, and the latter in Frankfort-on-the-Main, to spend five years in the good Fatherland. The cottage prepared for us, in the quiet Steffensweg, number three, was utterly innocent of carpet, and, according to American notions of a comfortable home, of many other requisites. Friendly hands, however, had provided some heavier articles, especially an abundance of colossal stoves, and had packed away, like bricks in a kiln, in two of the upper rooms, a long winter's supply of turf from the lowlands of still primitive and honest Frisia. The process of becoming established was tedious, and, out of Germany, would have been provoking. A chief difficulty lay in the utter impossibility of matching certain portions of furniture which we had brought with us from America. As to completing a bed-room set, or a China service, or getting any thing to suit any thing else, it was simply out of the question. For example, in endeavoring to find a bedstead of proper dimensions to fit an excellent mattress that we had brought along, I soon met with disappointment. There was not a cabinet shop in that whole city of ninety thousand

kind souls and ruddy faces, which I did not visit in vain
for the express purpose of procuring a bedstead of the
required proportions. Now they were too short, apparently as much so as that from which the feet of Tom Hood's
corpulent old uncle protruded, with a titanic feather bed
poised over him and a pigmy one beneath him. Now they
were too narrow, and of course had to be rejected. The
only approach to what I desired was a bedstead of the
precise length, but of only three-quarter width. The shop-
man was out, but his wife proved a worthy representative
of her lord. I insisted that the one in question was too
narrow.

"Not at all," she declared, "we never make them
larger."

"Well, then, I wish a larger one than you make."

"You are mistaken," she rejoined, "nobody ever wishes
a bedstead of different size from this. You are quite out
of the way."

"But I really am not," I ventured. "I have the exact
measurement here in my hand. I know just what I am
in search of, and must have it."

"Now *I* know what you want better than you do.
This bedstead is just the thing. Why, it is eternally
broad—*ewig breit!*"

There was now a positiveness and determination in her
manner well worthy of her sex in its roused and heroic
moments. It would have delighted Hawthorne, who
speaks of the grandeur of a woman's face after passing
through a great ordeal, to see this individual just then.
She so overawed me that I looked in enforced silence

toward the street door for timely escape. I am satisfied that if I had stood, and shivered, and argued in that cold shop for twenty-four hours, I could not have convinced her of the propriety of my having just what I was searching for. Subsequently, a humble cabinet maker was found, in an obscure street, who consented to run all the risk of losing what little reputation he had by adapting a German bedstead to an American mattress.

Now, in this whole matter I was wrong. The expectation of finding in Germany just what one is accustomed to at home, is simply an absurdity. The Germans have as much ground for fault-finding when they reach our shores as we have when we visit theirs, except when it comes to the serious matter of open beer-gardens on Sundays. The attempts of my domestic group to sustain the American style of cooking and general housekeeping in Bremen continued about six weeks, after which time we were ready to submit to all possible gravies ; in fact, to eat any thing, and that five times a day, that our Hamburgh cook and neighbor Behrens thought proper in civilized beings.

We had been in Bremen but a few hours before hearing frequent mention made of the Faulenstrasse. We found that this was the place where we were expected to buy nearly every thing we were to consume. My curiosity was excited to see it, and soon the desire was realized, and many times. It seemed to me, after awhile, that my feet gravitated toward it spontaneously, so naturally did they carry me thither for all purchases, from a tack-hammer to a French clock. I soon fell deeply in love with the short, quaint street, the petty briskness of its grotesque market, its good-natured shop people, and the doves that sauntered up and down the old worn stones in ostentatious independence.   And why should not the very doves share in their country's glory ?   Was it not their Prussia that had just left Austria bleeding and half dead at Sadowa ?

But after hearing the story of the origin of the Faulenstrasse, I loved it and its diminutive life with more intensity.   It runs thus, as the Grimms and other good tellers of German myths give it :—

Near where that street now stands there was once a thick forest.   The trees were old, but very strong and large.   Just on the edge of the forest there lived an aged couple, who had seven sons.   The father was an industrious man, cultivated his field with care, attended to his cow, and supported his whole family by his own exertions.   But it was very different with the seven sons.   True, they had long legs, broad backs, very strong arms, and well-formed heads, and were able to do a great amount of work, and relieve their father from all exertion.   But they were drones.

"Their parents were very kind and patient toward them.   The neighbors said of the seven large, lazy boys, that they had been spoiled.   By and by, every body in Bremen—which in those distant times was only a small Saxon town—became in a certain way acquainted with the sons of the old man, and many persons made sport of them.   Even the boys in the street would say, when one of them passed, "See there ! yonder goes one of the seven lazy brothers !"

The river Weser ran close to the field of the aged father. Often his seven indolent sons would go down to the bank and lie there, under the shade of an elm, and sleep many hours at a time. In the course of a few months the sailors found them out, and when the boats passed you could have heard the tars say, "Look under the tree; there are the seven lazy boys!" But the big boys did not like such expressions, and after hearing them a great many times they left the river bank, and found their way into the great forest.

They thought nobody would see them now. So they lay down in the thick moss, talked a little while about different useless things, and finally went to sleep. They kept up this habit a long time. But when autumn came, the boys and girls went through the forest to gather acorns and chestnuts. When they saw the seven lazy sons— who were almost grown men—they laughed at them, and cried out, "Here are the seven lazy brothers whom every body laughs at. The chestnuts fall right down on them, but they have not energy enough to brush them off, or even hull and eat them." So the brothers came home again. One would have thought that they would be ashamed to let their father do all the work. But they never offered to do a thing; and when they strolled off to lie on the ground and sleep somewhere, they never came back until their good mother had prepared their meal.

One day the eldest of the brothers said to the others, "Just think how every body laughs at us. We cannot go anywhere without even the children coming up behind us and pulling our coats, and crying out, 'What lazy fellows

these brothers are ! If every one were like them nothing
would be done.' Even school-teachers, when they want
to show their scholars the evils of idleness, say, ' Look how
the seven lazy brothers live. Never be idle, for you might
become as bad as they are.' Let us go to work ! Let us
do any thing honorable sooner than permit our good old
father to spend all his strength for us.' "

All the six remaining brothers roused up, rubbed their
eyes, and laughed at what the eldest had said. Finally,
he won them over to his side, and it was concluded unani-
mously that they should leave home, and seek a livelihood
in some other part of the country. At the dinner-table
they told their father what conclusion they had come to.
He laughed at them, and said, " You have been idle too
long, I fear, to become industrious now. But if you are
really determined to do some work, which is honest and
worthy, I will give each of you twenty-five dollars in gold,
and a new suit of clothes. But you must give me some
proof that you are sincere in your professions. I will give
each one of you an ax and a spade, and you must carry
the axes on your right shoulders, and the spades in your
left hands, and walk through Bremen. The eldest must
go first, and the youngest must be last in the procession."
The brothers looked at each other, and shook their heads.
They concluded that they could not do it. Then their
father said, " If you are not willing to make some sacrifice, and permit the world to see that you intend to be
industrious in future, I can put no confidence in your
resolutions."

The sons consulted further, and actually determined

to walk through Bremen with axes on their right shoulders
and spades in their left hands. The people came out of
their houses to look at them, with such implements of
work in their possession. Some persons cried out, "The
world must be coming to an end!" Others said, "That
is the most wonderful sight we ever saw."

On Saturday of the following week the old father gave
his sons the money and clothes which he had promised
them, and then they started off in procession. Their
mother said, "They will all be home again to-morrow."
Their father replied, "Well, I am not so sure of that. They
seem to be determined to do work of some kind. I think
they are resolved to mend their lives and set an example of
industry." The brothers wandered far from home. They
hired themselves out to a manufacturer, and worked with
great energy. They were very tired at first, and it seemed
to them that they could hardly live; but they adhered to
their resolution, and finally conquered. They gradually
rose from a humble to a high position, and acquired
much property. From time to time they sent home as
much as several thousand dollars to their parents.

One bright and beautiful May morning every body in
Bremen seemed to be out of doors. The old town clock
struck eleven, and just then you might have seen seven
men coming into town on foot. They were well dressed,
and had the appearance of gentlemen. In one respect
they looked like hard-working laborers; they had axes on
their right shoulders and spades in their left hands. The
people in the streets said to one another, "Can they be the

seven lazy brothers? They are evidently not lazy now. See how briskly they walk, how healthy they look, and how erect they hold their heads! But they really are the sons of that very old man who is now so advanced that he cannot work. Where have they been all this time?"

No one can tell what an excitement the arrival of the seven brothers made in Bremen, and how glad their old father and mother were to welcome them back to their humble cottage. There was a feast in the little house, which lasted several days. When they had been home some weeks, they said, " Let us not live in this cottage. There is not room to turn around. Our parents are very old, and we ought to provide better for them. We have plenty of money, and must build a new house."

A beautiful piece of land was bought half a mile from Bremen. There was no road that ran through it, nor was there any house on it. But the brothers had a splendid mansion erected on the place, and built, with their own hands, a road, though short, through the piece of land. It ran right in front of the house. " What shall we call our street?" said they one to another. After many fruitless attempts to devise a name, one of the brothers at last made the following suggestion :—

"Much of our life has been spent in idleness. What we have lost we can never get back again. Would it not be well to warn as many young people as we can from following our bad example when we lived in idleness? I suggest that we call our street *Faulenstrasse—Lazy-street.*" And no one said nay.

CHAPTER II.

A GERMAN YEAR MARKET.

ONE windy day late in November two immense beeves were driven through the streets of the staid old city of Bremen on a raffling excursion. They were dressed off as gayly as if they had just sauntered out of a milliner's shop, or had changed places with the pied Swiss Guard as the Pope's escort on Easter Sunday. Long ribbons of the brightest colors were streaming from their heads, while their natural horns were supplemented by others of brass, which towered above the head, and were so highly polished as to fairly dazzle ordinary eyes. The stately animals, besides having two drivers, were attended by a well-dressed man, who, with pencil and note-book in hand, waited upon the residents along the streets promenaded by the party, and offered them the opportunity of taking *thaler* chances for the ownership of the beeves. He was the duly accredited agent of a needy orphan asylum, whose funds were getting low, and whose fatted beeves were sent out in attractive style to help the treasury out of its difficulty by being raffled for. There is little doubt that the odd plan for raising charitable funds succeeded ; for in a land where the amusements, if not the traffic, of the week culminate on the Sabbath, it is not likely that the beeves begged in vain for a benefaction.

This peripatetic beef-lottery was the precursor of one of those institutions in Germany which is anticipated with great interest by all the young, and by many house-keepers, who hope to wreak ample vengeance on the shopkeepers by patronizing a class of itinerant venders, and supplying themselves with many articles that will last for a year. The Year Market is held in all the German towns of respectable size ; say, from a population of fifteen hundred to the largest cities. The almanacs contain the name of every place which is honored by such a visita-tion, and the date when it occurs. The German fairs—as those of Leipzig, for example—carry on a wholesale business in the main ; but the Year Market conducts a retail trade alone. There are certain dealers who do nothing but attend these Year Markets, having selected a series which they can visit in unbroken succession throughout the year. The market lasts a week or ten days, and when it ends, the dealers immediately turn their faces toward another. Some large manufacturing firms have vending companies always in attendance at them, when the poor goods that could not be sold in a more dignified way are offered at a low rate to the inhabitants of distant towns, who do not suspect the trick. But there are many who sell really substantial and valuable goods, only it is unsafe to make much of an investment, even if one has a special taste for such a style of trade. I heard a lady say that she bought a dress at a Year Market which proved a yard and a half less than the requisite amount ; she also bought quite a supply of sup-posed linen, which was found too late to be only cotton.

Our Year Market, when I visited it, had been for some days blowing its horns, drinking its beer, singing its songs, crying its wares, and telling its mercantile falsehoods. The prevailing articles seemed at first sight to be toys, gingerbread, and music. All the streets and alleys were alive with organ-grinders, and one was scarcely out of reach of their jargon either night or day. No mansion was too imposing for their attentions. I saw them in full possession of Senator Schuhmacher's doorway, and they enjoyed their leisurely stay as composedly as if sole proprietor of the premises.

The market-place and public square were filled with booths or stalls, chiefly made of boards, but in some cases of canvas. The external angles of the old Rathhaus and Cathedral were occupied to their utmost capacity. It was difficult to see where another booth could be thrown in. The outskirts of the market were occupied by the dealers in crockery and wooden ware. The stalls on the squares were arranged in streets, where every art of the shrewd tradesman was resorted to in order to effect a speedy and advantageous sale. Some of these streets were appropriated to specialties. There was one section where only cake was sold. Brunswick had sent its quota of bakers, who vied with the Nurembergers in massive piles of honey-cake and gingerbread. No one but a German shopkeeper could devise so many styles of cake ; there was every imaginable shape, size, color, flavor, and corresponding price. What a child would not buy, an older person would ; and so the salesmen were constantly confronted by adult customers, as well as by others who were so small as not to know that their six-grote piece would not buy all the gingerbread in Germany.

As I walked through the market, there seemed to be no limit to the toys.   Here, too, Nuremberg was largely represented.   The booths were much too small to hold even a small portion of the whole stock, so that many of the toys were strung up, twisted ropewise, and hung in variegated festoons from one stall to another, around the lamp posts, and every support made firm enough to bear the weight. Irregular mounds of toys, standing in every spare foot of space, rose as high as the little folks that crowded about them, and feasted upon them in bewilderment.   There was also a dry-goods department, where the Jews from Hamburg were the chief merchants.   The poor fishmongers were pushed into the background, while in close proximity to them were the soap-venders, lamp-oil traders, and other grocers whom the aristocratic portion of the guild would not allow to occupy the pigmy Broadways and Boulevards. The stationers make a very good appearance ; cap paper and Gillott's pens—I will not say how good—were marked at little more than half the shop prices.   The photographers had galleries in convenient places, in active operation, and in the stalls where collections were offered for sale you might buy a fair *carte de visite* of a celebrity which you had been wishing to get for months.

The Tyrolese and Swiss play an important part at the German Year Markets, as they have some of the best articles.   Their stock of carved wood-work is hardly inferior to that in some of the good stores of Geneva and Interlaken.   Their chamois-skin gloves, with other neatly gotten-up Alpine articles, cannot be bought anywhere at better advantage. The men and women having them for sale are gayly dressed in their peculiar cantonal costume. The Italians, like Mignon in "Wilhelm Meister," drift all the way up from the Mediterranean to the North Sea, with a large assortment of ordinary mosaics but good corals.

One part of the market is appropriated to puppet-shows, which are the great centers of attraction to the admiring peasantry, who come in throngs from all the surrounding country to enjoy their annual paradise of cheap amusement. There are shooting-galleries, circuses, zoological collections, pictures, natural curiosities, dwarfs, giants, and magic lanterns. Much attention is shown the children— a part of the population which is never forgotten in any department of German life. Amusements for their special enjoyment may be found, such as circular railways and hobby-horses moved by machinery. There is a band of music constantly plying its art in the open air.

One Tuesday, when the clock struck high noon, the balloons collapsed, the booths were knocked to pieces, the unsold stock was repacked, and the dealers hurried to take the first train for another Year Market. We were then relieved of the organ-grinders, though their places were but too well occupied by the screeching toys which the youthful population had in its hands and at its mouth. I dreaded to think of the impending wilder turbulence of a German Christmas, to which the bustle, joy, and excitement of many Year Markets combined are only as the dim shadows before the coming events.

CHAPTER III.

CHRISTMAS IN SHOP AND AT FIRESIDE.

ONE who has not seen the Germans at home in Christmas time—of all the year the most exciting—has failed to observe them under very favorable circumstances. The treasures of love, social feeling, and generosity, that lie buried in the great German heart in golden abundance through the year, are unlocked during this festive season. The universal feeling is evangelic—Peace on earth and good-will toward men. The German Christmas is quite a different thing from the American blaze of joyous excitement, which comes suddenly and is as soon gone and forgotten. The Christmas atmosphere prevails months before the twenty-fifth of December comes. I had been living in it ever since I landed, some solid weeks before gray-bearded Santa Klaus descended the chimney. I had not been in Bremen more than a day or two before a young man showed me a very good portrait of himself and sister, saying, at the same time, " Be careful not to let father know any thing about this, for it is to be a Christmas present for him."

The preparations for this scene in a German family are of a very useful character. Articles of clothing, handsome pieces of furniture, valuable books, and similar objects, appear to form a large proportion of the presents given and received by the adult members. The newspaper advertisements embrace offers of almost every conceivable thing which young or old could desire to buy and give to a friend. There is probably no branch of trade which does not receive a new impetus; every body seems to buy, and sell, and work, for Christmas. I do not question that even the sewing-machine agents sell more of their wares during the month of December than during the five preceding ones. I was in a large piano store one day, and almost every piano was labeled "sold." The clock merchants take good care to have an excellent assortment of new gilt clocks from Paris on hand, for they know right well that if they cannot serve their customers for the Christmas season, it will be many a long day before they can recover their lost opportunity. The same may be said of all classes of dealers.

Of course, at such a time as this, the booksellers are not oblivious to their golden opportunity. Books constitute an important share of the presents given and received, and every effort is made by publisher, binder, and seller, to make them worthy a post of high honor on the happy Christmas eve. The retail dealers, particularly, make enormous profits just at this season. But, however cold the weather, commend me to the outside of a German bookstore about Christmas time, rather than the inside. You may go to almost any bookstore·in Frankfort, especially on the Zeil—the Broadway of the city—and may call yourself fortunate if you can make your way through the throng of customers, and still more so if you can get any one to wait on you within ten or fifteen minutes after you have closed the door behind you; for, be it remem-

bered, that not to close the door is an offense to both proprietor and customers. A German child is taken into the
pure air when he is a fortnight old, and spends his childhood out of doors; but ever afterward pure air is at a
discount with him; he seems to think he has had enough
of it for his life-time, and to maintain a constant prejudice
against it. The best plan is, to know before you enter
just what you wish; have but few words to say; and get
out as soon as possible, if you have regard for your lungs,
feet, and hat. For pure air, and a refreshing sight of new
books, in all departments and styles of binding, a place
outside the window, if you can secure one, is far prefer-
able. Yes, if you can secure one; for often there are
such numbers at even the windows, that you must wait
your turn for a *stand*.

The German retail bookseller takes great pride in his
window, and you may expect to see in it the very best
specimens that his stock affords. As in the toy-shops,
every available inch, from bottom to top, is utilized. Little extra shelves are improvised, which fairly bend beneath
their burden of literature. To give variety and attractiveness to the scene, fine engravings, almost always Raphael's
Sistine Madonna, and sometimes oil-paintings, are sand-
wiched between the books. Beautiful quarto juvenile
publications are thrown open at the finest illustrations,
while a globe or map peeps out among the mass. Even
the second-hand, or, as they are more appropriately called
in Germany, antiquarian dealers—Schelm and St. Goar, for
example—try to give their shops a good sweeping, and, by
bringing out their choicest treasures, and adding to them

a good supply of new illustrated juvenile books, to present as good a window as their modern neighbors. In the antiquarian's shop, books are piled up and wedged in, with here and there solitary pyramids, with a compactness far surpassing what we used to see in Gowan's old store in New York, and attracting greater and more immobile crowds than Nassau-street or Paternoster Row ever dreamed of.

The booksellers who make the best gleanings during this universal harvest are those who reduce their prices the lowest, and get the name of selling the cheapest. But how can this be known to the general public? Only by extensive advertising. Suppose the Tribune, Times, or Herald, should issue two or three supplements every day or two, filled with catalogues of all the principal books on sale at Harper's, Scribner's, Appleton's, or Hurd and Houghton's. Yet that is just what these men do. For several weeks before Christmas, nearly a whole side of the Frankfort Journal, besides a surfeit of supplements, is almost daily occupied by full catalogues of books, ranging all the way up from six kreutzer to two or three hundred gulden.

When any article is bought for a Christmas present in Germany, the utmost secrecy is enjoined. Various subterfuges are resorted to in order that it be brought into the house at some hour of the day or night when the one for whom it is intended is either absent or asleep. And while the buying and selling are going on, there is a very busy plying of needles at home within closed doors. The young are making preparations for the older members ; the latter are not at all less industrious for the former ;

the servants work for their friends, and parents and children for the servants.   Each group has its own room, and
the business goes rapidly on within the locked apartments.

A few days before my first Christmas in Bremen I embraced an opportunity to walk through some of its busiest
streets by gas light.   There were no dark nights there ;
we were too far north for that.   The natural light, with
the full glare of gas, gave a good opportunity to see every
thing to advantage.   The toy shops were the centers of
attraction to old and young.   In the large windows there
were trees stationed, with slender gas pipes ramifying to
the outmost and uppermost branches.   The many little
cheerful jets shone down against the bright faces of the
happy children, who held their parents' hands and were
looking forward to their own good Christmas tree, which
might then be hidden in some obscure corner of their
home.   The trees were hung with all manner of little
gifts, each of which seemed to say, "Come and buy me,
parents, for your children's Christmas tree!"   The remaining part of the windows was filled with other articles
of attraction, each serving as a good advertisement.

I was struck with surprise, in one instance, at the mul-
tiplicity of objects which can be presented for sale in a
shop of only moderate dimensions.   I have had some experience of the pressure of a crowd in the Cooper Institute and the Academy of Music on more than one occasion,
when the alternative seemed every moment to be, beneath
the feet or above the shoulders of the swaying multitude ;
but I do not remember to have ever seen such density of
packing as I saw in this toy shop.   The salesmen could

not answer the questions of their customers, much less supply them with articles for purchase. When once you were inside of the shop, you might ask your neighbors when you could get out, but the answer would be one in which they would be as painfully interested as yourself. The great mistake was made in going in at all. But the trained skill in storing that shop with articles for Christmas use was the great marvel, after all. Every corner that was available for the smallest object, either lying or pendant, was occupied with something or other. How so much could be crowded into so small a space, and how so many people could get into the narrow door, and be served with any thing whatever, seems still very strange to me. I looked from the street toward the upper part of the house, and found it to be one of the old style of three or four centuries ago, with gable ends, curious wood carving, and little peaked windows in front. The rooms were all lighted up, and each window was densely filled with its Christmas variety of toys as far up as the top of the highest pane of glass. The shop, with its many customers inside, and its many more spectators outside, was only one of a great number of the same class which I passed during a walk of an hour or two in the evening.

The streets were busy with wagons passing to and fro, all laden with heavy and light articles which had been bought, and were now passing on to their cheerful mission in many houses. I noticed that many new shops were just now opened, and I have since learned that, when changes are made in business, or a new firm sets up for itself, the month or two before Christmas is regarded as

the most auspicious time. The windows of the butcher
shops were scarcely less attractive than those of the toy
and other stores. The little porkers, all ready for the
spit, were dressed in the most fanciful style imaginable,
each having a whole lemon in its mouth. Why it was a
lemon in every case, and not an orange or an apple, I
could not tell. Festoons of handsomely decorated sausage
were hung across the window, and even from one side to
another of the shop. It was, in a word, not any more the
plain shop which had been furnishing your table with beef
for months, but the establishment in its holiday splendor,
to which even the slain beasts were made, by every arti-
fice, to contribute their ornamental quota.

The great center of attraction to one section of Bremen
was a store of the better and larger class, which London,
Paris, and Nuremberg had filled from basement to garret
loft with a supply of Christmas merchandise. I had passed
Dittrich's many times before, but it had never attracted
my attention. The room which is entered by the street
door seemed at first to be all there was of the store, but
on one side there was another door which led into a second
room, with which there were still others connected ; while
in the rear of the first there was a flight of stairs which
led to an entire suite of rooms above, as extensive as the
ones below. Still above this there was a third story, which
was appropriated to a similar purpose to that of the floors
beneath. Each of the stairways of Dittrich's establishment had its class of articles ; each room had its genus,
the species of which found their localities in the various
pigeon-holes, on the counters, on the walls, around the

artificial trees, or on the circular tables. The variety of objects for sale appeared endless. One department was fancy carriages, which ranged in size from one which you could easily put into your pocket, to those large enough for practical use. Then there were every conceivable style and variety of each size ; and so of other classes of articles. There was one room for hardware. Nothing which could possibly be desired for a useful or ornamental present in that line needed to be asked for in vain. A very beautiful room was that in which were the morocco dressing-eases, traveling valises, ladies' sewing-cases, writing-desks, and similar articles, which had evidently been selected with great care, and were now arranged with equally good taste.

Following a habit which every American who has been in Bremen can appreciate, I did not finish my walk without sauntering to the great squares on which the old Cathedral and the City Hall stand. The latter space, especially, is still resplendent with its gray stone, mediæ-val glory. The entire square was surrounded by the pro-prietors of different articles for sale. Here were humble venders, who were not rich enough to have a shop, but had sufficient money to lay in a stock of toys or walnuts, and thus to make use of the approaching festive season to en-large their slender resources. Some of these persons had little booths, lighted up with gay lanterns, and decorated with the most attractive articles to the young and old who passed by. A large number of poor men sat on old low chairs, with bags of walnuts and a little measure in each, waiting to sell their stock. To one of the men who sold small tapers for Christmas trees, an old woman—most likely

his companion through the many years of lowly pilgrimage
—brought a smoking cup of coffee to strengthen his weary
frame.   The joy with which he received it, and the smile
which his smoking torch revealed upon his countenance,
were a scathing rebuke to the discontent which reigns in
splendid mansions in every season of the year.   Children
and parents—the most of whom were in happy poverty—
stood in groups near the little stands, wondering at the
beauty which they saw, but evidently not envious of those
who had the better fortune to be able to spend a few
grotes for toys or nuts.

The old Cathedral was surrounded by the tree market.
There were beautiful trees, all the way up in size from
the little branch which a small child could play with, to
the great tree which would require an effort to drag through
those wide German front doors.   The scene here presented
was worthy the study of both moralist and artist.   The
sale went on busily ; the poor were as eager to buy their
small trees for the gladness of their humble homes, as
were the rich for their more sumptuous mansions.   Truly,
the old time-worn figures on the Cathedral in Bremen
never looked down upon brighter smiles, happier hearts,
or greener Christmas trees, than they did that night.

Now I know that many a person will smile at all this
excitement about Christmas, and regard it as sheer nonsense.   A great mistake.   Beyond all the external excitement and decoration, there is a meaning which young and
old associate inseparably with Christmas.   The meaning
is, that Christ came to the world, and therefore the world
should be happy.   I have seen no undue excitement, not

one case of intoxication, nothing which would lead one to conclude that this festivity is at all associated with any form of immorality. On the contrary, as far as appearances go, the religious sentiment seems to be unusually active at this very time. I have never seen more people on their way to church than on the Sabbath preceding Christmas ; nor have I ever seen so strictly a religious Sunday-school exhibition as the one I witnessed on Christmas Day, when recitations and songs, full of joy and reverent devotion, were made the prelude to the disrobing of a tree which measured nineteen feet in height, and shed the brightness of its many lights upon a happy throng of old and young.

2*

CHAPTER IV.

OUT OF OUR FIRST BREMEN WINTER.—A DASH PARISWARD.

A N American who has not spent a winter in Germany,
with the high winds from the North Sea blowing
about him, and him about, for weary months, can hardly
appreciate the gladness with which one living as far north
as Bremen emerges into spring. The extremes of cold
and heat are not so great in the Fatherland as with us,
but there are compensating evils. There comes a short
cold spell, with snow in abundance ; and then you have
rain, wind, now and then a little grateful sunshine, but
ever a perplexing uncertainty as to what is going to happen next. The weather-cocks ought all to be hurled to
the street. The Germans of both North and South say,
that in summer as well as in winter it is never safe to go
out of doors without an umbrella, except when it is raining, for then you may be sure it will stop before you get
back again.

Nothing would content the bewintered occupants of
our little cottage on the Steffensweg but a positive pledge,
which I was compelled to repeat at every little interval,
that we would go off to the Paris Exposition as soon as
April should come. And when that welcome month did
arrive, it seemed that winter still held almost undisputed
sway all along the Weser. The cars were cold, and the
out-door air still colder ; and it was only after we had

crossed the Rhine at Cologne, and were going over the fields of Belgium, that we really felt the coming in of genial weather.

.There was good prospect of finding every thing on the Champ de Mars, the place where the Exposition was to be held, in a state of utter confusion, so uniformly had the papers outside of France declared that nothing was ready, and that the whole affair gave the promise of a ridiculous failure. But there was little truth in the reports. To be sure, not all of the buildings around the Palace had been completed, neither were all the paintings or the statuary in position; but the preparations were much further advanced, taking into account their magnitude, than could have been expected. The Exposition Palace, which was in the middle of the Champ, was of oval shape, and modeled after one of the rejected designs of the Sydenham Crystal Palace in 1851. The open center around which the building was constructed was a little plot of grass and flowers, furnishing a welcome relief to the eye. The building was divided into circles. Starting from the central open space, we came first to the inmost circle of chambers, which contained the paintings and sculpture of the different nations, each ownership being designated over the doorway. Having completed this circle, we continued outward, and walked around the second one. This contained the interesting class of articles approaching nearest to the fine arts. Thus, by completing one circle after another, the outmost one was reached, which embraced that portion of the machinery that was not in special buildings in the adjacent grounds. The machinery was in operation, and might be seen to advantage by ascending the high platform, which extended with the machinery, dividing it into two circles, around the whole building. The restaurants, though a part of the Palace, opened only from the outside. Now, cut these circular suites of rooms into segments, extending straight and broad walls from the open space in the middle through the exterior wall of the edifice to the grounds outside, and you have the nations. The classes of articles on exhibition were the circles ; the nations were the *radii*.

The American department had, for some reason or other, been unduly thrown into the background. Maximilian was then in Mexico, and Louis Napoleon had gained nothing by our war. The space to which we were confined was altogether too small, and it was not surprising that this attempt to put Brother Jonathan into a strait-jacket, which he has never been used to, either on sea or land, produced a dispiriting effect on him. But our people had no ground to be ashamed of their representative art and industry in the Exposition. Our catalogue embraced a very satisfactory diversity of articles, and, on inspection, it was clear enough that these were well worthy of being placed beside the best fruits of the toil and skill of the most advanced European nations. I noticed that the main entrance to the room containing our paintings was flanked on the right by a magnificent portrait of Fletcher Harper, Esq., of New York, and on the left by one of General Sherman. Church's " Niagara," Bierstadt's " Rocky Mountains," and Story's " Marbles," were popular centers of attraction.

One morning we took advantage of an early hour, when it was raining very hard, to visit the Exposition, and enjoy a comfortable stroll through those parts which, because of the throng, it was impossible to visit late in the day with any comfort. Our luck gave us the opportunity to see the Empress Eugenie, who, on our arrival, was already inspecting the objects of special interest to her. A light rope barrier, stretched across the entrance of one of the largest jewelry-rooms, was the only intimation to persons near by that she was within, looking at the brilliant array of a French artificer, and witnessing the cutting of diamonds. There were no bravoes. She was plainly clad in a black silk dress, the lower part of which had its full share of white Paris mud. Her gloves, of undressed kid, looked as if they might have been worn for months. It was clear, that in personal appearance she had been flattered by none of the portraits in the shop-windows, or in Versailles, or the Luxembourg. Her real age was about forty-two, and yet she would not be considered over thirty, at the furthest. She was of medium height, had blonde hair, and a tolerably full face. If there was any exception to her rare combination of personal charms, it was a slight rotundity of the shoulders. To the gentleman who exhibited his jewelry to her she was very affable, and expressed her admiration freely. As she passed, there was no one who bowed to her whom she did not recognize. She was attended by two maids of honor, who, in state and rich costume, made ample amends for her *négligé* appearance. No one would suspect that amiable-looking woman of being a thunderbolt of Spanish

fire ; the defier, when the notion struck her, of the man
who made the Countess an Empress ; the great hope of
the Ultramontanes of Europe ; and the highest representative of the broken-down and doomed temporal power of
the papacy.

The Empress Eugenie had just then her secret burden
of political care, already fearfully augmenting, by the com-
plications of France with Prussia, and by the doubtful
recovery of her son. She was probably more wretched at
heart than any one who looked at her, for the clouds had
been growing very thick about the French Government of
late, and she had perception enough to know a cloud when
she saw it. It was not long, however, before she felt all
the violence of the blast. Only three years more were
needed to bring about Metz and Sedan ; to send her husband within the portals of Wilhelmshöhe ; and to make her
a fugitive by night from her maddened and stricken capital to modest English Hastings. The story of her escape
now belongs to history, and forms no dull chapter in the
record of the misfortunes of royalty. I give its details as
told by one of her two companions in flight. Her last
three days in the Tuileries had been passed without news
from the Emperor and his army, and the mob was getting
wild in the streets. She sent for Trochu and begged, in
the event of the rabble breaking into the palace, that he
would protect her with his army of defense. A bow
and a pledge—"*Pour entrer dans les Tuileries on passera
pardessus mon corps*"—seemed enough. But Trochu's
memory was very short. He sent no word of the violence
of the people, and but for the Prince Metternich, Eugenie

would have fallen a victim to their rage. Accompanied
by this man, another gentleman, and Madam Lebreton,
she reached the street, when the two ladies were left alone
in order to escape detection. Just as they entered a
fiacre, a *gamin* recognized the Empress, ran after the
vehicle, and shook his fist. But he did not betray her.
After proceeding some distance the ladies left the *fiacre*,
proceeded down a narrow alley to another street, took a
second conveyance, and drove to the only address the
Empress remembered—Dr. Thomas W. Evans, the American dentist. He immediately ordered his horses and carriage and drove with the two ladies as far as the horses
could go beyond Paris, where other horses and carriages
were provided. Only for a short distance the three took a
train. The rest of the journey to Deanville, on the coast,
was made in wretched carts. At the hotel the fugitive
Empress feigned sickness, and a little food was taken to
her, while a gentleman went on board Sir John Burgoyne's
yacht, which happened to be lying in the harbor, to inquire if he would give her passage across to England.
Both Sir John and lady expressed their willingness, and
with great courtesy placed the "Gazelle" at her disposal.

The Empress, Dr. Evans, and Madame Lebreton em-
barked at midnight; but, as there was only little water,
the yacht could not leave her moorings until morning,
and the cries of "Vive la Republique" were constantly
heard. Madame Lebreton was greatly troubled, and constantly inquired if the yacht would soon be under weigh.
Eugenie, however, was very calm, and, though ill, slept
soundly. In due time the boat reached the English coast.

Then came a long suspense—then a hurried visit to the gray and silent prisoner in Germany—and then the quiet life of the three exiles, and now of two, at Chiselhurst.

But we must return to the Exposition. To many persons the buildings outside the Palace were more interesting than the Palace itself. Some were a good distance off, and others near at hand, but all connected by winding walks, with each intervening spot of ground covered with grass, flowers, fountains, monuments, and statuary. The most splendid of these edifices was the Imperial Pavilion, which was shaped something like a flat clover-leaf, and was adorned with more rich and expensive furniture than could make five hundred peasant homes happy. There were many model buildings; such as a plan for an improved style of tenant-houses, a Turkish mosque on a large scale, a Turkish school, a Pompeian museum, and a Saxon school-house. One building was devoted to the exhibition, by work in relief, of the topography of the entire district of the Suez Canal. There was an Egyptian temple, sixty-three feet wide and ninety-three feet long, surrounded by immense columns, covered on all sides, from base to roof, by hieroglyphics, and standing back of an entrance guarded by an avenue of immense granite Sphinx. One could imagine himself at Edfou or Philæ. The Mexican temple was one of the greatest curiosities. It was a resurrection of the temple of the Montezumas. All the attendants were dressed in the Mexican costume,

The British and Foreign Bible Society had a house, in which could be seen a copy of the Bible in all the versions in which it had as yet been printed. Besides this, there

was a house where the Scriptures were gratuitously distributed in separate books in all the principal languages.
The German could get Romans at one window; the
Frenchman, John's Gospel at another; the Spaniard, the
Psalms at another; and the Italian, Hebrews at a fourth.
The Religious Tract Society of London had a house for
the free distribution of its publications. One of the buildings contained a miniature Jewish tabernacle, and plans
of the architecture of all the Bible lands. This was one
of the best-prepared and most valuable objects to be seen
at the Exposition. It would have been an ornament to
the best theological museum in any country. It was, in
fact, a museum of itself. The Evangelical Hall was to
me, however, by far the most interesting object of the entire Exposition. It occupied a central position, and Protestant services were held in it, in various languages, during
the summer. The dedication was a scene of great interest. We heard William Monod, Lord Shaftesbury, the
aged Guizot, and other men of note, make addresses. On
leaving the hall we made the acquaintance of Emile Cook,
who later, in 1873, became one of the delegates from
France to the New York session of the Evangelical Alliance, and on his return home suffered a double shipwreck
on the "Ville du Havre" and the "Loch Earn," and
afterward died through his exposure, in Nimes, in Southern France. The smile he wore when we first saw him
lost none of its sweetness by his sufferings and dangers
in the Commune, and the sorrows through which he had
to pass as a struggling French Protestant.

CHAPTER V.

ACROSS FRANCE TO STRASBOURG.

I N preparing to leave Paris for the journey homeward
and workward, the road to Strasbourg and thence down
the Rhine presented the strongest inducements. The way
winds through the section celebrated for champagne wine.
There is no doubt that nearly all the wine which is produced here is used for admixture; the greatest care and
a high price can ever buy the veritable champagne,
even in France and Germany. What shall we say of
New York? There are districts in France that naturally
produce poor wine, which is carefully made to imitate
champagne, and is sold as such, after having been passed
through an apparatus which charges it with carbonic acid
gas. In this state it is bottled, labeled "Champagne,"
and in ten minutes is ready for the market. There is no
attempt made in France to keep this a secret; nor ought
it to be one in any part of the world. There are companies
in Paris, Cette, and other French cities, which carry on
the adulteration to a large extent.

One of the most obscure villages on the short section
of the Meuse which the railway traverses was the birth-
place of Joan of Arc. The little church, as we saw it,
stood in dingy contrast with the blossoming fruit-trees
that half hide all except its humble spire. It was in a
neighboring field that the simple peasant girl served as

a shepherdess until, as she professed, she heard in the gloomy woods near by—the *Nemus Canutum* of the Romans, and the Bois Chênus of the French—the voices of St. Margaret and St. Catharine calling and counseling her to deliver France from the English conqueror, a result which was reached by the coronation of Charles VII. at Rheims. The only favor which she would accept for her services was that her native village, obscure little Domrémy, should be exempted from taxation. So, from her time down to the French Revolution, the space opposite Domrémy, in the registry-book of taxes, was filled by, "Exempt for the sake of the Maid."

In the neighborhood of Nancy, the face of the country becomes more picturesque. The number of old walled towns, in all their mediæval simplicity, increases. The hill that is not crowned with a village has at least a castellated ruin which may appropriately be compared with not the least along the Rhine. The castles are in hopeless decay in nearly every case, and half overgrown with ivy. Many of the great old archways are still preserved, and may be seen far in the distance. The peasants were plowing their historic fields in a half-asleep way, and used the agricultural implements of the olden time. The plow, which was steadied in part by an old-fashioned pair of wheels, was drawn by two horses. The women worked with the men, as in Germany. There were very few children in the fields, a fact which may be accounted for by the new stringent educational laws of France. All the men wore blue blouses.

Nancy is a very beautiful city. It has a population of

fifty thousand, and is the capital of Lorraine. The inhabitants are very proud of their home, and regard its beauty
as unsurpassed. At a station near the city a good-natured
old peasant man, clad in the inevitable blue blouse, took
a seat next to me in the car, and having offered a pinch
of snuff—which he seemed to consider an introduction—
commenced conversation about the beauty of Nancy.
" The people of Paris think their city very fine," said the
old man, with an expression of compassion playing over
his ruddy face, " but they don't know any thing about
lovely Nancy. Nancy! How could a city be more lovely
than our Nancy? Just see how it lies—right in the middle of that rich plain! Where are you from? O, I do
hope you can stay awhile in Nancy, and see the finest
place in the world !" The old man went all the way to
Strasbourg, and he proved to be an entertaining and not
uninstructive *compagnon de voyage.*

For want of time to stop at Nancy we were compelled
to be satisfied with the accounts of the Guide-book and
the old peasant, until the opportuity came to read once
more the history of the country in the " Chronicles " of
gossiping old Froissart.

People visit Strasbourg to see the Minster, which is well
worth a long journey. Having passed through the tedious ordeal of getting baggage, elbowing through a trouble-
some crowd of guides, and securing lodgings for the night,
we started immediately through the narrow, winding
streets to see the Minster. The sun was about an hour
high, and there was yet time enough to take a good glance
preparatory to a better view next morning. Nothing but

the spire could be seen above the high-peaked houses, until reaching the short street in front of the Minster. The effect of the first view is almost overwhelming. The multitude of elaborately carved figures over the deeply receding doorways, the infinitely varied and rich open stonework above these, and the magnificent spire, four hundred and sixty-eight feet high, standing in kingly majesty above all, produce an impression rarely equaled on witnessing a triumph of human skill. A stairway of three hundred and thirty steps leads to the platform, or roof. On this the guide has his house, where he and his family had lived, as he told us, twenty-three years. The last half hour of clear sunlight afforded time enough to enjoy the wide prospect. Strasbourg, with its curious bridges, picturesque old dwellings, neat little squares, gray churches of a far past day, and muddy, winding little Ill, lies below. In the east, the Black Forest extends many miles, and finally bounds the horizon. Away off in the west, the Vosges Mountains, standing out like sculpture, forbid a wider view of the Alsace ; while in the south, the Jura range may be distinctly seen.

The next morning there was a funeral service in the Minster, at which we were present, and heard the organ. The interior of this marvelous edifice is in keeping with its exterior. The marigold windows of richly-stained glass ; the graceful and luxuriant stone tracery ; the great Gothic columns, supporting their harmonious systems of arches ; the long and unobstructed aisles ; the celebrated astronomical clock ; the immense organ, with its hidden world of melody ; and that exquisitely beautiful and lonely pillar,

ornamented from base to capital with statues in stone,
among which Sabina, the daughter of the architect of the
Minster, and the only one who could complete the interrupted plan of her father, stands, leaning on her hand,
looking intently through the centuries at each stroke of
her mute and motionless stone workmen.

Severe, indeed, has been the change in Strasbourg the
Beautiful, since that calm and peaceful morning. The
bloody chasm between the scene at Ems and the Peace of
Versailles, tells the whole story. Strasbourg was among
the fearful French losses. It was on the evening of
September 27, 1870, when the white flag floated from
the Minster spire, that the people felt that they could
crawl out of their cellars and caves for the first time with
safety for six weeks. For thirty-one days the terrible
iron hail had hurtled on roof and cobblestones. The first
number of the German official paper published in the city
after its surrender contained a paragraph of appalling interest, namely, the number of shots fired by the Germans
into the city during the bombardment. Two hundred
and forty-one guns were employed by the besiegers ; on
the Prussian side, 30 long, and 12 short, rifled twenty-
four pounders, 64 twelve-pounders, 19 fifty-pounders, 20
twenty-five-pounders, 30 seven-pound smooth mortars ;
on the Baden side, 4 twenty-five-pound mortars, 6 sixty-
pound mortars, 16 rifled twelve-pounders, 16 rifled twenty-
four-pounders. From these 241 guns, 193,722 missiles
were cast into the city, 162,600 from the 197 Prussian
guns, and 31,122 from the 44 Baden guns.

Altogether, it is estimated that the bombardment of

Strasbourg cost the Germans about two millions of thalers, every shot representing the worth of twelve thalers. The actual bombardment lasted thirty-one days ; the average number of missiles sent each day into the city and fortress was 6,249 ; in every hour, 269 ; in the minute, from 4 to 5. The total number of houses destroyed was 600 ; inhabitants killed, 300 ; wounded, 2,000 ; homeless and breadless citizens, from 10,000 to 12,000.

On the 21st of August preceding the surrender, public service had been held for the last time in all the churches ; then these were either closed altogether, or only served to shelter the helpless and destitute. But the people showed a disposition for prayer-meetings ; and one was organized on the 4th of September, which continued on week-days until the surrender of the city. On the very first Sunday of the service in St. Thomas's church, a shell struck the chief door a few minutes before the close of the worship, and on the following day one fell directly within the church.

Singularly enough, almost the very first shells that fell into the city destroyed the edifices of learning and the rich libraries. On the second night of the bombardment, a bright light overspread the whole city, changing night into day. A thrill of horror pervaded the entire population when it was known to proceed from the New Church, formerly the Dominican Church, but since 1868 the chief place of Protestant worship in Strasbourg. This was the scene of Tauler's memorable sermons, of Hedia's defense of the doctrines of the Reformation, and, later, of the eloquent utterances of Blessig and Redslob. Even

the solid old walls, for the most part, fell, and not a trace
was left of altar or pulpit, of the remarkable paintings on
the walls, or of Silbermann's celebrated organ.   Tauler's
monument and the tombs of Blessig and Redslob were
almost the only objects that escaped the flames.   In the
choir of the New Church were the two great libraries of
the city—the Public Library and the Seminary Library—
and of both these nothing has been left but a pile of cin-
ders.   A friend, one of the first to enter the city with the
German troops, has given me, as a *souvenir,* a few charred
leaves from a rich vellum missal.   The tracery is still very
distinct.   On the same night that the Library burned, the
finest houses in the city fell before the fury of the bombs.
The Aubette, situated on the Kleber Place, containing the
city Museum of Paintings and Sculptures, fell a victim to
the flames.   The Minster alone remained, and though
many sad traces of shot and shell are visible, the walls and
spire of the finest complete specimen of Gothic art in the
world are still standing.   On the night of the 25th of
August it was on fire, but, by great exertion, was nevertheless rescued.

M. Colani was the great light of the Protestant Theo-
logical Seminary, which adjoined the place where the St.
Thomas Church stood, and, in part, was likewise burned.
I had become acquainted in various ways with his the-
ology, but chiefly through his " Revue de Théologie."
The spirit of this review may be inferred from the title
of the first article in one of the numbers for 1867 : " The
Pretended Discoveries of M. Tischendorf."

M. Colani is one of the leaders of French Rationalism, or

" New Theology," as its adherents term it. On the morning when I heard him, he was lecturing on Moral Philosophy. His lecture-room might hold seventy-five students, but there were but twenty-five present. Some took full notes, but others only made a stroke of the pen now and then. M. Colani looked as if yet on the sunny side of forty ; he had coal black hair, a fine eye, and a very fine expression. He probably had a brief before him, but did not use it. His voice was not monotonous or harsh. He rather talked than lectured, and looked at the students at his left nearly all the time.

M. Colani has exhibited great energy from boyhood. When very young, he hoped to be professor in Strasbourg, and he worked for it. There was strong opposition to him, but at last he carried his point. He is a popular preacher, perhaps the best of all the New Theologians. Poor in boyhood, he has fought his way up to an easier life. As for M. Colani's capacities and pluck, he deserves high praise ; but as to his mistaken theology, the storms of time will serve it no better than they have treated all the other pasteboard houses that his theological ancestry have planned and reared.

3

CHAPTER VI.

NORTHWARD BY THE RHINE.

THE northward railway from Strasbourg, along the west bank of the Rhine, is in full view of the Haardt and Vosges Mountains, and sometimes winds close under their renowned peaks. There is no guide-book which does even half justice to the section of this road, which begins at the outskirts of the plain in which Strasbourg stands and terminates at Neustadt, where the road runs eastward and leaves the Rhine no more. This is but a short portion of the whole distance from Strasbourg to Bingen, where the real beauties of the Rhine begin, and where it first becomes actually necessary to take the boat. But there is combined in it such a pleasing variety of scenery and historical associations that when one once gets home he regards it rather as a valuable casket which he has brought with him, than as an immovable range of castellated mountains and beautiful Swiss-like vales, almost every foot of which seems to have its place in history.

In the olden times the Haardt and the Vosges served as a mountain barrier for both the Germans and French, who contested it in turn from century to century, and only ceased to fight when they had well-nigh eaten each other up. At every short distance some new peak, with its extensive ruins of a castle erected on the still older foundations laid in the Roman period, starts up suddenly into view

—an ivied and tottering witness of the long-past and almost stagnant centuries of romantic but cruel glory. Some of the towns at the base of the mountains were so often besieged and retaken that they never knew what security was. Landau, for example, has been an object of contest in every great European war, from the fifteenth century; and its history is little more than a succession of sieges, blockades, bombardments, captures, and surrenders. During the Thirty Years' War it was taken eight times by the troops of Count Mansfeldt; by the Spaniards, Swedes, Imperialists, and French. Its history since then has been but little more peaceful.

There are several important ruins whose history, if written at length, would require many a page. But there is none that can be regarded with greater interest than the Castle of Trifels, which was once the prison of Richard Cœur de Lion. The storms of war and time have broken down stone after stone of the thick walls and compact archways, and the only tolerably perfect fragment left is the one square tower, which stands out clearly in front of the dark green background of the Haardt. The subterranean dungeon in which the imprisoned king was confined, and watched night and day by guards with drawn swords, is still pointed out. First captured by the treacherous Leopold of Austria, and basely sold by him to the Emperor Henry VI. for thirty thousand marks of silver, he was kept a prisoner in the Trifels dungeon from 1192 to 1194. The story of his release is one of the most romantic in history. His faithful minstrel-friend, Blondel, went from prison to prison, with- harp in hand, hoping somewhere to learn of the lion-hearted king. At last he came to the Trifels, and playing the songs of England's merrier days, the royal troubadour responded, and thus told England and his jealous brother John that he expected to wear the crown of the Plantagenets again. The King of France wished to have him kept perpetually in prison, but the imperial jailer, Henry VI., was compelled to release him on terms agreed upon by England. A ransom of one hundred and thirty thousand marks of silver was the price of his liberation.

The Castle of Trifels has been the prison-home of many other royal captives. It was always a favorite residence of the German emperors, and was for a long time a place of combined magnificence and strength. Frederic Barbarossa, as well as many of his predecessors and successors, held his court here, and the regalia of the empire were deposited here, as the securest place to be found. Ever since the Thirty Years' War, when it was taken by the Swedes, it has been a ruin. The walls of the donjon are very thick, and forty feet high. The chapel has been stripped, and its marble pillars placed in the church of a neighboring town. The ruins stand fourteen hundred and twenty-two feet above the level of the sea, and command a fine prospect of the surrounding country.

Our road emerged from the interesting and romantic mountain section as suddenly as it had entered it. By and by the lofty Königsstuhl, rising high up to the eastward, called to mind the finest of all the castles—that of Heidelberg—lying at its base. Passing by Mannheim, we were soon in Worms. The Luther elm, about a half mile west of the city, is still standing. While resting on the seat around its great trunk, one hot and dusty summer afternoon, in the student days of auld lang syne, a plain peasant told me the tradition of the tree : that Luther, on his way to the Diet at Worms, was met at that spot by the friends who told him that if he went into the city he would be killed ; and that he replied, " I will go to Worms though there are as many devils within its walls as there are tiles on its houses ! " " The Reformer had a little riding-switch in his hand," continued the peasant, " that he had pulled from a tree in the Thuringian Forest, through which he had passed. He quietly stuck it into the ground, and said, ' As this little switch will become a great tree, so will the Protestant Church in time become very great.' "

We had a couple of hours to take a hasty view of Mayence, which I have since supplemented by several visits. The old Cathedral is one of the most gloomy churches conceivable. It is very large, and its history, dating from the tenth century, is interesting ; but the miniature Virgin Marys and the crucified Saviours in its frequent altars were dressed off in such fanciful baby-clothes, faded paper flowers, and dusty tinselry, that one scarcely knew which was the more disgusting, the heathenish idolatry or the ridiculous taste. The floor consists largely of burial slabs, the inscriptions on which are nearly worn off by the roughly-shod soldiers who have been quartered there in war-time, and by many a dead generation of worshipers. The tablets around the church are very legible ; one of these is to the memory of Charlemagne's third wife, Fastrada. Through the " beautiful doorway " we passed into a large court, one side of which was limited by the church, and the other three sides were surrounded by cloisters. The colonnade around the cloisters gave them an Italian appearance. The broad stone floor of the cloisters, like that of the church, was nothing but closely-placed slabs, covering the dust of hundreds of dead and forgotten people, who were known at their day for their devotion to Roman Catholicism or their bravery on the battle-field.

About dusk we reached Bingen, on the Rhine, where we left the cars and selected a hotel for the night. The moon shone clearly down on the ruined castles opposite, and on the little square Mouse Tower, in the middle of the river, whose legend has been beautifully rendered by Southey in his poem on the "Tradition of Bishop Hatto." Forgetful of the long journey of the day, and also of the remaining weariness from a fortnight's constant walking in Paris, we could not leave the banks of the Rhine at Bingen until late in the night. The swollen waters foamed and hissed as they broke against the sluggish boats nestling along the river-side. One by one the lights in the houses were put out, and the town soon became as quiet as a village of the dead. It was a rich feast we had, watching the moonlit Rhine until far into the night. When we returned to the hotel, Boots, whose highest idea of propriety was that a man should go to bed at an honest hour, and pay him a good *trinkgeld* on leaving, gave us a very disapproving welcome. He saw no sense in our errand to Bingen. But poor Boots had never read Simrock's "Legends of the Rhine," nor Victor Hugo's "Rhine," nor any history of Father Rhine.

The next morning we took the first boat down the river.
The steamer was not equal to our "Dean Richmonds,"
"Daniel Drews," or Sound boats.   The morning mist
half hid for awhile some of the highest terraces along the
mountain banks of the river, but it obscured no castle,
and soon disappeared before the bright sun.   It required
a careful look-out in order to single out the castles as we
quickly glided by them.   Rheinstein is one of the best
preserved.   It stands on the sharp point of a rock, and
has been restored to its original shape.   Then came the
picturesque, turreted ruin of Sonneck ; the Devil's Ladder,
crowned by the Castle of Nollingen ; Stahleck, whose lofty
Gothic, pointed windows still retain in a perfect condition
the most delicate tracery ; the Pfalz, rising like a water-
deity from the middle of the river, where Louis le Débon-
naire retired to die, "lulled by the soothing music of the
gurgling waters ;" the Castles of Gutenfels, Schönberg,
Reichenberg, the Cat, and the Rheinfels ; then Lahneck,
and, last before reaching Coblentz, Stolzenfels, (Proud
Rock.)   Opposite Coblentz stands the German Gibraltar,
Ehrenbreitstein, (Honor's Broad Stone.)   Below Coblentz
are the Castles of Hammerstein, Rheineck, Rolandseck,
and the famous Drachenfels, (Dragon's Rock.)   Each of
these castles, and many of the lesser ones which I have
not named, have a very interesting history, which it would
require volumes to give in detail.   But it is the same old
mediæval story of love, hate, war, plunder, secret murder,
and occasional self-sacrifice.   There is a philosophy and
progressive utility in history, we must all grant ; but
the man who can prove how these robber-knights of the

Rhine have contributed to the fund of human development
deserves a prize from the French Academy.   But who can
be utilitarian in the presence of such rare natural beauty
and rich historical associations ?   Rather, let us sing with
Planché, the tenderest of all Rhenish minstrels :

" Thy scenes, forever rich and new ;
Thy cheerful towns, thy Gothic piles,
Thy rude ravines, thy verdant isles ;
Thy golden hills with garlands bound,
Thy giant crags with castles crowned !

" The Rhine ! O where beneath the sun
Doth that fair river's rival run?
Where dawns the day that on a stream
    Can in such changeful beauty shine,
Outstripping Fancy's wildest dream,
    Like yon green, glancing, glorious Rhine?

" Born where blooms the Alpine rose,
    Cradled in the Boden-see,
Forth the infant river flows,
    Leaping on in childish glee ;
Coming to a riper age,
    He crowns his rocky cup with wine,
And makes a gallant pilgrimage
    To many a ruined tower and shrine.

" Strong and swift, and wild and brave,
On he speeds with crested wave ;
And spurning aught like check or stay,
Fights and foams along his way,
O'er crag and shoal, until his flood
Boils like manhood's hasty blood."

We stopped twelve hours at Bonn, visiting the University, whose buildings had once been a palace ; its magnificent library ; its valuable museums ; the Minster ; the
squares ; and other places of interest.   Professor Lange, the
author of the " Bible Work," and I know not how many

other books, lives in a plain, modest dwelling in the newer
part of the city. I had a special interest in seeing him, for
I had long been translating his " Commentary on Romans,"
and breaking his sesquipedalian periods into many fragments. He lives within unpleasant hearing of the railroad
whistle, but as he is a man of progressive nature, and knows
how to push his way well through the great theological
crowd of Germany, he does not despise proximity to the
symbol of modern speed. He enjoys the good fortune to
have a daughter who knows where every book in his library belongs, who is the only one permitted to touch the
theologian's books and papers, and knows enough of her
father's business, studies, and plans to aid him by her taste,
industry, and reliable fidelity. We saw in the University
the lecture-room where Lange reads. The desks and seats
are ink-covered and mutilated to a degree worthy our most
successful congressional whittler. Let any one who would
form a correct idea of the contentment of the learned men
of Germany, walk into this lecture-room and see for himself
that the greatest commentator in Europe reads his lectures
to an eager auditory from a diminutive desk no larger than
the frail stand which supports a chorister's note-book, and
sits meanwhile on a narrow, unpainted, three-legged stool,
which is so uncomfortably gauged as to make its occupant
neither sit nor stand, but do half of both. How Lange, or
any man but an acrobat, can keep his equipoise on such a
nondescript stool, and read from such an aspen-leaf desk, is
more than I can easily imagine. But of his doing it, the
well-used and antiquated appearance of both are ample
proof.
3*

CHAPTER VII.

MEALS AND SERVANTS.

N O stranger can reside in Germany for a considerable length of time, and form even a moderate acquaintance with the citizens, without becoming impressed by the contentment, frugality, and union usually reigning in the German domestic circle. The family of many a man doing a large business, and moving in society of the highest respectability, often occupy but one floor, and every room is furnished with great simplicity. One seldom observes a disposition to occupy the whole of a large house. Just enough rooms to satisfy every requirement, and they generally much smaller than Americans are accustomed to, are all that are desired. A man's business may increase every year, and yet he does not seem to be troubled with the thought of getting out of his modest apartments into larger ones, or of buying a house for its entire occupation. The disposition, on the increase of wealth, to enter a more aristocratic circle by buying a stately mansion on a fashionable street, beautifying it with costly furniture, giving great entertainments, and appearing every afternoon with a grand equipage, is not a part of the German's character. If he indulges in all these luxuries on any thing less than an immense fortune, the presumption is, that either he or his wife has been to America. The first thing a wealthy German thinks of—unless his tastes elevate him

quite above material pleasures—is to store his cellar with
wines of the oldest vintages, and to surround himself with
an abundance of servants.

The breakfast is very simple—indeed, it is never called
breakfast, but only *coffee.* Not an inch will the real German move from his house, or scarcely in it, until he has
had his coffee, which is accompanied by a biscuit or two,
without butter. The scholar will not open a book, or
take up his pen, until he has had this light repast. At
ten o'clock, a lunch of bread and cheese, or something of
a similar character, is generally taken. The dinner, invariably introduced by soup, consists of substantial and
nutritious dishes, and closes with bread and cheese. In
the middle of the afternoon coffee is again taken, and a
light tea, at about half past six, closes the meals of the
day. In summer afternoons many families take their
coffee in little arbors in the front garden. The garden
may be very small, but, by dint of management, enough
of its narrow dimensions are subsidized into space for a
little table, surrounded by half a dozen seats, over which
rises a vine-covered lattice. Where there is no spare
ground, but the veranda reaches the street, even one end
of the veranda itself is often divided into a little room,
which is half screened from the street by some ingenious
device, and supplied with chairs, table, and pictures.
These pleasant little nooks are usually occupied a large
part of the afternoon by the ladies, in pleasant summer
weather, who there converse, sew, sip their coffee, and enter-
tain their friends, and, in the evening, are joined by the
gentlemen, on their return from their places of business.

J. Ross Browne, in his "American Family in Germany," is the only author I know of who does justice to the servants. The German servant is regarded in America as more nearly perfect than one of any other nationality. There never was a greater illusion. From the time an American lands on the Continent, the probability is that the difficulty in obtaining good servants will be found just as great there as in America. We have never had poorer domestics than during our German residence. I have certainly heard as many lamentations over inferior ones on that side of the Atlantic as on this, during an equal period. The truth is, that a large class of the best servants there lay by their savings for many years, and no sooner do they gather up enough to pay their passage, than they sail for America. When they reach this country they immediately think of independence and matrimony. Both the jewels that we brought home from the Fatherland with us formed intimacies on shipboard with emigrant men they had never seen before, and the result was, that they lived with us but a month after reaching this country.

The frequent and sudden changes of servants in American families are not known there. The time for them to enter or leave a place of employment is the first of April or the first of October, but the hiring goes on all through the year, and many families engage their new servants six months, or even a year, in advance of the time when they are expected to enter upon service. If your cook gets angry and leaves your premises without giving you three months' warning, she can be at once arrested and put in prison. If you discharge her without giving her three months to get a new home, she can make you pay her full wages and board for that length of time. Thus, nothing is gained on either side by the premature sundering of relations, and both parties are compelled, in self-defense, to exercise great forbearance.

The wages of a servant doing general house-work in a small family average from three to six thalers a month. This has the appearance of being a small sum, but, if all the perquisites are taken into consideration, there is little difference between the wages there and in New York.

I will mention a few of these perquisites, though it must not be understood that the category is by any means exhausted. Just as soon as you hire a girl for work in your family, you must give her a thaler to bind the bargain. Then, as soon as she enters your service, you must pay two thalers to the hospital, which is conducted very well, and whither she is to be taken, free of further charge, in case of sickness. If you are invited out to an entertainment, you are expected to leave a thaler in the hand of the domestic who was the first to welcome you at the door, and the last, after finding your hat and coat, to see you from it. When Christmas comes, you are further expected to give a sum ranging from five to twelve or fifteen thalers, accompanied with a present from each member of the family. When the Year Market arrives, any less present than a new dress is not considered respectable. Every time a new " olive-plant " takes its place in your domestic circle, you must give the aforementioned individual a new dress, and, no matter how many servants may be in your employ, each one must receive the same favor. If the servant is the

lucky individual to see your child's first tooth, nothing but
a dress, or its equivalent, is regarded a worthy remuneration for the valuable discovery.   If this present is with-
held, the child to whom the tooth belongs is foreboded, at
least by *one* individual, never to prosper.

In addition to these things, the servant in your employment gets fees from certain tradesmen.   If she goes to
the baker for bread every day, she receives a percentage,
for her bringing it saves his sending it.   When New-
Year's Day comes, the accumulated bills for the whole of
the past year begin to rain in on you for payment.   If any
thing is bought after that day, and it is not paid for on the
spot, the German tradesman does not ask for his money,
nor does he seem to want it, until the following January,
when the bill comes.   By the middle of January, when all
the bills have been brought in, it is not respectable for the
person having to pay them to take them himself and settle
them ; so, to save your credit, you give them to your servant, who arranges the whole matter, and brings you back
your receipts.   For this service she receives a percentage,
at the option of the tradesman.   A butcher, for instance,
pays to the girl settling his bill at least one per cent., and
so with the baker, and the rest.

It is very plain, from this arrangement, that the motives
for extravagance and wastefulness on the part of servants
are more strongly appealed to than those of economy.
But, however great the sum you wish to pay out, there
need be no fear of intrusting the money with the bills in
such hands for settlement.   Whatever temptation to dis-
honesty may arise is checked by stringent police regula-

tions. If a servant leaves home without the consent of her employer, she only gets more inextricably involved in a net-work of trouble with every step she takes. She cannot even ride on the cars without a traveling-pass, and this would be impossible to obtain if her record was not perfectly clear where she had been employed.

In consequence of the large number of perquisites which the German servants receive, the whole of the wages, and often some of the money received as presents, can be placed in the savings-bank. Many of the German servants never expect to lay out one cent of the money received as wages. The attention of a number of wealthy Germans has been directed to the wants of superannuated and infirm servants, and, in a number of German cities, there is a special fund for their relief.

CHAPTER VIII.

OTHER SHADES OF GERMAN LIFE.

A PROMINENT thing that strikes the attention of an American in Germany, when he begins to get a little insight into the life of the people, is the equality and sympathy existing between parents and children. There is no country where parents take more pains, and occupy more time, to enter into the very hearts and lives of their children, than there. They make them acquainted very early with their plans, talk with them as to older people, never go on an excursion or journey without them, and search every-where for whatever will minister to their amusement and instruction. In no home could I sooner expect to find a father turning himself into a donkey, a horse, an elephant, or a barrel on his parlor floor, for his children to bridle him, ride him, spur him, roll him over, or do with him what they please, than in a German one—and the clergyman's as soon as any other. There are probably five juvenile household games in Germany to one anywhere else, and the parents exercise a wise discretion by having frequent entertainments for their children, and providing every thing possible for the amusement of all, to make their home the most attractive spot on earth to the little folks. The child that asks a question is not met with a blurt answer, but with such a reply—as pleasant and instructive as the parent knows how to give—as naturally promotes other inquiries and gives stimulus to the mind.

One of the causes of the equality between the old and young lies in the fact that the child—at any rate the eldest boy—is expected to follow his father's business, and must early share his plans. The same house, the same employment, and I should not at all wonder if sometimes the same generations of customers, are identified with the same family and name, from century to century, in defiance of changes of governments. If Luther and Melanchthon should rise from the stone floor of the old Castle. Church in Wittenberg, and take a shopping stroll together, it would not be unlikely that they could buy books, stationery, clothing, and groceries, and get a large class of wants supplied, at about the same shops that they had patronized three hundred years ago.

But there is a far deeper cause—the Germans love children, and the more they have the greater their joy. This was the case as long ago as the time of Tacitus, when they were in their barbarous period, and has been declared by historians and expressed in legislation at various intervals since then.* So soon as another child is added to the number, the father is expected to communicate by letter the fact to all his near and remote relatives and friends, and in due time he has every reason to expect congratulatory letters from them in return. The act is stated in

---

* Numerum liberorum finire, aut quemquam exagnatis necare, flagitium habetur: plusque ibi boni mores valent, quam alibi bonæ leges.—*De Moribus Germanorum*, cap. xix. Compare the many safeguards provided for the young by the Salic law. Tit. xxviii. De Homicidiis Parvulorum.

the papers, and then more letters come. The little
stranger is fairly smothered with presents. When the
baptism comes, which is expected to take place within a
very few weeks after birth, a great feast is given, and
friends from far and near come. Each is expected to
bring a gift of some kind, usually money, which is immediately put out at compound interest for the future
benefit of the little recipient. The pastor makes an address, the Bible is read, prayer is offered, the rite admin-
istered, prayer again, and then eating and drinking and
conversation.

One of the beauties of all German festivities is the
early hour at which they are held. Places of amusement
are opened early in the evening. Concerts and lectures begin at six, or thereabouts, and the theater-pro-
grammes announce the performances to begin at nearly
the same time. The streets are quiet at ten. When
the German returns from any public place of literary,
musical, or other entertainment, he takes a meal before
sleeping. I have seen hearty meals enjoyed late at night,
just before retiring, and asked myself the question:
" What on earth must these people dream about?" Yet
the next morning they were up as soon as I, and as hard
at work, too, but taking only their cold biscuit and cup of
coffee for their breakfast. They have the art of digesting asleep, physiology to the contrary notwithstanding.
Two lunches and three meals a day are the German rule
—not so much at once as we Americans consume, but
about as much in the long run. The German eats less
meat than the American. No dinner is regarded complete

without beer or wine. Bread is always supplied by the
baker, usually twice a day. We did not eat a hot biscuit
for five years, less beeause we did not want the article,
than because no bakcr could, or would, supply it. Baking
is a flourishing and lucrativc business. Once I told an
enterprising young bakcr that he ought to go to America,
for he could make his fortune there.

" Not I," he answcred ; " the business is not respectable
enough there ; for thc bakers only make cake, and the
people bake all their bread at home ! "

But little confectionery is uscd in Germany ; ehildren
do not get aeeustomed to the taste. Fruit cake and pound
eake are very seldom seen, and only on festive oceasions
does even light cake find its way to a Gcrman tablc.

In Frankfort all our milk was supplied by little carts,
with only a few eans, drawn by donkeys. In some towns
it is drawn to eustomers' doors by dogs. Women generally servc it out.

The art of kecping a hotcl and condueting a shop is
earried to great perfection. A lady from Europe, who
was once in New York, told me that it seemed to her,
whcn shopping in our metropolis, that all the clerks werc
" angry with her." In Europe, and particularly in Germany, the customer is treated with the greatest suavity
and attention. Every eare is takcn that your exact want
be supplied, so that you come again, and keep coming.
If you buy nothing, there is seldom the least change in
the shopkeeper's demeanor. The person who has waited
on you generally comes from behind thc counter, attends
you to the door, and closcs it after you—and this whcther

you buy or not. All parcels must be sent to your home. If you buy a quire of paper, the shopkeeper will insist on sending it to your house. At least, such has been my experience. It is not considered refined to carry a parcel at all. An umbrella or cane is the most that a gentleman is expected to burden himself with. I was a dull scholar in conforming to this custom, and often paid the penalty for carrying home a little package by having even the school-children look at me in wonder. You are expected to take off your hat on entering a shop, and keep it off until you leave. You are treated with marked disapproval if you enter a banking-house, or any police or government office of any kind, with undoffed hat.

The shops are generally conducted by young women. I suppose that nine tenths, at least, of the shopkeepers of Frankfort are women, and that they do their work well no one can doubt who goes to buy. The marketing is done by the ladies. A man is never expected to do it—only his wife. But Americans will never learn this.

On taking up your residence in a German town or city, you are expected to choose your own society. You must make the first call always, or you will get none. But that first call is very soon acknowledged. Persons who are only on a formal and simply occasional visiting acquaintance with you must be treated with all deference, sometimes painfully punctilious to an American, or you will wake up some morning and find that you have lost all your friends. If you make a journey or go to the springs, you must make your parting visits ; and when your return, you must show, by a prompt call, that you are back again,

and wish to continue the old relations. The forenoon—
say about eleven or twelve o'clock—is the fashionable visiting time. New-Year visits are not so common there as
in America. It is quite customary, instead of calling personally, to send your card by a special messenger. This
means congratulation, and every thing else that is implied
in a personal visit.

The clergy are a more secluded class in Germany than
with us. They dare not, as a rule, touch political questions, unless on the Government side ; for their positions
are dependent on the consistories, in most instances, and
the consistories are controlled by people in sympathy with
the Government, or connected directly with it. The salaries are not so high as an American expects, but there are
more perquisites. One of the oldest, most popular, and
most learned pastors of Frankfort receives a salary equal
to only five hundred and sixty dollars, American gold,
besides fuel and gas. But he never performs a baptism,
attends a funeral, or hardly any pastoral office, without
a *douceur.* There are generally a senior and a junior
pastor, who preach alternately, the junior being always
expected to step into the senior's place in due time.
When pastors become infirm they are "pensioned," and
have no more care. Then, like Bushnell, they often go to
writing books. The hour of service is nine or ten in
the morning, and four or five in the evening. Our popu·
lar evening service is not known. The churches close at
such an hour that the attendants—sometimes the pastor
as well—can go to the theater afterward. A clergyman's
presence at a place of social entertainment is never con-

5

sidered a requisite. I have frequently observed that the
chasm between the German clergy and laity, in their
entire social life, is very much greater than in the United
States.

Every theological candidate must have previously passed
through the University in order to become one. When
a clergyman once finds a pulpit, he can look upon it as
his permanent home, if he be at all judicious. The
American thirst for novelty and change in the pulpit, on
the slightest pretext, has never yet invaded that land.
Literary merit is considered a great advantage for any candidate. When a German writes a book, all doors open
before him. Pulpit exchanges very rarely occur ; the pastor must be the only one to look his people in the face.
He always preaches without notes. The delivery, however, betrays generally a *memoriter* preparation.

No pastor must be suspected of sympathy with the
" sects." A leaning toward Presbyterianism, Baptism, or
Methodism, as distinct organizations in Germany, costs a
German pastor his position, his friends, and prospects.
Hence the cold hand extended to evangelists from abroad.

The "law's delay" is a terrible and painful reality in
Germany. Better never commence a suit unless you
are willing to lose double the sum at stake, and wait a
year or two before you have the satisfaction of knowing
it and the privilege of paying it. You can neither enter
nor leave the world without all sorts of formalities, and the
buying of enough certificates to set an army in motion.
A clergyman, a neighbor of mine, in order to marry the
lady of his choice, who was a Swabian, was compelled to

procure twenty-three different certificates before they could be pronounced "man and wife!" The most of these, of course, had to be paid for. I was fined once for not registering the entrance of a servant-girl into my household within a few specified days after the occurrence, and that when I was from home. I was told that imprisonment, or appeal and a regular lawsuit, would be the only relief. If you find an article—say a watch-key—in the street, you are expected to take it to the police-bureau, and that watch-key is regularly advertised. If no owner claims it, it is returned to you within just two weeks, or if you are so charitable, it is sold for the benefit of the city poor. On going to any public office, you have sometimes to wait hours for admission. I have learned never to go without a book or two in my pocket. Mr. Greeley could have gotten through all the newspapers in the pockets of his three coats during the process. When once you are in, you are treated very politely, as a general rule, and as leisurely as if the very sun was standing still, and nobody waiting to follow you. To an American, all this is very tantalizing ; but the Germans—the storm spare their patient souls!—never seem to be worried, or to imagine that they are losing in this way big slices out of their life-time.

CHAPTER IX.

THE GERMANS AND THEIR GARDENS.

THE art of taking care of a garden is cultivated and understood in Germany to a remarkable degree. No sooner does February furnish an hour or two of pleasant sunshine and spring-like air, than every plain man or woman who hopes to realize some pecuniary benefit from a little patch of ground, is engaged in preparing it for fruitfulness. Indeed, one is reminded, all through the winter, of the garden work of the coming spring. Every thing that possesses the slightest amount of fertilizing nutriment is saved with the greatest care, and applied to the ground during the intervals of thawing weather throughout all the winter months.

The question does not seem to be asked, when spring once opens, whether there will be any more frost or not. But the art of gardening is so well understood, together with the kind of plants best suited to the stage of the season, that a subsequent frost is not very likely to affect injuriously any vegetables that those prudent gardeners have ventured to plant. In February the gardeners in and about Bremen set out many vegetables and flowers, right fresh from the hot-beds. These no sooner take root than the cold weather, with whole weeks of frost and sleet, returns. Any body who would look with American eyes at those gardens after such a trial would very naturally conclude that every plant is killed. I thought so, for the appearance forbade a different conclusion. But two or three weeks of real spring weather showed that the gardeners knew just what they were about, and that their plants seemed to be really more vigorous in consequence of their frosty discipline.

There is no disposition in Germany to deny any body the privilege of working in the garden who has the power. Just opposite my study-window in Bremen there were several lots which were owned by different persons, but were cultivated by women as well as men. Generally, the sexes work together ; but so far as appearances go, the women know as well how to use the spade and hoe as the men. Indeed, there is no doubt that they are quicker in their movements, and really accomplish more in the field in a day. There is a general disposition on the part of the poor to have a piece of ground, no matter how small, how angular, or how poor it is. Depend upon it, it will soon be dug over, two spade-depths down ; it will be filled with fertilizers ; and its surface will be as smooth and clodless as if raked by the softest fairy hands that Hans Andersen has ever told us about. The gardens are planted with mathematical exactness. You may glance at the largest of them, but not a plant will be found out of place. The divisions between gardens under different proprietors are often only imaginary lines, there being two important objections to fences between them ; first, they cost too much ; and second, they occupy altogether too much valuable ground. Where a fence would be, the real German gardener can raise a large quantity of vegetables. This

4

economy of ground is surprising, and stands in very favorable contrast with the wastefulness of land every-where met with in America.

The care bestowed on vegetable gardens is exhibited, with even more skill and taste, in the cultivation of flowers. The Germans love flowers.   According to the old geographers, there never was a time when they did not.   They would submit to any ordinary denial sooner than be without them.   I believe if Herr Hofgartenrath Blumenliebe were required to pay a tax on every flower that hangs on each fuchsia, or hyacinth, or rose-stalk that grows in the windows of his house, he would submit to the publican's demand without a murmur, sooner than abandon the blissful ownership.   This love of flowers is clearly as common to the poor as to the wealthy classes.   The wealthy have their conservatories.   No house of respectable size is considered complete without one.   And it is not placed in the rear, where nobody can see it, but often on the street, just at the very angle of the house where the most people would be likely to see the flowers in passing.   The flower-pots are very beautiful, some of them in the old Etruscan style, others having rich arabesques, and still others ornamented with beautiful designs from common life.   Inside these costly and beautiful flower-pots stand the real ones of burnt clay, in which the plants themselves are growing.

But while the universal pains bestowed by the affluent on plants of the rarest and most beautiful variety is admirable, the almost paternal care lavished by the poorest and humblest on such flowers as they can have is touching.

The family that is crowded into a single story of a small house is sure to have each window, however small, occupied by flowers. Then every little projection—a rebellious brick, or a dissatisfied piece of timber, or a shelf nailed to the original window-sill—is burdened with flowers. They are healthy plants, too, for they seem to be always in blossom, and the leaves are of the freshest verdure. I call to mind at this time the flowers in the windows of a dilapidated house near our Bremen cottage. This house was probably not less than a century and a half old, and was occupied by a very poor family. I never knew the children to be clean or neatly clad ; but the flowers that bloomed in luxuriant beauty in those old-fashioned windows were worthy of the best mansions on Fifth Avenue. Nor is this any exception. In the narrowest streets and obscurest lanes of the city, in town as well as in country, there is a love of flowers, and a skill in training them into thrift and beauty, confined to no class or condition, and exhibited alike by small children and very aged persons.

There is no time in the year when flowers are not salable. The flower-stores are judiciously located on street-corners. But a flower-store in Germany is a very different thing from those in John-street, or the flower-stalls in Washington Market. There is something else to be seen in them besides monotonous drawers, with labels of all the plants in botany, or parcels of seeds, or clusters of dried bulbs, or packages of shrubs ready for planting. First of all, there are the living plants, arranged with exquisite taste on terraced stands at each of the large windows, and blooming in tropical splendor and beauty. These windows are a complete study. Any body who loves flowers can stand and look at them by the hour; and he may be sure that when he returns a day or two later, while he will probably find some new plant added and some fading flower withdrawn, he will observe no diminution in the surpassing loveliness of the scene. These flower-stores are not mere vernal institutions, but are as permanent as the banks of the Rothschilds, continuing from January to January again. Yet at these establishments seeds of all possible varieties may also be obtained. Probably no plant, either ready for ornamenting a street window or to be grown from seed, will be asked for in vain.

But then there are other flower-stores of an humbler kind. There are little booths erected in a quiet place under the shadow of the old cathedrals, and kept by old women. The lowly saleswomen may be found there, with their little kettles of charcoal embers and pots of coffee, during the very coldest weather of the winter. They have beautiful bouquets of dried flowers, which have all the appearance of fresh ones—thus highly is the art of taking care of flowers from first to last cultivated. But they have fresh ones too, and already in bloom. In cold weather these cannot be exposed; but if you ask one of the old women for one, she will take a quantity of wrapping-cloth from her low table or padded basket, as carefully as if uncovering her youngest grandchild. She shows you in time the very plant you desire. I could seldom stop to ask for a plant without taking quite a supply away with me. I was always conquered by the aged saleswomen.

In addition to the private care and culture of flowers, the municipal authorities bestow all pains upon them in the public parks and gardens. This is not merely the case in one, but in all the German cities. The Wall in Bremen and the Anlage in Frankfort are parks, which extend from one end of the city to the other. They are the peaceful and beautified remains of the old ramparts, and are now the great promenades of the inhabitants. The walks are well laid out, flowers and trees being distributed in such a way as to present a constant change of scene. Some of the flower-plots are very large, and are cultivated with the strictest care. On the Bremen Wall there were, even in spring, long and winding borders, and flower-beds of blooming hyacinths and crocuses, which reminded one rather of Italy than of the fifty-fourth degree of north latitude. Then the beds of roses and the endless variety of other flowers daily underwent the treatment of those painstaking and matchless gardeners. And if they succeeded thus early in the season in bringing their horticultural charges to such a high state of beauty, what must have been their success in the later spring, and in all the summer months ?

On all festal occasions there is exhibited a fondness for floral adornments which is equaled nowhere else, with the single exception of Holland, the paradise of tulips, dahlias, and other bulbs. But there is not the lavish expense in providing rare flowers that is now becoming common in this country. In Germany those used at festivities are such as the season produces, and are supplied at moderate cost. At funerals all friends and acquaintances bring

flowers in many designs, while the procession to the
cemetery is preceded by the servants of the family, or
of the neighbors, bearing in their hands flower-pots containing choice roses and other plants, which, when the
interment has taken place, are planted on the grave. And
no grave is ever forgotten. Every one is tenderly cared
for, not only by one of the many special gardeners belonging to the cemetery, but by the family to whom it is of
saddest interest. Often generations visit it, and keep it
beautiful and fragrant. A watering pot is provided,
locked to the inclosure, and detached and used by loving
hands at frequent visits. All through the summer the
grave is tastefully covered and surrounded with exquisite
flowers, which, when autumn comes, are transferred from
their evergreen fir and arbor-vitæ associates to the hot-
house to reappear with the following spring.

That the constant presence of flowers exerts a good
influence on German character, I have no doubt. The
vicious are, in a measure, restrained from the commission
of crime ; the children learn to be happy by the sight
of them ; the poor are withdrawn from contemplation
of their poverty, and learn from their republican flowers
that God does not confine his love to any privileged class ;
while all are unconsciously, but surely, influenced to a love
of natural beauty and reverence for its divine Author.

II.

SCHOOLS—GREAT AND SMALL.

The thing is not, to let the Schools and Universities go on in a proxy and impotent routine; the thing is, to raise the children of the nation even higher by their means.

WILHELM VON HUMBOLDT.

CHAPTER I.

THE increasing attention bestowed lately on the schools by European legislators is a gratifying evidence of·progress in meeting a great popular want. It was one of the very first questions to which the English Parliament, on the accession of the Gladstone ministry, addressed itself, and there are few Englishmen or Americans who read the reports of the long discussion in that body, and especially the elaborate speeches of Messrs. Melley and Goschen, who were not astonished at the statistical revelations of popular ignorance in Great Britain. Mr. Bright, in his address at Birmingham, in 1869, after saying, with his usual candor, that the education of the masses is "infinitely below that of Prussia, and, I think, also of Switzerland, and infinitely below that of the corresponding class—if there be a corresponding class—in the Northern States of the American Union," recalled the memorable words of his lamented friend, Cobden, that the Prussians "were the Yankees of Europe, and from their education would be the most powerful nation in Europe, because they had followed to a very large extent, although not exactly in the same way, the system of the United States, of endeavoring to give a sound education to their whole people."

In no country has there been a greater increase of

4*

legislative zeal in the cause of public education than in France. In the year 1866, the Emperor Louis Napoleon declared, at the opening of the Corps Legislatif, that, within nine months, thanks to the school-teachers, thirteen thousand new courses of study had been opened for adults. A map, projected by M. Durny, represents all the Departments in light or dark colors, according to which the state of education may be determined. Eleven Departments show a percentage of $\frac{10}{15}$ths of the population without any education; twelve, of $\frac{16}{23}$ths; twenty-three, of $\frac{24}{35}$; and twenty-six, of $\frac{31}{48}$. The least educated district is Bretagne, and, indeed, central France in general. In the Department of Doules, public instruction is more general than anywhere else in the country. An effort has been made to establish evening-schools for adults. The thirty thousand teachers have already taken up the measure, and such schools have been established in 22,947 parishes. In the Alsace, before its transfer to Germany, parish libraries had been established in many districts, and some of them embrace many thousand volumes.

The ignorance prevailing in the Latin countries of the South is simply amazing, and the legislator has a task before him there which will tax to the utmost all his educational zeal. In Italy, according to official returns, out of a population of twenty-seven millions, eighteen millions can neither read nor write. In 1866, 1,314,938 children attended school—therefore, only about one sixteenth part of the population of that date. In Upper Italy about 46 per cent. of the population are without any instruction whatever ; while in Lower Italy, 86 per cent. of the popu-

lation are without instruction. Only in a few districts—
for example, in Turin—is there any special zeal for primary
school education. In that city, the school-children constitute one eighth of the population.

In Spain, which has a population of seventeen millions,
nearly twelve millions are unable either to read or write.
A late official report says: "It is very easy to see how
public education is conducted, when we are informed that,
out of 72,157 municipal councilors, 12,479 can neither
read nor write; besides these, 422 burgomasters, 938 ad-
juncts, and 11,119 nagadores of the municipalities, can
neither read nor write." Popular education was one of
the gravest, but one of the first, problems which the new
Provisional Government, after the dethronement of Isa-
bella, was called upon to solve.

Portugal seems, however, in some respects, to be quite in
advance of her Spanish neighbor. Elementary education
is gratis and obligatory. Parents and guardians are required to send their children to school, under a penalty of
from fifty cents to one dollar. If children reach their
eighteenth year without being able to read or write, their
parents or guardians lose all political rights for the space
of five years. Instruction is secular, the priests not being
allowed to interfere with it in any way whatever. In
every school, the exercises open every day with prayer
from a prayer-book; besides, every teacher must take his
children every Sunday to mass, and see that they are all
provided with the Church prayer-books. He teaches
them the fundamental articles of the Christian (Catholic)
faith, and prepares them for their first communion. He

also reads with them, from an approved translation, the
Gospel lessons for the respective Sundays, and, after
preaching, goes through the principal parts of the sermon
with his scholars.

The provision made by Sweden and Norway for popular
instruction is highly creditable, and the Government is
constantly devising larger measures.   From the recent
report of the inspectors of the condition of the national
schools of Sweden and Norway, we learn that the national
schools in the year 1868 cost altogether 3,337,900 Swedish thalers, or 0.80 thaler per each person of the population ; of which the Government bears 1,208,203, and the
parishes 2,129,717.   The body of this sum, or 2,534,851
thalers, was expended for salaries of teachers.   The.Gov-
ernment estimates, granted by Parliament for public
instruction for 1871, for the higher schools, which in
Sweden are called Elementary Educational Establishments,
but which are really like the German gymnasia, amounted
to 1,688,619 thalers, and for the National Schools, 1,191,500
thalers.   Besides this, the estimates for the seminaries for
the education of female teachers and others amount to
82,761 thalers.   This makes a total of 2,962,880 thalers.
To the support of the National Schools, however, come
one and a half millions from another source, besides the
yearly interest paid for the building and repairing of
school-houses, (between 2,000 and 3,000 in number,) which
amounts to between 800,000 and 900,000 thalers ; 2,500
thalers are likewise given to an establishment for idiots.
For the support of science and the fine arts, are granted :
For the Royal Library, which will receive the name of The

National Library, besides 55,000 thalers toward the foundation of a new edifice, whose completion is to cost
480,238 thalers, the sum of 27,850 thalers; for the two
Universities, 466,551 thalers; the Government archives,
20,040; the National Museum, 25,550; the Caroline
Institute, 75,051. The academies receive as follows:
Swedish, 12,000; Scientific, 14,710; the Fine Arts, History, and Antiquities, 16,450; the Liberal Arts, 53,600;
Music, 30,300; and the National History Museum, 43,950.

It may be affirmed with safety that all the great movements toward popular instruction in these Continental
countries have taken their rise from Germany. The geographical position of the territory has been as important
a factor in this respect as, in the sixteenth century, in the
diffusion of Protestant sentiments. The German school
is the growth of centuries of repeated experiment, patient
labor, and careful observation. Pedagogy, long before
Pestalozzi's day, was elevated to one of the most respectable and elaborate sciences, and, as applied in Germany, is
nearer perfection than anywhere else in the world. There,
more than in any other country, fitness is the condition
of the teacher's holding his place; and in no other land is
the relation between teacher and pupil so beautified and
sweetened by such a large element of real sympathy and
friendship. The teacher does not consider it beneath his
dignity to place himself on a level with his scholar, to
ascertain his tastes and cultivate them, to ferret out his
plans and criticise them as a friend, and not to stand
aloof from him in his sorrows. A boy or girl, therefore,
placed in a German school of average respectability, is

almost sure to find among the teachers very congenial friends and sympathizers. This is especially true if the boy or girl is from America; for if a German teacher shows any partiality it is to his American pupils.

But no degree of excellence makes the German fully satisfied with his schools. The Prussians, or rather all the members of the Teutonic family represented by the German Parliament, are continually legislating on them. In the Prussian provinces, and in the Kingdom of Saxony, a half per cent. of the children are without instruction ; in the province of Brandenburg, there is a still less percentage than this ; while in Westphalia, there is a little over one per cent. In the provinces of Posen and Prussia, where the language presents the greatest difficulties, the percentage is about sixteen. In Bavaria, the percentage of children unable to read or write ranges from four to nineteen.

The Germans take the lead in teachers' associations. About the first of June, every year, they hold their Convention. The General Convention of Teachers in 1867 was attended by seven hundred and ten teachers, five hundred of whom were from the kingdom of Prussia. The number of clerical teachers was small.

Since the German and French war, the legislation on schools in Germany has taken some new forms. The disposition is, clearly, to reduce the traditional use of the Latin in the lecture-rooms ; to give less attention to the French and more to the English ; and to develop more than ever the critical study and use of the German language and literature. The French standards are now at a discount. There is, likewise, an effort now making throughout Germany to contract the bounds of religious instruction as closely as possible. At present, only two or three hours are devoted weekly to the subject. The biblical history of the Old Testament is almost totally neglected. In the Kingdom of Saxony, a controversy has broken out on the use of the Bible in the public schools. A Chemnitz teacher, by the name of Stahlknecht, has asserted in a work that a selection from the Bible, a so-called "School Bible," is an unavoidable necessity for Christian training, as many objectionable passages in the Old Testament can only exert a corrupting influence on the children! In 1853 a number of clergymen and teachers, among whom was the highly respected Hausschild, petitioned the Ministry for the introduction of a selection from the Bible; and in 1862 the Legislative and State Council at Chemnitz declared for the same. The Pedagogical Union has approved of this petition, and a number of clergymen and teachers have been called into Council to discuss the question, whether one of the existing selections or a new one can be best employed. Whatever these agree upon will be introduced into all the schools. In several of the German countries this question has elicited considerable discussion, and a number of selections of biblical history have been employed, the most of them having the old rationalistic sense.

CHAPTER II.

THE KINDERGARTEN.

THE Kindergarten, an institution now regarded a necessity by the Germans, is both the most elementary and the youngest of the German school systems. The first one was established by Frederic Froebel, less than forty years ago, since which time a great many have sprung up in various parts of the country. There are now Kindergartens in all the principal German cities, and in Great Britain and the United States. The principal center for the training of teachers is Weimar, and in Hamburg the most of the rapidly increasing literature on the subject is published. The Kindergarten is a school for children ranging from, say four to ten years of age, where no books are used, and all instruction is imparted by teachers through the medium of stories, games, and some light physical labor, when the most studious effort is made to keep out of the minds of the children the idea that they are really at school, and are all the while being prepared for one of a higher grade. It derives its name from the fact that each scholar has a little garden in the school grounds, which is his sole property, and where he can carry on all his operations of husbandry to his liking, and indulge his horticultural hopes to his heart's content.

The Kindergarten takes its rise from the educational

revolution in Germany and Switzerland effected by Campe, Pestalozzi, Salzmann, and Rousseau. The founder—Frederic Froebel—took Pestalozzi as his model, and was even a teacher in Pestalozzi's institution at Yverdun, from 1808 to 1810. He was born on April 21, 1782. In 1799 he went to Jena University as a student, but, after a short experience in study and nine weeks in prison, he became a farmer. His father died in 1802, when the son became a forest-keeper in the neighborhood of Bamberg. In 1805 he went to Frankfort, in hope of becoming an architect, but neither this nor any other occupation seemed to suit him. He studied in Göttingen in 1811, and in 1812 went to Berlin University. He then directed his attention to education, and particularly to the education of young children, and issued publications at frequent intervals in favor of his new views. He commenced his Universal German Educational Institute in Grieshcim, which he followed by others in various places. His principle or formula of education was this: "Do this, and see what results, in this particular respect, from your action, and to what knowledge it will lead you." He would unite thinking and doing, perceiving and acting, knowledge and ability, in the most intimate relations. His great themes of instruction were, religion, physical exercise, contemplation and comprehension of the outward world, and language. Religion —the Christian religion—is the foundation of all knowledge, as well as of all the relations from which all our knowledge receives its life and importance, and to which all our knowledge and capacity, and their fruits, return. We find, however, not only the principles of our Christian religion revealed in the Holy Scriptures, but also in the life of the individual man, in that of mankind in general, and in the whole sphere of nature. Hence, Froebel founded his religious instruction, formally, on the threefold revelation of God, in and by the Holy Scriptures, the life of individual man, and the whole organism of nature.

Language, counting, drawing, and singing were taught by him in a peculiar way, so that instruction might be imparted without the pupil feeling the burden of it. He began to teach his pupils piano-music by first having them exercise on some other object, and, after the fingers had become skillful, he took them to the piano. He had his pupils begin Latin by reading Cæsar's "Commentaries," and commenced his instruction in Greek, not by grammatical rules, but by making them attack the "Iliad" at the very outset! Froebel's collected works were published in three volumes, in Berlin, in 1862-3. His most popular work, and the one which has had most influence in propagating his sentiments, and founding Kindergartens in Germany, is, "Come, let us Live for our Children"—*Kommt, lasst uns unsern Kindern leben.* (Blankenburg: 1844.)

Perhaps a better idea cannot be presented of the working of a Kindergarten than a description of the way in which the principal one in Bremen is conducted, and which I had occasion to visit, and in which I had a personal interest. Many of the children were so small that they needed to be conducted thither by older persons. The little folks were met at the door by a servant, who relieved them of hat, coat, shawl, and lunch-box, care being taken, however, that each child aid in adjusting his own things, and having a fixed place for all. The proprietress —Miss Grabau—was assisted by two other ladies. The school was divided into two classes, either one or the other of which was nearly always in the large hall for exercise, or working in the little gardens out of doors. In the school-room, each scholar was provided with a very neat and comfortable desk and chair, and was taught to regard them as his own property. The employments were worsted-work, knitting, elementary drawing, and every other imaginable thing which is supposed to furnish such young fingers and minds with combined skill and amusement. The children had patterns before them for every thing they were to do, and the teacher personally superintended them in each little labor, when every pains was taken to impart as much elementary instruction as possible. For example, if a little girl was at work on a bookmark or a lamp-mat, she was taught imitation, combination, perspective, counting, and the alphabet. As soon as a child was tired of one employment, the mind was immediately diverted by the teacher to another, to prevent weariness.

The room for exercise was very large, and, like the school-room, neatly ornamented with pictures ; and when the children were in it they were under the care of a teacher, who had them go through many gymnastic exercises. This was the most interesting feature of the Kindergarten. The children, boys and girls promiscuously, were directed to assume a certain position. It might be that of a regiment drawn up in a line of battle. The teacher then commenced a story about a certain battle ; then came some stirring song, when all sang it together, after which the battle commenced in right good earnest. After the great victory was won, the teacher narrated a peaceful story in verse, which the children had been also previously taught, and which they repeated with her, going through with all the gymnastic exercises suggested by the verses. For instance, she told of a great pigeon-house, out of which the pigeons came, one by one. Some flew slowly, and some more rapidly ; others went off and hopped around on the ground, while others lighted on the chairs ; some got tired, and others fell down ; and thus the supposed movements of a whole flock of pigeons were represented by the children. Afterward, the teacher began to tell in prose about an old blacksmith, and by and by she reached the verses descriptive of his anvil, bellows, red-hot iron, and great hammer, when the children sang with her, and the whole room was transformed, for a time, into a great smithy, and all the little folks industriously and laughingly playing blacksmith. Another song described a walk over a heath, where, at last, a great pond was reached. The frogs were heard to croak, and seen to leap into the pond. During this time the entire class became a large group of similar croakers.

A song runs thus, during the singing of which the children go through all the motions common to cooperage :

"I am a cooper, and barrels I bind,
And on my brow perspiration I find ;
But happy and merry I always am found,
And with this my hammer I pound,
I pound, around, around, around, around."

In all these imitatory exercises the children preserved strict order, but their risible propensities were not at all restrained. Just as soon as the slightest fatigue or decrease in interest was observed the exercises were changed, when the class was immediately taken into another room, or else into the garden. About one half the time seemed to be devoted to the gymnastic and horticultural employments, and the other half to the light manual labor at the desks in the school-room proper.

There are a great many of these half-poetical and half-prose stories, having somewhat of a theatrical character, taught and performed in the Kindergarten. I have at hand a volume which contains fifty in all, profusely illustrated. Some of the titles are: "The Mouse and the Cat," "The Ants," "The Stork and the Frog," "The Butterfly," "The Grasshopper and the Worm," and "The Horse-chestnut Tree." Each of these stories requires, perhaps, from ten to fifteen minutes to repeat and perform.

The exercises and employments at the Kindergarten are sure to be brought away by the children, and enter largely into their home-life. The two little folks that went out of our doorway every morning to Miss Grabau's school, had not been in attendance more than a few weeks before they were hopping about the premises like frogs, leaping like deer, springing like cats, and, as nearly as they could, flying like swallows, barking like dogs, swimming like fish, swinging like tree-tops, sailing like boats, and chattering like magpies.

It is difficult to decide whether the Kindergarten is very

superior to the usual schools first attended by children. It is by no means likely that it is all that its warm admirers imagine it to be, and it is equally probable that many of the principles which are applied in it, without any books, and only by illustration, might be employed very advantageously in connection with attractive and appropriate books. A certain amount of the Kindergarten introduced into our ordinary elementary school would certainly be an improvement. Too much cannot be said for the physical influence of the gymnastic exercises, which, indeed, constitute the most beneficial feature of the institution. It is to be regretted that, despite Froebel's generalizations on religion, there is but little cognizance of Christianity taken in the purely German Kindergarten—thus showing its barren Pestalozzian origin, and Froebel's own depreciation of it to a level with outward nature, and the revelation natural to the human mind. After all the lessons taught the children, there is scarcely one that might not have been taught them, so far as a practical religious spirit is concerned, in the palmy days of English Deism, or even in the time of the "gods of Greece," which Schiller sighed to have back again to the world.

CHAPTER III.

THE FRANKFORT SCHOOLS.

THE schools in Germany, to which any foreign pupil has access, are very varied in scope and facilities. Those of Frankfort have the name of being the best in the country; but it is not likely that there is any further foundation for the celebrity than their being simply so frequented by English and Americans as to have become specially adapted to the practical Anglo-Saxon tastes, and more widely known across the Channel and the Atlantic than are the other schools. In Frankfort the two classes of male schools to choose between are, the public schools, supported by the State, and the private or select schools. In the former the teachers are just as competent as in the latter, and the annual tuition is not over seventy gulden, or thereabout. The buildings are commodious, but generally of very defective ventilation, and have a gymnasium and play-ground. Here, too, the American boy has the best opportunity to learn German; for nearly all his associates are Germans. But, then, he cannot receive as much attention from his instructors as he would like, and must frequently employ private aid, because in most of these schools there are too many students for the number of teachers. Care should be taken, in placing young Americans in German schools, to avoid those where other Americans or English are studying. Neither German nor French can

be learned to advantage in such associations. The following is the plan of studies in one of the best schools in
Frankfort-on-the-Main :—

STUDIES AND HOURS IN THE MEDIUM CITIZEN SCHOOL.

Number of the Classes.

	VII.	VI.	V.	IV.	III.	II.	I.
Religious Instruction (hours) ...	3	3	3	2	2	2	2
Instruction by Intuition.......	4	2	.	.	.	.	.
Writing from Dictation........	11	.	.	.	.	.	.
German......................	.	9	6	4	4	4	4
French......................	.	.	5	5	4	4	
History.....................	.	.	.	2	2	2	3
Geography	.	.	2	2	2	2	2
Natural History..............	.	.	2	2	2	2	2
Physics	.	.	.	.	.	3	3
Arithmetic and Algebra.......	6	6	5	4	4	4	4
Geometry	.	.	2	3	3	3	3
Penmanship.................	.	4	4	3	3	2	2
Drawing....................	.	2	2	2	2	2	2
Singing	.	.	2	2	2	1	1
Fencing.....................	2	2	2	2	2	2	1
Hours per week.............	26	28	28	32	33	33	33

In this elementary school there are seven teachers ; the
number of scholars is three hundred and twenty-nine,
and the ages of the pupils range from eight to fourteen
years. America is certainly not the only land, it is clear,
where the teacher is overworked.

All things considered, the best course for the young
American who simply goes abroad to study the modern
languages and the ordinary branches preparatory to business or a collegiate education at home, is to enter one of
the select schools. If he is already a young man, and has
been through an American college, he should go at once
to a university, where, in addition to lectures, he can get

private instruction on any subject that he may wish. The select, or boarding, schools have every facility for real progress and success—able teachers and plenty of them, chemical apparatus, charts, and what not. The student can board in the institution, or, if he prefer, elsewhere, and attend as a day scholar. The price of board and tuition in one such school, near Hanover, whose catalogue I have before me, is, for boys of eight to twelve years, $250 (gold) ; of twelve to fifteen, $300 ; of fifteen to eighteen, $450. There is a reduction of these prices where brothers enter together ; but these terms are rather above than below the average. Here the scholars are trained with a view to their proposed vocation, without undergoing what might be called waste studies.

In Frankfort there are about ten schools for boys and twenty for girls. In Heidelberg, Stuttgart, Brunswick, and all of the more western German towns and cities, there are excellent schools. I do not mention the names of any of them, for it would be doing injustice to many, equally good, that would be omitted. The schools which advertise the most in England and America do not enjoy the best reputation at home. The finest schools, as a rule, have as many pupils as are desired, without advertising. The number of students in a German select school averages, say, about forty.

Some Americans and English, to secure religious oversight for their children, place them under the care of pastors, in whose families they live, and by whom they are instructed. In some respects this is a good plan, but it has the disadvantages resulting from being educated in

5

a very narrow circle. Some of the pastors, too, are not always what every body would call safe spiritual guides. A young American, who was studying in Frankfort, told me one day that a pastor of his acquaintance had lately requested him to take the twelve o'clock Sunday train, in order to attend the theater that afternoon in Darmstadt, where a piece of unusual attractiveness was to be performed.

"But you preach at eleven o'clock, and you cannot catch the train?" was the answer.

"O! that don't make any difference! I can hurry up my closing prayer, throw off my robe in the vestry, and go directly from church to the depot, and thus be in good time to catch the train!"

The American, who, by the way, had had faithful pastors and Sunday-school teachers at home, in New York, declined the invitation, the importunities of the pleasure-loving pastor to the contrary notwithstanding.

The Germans do not like male and female schools together. They profess to have excellent reasons for opposing them, and you seldom hear of one being organized. There are, nevertheless, good seminaries for ladies, where religious instruction is not neglected, and where special attention is paid to speaking and writing the modern languages, the teachers of which are generally natives of the countries represented by them. Notwithstanding the usual opposition of the Germans to mixed schools, there is a good male and female seminary near Frankfort, which is patronized by many Christian parents, who have expressed full satisfaction with the establishment. The terms in this institution are, in round figures, $200 (gold), for board and tuition.

If parents do not wish their children to pay special attention to the modern languages, they will do as well to keep them in schools at home, where instruction in practical branches and in the elements of the classics is unsurpassed. If they wish their children to go abroad for a length of time—and less than a couple of years is not advisable—they should take special pains to see that they are placed in a boarding school where the proprietor and instructors are of evangelical sentiments, and have at least some respect for the American Sunday, and, the children being placed under them, that their time be occupied in such studies as will be of the most use to them on their return to America. As a rule, •education abroad should be deferred until a broad foundation is laid at home.

The cases are rare where young ladies should be sent abroad for instruction. Where parents have sons and daughters whom they desire to be educated in Germany or France, their best course is to go abroad themselves, and take their children with them. In Dresden, Berlin, Hanover, Frankfort, and other cities, there are many American families living, the direct object of whose going abroad was that the children might attend German schools. The more one thinks of this plan, the more reason he will find to admire it. Living is as cheap there as in America, but not much cheaper. However, to a wise parent an undivided family circle abroad is much more desirable than unintermitted business enterprises at home.

CHAPTER IV.

PROTESTANT SCHOOLS IN AUSTRIA.—SCHOOL REFORMERS.

ONE of the most important questions connected with the whole recent reformatory movement in Austria, going steadily onward ever since 1866, is that of the schools ; and the abrogation of the Concordat has been the means of restoring to the Protestants a freedom of instruction not enjoyed by them since the days of the Reformers. There was a time in Austria when schools were in a very flourishing state. As soon as the Reformation broke into the Catholic darkness and pervaded the country, the Bible immediately became a popular book, and schools at once improved in the cities and villages wherever the Reformation had the slightest influence. The nobility, who were at first favorable to the cause, which was commenced by Huss and continued by Luther, sent to Germany, and especially to Wittenberg, for teachers ; and the more strength the Reformation gained in Austria, the more vigorous was the growth of schools. But in the very places where the people showed a preference for Romanism, the schools either went down or became very poor. It was a prominent object of the Catholics to impede, or even exterminate, these new Protestant schools, and they carried on their conflict with great bitterness. Owing, however, to the influence of the Court, and to the hostility of the Catholic nobility, Protestantism was oppressed more and more, and those who refused to renounce their faith were required by cruel religious edicts to leave the country, as in the case of the Evangelical Salzburgers.

The political history of Austria during the seventeenth and eighteenth centuries reflects very clearly the history of the schools. Austria was a thoroughly Catholic empire, and the last vestige of Protestant liberty therein was destroyed in 1629, under the government of Ferdinand II.; and though a little leniency was shown under his successor, no openly professing Protestants were to be found any longer in Austria, and those who were Protestants at heart instructed their children privately in the Bible, and in the old devotional books and sermons left them by their forefathers. In order to prevent the people from ever yielding to Protestant heresy again, the instruction of all the children in the land was placed in the hands of the Catholic clergy; Catholic priests were placed over small circles or districts, and had charge over all the books, and oversight over all the teachers. The Emperor Joseph II. designed to pursue a better course, but his failure was partly owing to his being in advance of the public sentiment of his country, and in part to the shortness of his reign. · However, the first important step within the century was taken by this ruler, who issued the Patent of Toleration, on 'the 13th of October, 1781. This served as the official invitation to the Protestants to show their colors. They immediately began to form congregations, called their pastors in part from Hungary and in part from Germany, and immediately established schools on a good foundation. Of course, they were compelled to organize their schools according to the Catholic laws in existence, and were naturally very much cramped by them. In a short time the Protestant schools became very flourishing, and had the name of being the best in the empire. They were distinguished not so much for a better organization, for that was a matter of law, but for the greater skill in teaching, the freer action of the minds of the children, and, above all, for the scriptural character of the instruction. But after this time new shackles were placed on the Austrian Protestant schools, and it has only been since the recent reform commenced, after Austria's humiliation in the war of 1866, that the Protestants have been assured a freedom of instruction which had not been so fully enjoyed since the days of the Reformers.

A Protestant normal school has been commenced in Bielitz, Austria, and if we may take its past progress under oppressive laws as a mark for the future, its growth will be very rapid, and its influence will be felt in the elevation of Austrian Protestantism. The Austrian Ministry approved of its statutes and plan of instruction as long ago as the 10th of August, 1867, and guaranteed that the seventeen hundred florins still unprovided for should be paid out of the State-treasury, and that the opening of the seminary might take place at once. The school commenced with a director and four teachers, and the Gustavus Adolphus Union gives it an annuity of three thousand florins. Two other important Austrian schools deserve to be mentioned, one in Vienna and the other in Gratz, both of which are thoroughly up to the requirements of the times, and great good may be expected from their future operations. The former school-building is an ornament to the new part of the city of Vienna, and its arrangements for instruction are hardly surpassed in Germany. The board of managers consists of four Lutheran and two Reformed persons, and, besides the director and three catechists, there are twenty-two male and female teachers. The present director is Dr. R. A. Jacobi. There are over one thousand scholars in attendance. The charges for attendance are very moderate ; a scholar paying, on entering the primary department, five florins ; (the Austrian florin is equal to about fifty cents in gold) ; on entering any further class, two florins ; and the subsequent yearly payment ranging from seven to fifteen florins. The school at Gratz consists of four classes, which are taught by a director and three teachers.

The first general session of the Austrian Teachers' Association took place in Vienna, on the 5th of September, 1867, and lasted two days. There were in attendance one thousand six hundred and twenty-seven teachers, and the prevailing spirit of the meeting was, that perfect religious liberty is a necessity for the proper instruction of children. As a matter of course, the greater portion of the teachers were Catholics ; but there was no disposition to abridge the liberty of speech of their Protestant associates, and Catholics as well as Protestants united in claiming the absolute separation of the clergy from all interference with the instruction imparted in the Austrian schools. This teachers' meeting, the first of the kind in Austria, and attended by so great a number of members, had an influence in moving the Government and the Emperor to adopt the reformatory measures which have since successfully culminated. The ultra course taken by the Vatican Council, in adopting the dogma of the Pope's infallibility, has alienated all the liberal Catholic sentiment from the Church party, and it affiliates cordially with that of the Protestants in further aggressive measures in behalf of perfect confessional and educational liberty. Our American Consul in Vienna told me that Austria was the freest country in Europe ; and, certainly, I neither saw nor heard any thing in conflict with his opinion.

The General German Teachers' Association held its session in 1870, in Vienna, where the most pronounced course was taken for completely breaking loose from the traditional conservatism of Austrian education, and for a reorganization of educational facilities. The proceedings were of such a character as to attract the attention of all Europe. I regret to say, that the evidences of reaction against the long bondage were too evident in a disposition to cast off all authority, the Bible not excepted.

The tendency in Austria now is, to thoroughly popularize education throughout the empire, especially in the direction of the study of natural science. The languages have held a long sway, but on every hand an effort is making to give the study of nature a predominance. The defects of the Austrian gymnasia are claimed to concentrate here. In 1849 the distribution of time in the lower gymnasia was ten hours a week to the study of natural history and physics, and eleven to the classics ; afterward, two hours were taken from the former. The Imperial School Inspector of Gratz, Herr M. Wretchks, has

written a little work in defense of the proposed reform,
and states his case very pointedly. He claims, that according to the present arrangement for natural science,
only doctors and apothecaries seem to be kept in sight,
and that the great mass of students are constantly drilled
in the languages, to the utter neglect of physical studies.
He urges, as a principal relief from the evil, that the
number of professorships in the various gymnasia be·so
increased as to throw the whole field of nature open to
every student ; and, further, that there should be more universities. His second position, however, is by no means
defensible ; for, if the history of the German universities
proves any thing, it proves this : that it is not the great
number of universities, but the magnitude of the facilities
of the few, that develops both teacher and student, and
elevates popular instruction. What a different aspect
would be presented in Germany to-day, if the wealth and
intellect concentrated in the Berlin University were scattered into half a dozen puny ones in different parts of the
country !

Dr. Fischhof, in his " Oesterreich und die Bürgschaften
ihres Bestandes," throws a stronger light on the present
state of education in Austria than any other writer with
whom I have met. His attempt, throughout his excellent
work, is to compare his country, Austria, with other leading nations, and to show wherein she stands in need of improvement. The low stage of education seems to be the
subject which he has made a special study. In Switzerland, he says, the fifth part of all the government expenditure is appropriated to education and worship ; twenty

5*

per cent. of the taxes paid by the Swiss are, therefore, applied to improving the education, morals, and religious sentiments of the population. In Austria, on the contrary, only one and a quarter per cent. of the government expenditure is appropriated to worship and instruction. Still, it must be allowed that all the great countries of Europe stand, in this respect, far behind Switzerland. France applies only four and a half per cent. a year for instruction, while Switzerland uses in the training of its youth nearly fourteen per cent. of its whole income. If Austria should make, proportionately, as good provision for education as Switzerland does, she would have to give 44,000,000 gulden, while she really gives but 5,500,000. Switzerland, which has a population of 2,500,000, has 7,000 elementary schools; 260 higher and industrial schools; 47 gymnasia; 3 universities in the German language; 3 academies, after the model of the French universities, in the French language; and one polytechnical institute. If Austria, with her 35,000,000 of inhabitants, should stand equal to Switzerland, she would have 98,000 elementary schools, 3,640 higher and industrial schools, 658 gymnasia, 84 universities, and 14 polytechnical institutes. But in 1865 she had really only 29,200 elementary schools (and many of them in utterly destitute circumstances), 134 dependent elementary schools, 71 independent ones, 236 gymnasia, 7 universities, and 8 technical academies.

Dr. Fischhof gives the following statement of the special educational institutions of Austria: 3 Theological Faculties, 11 Law Academies, 4 Commercial Academies, 6 Chirurgical Institutes, 4 Forest-culture Institutes,

1 Agricultural Academy, 82 Theological Schools, 16 Obstetrical Schools, 28 Agricultural Schools, 7 Nautical Schools, 5 Mining Schools, 3 Military Academies, 8 Special Military Schools, 8 School Companies, 9 Military Training Schools, and 4 Cadet Institutes.

This author proceeds to show that it is not a mere accident that Switzerland pays the great attention that she does to the subject of education. The main root of the matter is the free spirit of the people. He then attempts to prove this further by the state of education in the United States of America, and pays a very high compliment to our system of popular instruction. He gives the most elaborate and reliable statistics of education in our country, and shows by these that education in America is far in advance of that in any other country in the world. He calls attention to the fact, too, that not only do the children in the common schools receive their education free, but that even their text-books and writing materials are supplied gratuitously.

In reference to schools of a higher grade, and the Universities, Dr. Fischhof claims that Austria remains far in the background, and must make immediate and rapid advances if she would stand on a respectable footing with other important nations. He says, that while the Government should give all the aid it can to those higher institutions of learning, the people should take the matter in hand themselves, and show that they can go along independently of the Government. He again adduces the United States in support of his position, and defends the voluntary promotion of education by the people in a way highly gratifying and complimentary. He prophesies that the time is not far distant when America will take the lead of the European nations in the splendor of her educational achievements. In order that Austria promote the cause of university education, the power of the Government over the universities must be diminished, and left largely to the managers of the universities themselves.

Looking at the testimony of history, the growth of the Italian universities, centuries ago, is largely attributable to this cause ; and the achievements of the Universities of Utrecht and Leyden, in Holland, were the direct results of the free footing which they enjoyed. And the twenty Universities of Germany prove beyond a doubt that their prosperity and constant success have been the direct outgrowth of the greater or less independence which they have enjoyed. In Great Britain, rich and liberal as she is, the two great Universities, Oxford and Cambridge, are still measurably beneath the yoke of the Established Church. The only university in England abreast of the spirit of the times is the London University, which was founded in 1828 by a stock company. Our author here falls into an error, in omitting just as important a one, the Manchester University, newly endowed and now clothed with full university functions.

Dr. Fischhof, in continuing his comparative statement, says that France has seventeen large academies and but one university, namely, that of Paris. This institution has all the completeness of the German universities. The Austrian institutions of a higher grade have only one, two, or at most three Faculties. Switzerland has one university for every 400,000 inhabitants, while in Germany there is one for every 2,000,000, and in Austria only one for every 5,000,000.   Dr. Fischhof attributes a large measure of the great achievements and prosperity of higher education in the United States to the fact that instruction is not a subject of legislation by the General Government at all, but that it is left to the individual States ; and he does not pass over Washington's earnest wish that there might be one model university.

CHAPTER V.

THE MACHINERY OF THE GERMAN UNIVERSITY.

EVERY one confesses the magnitude of the German University, and its important relation to the whole life of the Continent. Madame de Staël was saying nothing new, even in her day, when she declared, "The literary glory of Germany depends altogether on these institutions." Sir William Hamilton's remarks on their growth is well worthy of remembrance :—

" By Germans themselves, German universities are admitted to have been incomparably inferior to the Dutch and Italian universities, until the foundation of the University of Göttingen. Münchhausen was for Göttingen and the German universities what Donza was for Leyden and the Dutch. But with this difference : Leyden was the model on which the younger universities of the Republic were constructed ; Göttingen, the model on which the older universities of the empire were reformed. Both were statesmen and scholars. Both proposed a high ideal for the schools founded under their auspices ; and both, as first curators, labored with paramount influence in realizing this ideal for the same long period of thirty-two years. Under their patronage, Leyden and Göttingen took the highest place among the universities of Europe, and both have only lost their relative supremacy by the application, in other seminaries, of the same measures which had at first determined their superiority.

" From the mutual relations of the seminaries, States, and people of the empire, the resort to a German university has, in general, been always mainly dependent on its comparative excellence ; and as the interest of the several States was involved in the prosperity of their

several universities, the improvement of one of these schools neces-
sarily occasioned the improvement of the others. No sooner, therefore, had Göttingen risen to a decided superiority through her system
of curatorial patronage, and other subordinate improvements, than
the different governments found it necessary to place their seminaries,
as far as possible, on an equal footing. The nuisance of professional
recommendation, under which the universities had so long pined,
was generally abated; and the few schools in which it has been tol-
erated subsist only through their endowments, and stand as warning
monuments of its effect. Compare wealthy Greifswalde with poor
Halle. The virtual patronage was, in general, found best confided to
a *small body of* curators; though the peculiar circumstances of the
country, and the peculiar organization of its machinery of government, have recently enabled at least one of the German States to
concentrate, without a violation of our principles, its academical patronage in a ministry of public instruction. This, however, we cannot now explain. It is universally admitted, that since their rise
through the new system of patronage, the universities of Germany
have drawn into their sphere the highest talent of the nation; that
the new era in its intellectual life has been wholly determined by
them; as from them have emanated almost all the most remarkable
products of German genius in literature, erudition, philosophy, and
science." *

In former times the universities—Leipzig for example—
were largely sustained by extensive landed estates. But
these, from various causes, have passed out of their possession, and the support of the universities now devolves
upon the appropriations of the State and the fees of
students.

The following account of the expenditures and income
of the nine universities of Prussia, and of the Academy

* " Discussions on Philosophy and Literature." Second London edition,
p. 381.

of Münster, has been laid before the German Parliament, and may therefore be regarded correct :—

The yearly appropriation for these ten institutions amounts to 1,492,211 thalers ; of this, 862,911 thalers are derived from State funds, and the remaining 629,300 from the investments of the several institutions.

This entire sum is consumed as follows : 613,201 thalers, for salaries of professors and teachers ; 534,672 thalers for institutes, museums, and university worship ; 184,052 thalers for commons and stipends of students ; 70,491 thalers for curators, university discipline, and administration ; 42,261 thalers for repairs and taxes ; 47,534 thalers for incidentals and additions to salaries. Of the various institutes connected with the different departments of the universities, those of Berlin and Göttingen receive the highest sum ; the former, 221,683 thalers ; and the latter, 181,930 thalers. The remaining universities fall in the following order: Bonn, 151,372 thalers ; Halle, 127,485 thalers ; Königsberg, 117,432 thalers ; Breslau, 117,402 thalers ; Marburg, 95,221 thalers ; Greifswald, the only university which receives no support from the State, but sustains itself solely upon the income from its own property, applies for its institutes 94,100 thalers ; and, finally, the Academy at Münster, 22,376 thalers.

The sum of 613,201 thalers, for paying the salaries of professors and teachers, is thus divided :—

Seventy-five professors in ordinary and nineteen extraordinary in the theological faculties, 97,122 thalers ; fifty-nine professors in ordinary and seventeen extraordinary in the law faculties, 89,278 thalers ; seventy-seven professors in ordinary, and forty-three extraordinary in the medical faculties, 108,192 thalers ; two hundred and nine professors in ordinary, and eighty-six extraordinary in the philosophical faculties, 302,042 thalers.

The remainder of the whole sum is applied to lectures, teachers of languages, and instructors in fencing, music, riding, and dancing. The average support of a regular professor is 1,246¼ thalers ; the theological professor receiving a little more than any of the rest. The average in all the faculties is as follows : A professor in ordinary in the theological faculty receives 1,262¼ thalers ; one in the law faculty, 1,258¾ thalers ; one in the medical faculty, 1,223¼ thalers ; one in the philosophical faculty, 1,257¾ thalers.

The highest average salary in any one university is received by a regular professor in Berlin, who gets 1,568 thalers. Then follow Kiel, with an average salary of 1,446 thalers ; Göttingen, 1,445 thalers ; Bonn, 1,349 thalers ; Halle, 1,259 thalers ; Griefswald, 1,252 thalers ; Breslau, 1,134 thalers ; Königsberg, 1,097 ; Marburg, 1,069 thalers ; and at the Academy of Münster the average salary is only 842 thalers. The salaries of professors extraordinary are so varied that an average cannot be arrived at. They range from 200 to 1,200 thalers. Of instructors in the universities who receive no salary whatever, there are five professors in ordinary, (two at Göttingen, two at Breslau, and one at Bonn,) and forty professors extraordinary. Of the latter, there are five theologians, four priests, eighteen in the medical faculties, and thirteen in the philosophical faculties.

Of the sum applied to institutes and museums, the

greatest proportion is drawn by the medical and natural
science departments. The botanical gardens and herb-
aria alone require almost as great a yearly appropriation
as all the libraries of all the universities, for they cost
54,541 thalers ; the latter, 57,928 thalers. The Göttingen
library receives yearly 15,324 thalers ; the Bonn library,
8,104 thalers ; the Königsberg library, 6,583 thalers ; the
Breslau library, 5,738 thalers ; the Halle library, 5,245
thalers ; the Marburg library, 4,790 thalers ; the Greifswald library, 4,335 thalers ; the Kiel library, 4,306 thalers.
The university library at Berlin receives 3,503 thalers—
a very small sum. But it must be remembered that the
great royal library of Berlin is open for all university
purposes, and is very richly endowed by State funds.

The division of labor practiced in the German universities is carried to a marvelous extent. The professors
are allowed much liberty in the choice of themes for their
courses of lectures ; yet care is taken that no topic of
importance be neglected. Unquestionably, one of the
great causes of the prosperity of the universities, of the
literary activity of the instructors, and of the powerful
incentives to labor which the students carry home with
them, lies in the act that men are invariably chosen for
professional positions with careful regard to the special
departments of study in which they have manifested taste
and capacity. All considerations must yield to that of
complete adaptation of the man to his topic. If the professors were compelled to conform to the notions of others
in their lectures, and the lectures were, therefore, not the
direct outflow of the favorite thinking of the teacher, the

German university would soon lose its traditional influence. In this respect, as in others, it is essentially a republic, and has been for many generations, whatever the character of the government holding jurisdiction over it. In order to show how far this division of labor is carried, and how much is conceded to the individual taste of teacher and student, as well as to give some notion of the wonderful intellectual machinery in constant operation in the German universities, I present an abstract from the prospectus of five representative theological departments. There are four faculties in all the universities, with but an exception or two: theology, law, medicine, philosophy. Political science, philology, history, and, in fact, all subjects not embraced under theology, law, or medicine, are grouped under the last head. From the number of lectures, and the specialty of the themes in the theological department, those of the three remaining faculties may be pretty well imagined.

BERLIN.—*Dorner:* Theological Encyclopædia and Methodology ; Special Christian Doctrine ; Exercises in Systematic Theology. *Rüdiger:* Genesis ; Chaldaic Language, and the Book of Daniel ; Introduction to Old Testament. *Benary:* I. Samuel ; Psalms ; Hebrew Language and other Semitic Dialects. *Kleinert:* Isaiah ; Biblical Theology of the Old Testament ; Significance of the Old Testament for the Church of the Present Time ; Theological Disputation. *Dieterici:* Minor Prophets. *Vatke:* Introduction to Old Testament ; Doctrines. *Strauss:* History of the Old Testament, including Biblical Archæology ; Catechetics ; Homiletics, and Homiletical Exercises. *Messner:* Introduction to New Testament ; Christology of New Testament. *Brückner:* John's Gospel ; Homiletical Exercises. *Twesten:* Epistle to Hebrews ; Moral Science ; Symbolical Basis of the

Evangelical Church. *Piper:* History of the Church (first period) ; Archæology, and Patristic Exercises in the Christian Museum ; Doctrinal Explanations from the Monuments. *Weingarten:* History of the Church (first period) ; Tertullian's Apology ; Introduction to the Apocryphal Books of New Testament. *Semisch:* Church History (second period) ; General History of Christian Doctrines ; Doctrinal History of the Middle Ages. *Schmidt:* History of Rationalism and Pietism ; History of the Œcumenical Councils. *Steinmeyer:* Practical Theology ; Catechetics ; Practical Homiletics.

BONN.—(Protestant Theological Faculty.) *Lange:* Theological Encyclopædia and Methodology ; Biblical Theology ; Doctrinal Theology. *Kamphausen:* Hebrew Exercises ; Isaiah ; Gospel of Luke. *Hundeshagen:* Epistle to Philippians ; Church History (first period). *Christlieb:* First Epistle to Timothy ; Homiletics ; Pastoral Theology. *Krafft:* Life of Christ ; Recent Church History. Exercises in the Theological Seminary conducted by each of these men.—(Roman Catholic Faculty.) *Floss:* Theological Encyclopædia ; Church History (first period) ; Recent Church History ; Moral Theology. *Reusch:* Introduction to Old Testament ; Mosaic Account of the Creation ; Book of Wisdom ; Exegetical Exercises. *Langen:* Introduction to New Testament ; Augustine's Writings ; Mark's Gospel. *Kaulen:* Psalms ; Hebrew Exercises. *Hilgers:* Epistle to the Hebrews ; Symbolism. *Dieringer:* Dogmatic Theology (first part) ; Doctrine of the Church ; Homiletics ; Homiletical Exercises. *Simar:* Dogmatical Theology ; Call to, and Preparation for, the Ministry ; Catechetics.

HALLE.—*Kähler:* Theological Encyclopædia and Methodology ; Biblical Theology of the New Testament ; The Johannean Doctrinal Idea. *Riehm:* Introduction to Canonical Books of Old Testament ; History of Old Testament Exegesis ; Elucidation of Prophecy of Isaiah (both parts). *Schlottmann:* Genesis ; Biblical Theology of the Old Testament ; Hegel and Schleiermacher ; Exercises in Old Testament Exegesis. *Böhmer:* Prophecy of Daniel. *Jacobi:* Introduction to the New Testament ; History of Doctrines ; History of the Doctrine of the Inspiration of the Scriptures ; Church History.

Tholuck: Synoptic Gospels; Sermon on the Mount; Exercises in New Testament Exegesis. *Beyschlag:* Exegesis of Christ's Parables; Epistles to the Romans; Life of Christ; Exercises in Homiletics and Catechetics. *Dähne:* II. Corinthians; Epistle of James. *Guericke:* Epistle to the Philippians; Church History (first period.) *Wuttke:* History of Deism and Rationalism; Ethics; Exercises in Dogmatics and Ethics. *Julius Müller:* Introduction to Dogmatics; Dogmatic Theology; Practical Theology. *Kramer:* History of Later Pedagogics.

LEIPZIG.—*Kahnis:* History of Doctrines; Theological Encyclopædia; History of the Church in the Middle Ages. *Luthardt:* Dogmatic Theology; Epistle to the Hebrews; Characteristics of New Testament Scriptures; Doctrinal Exercises. *Lechler:* History of Christian Missions. *Delitzsch:* Genesis; Song of Solomon; Matthew's Gospel. *Fricke:* Epistle to the Galatians; Life of Christ; Christian Ethics; History of the Bible. *Tischendorf:* Introduction to the New Testament; Palestine. *Hölemann:* Epistles to the Thessalonians; Scriptural Idea of God. *Hoffmann:* Symbolics; Practical Theology; Catechetical Exercises. *Schmidt:* Epistles to the Corinthians; Christian Apologetics. *Brockhaus:* Church History (first period). *Mühlau:* Book of Job; Hebrew Syntax; Epistle to the Colossians; Exegetical History of Old Testament. *Kautsch:* Isaiah; History of Israel in Time of the Kings. *Schürer:* Introduction to New Testament; Exegetical History of New Testament.

BASLE (Switzerland).—*Hagenbach:* Later Church History (from 1555 to the Present Time); Theological Encyclopædia and Methodology; Elucidation of the Reformed Confessions; Exercises in Church History and Homiletics. *Stähelin:* Introduction to the Prophetical and Poetical Books of the Old Testament; History of the Jews; Dialectical Exercises. *Müller:* New Testament Introduction; Historical Basis for Higher Criticism; Commentary on Epistles of John, James, Jude; Elucidation of Works of Philo. *Riggenbach:* Commentary on the Synoptic Gospels down to the Passion; Catechetics; Theological Society. *Schultz:* System of Doctrine; Prophecy of Isaiah; Exegetical Society. *Von der Goltz:* Epistle to the

Romans; Symbolics; Doctrinal Society. *Preiswerk:* Hebrew Grammar; Exercises in Hebrew Writing. *Stockmeyer:* Homiletical Exercises.

Besides the theological faculties in these five universities, there are six Theological Professors in the University of Berne, Switzerland; fifteen in Breslau (Protestant and Roman Catholic faculties); six in Dorpat; ten in Erlangen; eight in Freiburg (Roman Catholic); five in Giessen; thirteen in Göttingen; four in Greifswald; nine in Heidelberg (Rationalists); seven in Jena; seven in Kiel; seven in Königsberg; seven in Marburg; nine in Munich (Roman Catholic); eight in Münster (Roman Catholic); eight in Prague (Roman Catholic); four in Rostock; fourteen in Tübingen (Protestant and Roman Catholic faculties); ten in Vienna (Roman Catholic); nine in Würtzburg (Roman Catholic); and eleven in Zurich (nearly all Rationalists).

The German University is a commonwealth in itself. Its laws and the administration of them are almost totally cut off from the State. The student is, in fact, a citizen of one country, while the man from whom he takes his lodgings belongs to another; if they are both sentenced to prison, the judgment is pronounced by different courts, and they are confined in different places. This has been the case ever since the origin of the universities, and the students have been favored with many immunities of which the ordinary burgher has been deprived. Recently, however, a disposition has arisen among the students to have the university court entirely abolished. Herr Studiosus has arrived at the conclusion that the university laws have not kept pace with those of the State, and he demands that his whole guild shall be placed on exactly the same footing with other citizens. He hopes in this way to acquire liberty, I imagine, of fighting duels to his heart's content. Heidelberg University has already abrogated its court. It is difficult to imagine how any one can have greater freedom than the German student. He can do what he pleases within the bounds of morality, and sometimes outside of them. The professors, as such, have nothing whatever to do with discipline, and their relation is purely that of teachers to pupils. The students may absent themselves from lectures as much as they choose, and if they are disorderly, and wish to play a prank by locking the lecture-room door—though just such sophomorical nonsense is never dreamed of in Germany—the humble beadle is the disciplinarian ; and yet, poor wight, he can only report the offenders to the university judge. When will the day come when the whole police system of our American schools will be abolished ? When our young men are trusted, and regarded as gentlemen and equals, a new hour will have come in the development of our educational life.

The whole university system of Germany is now undergoing serious reconsideration.* The last twenty-four years have wrought such changes in it that the best educators

---

* Among the most recent German works treating the need of immediate university reform, are :—(1.) Meyer, "*Die Zukunft der deutschen Hochschulen.*" Breslau : 1874. (2.) Reusch, " *Theologische Facultäten oder Seminarien ?* " Bonn: 1873. (3.) Holtzendorff, "*Die Gegenwart.*" (Nos. 27, 28,) 1873. (4.) Ravoth, " *Zur Revision und Reformirung der Lehr und Lern-methode an den Universitäten.*" Berlin : 1874.

are concerned as to the future. The present alarming decline in the number of students attending the Berlin University cannot be accounted for on the ground of increased expense of living. The new attention given to mechanics and natural sciences has brought into successful working a large class of polytechnical and other institutions of popular grade that have made fearful inroads upon most of the universities. Their old methods are too heavy, and the crisis of uncertainty as to what new ones to adopt is painfully present. Singularly enough, while some Americans are slavishly following in the footsteps of the Germans, and boasting that they are reproducing here the faultless German university system, the Germans themselves are proposing to change to the English and American plan. They say their own, as it now is, is *effete*, and that the lack of unity in theology and general spirit in the German university is proving fatal.

Years ago, Dorner lamented the absence of the ethical element, and his jeremiad is more in place now than when he uttered it. Holtzendorff proposes that the university buildings of Berlin be removed, and that dormitories be built for the accommodation of eight hundred students. Nothing but this, he claims, can bring individuality to the university work and life. In December, 1873, a building was opened in Sebastian strasse, Berlin, where eighteen young theologians, five philologians, and two mathematicians, found accommodation ; and the disposition for students to group has increased ever since, and will likely extend to all the universities.

TABLE OF THE GERMAN UNIVERSITIES:

Including the few others, identical in language, and generally
ranked with those of Germany.
1873, 1874.

NAME AND LOCATION.	Date of Foundation.	Professors In Ordinary.	Professors Extraordinary, and other Teachers.	Total Instructors.	Number of Students.
I. GERMANY.					
1. Berlin....................	1809	55	130	185	3,051
2. Bonn	1818	58	45	103	834
3. Breslau...................	1506	49	58	107	1,022
4. Erlangen	1743	34	21	55	408
5. Friburg...................	1457	38	13	51	294
6. Giessen	1607	34	23	57	325
7. Göttingen	1737	56	48	104	979
8. Greifswald	1456	34	20	54	531
9. Halle	1697	45	47	92	961
10. Heidelberg...............	1386	40	68	108	883
11. Jena.....................	1558	26	38	64	425
12. Kiel	1665	34	24	58	174
13. Königsberg	1544	44	30	74	581
14. Leipsig	1409	55	92	147	2,845
15. Marburg.................	1527	32	32	64	392
16. Munich..................	1472	66	45	111	1,128
17. Rostock	1419	27	7	34	126
18. Strasburg...............	1566	50	24	74	405
19. Tübingen................	1477	41	36	77	896
20. Würtzburg...............	....	..	..	54	880
II. GERMAN AUSTRIA.					
1. Gratz	1486	42	30	72	722
2. Innspruck	1673	38	20	58	640
3. Prague...................	1347	51	62	113	1,442
4. Vienna...................	1365	79	143	222	3,440
III. SWITZERLAND.					
1. Bâle	1460	30	30	60	150
2. Berne	1834	30	32	62	315
3. Zurich...................	1832	33	42	72	462
IV. GERMAN RUSSIA.					
1. Dorpat...................	1632	38	28	66	756
Total.....................		1,159	1,188	2,398	25,067

6

CHAPTER VI.

HEIDELBERG UNIVERSITY.

THE one who grows weary of Heidelberg is deserving of compassion. My first visit to the lovely little city, in 1857, was for the purpose of immediate matriculation in the university. In three days I expected to be an exemplary student, hearing and copying at least three lectures a day, and spending not less than one hour in the twenty-four in the famous library. But it was two full months before I could get within the lecture-rooms, so enticing was the scenery without. And, to be candid, I never matriculated at all in Heidelberg, but heard lectures at irregular intervals. In spring and summer, the promenades and hill-sides are simply perfect. The walks to the Molkenkur and Wolfsbrunnen, the stiff climb to the Königstuhl, and a scramble among the never wearying ruins of the Castle, with its chaos of ivy, never seemed to me a reality, but rather a magic spell, whose only drawback was the apprehension that it would soon be broken. From the Castle Terrace, where I have lingered many a time by the whole afternoon, one has a view of the vine-clad slopes across the Neckar; of the desolate place where Strauss, the author of the "Life of Jesus," used to brood away his melancholy hours; of the Philosophenweg, where Hegel, cogitating the system that was destined to take such a violent pantheistic hold on German theology, walked to and fro until every pebble and shrub became familiar to him ; and of the dwelling which will be remembered and visited for many years as the cheerful home of the sweet-spirited Bunsen.

The following account of the Heidelberg professors, and of their brethren elsewhere, is the result of various opportunities to visit the institutions where they labor, to hear them in their lecture-rooms, to enjoy many delightful hours at some of their peaceful homes, to accompany some of them on their walks, and, above all, to be aided by many of them in directions for study. So far as Halle is concerned, I had the privilege of a period of uninterrupted study and daily contact with its great minds.

A feeling of sadness comes over any one not in sympathy with the prevailing theology in Heidelberg, who remembers what was taught there fifteen years ago, when its principal chairs were occupied by men of evangelical sentiment. The genial, original Hundershagen was there then, but went later to Bonn. His mantle seems to have fallen on Christlieb. Not even Herder himself lived more in the Old Testament period, or clothed it with a fresher life, than the magnificent Umbreit, the most eloquent German professor whom it has ever been my fortune to hear. But he has fallen, and his poetry has long ago become a living reality. The seat of Rothe, who was himself the very personification of his own great ethical system, is occupied by another. The places of these men, and of a few more of similar spirit that might be mentioned, are filled by others of laxer—they call it more liberal—theology. The consequence is, that the number of theological students in Heidelberg has so diminished within a few years as to have become a serious question for the Baden Government. All recent attempts to reinforce the theological faculty by the accession of the best theologians from other universities have failed, and must do so, so long as the theology at Heidelberg maintains its present negative tone.

Hitzig is now climbing up among the Nestors of German learning, for he has well passed his threescore. His has been a life of real study, all of it spent in academic seclusion, and may be taken as a specimen of German professorial circulation from university to university, in answer to calls to and fro, from north to south. When seventeen years old he studied theology at Heidelberg, and in the following year went to Halle, and sat at the feet of Gesenius. In 1828 he became Professor of Theology at Heidelberg, and four years afterward went to Zürich in a similar capacity. He returned once more to Heidelberg, in 1861, where he now gives the ripe results of his long study. He lectures, as occasion requires, on all branches of Old Testament science, certain subjects connected with the New Testament, and on the languages of the Semitic stem. Now that Tuch is gone, he stands with Ewald at the head of the Old Testament negative critics of Germany. He appeared as an author as long ago as 1831, and his first work, the "Idea of Criticism Practically applied to the Old Testament," gave evidence of a taste and learning which have ripened in his translation and exposition of Psalms, Proverbs, Ecclesiastes, Song of Solomon, Jeremiah, Ezekiel, Daniel, the Minor

Prophets, and lesser works of like import. His criticism is bold, and, if very learned, yet betrays far less sympathy with the truths of revelation than patience and thoroughness of research.

Hitzig is tall, angular, and awkward to excess. If the veriest countryman who brings vegetables to the market-floor of Faneuil Hall were placed on the rostrum of any senate, he would not present a more abominable violation of all the maxims of elocutionary taste' and ease than this same archæologist. Hitzig looks for all the world as if he might be some long-lost and forgotten hieroglyphic, suddenly fished up from the slimy bank of the Nile or Euphrates. His very clothing appears as if it might have been made for any other gaunt man sooner than for him. His arms are as long as Lincoln's, and, while lecturing, he folds them and swings them about as if practicing some system of gymnastics of which Dio Lewis has never heard. He sits down and rises again at intervals, poking out and twisting his long fingers as if trying to make a knot or braid of them, or to practice upon his auditors some ancient alphabet for the deaf and dumb. His gloves are hardly at rest on one side of his desk before they have to emigrate to the other. His notes are of immense quarto size, and every time he wishes to turn them over he has to go through the motions similar to those of a man reading all sides of a double-sheet newspaper without cutting the leaves. Like nearly all German professors, he wears a ring—some of them indulge in several. Hitzig's ring, having to be an antique, or else not at all to his taste, is set with some immense red stone, whose brilliancy contrasts

pleasingly with his dull brown notes, three minutes' use
of a paper knife on which would have saved an immense
amount of manipulation.

Hitzig, in the only lecture I have heard by him, was in
his element. His subject was the social customs, mode
of travel, and hospitality of the ancient Jews. He seemed
to have just taken a journey to, and spent half a life-time
among, the inhabitants of Palestine at the time of the
Judges. He showed how the Jews differed from other
nations in social habits, and he seemed as thoroughly domesticated among them as Boeckh among the Greeks and
Romans. The wayfarer did not pay when he had nothing
to pay with. A little present for a night's lodging was as
much thought of as the payment of a large bill. When
travelers met or separated they kissed each other, and
inferiors touched the ground with their mouths or fore-
heads in greeting a superior. The Hebrew, of course,
knew nothing of the coffee-house, but he was well treated
when away from home. All these familiar points were
enlarged upon, and abundantly, but not tediously, illustrated. Hitzig, with all his antiquarian taste and appearance, has a ready store of wit, and often uses a digression
to allay the explosive laughter that some almost waggish
remark excites. Such things as the following are not
uncommon. To illustrate the abusive epithets common
among the Jews, he gave an authenticated instance of the
meeting of an aristocratic and a plebeian Hebrew: "How
do you do, you dog?" "Thank you. Your dog and his
three little pups are quite well!" He adduced authorities
in abundance for all his general statements, and, incon-

sistently enough, used the Bible, as well he might, as his chief authority, though it is too well known that he denies exegetically the authenticity of the very books which he uses as his strongest corroborative evidence. On the topography of Palestine, our American Robinson is his great stay, as he is of all men of learning in the same department throughout Germany and Great Britain. In order that the students might not lose any important term, Hitzig wrote, from time to time, on the blackboard, the original words, in the different Oriental languages concerned, and so readily and beautifully as betrayed his perfect familiarity with the Hebrew and its cognates.

Schenkel, also of the Theological Faculty, has great popular power as a speaker, and it is impossible for any one to go to sleep while hearing him, or to forget what he says after leaving his presence. He is forcible, sometimes very eloquent, but brimful of inconsistencies, and sometimes contradicts himself more than once in the same hour. He speaks, apparently, with utter self-forgetfulness, and in a short time can work himself into a perspiration, his cravat-bow around to the nape of his neck, and the pens out of the hands of his hearers. A lecture on the temptation of Christ, indicates both his style and theological tone. " The temptation of Christ," said he, " is no religious incantation, like Mephistopheles in Faust ; neither was it an historical occurrence, as presented by the New Testament ; much less was it a myth, as Strauss holds. It has simply an historical germ, as with the miracle of changing the water into wine at the marriage at Cana in Galilee, but was not a fact in its particulars. The New Testament

account of Christ's temptation is Oriental, and is a narrative framed according to the idea of what the Church
afterward thought Christ to be. Evil is reflected in the
temptation. Christ, in order to be ready for his mission,
was compelled to resist the principle of evil, and this is
the meaning of the Satan described by Matthew. Christ
felt that he could save Israel, and in his resistance of the
principle of evil he showed his capacity for accomplishing
his object. He felt that his call was to pour balm into
the wounds of his times. The first questions which Christ
had to ask were: 'Am I not the Old Testament Messiah?' 'Am I not the Son of David?' The temptation now came to say: 'You are this very person, and
you can best prove it if you will do what I tell you—
namely: restore the glory of Jerusalem and the splendor
of Israel.' The temptation to enjoy himself, to receive
honor from men, to have great power, was strong, but it
was all an inward feeling. He was tempted to believe
that the Messianic kingdom was merely to take the prophecies of the Old Testament in their literal signification.
The Jews were full of the Old Testament Messianic idea,
and Christ was inwardly tempted to accord with it. His
whole triumph over these inward stirrings was his great
preparatory work for the accomplishment of his design.
He did not proclaim himself the Messiah."

All of Schenkel's lectures abound, just as his books,
in thrusts at the prevailing evangelical theology, and at
the orthodox view of scriptural authority. When he
preaches, the churches are crowded, just as they would be
if any man of his capacity as an orator should speak on

any subject not kindred to theology. The people hear him and read his writings, because he speaks and writes freshly. As a thorough scholar, a profound theologian, a man entitled to the claims he makes, he commands the respect of no mind in Germany not in harmony with his negative views. He is, confessedly, the most complete theological charlatan of Germany. If his efforts shall have the result of making the orthodox divines throw away their stilts, tread squarely on the ground with the people, and use the language of the hungering masses, they will not be in vain. Already there are gratifying signs that he and his school are unintentionally exerting this very influence. I counted but seventeen students in his lecture-room when I heard him last. According to very late accounts, he has but two. If one should enter the large halls of the evangelical theological professors at Halle or Berlin, he would have to go early to get a good seat. The young men of Germany are on the side of orthodox theology, and this is only one of the proofs.

Dr. Gass fills the chair of Systematic Theology, made vacant by the death of the beloved Rothe. One would suppose that history would be more to his taste, in view of his elaborate " History of Protestant Doctrines," on which his reputation chiefly rests. He has his notes beside him, but uses them very little. He is small-sized, and has the air of the cultivated gentleman, and of the lover of society quite as much as of books. Dr. Gass has a pleasant voice, but never makes a surprise, like Hitzig in an adjoining room. In a lecture on angelology and demonology, he said: " The idea of angels has never

6*

been a part of the Christian faith. All the principles of our religion would be the same without them. Such beings exist, nevertheless, and carry out God's purposes for human welfare. 'They encompass his whole government, and constitute an important part of it. In answer to the question, 'What are the angels?' the New Testament gives but little information, and speaks only of their acts. The belief in angels is very important, for it colors and animates the whole realm of space. The belief in demons has always had a hold on the moral life of man. Christianity, by refining it, is distinguished in this respect from all dualistic and gnostic systems of antiquity. The scriptural idea of Satan, and of demons in general, is, that they represent general principles. The figure of Satan in Job simply shows how near the principle of evil could appear in God's presence. The New Testament representation of Satan and demons bears traces of the religious systems of heathendom. The whole idea of the accounts of Satan and demons in the New Testament is simply to represent the conquest of sin over all opposition."

After leaving this lecture it was difficult to tell exactly what Gass thought of Satan, whether he be a person or not. I asked my friend what he understood the learned Doctor to hold on this point, confessing my own failure to catch any clear idea of his meaning. "Oh!" said he, "he means that the quality of actual and veritable personality inheres in that character, but that, after all, if we would understand Satan, he must be metaphysically construed." I was now ready for dinner.

CHAPTER VII.

HALLE.—TWO OF ITS NESTORS.

ONE does not need to walk over five minutes from the railway station of Halle before being convinced that he is in a really German university town. Excepting some new buildings in the suburbs, the main features of the place must be very nearly what they were centuries ago. An old round tower occupies a prominent position as you enter the long, narrow, cobble-stone alley, which is inclosed on the left by the same rough high wall that was a part of the fortifications in the Middle Ages. On the right are lodging houses for the students, some of whom may be seen leaning over the broad window-sills, half enveloped in clouds of tobacco smoke from their long pipes. By taking a broader but more circuitous street to the University, a bookstore is seen at every few paces. The windows are plentifully supplied with the later works of the Halle professors, the spare interstices being filled with their portraits. I was glad, on one of my later visits, to buy at a shop an excellent *carte de visite* of Tholuck, representing his bloodless, leathery, wrinkled face, better than any portrait of him I had seen. The bookstores increase in number as you approach the University, until you reach the last one, Herr Petersen's, in which velvet-coated and long-booted students ; books and pamphlets, stretching from Faust's day down to ours ; maps, old, new,

and nondescript ; and tobacco smoke, that creeps up through
the great barrel stems that have long since lost their cherry
perfume, exist in such heterogeneous intermixture as can
be found only in an antiquarian bookstore of a German
university town.

Julius Müller, the author of the " Christian Doctrine of
Sin," and celebrated throughout Europe for the best course
of lectures on "Dogmatics" in any university, is now preparing his "Doctrinal System" for the first time for the
press, and proposes to issue the work shortly in three volumes.   The last few years have made great changes in his
appearance.   He is more bent, has donned the skull-cap
on account of baldness, and reads with less vigor, and in
a thicker and weaker voice, in which the nose seems to
play as important a part as the tongue.   But there is the
same pleasant face as before, and all accounts agree that,
with the exception of a slight loss of memory, his mind is
as strong as ever.   The last time I heard him, his audience consisted of about seventy-five students, two of
whom smoked cigars during the whole of the lecture.
The lecturer did not take any notice of it, nor did any of
the students ; it seemed to be only a common occurrence.
Whenever the professor was not understood, a loud hiss
here and there from the students was a signal for repeti-
tion.   Müller always repeated when thus invited.   His
notes were very brown, and probably had been used many
years.   I noticed that he looked now and then closely at
the additions on their margins—the only new growth that
the plant had taken since it first bloomed.

The lecture was a clear statement of the relations of

religion to social life, of the grounds of real social freedom, and of the utility and necessity of overcoming individual peculiarities for the public good. It was just such
a lecture as one would expect from Müller—profoundly
learned, fortified by the strongest authorities, and, best of
all, in perfect harmony with the Scriptures. When the
hall-clock struck the hour for the professor to cease, he
kept on reading toward the close of his section, amid the
general buzz of his auditors, who were evidently determined to hear no more, but busied themselves with cork-
ing their inkstands, folding their notes, and finding their
way to their hats, canes, and the door.

I was surprised to see how well Tholuck looked, compared with his delicate and even death-like appearance in
former years. His lecture-room was well filled—a test of
his undiminished hold on the students. He lectured on
the twelfth chapter of the Gospel of John. One of the
students had a copy of the last edition of Tholuck's
"Commentary on John" before him, endeavoring in this
way to follow the lecturer. But this was impossible. The
old body was so vitalized by new blood, that he was compelled to close the book frequently, and hear the newest
and freshest thoughts of the man who was giving to his
audience a better commentary on the Fourth Gospel than
he had ever given to the printer. Tholuck was almost blind,
and had to bring his notes well nigh into contact with his
face in order to decipher them. When he leisurely laid
them down, and looked right out upon the students as if
he could see the most distant face and into the deepest
heart, he always said what took firmest hold, and was

destined to be kept longest in mind. I could compare this scene, which occurred perhaps five or six times during the lecture, to nothing better than a man casting handfuls of diamonds to his children.

Tholuck is compelled to do the most of his writing now by dictation, and, indeed, for many years has been making use of one or more amanuenses. He was thought to be on the consumptive's death-bed when about twenty years of age, but he is now threescore and ten. He has been ascetically careful of his diet and the general treatment of his body, and constantly observes his clock-work distribution of time for literary labor. Between eleven and twelve in the morning he walks up and down the short, covered promenade in his garden, or far out on a country road. Here, in this only idle hour at home, he examines theological candidates for orders, transacts business with all who have accounts to settle, receives calls from men who come to consult him on important ecclesiastical questions, and renews acquaintanceship with the old students whom many miles and years have kept aloof from his presence. But in the midst of the most pressing duty, whether on his promenade or in his study, Tholuck always has time to grasp an American's hand, and talk with him at leisure. He remembers his American students with great interest; still knows their names perfectly well; inquires about certain ones with fatherly love; and even ventures to predict their path of life in the great theological world. He complains, with a sigh, that there are now few Americans at Halle, and wants to know, half querulously, what has become of them all. When asked what message he desired to be conveyed to his friends, readers, and co-workers beyond the sea, he looked toward the blue sky, and, a smile playing over his face, replied in a voice full · of pathos : " Tell them I am still working hard here for the higher work of heaven ! "

In Germany they celebrate every thing—birthdays, baptismal-days, wedding-days, days of induction into office, of receiving degrees and titles, and, indeed, all manner of days around which one can hang a scrap of interest or romance. Any excuse is regarded better than none in order to have a resting spell, an extra dinner, a little congratulatory poetry, and all one's friends at the board. You are hardly over one of these scenes before another one is upon you, and life in the Fatherland is one continual celebration. Such an event as the completion of a half a century of steady work in the halls of a quiet German university must be numbered among the " white days " of life, and the year 1870 was distinguished by two of these in Halle alone, the former being that of Professor Leo, the well-known historian, and the latter that of the still better known Tholuck. I remember often passing Professor Leo, years ago, in the dirty old streets of Halle, and little dreamed that the brisk little old man—his white, round head crowned jauntily with a hat that might once have been black, and have had some shape—had then been writing and lecturing history for thirty-six years. But he has survived it all, and has, probably, a half dozen more books slumbering in his busy brain. As to how many new courses of lectures, essays, and political articles he is incubating, who will dare to guess ?

From December first to the third, 1870, the close of
Tholuck's half century of work in the University of Halle
was celebrated in a manner worthy of his great name, and
the thousands of his grateful disciples. The intimate personal relations which he has cultivated with the students,
from the very day he entered on his duties in the university, account in a large measure for the great numbers
from all parts of Germany who were present at the gathering. The festivities commenced in the Crown Prince
Hotel, where the dining-hall was filled with guests.

Tholuck delivered an address to them, calling them " not
disciples or admirers, but friends in Christ," and giving a
retrospect of his labors as an instructor and an author.
He told of his conversion, and that he had made it his
object not to be a " book professor," but a " student professor," and that it had been said truthfully of him that
" he cultivated rather the society of candidates than pastors, and of students than candidates." He had been sent
to Halle to fight the prevailing Rationalism, and long ago
it gave way to a better state of things. He urged his
auditors to have but " one passion—Him, only Him."
Early on the second morning of the celebration, the University Musical Club serenaded the doctor with a choral:
" Praise the Lord, the mighty King of Glory!" The aged
man said, in his acknowledgment, that above all things
for which we have to thank God are a knowledge of our
sinfulness, and real penitence. The congratulations of
friends began at ten o'clock, in Tholuck's own home,
where, unfortunately, only a few could gain admittance.
All the halls and stairways and every available spot were

occupied, either by the friends of the doctor or by the multitudes of wreaths, bouquets, and garlands that they had
brought and piled into pyramids.

But the testimonial Kögel brought with him, from
the Prussian Ministry of Public Worship—the Star
of the Red Eagle of the second class, with oaken
branch—was most prominent. This was old Kaiser
William's tribute. Court-preacher Hoffmann was the
bearer of the salutations of the Ecclesiastical Council,
and called Tholuck "one of the outmost guards in
the conflict of the Church, a veritable Church Father
of the nineteenth century;" and nobody, not even the
Rationalists themselves, will question the merit of the
term. The rector of the Halle University acknowledged
the services of Tholuck for science, the Church, and the
University, and presented to him a special semi-centen-
nial production in Latin, by Professor Schlottman, entitled "The Union of the Roman and German Nations."
In replying to this, the doctor told the process of his
dealing with the Halle skeptics in his younger days, and
that, notwithstanding, he had never wanted for friends in
all the four Faculties. The congratulations of the students
were embodied in a neat speech by one of the number;
the Theological Faculty congratulated through its dean;
the various universities throughout Germany were represented personally by their very brightest stars; and the pastors of different cities sent one or more thither, to say that
their love and admiration were unabated. An album,
containing the portraits of all the amanuenses who had
served the doctor through his long life as an author, was

presented by one of the number, himself now a leading
German ecclesiatie—Superintendent Müller, of Bielefeld.
The Gustavus Adolphus Society, foreign and home mis-
sionary organizations, and I know not how many other
associations—many of which had received their very life
from his sympathetic pen—sent representations. Professor Jacobi, the Church historian, touched the deepest
chord in host and guests when he read a letter to the
doctor, written and signed by theologians in the German
army at that very hour before Paris, expressing the same
feeling of gratitude, undiminished love, and fervent prayer
for many a year of good work for the old man. One of
the signers was mortally wounded, and his signature was
in a trembling hand. A sum of money "from unseen
friends," amounting to four thousand and seven hundred
thalers, was presented as a Tholuck fund for the education
of indigent theological students. There were contributions from England, Holland, and America.

In the afternoon more than three hundred guests sat
down to the dinner. Toasts followed in abundance. Frau
Tholuck, a Swabian by birth, was one of the centers of attraction and compliment, and a toast was presented to her
by Court-preacher Hoffmann, who had witnessed her marriage long since in the Castle Church of Stuttgart. An
American was present, and expressed the attachment of
his countrymen to the character and writings of Tholuck.
Another guest offered a toast to the University of Halle,
which has the honor of conferring the doctor's degree on
the three most noted leaders of the German army not
identified with the royal family. Think of it—Dr. Von

Bismarck, Dr. Von Moltke, Dr. Von Roon! The dinner closed by singing the old hymn: "Let all praise God!" In the evening there was an immense torchlight procession by the students, and far into the night the quiet Halleans heard Luther's hymn, "A strong tower is our God," reverberating through their crooked streets. Tholuck urged his theological serenaders to compensate for the chasms of war by deeper and truer spiritual life.

The guests started for their various homes the next day, happy to have seen once more, and probably for the last time, the old teacher of their youth—himself, perhaps, the youngest of them all; for, like Schleiermacher, Tholuck seems to have made a bond with youth never to part company. It would have been just like him of the laboring oar to rise as early as usual the morning after the festivities to his honor, more full of literary plans for the future than when, half a century previously, the apparently dying consumptive entered the lists with a learned book on the "Sufism, or the Pantheistic Theosophy of the Persians."

The two things that struck me most of all he said during the celebration were, first, that though he had "always been *bent*, he had never been *broken;*" referring to his continual sickness from childhood, and to his unceasing work under it; and, second, that he was on the most friendly terms with every one of his eighty-four associate professors.

Truly, that sun is going down in a cloudless sky. Long may the students still call the man of their love, "The eternal Tholuck!"

CHAPTER VIII.

THE BERLIN UNIVERSITY.—LEADING PROFESSORS.

THE Berlin University is the center of German learning. Göttingen may surpass it in law and history, Vienna in medicine, Munich in chemistry, Leipzig in languages, while Halle is its rival, if not superior, in theology; but no German seat of learning is so thoroughly cosmopolitan, and makes such liberal provision for the culture of its students. On passing down Unter den Linden, and turning to the left at the equestrian statue of Frederick the Great, one sees at the left the university building. It was formerly the palace of Prince Henry, the brother of Frederick the Great, and was built 1754–64. It was given by Frederick William III., in 1809, for its present purpose. It sprang into existence during the agony of the Napoleonic supremacy. It contains only the lecture rooms and scientific collections. The zoological museum is one of the richest, most complete, and best arranged in Europe. The mineralogical and anatomical collections are also of a very superior order. The library building stands across the street from the university, and reminds one of a huge old-fashioned bureau. In fact, the capricious Frederick the Great gave his architect a chest of drawers for the model, and made him conform to it. It is surmounted by the Prussian flag, and a guard of soldiers plays the formality of its protection. There are six hundred thousand volumes and fourteen thousand MSS. in the library, every one of which is carefully recorded in its catalogue of eight hundred and eighty-seven folio volumes. The most important works are never permitted to be taken from the library. There is one room in which those who wish to consult books can read and write at leisure. There is nothing imposing in the appearance of the university building ; it is dingy, devoid of all architectural display, and, with the exception of the refreshing little plot of grass in the front court, is uninviting in the extreme. But a day spent under its roof in hearing the lectures of its professors, and seeing its throngs of students, gathered from all parts of the world, gives one an idea of the magnitude of the intellectual influence of the university upon the age, which cannot be derived from the most faithful description. In the quarter-hour interval between the lectures, the halls are thronged with the professors of all the departments, hurrying to and from their lectures, with students of many nationalities, and with visitors anxious to hear, though but once, the men whose books they had been for years feeding on.

On the register posted at the entrance of the building I counted, when last in Berlin, the names of one hundred and twenty-six professors and licentiates, many of whom lecture every day in the week, and some oftener, though the most infirm only read once or twice. The aged Ranke was doing good service still ; the elder Nitzsch was likewise kept at his post. His son, if his dry lecture on Romans which I heard be a fair specimen of his exegetical skill, gives but little evidence of his father's acuteness.

Hengstenberg, who died in 1869, was still in the harness. He was erect in form, quick in movement, and to all appearance a rare picture of health at sixty-five. He walked rapidly through the hall, and evidently knew well how to elbow his way adroitly through the crowd toward his lecture-room or pen. Lepsius, the Egyptologist, looked as abstracted as if his heart were nearer the pyramids than Berlin. Twesten, short, redfaced, and grandfatherly, might be distinguished in a moment by his picture. Piper, one of the pleasantest faces in all the throng, hurried hastily up to the third story, where he could feed upon his rich little museum of Christian antiquities. Semisch, the successor of Neander and Niedner, gave promise of twenty years of useful work. He appeared to be brimful of his theme, and seemed conscious of his responsibility in continuing the labors of his celebrated predecessors. Suddenly the bell struck the hour for lectures to recommence, the long halls were vacated as by magic, the lecture-room doors were closed, and not a sound could be heard but the Babel of professors lecturing.

It is now nearly fifty years since Twesten, with great hesitation, consented to leave his professorship in the University of Kiel, to take the great Schleiermacher's vacant seat in Berlin. He is about eighty-five years old, and still stands firmly at his post, lecturing a goodly number of times a week on Encyclopædia and Methodology, John's Gospel, and the Symbolical Theology of the Evangelical Church. He is short and stout; has a thin, gasping voice, though a broad mouth; parts his scant hair in the middle; wears the padded white cravat of the old

school ; and has the habit of commencing his lecture before he is fairly in his chair. I saw his lips in motion
some time before it was possible to catch a single sentence, and sometimes not a word of a sentence. He has
his notes before him, but seldom consults them. The
lecture I last heard—one of his course on Symbolical
Theology—related to the morbid and abnormal phenom-
ena of Christian life, in which he spoke of the part which
fanaticism had played in the history of the Church. True
faith, he said, consists in the harmonious union of nature
and the supernatural. Fanaticism becomes superstition
when it unites nature and the supernatural improperly.
Superstition does not do justice to the natural, and unbe-
lief does not do justice to the supernatural. In all that
Twesten said there was not the slightest indication of
mental imbecility. He has ripened into a sweet old age.
His face might well be the study of a Fra Angelico, wishing to portray cheerfulness, simplicity, and love, crowning
a long, hard-working, Christian life.

Hengstenberg had to lecture in a large room. His
course on Psalms was so largely attended that, according
to his own statement, there was not a single vacant seat.
He walked quickly to his chair, said " Gentlemen," and
then read such a clear and concise lecture as one would
expect from a man who is impressed with the magnitude
of his theme, and the part his auditors are to take in the
Church of the future. The Scriptures, he said, are inspired not merely in a general, but in a special respect.
Reason does not know how to decide between what may
and what may not be inspired. Inspiration is elevating,

purifying, and hortatory. A writing must be pure if it belongs to the Scriptures. The Old Testament is the only remnant we have of the antediluvian period. Revelation and inspiration belong to each other; each is the complement of the other.

Hengstenberg's peculiar manner of delivery was odd enough to disturb the sobriety of any one who was not a regular attendant upon his lectures. He had a drawling, harsh voice when on a high key, but his lower tones were not unpleasant, yet often so low as to make his words unintelligible. Though he would call his posture sitting, he yet turned in his chair; stood up; sat down again; wheeled around on one side; rested his elbow on the back of his chair; looked out of the window at the falling leaves; then sprang up again; pulled his chair into position, or out of position, as the case might be; dropped down into it again; wheeled round; tugged at his coat; buttoned and unbuttoned it repeatedly; and all the while read a manuscript which it was a wonder, amid all his odd twichings, was not torn into fragments, and scattered all round him. Thus his lecture went on until the clock-stroke stopped his gyrations, and sent the galvanic man out of the room. His voice was as convulsive as his body. He might say one half of a word in a whisper inaudible to many of his students, while the other was roared out with a lion-like violence that called to mind some of his editorials in the "Evangelical Church Gazette."

Dorner is one of the best thinkers, warmest hearts, and most useful men in the theological faculty. He is deeply

attached to the Mediation Theology—indeed, is one of
its most industrious cultivators. Not one of the elder
theologians whom I heard suggested by manner and language as forcibly as did he that sense of the intensity
of life which was the great characteristic and real mag-
netic secret of Arnold of Rugby. He is of slight build,
has a pleasant face, long, disheveled hair, and a forehead
bisected by a bulging, perpendicular vein. Throughout
his lecture he moves mechanically back and forth in his
chair, introduces his snuff-box at leisure, and gives his
watch-guard as thorough a handling as the subject of his
lecture. He lectures on dogmatic theology. The students are deeply attached to him.

Semisch and Steinmeyer are in the prime of life, and
stand midway between those we have already named and
their juniors, who are working up into position. The former professor is second from the sainted Neander in the
chair of Church history, but has few of that great man's
rare qualities. Semisch lectures to a large audience. I
once heard him give a charming picture of the decline
of paganism before the enthusiastic devotion and mission-
ary spirit of the early Church. At a certain point in his
lecture he laid down his notes, arose from his seat, closed
his eyes, put his hand to his face as if in extreme pain,
and made quite a lengthy and, to me, alarming pause.
All the students dropped their pens. My first thought
was that he was suddenly taken ill, perhaps had apoplexy.
But it proved to be only his usual way of delivering his
extempore episodes. He spoke about ten minutes very
earnestly, without once looking at his notes, and then sat
7

down to them again, when the students resumed their writing. This was really the best part of the lecture, but it is just these portions of the university lectures that are not expected, either by professor or student, to be noted down. The students call them *expectoration*, by which they mean, talking from the heart.

Steinmeyer has been an author ever since 1844, when he published an excellent little volume of lectures. His principal work is, " Contributions to the Understanding of the Scriptures," a work which has had the success of reaching several editions. He is celebrated as a lecturer for his course on practical theology. He has the appearance of a refined, Christian gentleman ; is pale and thin in person ; does not yet wear glasses ; and is known to prepare himself specially for the delivery of each lecture. He has paid more attention to his elocution than most of his colleagues, stands as he speaks, and moves about in Beecher-like freedom. He has the peculiar habit, in the early part of his lecture, of laying the forefinger of his right hand lengthwise his nose, and keeping it there until he finishes the point he is trying to make. The Church, he says, is one, whether in heaven or on earth, in the past, present, or future. The Church is the mother of the congregation ; it springs directly from Christ, is a Divine institution, and cannot be imitated. The congregation or parish is only a member of the Church. It is the *ecclesiola in ecclesia*, just according to Spener's idea. How must the congregation be treated ? It must be trained in the Lord by faithful pastors, preachers who regard themselves not as the masters, but as the servants of the

Church. The preacher is not responsible to the parish for the faithful discharge of his duty, but rather to God ; for the Church never called him to preach—he was called from heaven. The preacher does not derive his commission from the congregation ; he takes nothing from them, but takes all to them from God. All the duties of the preacher may be summed up in one term—"those who take care of the sheep ;" he is the pastor.

Messner's theological stand-point may be imagined from the fact that he is editor of the "New Evangelical Church Gazette," the German organ of the Evangelical Alliance. He read a carefully prepared and scholarly lecture on Paul's Epistles to the Corinthians. He had but fifteen hearers, but, like all who have become illustrious in the German universities, he must commence at the bottom of the heap. The top is as much for him as for any one else, but he is too dry ever to reach it.

Kleinert is thought by many to be the most gifted, as he is without doubt one of the most evangelical, of all the younger theologians.

The prince of the philosophical faculty, Trendelenburg, died a few months since. He went to Berlin as the successor of Schelling ; he was a prolific author, the most of his works having clustered around his favorite theme, the Aristotelian Philosophy. His great work, "Logical Investigations," appeared over thirty years ago. In this he laid down the principles of what is the nearest approach to an original system, which he has elaborated in his later works, "Niobe," "The Moral Idea of Right," and the "Cologne Cathedral." He lectured, of course, in one of the largest halls, and always had an immense number of students. In person he was tall, neatly attired, and wore the heavy, hand-broad cravat, such as are seen in the faded, stiffnecked portraits on the old palace walls of Germany. His manner was dull and sluggish in the extreme, his voice was scarcely more than a hoarse, rough whisper, quite in contrast with the Ptolemaic "music of the spheres," which he so drowsily descanted upon. It was a rare thing for any stranger to catch two consecutive sentences. Even many of the students in regular hearing occupied their time about equally between taking scrappy notes and making ear-trumpets of their hands. Trendelenburg was a great philosopher, but his elocution was barbarously poor—hardly equaled in its line even in the British Parliament.

CHAPTER IX.

THE University of Munich is a Roman Catholic institution, and is the principal school of learning in Bavaria. It was founded in 1472, first located in Ingoldstadt, afterward removed to Landshut, (1800,) and finally established, in 1826, in Munich. It is situated on the Ludwigstrasse, a very quiet street, yet one of the most splendid in Europe, and, with the opposite Priests' Seminary, forms a large quadrangle, which is ornamented by two fountains, copied from those in St. Peter's Place in Rome.

For many years Doellinger has been the leading professor in the Roman Catholic University at Munich. He has long been the acknowledged leader of the liberal wing of the Romanists, and, as a penalty for his independence, has been publicly excommunicated by the Pope from its fold. This last exercise of papal authority against a recalcitrant son came to pass on this wise : The convocation of the Vatican Council in 1870 was the signal for new discontent throughout the length and breadth of the Roman Catholic Communion. Père Hyacinthe, in Paris, was not the only one who saw in the coming Council true cause for alarm, knowing full well that every effort would be made by the Pope to impose additional restrictions upon the whole Catholic body. Every liberal Catholic, however, looked to Germany for the leadership of the advanced section of the Church, and the expectation was not in vain. For a long time Doellinger had been protesting against the ultra measures of Catholicism, and he never grew weary of demanding that it adapt itself to the different nations, and to the growth of intelligence throughout the world. He did this through no sympathy with Protestantism, but in the interest of Catholicism, for he believed that only in this way could it preserve its life, and grow in strength and influence. Being himself an ardent member of the flock, he was desirous of doing all he could to secure and perpetuate its integrity. It was, accordingly, of a piece with his whole life that he should give timely alarm against the probable adoption by the Council of the dogma of papal infallibility, but his protest did not prevent the act. When the dogma was adopted he did not blindly and tacitly acquiesce, but wrote and spoke against it with unwearied diligence, never showing any bitterness, but proving with the logical skill and clear style that distinguish all the fruits of his busy pen, how absurd, and, in the end, void, would be the new offense to the common sense of every impartial man. Then came reprimand and threat from Rome. And last were heard the thunders of excommunication, with its great catalogue of woes, reminding one of the curse of the Cardinal of Rheims, pronounced on the sacrilegious jackdaw that stole the ring of his holiness. It ran thus, if we can believe the poet :—

> " The Cardinal rose with a dignified look :
> He called for his candle, his bell, and his book.
> In holy anger and pious grief,
> He solemnly cursed that rascally thief!

He cursed him at board, he cursed him in bed :
From the sole of his foot to the crown of his head.
He cursed him in sleeping, that every night
He should dream of the devil and wake in a fright.
He cursed him in eating, he cursed him in drinking,
He cursed him in coughing, in sneezing, in winking ;
He cursed him in sitting, in standing, in lying ;
He cursed him in walking, in riding, in flying ;
He cursed him living, he cursed him dying !
    Never was heard such a terrible curse !
        But what gave rise
        To no little surprise,
    Nobody seemed one penny the worse."

But we must go back a little, for the whole life of such a man as Dr. Doellinger is a matter of public interest.

John Joseph Ignatius Doellinger was born at Bamberg, Bavaria, on the 28th of February, 1799. The family had long been distinguished for remarkable talents, and the father of young Doellinger was, in his day, celebrated throughout Germany as a physiologist, physician, and naturalist. His portrait and bust are frequently to be met with in the scientific cabinets of Bavaria. He was professor in the University of Bamberg at the close of the last century and the beginning of the present, and was regarded, in consequence of his discoveries and writings, as a leading authority in various departments of natural science. The son, chiefly through his mother's influence, was destined for the study of theology, and this tendency was given to his early life. In the year 1822 he was consecrated a priest, and appointed chaplain of Oberscheinfeld, a village in Bavaria. His natural desire led him to teaching, and in the following year he received an appointment as teacher in the Lyceum at Aschaffenburg, near

Frankfort-on-the-Main.   In 1826 he was elected Professor of Church History and Church Law in the University of Munich, where he received immediately various honorary offices, and was nominated and appointed chief librarian of the University library.   Doellinger soon attracted attention as professor because of the thorough and enchanting style of his lectures.   His method was calm, argumentative, and abounding in surprises.

Once, during an Easter ramble, it was my privilege to be present at one of his lectures on Church history, and to note some of the characteristics of the man.   He was to lecture at eleven o'clock in the morning, and a moving crowd of laughing young priests, with shaven crowns, and black coats reaching to the ankles, indicated his lecture-room.   The room was capable of accommodating from three to four hundred auditors, but the seats were not more than two thirds filled.   The lecturer entered in the most quiet and deliberate manner possible, and, hardly looking at his hearers, calmly laid his notes upon the high desk before him, and commenced his lecture as quietly as if talking to a group of little children.   He was in his element, evidently, when standing before his quiet audience of theological students, among whom one could easily perceive a goodly admixture of foreigners.   While his voice was very low, it was also as distinct as a clarion, and audible at the nether end of the great hall.

He seemed to be talking to two or three young friends on a subject which was uppermost in his mind, and which he seemed to think should be the same in theirs.   From the way in which his liberal theology quietly exuded here

and there, one would judge him to be one of those men
with whom you cannot talk ten minutes without seeing the
very inmost heart, and without being warmed anew by their
sympathy. If he had been lecturing on the Tower of
Babel, there is not a doubt that he would have found some
moment, some golden opportunity, to let fall a sentence
or two in favor of bold and liberal thought, and of the
largest freedom to the conscience. This he did abundantly when I listened to him.

He was lecturing on modern Church history, and it
would have been impossible to select any one of his course
in which all the peculiarities of his theological views
and methods were more completely combined than in this.
His theme was "English Puritanism and its Relation to
the Established Church;" but he did not hesitate to cross
the channel repeatedly, and even the intervening centuries,
too, in order to weigh Continental Calvinism in the Catholic balance, and to strive to show the unfitness of the
whole system for the religious demands of the present day.
But Calvinism is Protestanism, he continued, in its un-
mixed state, while Lutheranism is only a corrupt form of
Catholicism. The Anglican Church has never been free
from vestiges of Catholicism, and these are now its saving
principles. During every period of its history, men have
stood up within its fold and called aloud for a return to
the faith which it had abandoned. Just here Doellinger
embraced his opportunity to laud Pusey and his whole
ritualistic crew, yet he did it so calmly and jesuitically,
that his mine of secret enthusiasm became hardly perceptible for a moment. In consequence of the continued

7*

sympathy of the Anglican Church for Catholicism, Doellinger held that its separation from the Papacy must be regarded as only temporary and accidental, and that all good Anglicans must labor to restore the unity. Under the reign of James I., the Anglican Church assumed a new form. When Arminianism came in as a theological element, it acted as an accession to the Catholic strength, for Arminianism was nothing else than a confession of the Catholic doctrine of justification by faith. One of the most remarkable features of English Calvinism is, that it did not perfectly control all English theology, as the Augsburg Confession has controlled Lutheranism. The reason is, that the English mind would not submit to be brought within such narrow limits, and thus England stands a chance of being again controlled by Catholic theology. The Romanizing tendencies there are now very strong, and constantly on the increase.

The sketch of Archbishop Laud and his influence on posterity was worthy of Pusey himself. Cromwell's character was very fairly described, and there can be no ground of complaint at Doellinger's estimate of the constant vacillations of Anglican theology, in consequence of changes in the Government and of French influences. He spoke almost wholly of Protestanism, yet he did not utter one word of abuse. He appeared as impartial as justice itself, and seemed to forget nothing, yet not to say a superfluous word. The whole force of his lecture was this : Protestantism is always vacillating and inconsistent ; it is the tool of the times, the plaything of revolutionists and madcaps ; but real Catholicism stands high above them, and if we

all unite to develop it as the times require, it will accomplish what it used to do—control all the movements and
thinking of the eivilized world. Doellinger's theology is
very attractive to many of the English Catholics and
ritualistic Anglicans, who are said to visit him in large
numbers. He is known to admire warmly both the English Government and people. Those who know him
personally say that he is already a "half-Englishman."

Doellinger is slightly above medium height; he stands
while lecturing, contrary to the custom of many of his colleagues, and does not wear the priest's robe. There is
nothing about him that would lead you to think him a
priest; while every student before him had the tonsure,
the black stockings, and the long black robe dangling about
his feet. When lecturing, his pale, wrinkled, angular face
sometimes lights up with an intrusive smile, a tell-tale
sprite, that reveals where his real feelings and opinions lie.
He now reads from his manuscript, and now speaks ex-
temporaneously ; does not hurry ; seems for the most time
utterly destitute of passion, and is the very personification of sincerity and simplicity. Awhile after the lecture
I heard, I happened to pass him on the street, on the same
day, and had a nearer view of him than when listening to
his lecture. His thin form was slightly bent ; his face,
now not kindled by the presence and light of his students,
wore a sad expression, which was deepened by the lines
that age had been making, but which I had not noticed
before. Some of his features, especially the nose, had an
emphatic Jewish cast. There was a blandness in his manner which could not fail to impress any one who observed

him ; there was probably not a man who walked along the
beautiful Maximilian-street in Munich that whole day,
before whom the most diffident school-girl would have
felt less hesitation in stopping to ask the time of day.

A word on Dr. Doellinger's home, the shop where this
Vulcan forges his thunder-bolts. Like all Germans, he
does not occupy a whole house, but only a story, well-to-
do as he unquestionably is. His apartments are spacious,
and have the air of quiet comfort, if comfort can be sup-
posable in the home of the celibate. Here is a prayer-
stool, embroidered by some admiring one, perhaps a nun ;
there you see a pot of flowers, with I. H. S. inscribed on
it in gilt letters. He has twelve large rooms, nearly all of
which are occupied by his immense library. With the
exception of a few Englishmen, it is believed that Doellinger has the largest private library in Europe. He has
certain sections of his books marked according to the
countries whence he has derived them. "From Spain"
are 1,003 volumes ; "from France," 2,000 ; but far the
greater number are from thinking and writing Germany.
He calls his books his " better half," and he spends nearly
all his in-door hours before his great writing-desk. Every
body receives a cordial, but not demonstrative, welcome,
just as in other days at the doors of Montalembert and
Lord Acton.

No one can visit the halls of the University of Munich
without being reminded of the philosopher Schelling, who
lectured there in the meridian of his fame and strength.
One of his students thus recently wrote, in an article in
the Augsburg " Allgemeine Zeitung," " The Master in his

Lecture-room, about the year 1840 :" "Students thronged about the doors of the University long before the clock struck eleven, when the lecture was to commence. Old men from all parts of Europe were among them, equally eager to gain admission. There was a beadle at each door, and if any one tried to enter without a ticket of admission he was bidden peremptorily to retire ; whether prince or peasant, there was no exception.

" This was Schelling's express order. His fear was, that somebody would publish what he said in his lectures. He cautioned his audience in the strongest language against publishing him, as he wished to give the finishing touches of his system to the world with his own hand, lest the public might be deceived about his opinions. This careful watching of his audience was almost a disease, which grew upon him after somebody once slipped into his lecture-room, and afterward published in a North German literary journal a fragment of one of his lectures on the ' Philosophy of Revelation.' After the unpardonable offense became known to Schelling, he convulsed his audience after the manner of a Jupiter Tonans, by railing in philosophic (?) madness at the indiscretion of the Tantalus, who, by the way, was a Hegelian, and said to be Hegel's own son. In the fifteen minutes that elapsed before the lecturer appeared, many languages could be heard at once. French, English, Modern Greek, Russian, Servian, Hungarian, and other tongues were spoken in that one lecture-room, until the greater one appeared and silenced them all.

" When Schelling entered the door there was profound

silence.   All the people arose from their seats to do the
old man reverence, and seated themselves again when
he became seated.   The little gray-haired, blue-eyed, pug-
nosed philosopher took a thorough survey of his audience,
which saw only the massive, Socratic forehead of the
man, and thought only of what he was going to say.   He
was clad in brown coat and black pantaloons, his toilet
having been arranged with scrupulous care.   His first act,
after looking leisurely at his audience, was to draw his
snuff-box from his pocket and take a pinch, when he laid
the box down on his desk for further use.   He then took
out the large leaves on which his loose notes were
written.   But soon the man was lost in the thinker, and
notes were discarded, as useless scaffolding around the
finished temple."

CHAPTER X.

THE UNIVERSITIES OF EUROPE.—DOELLINGER'S SURVEY.

DOELLINGER was installed Rector of the University of Munich in the year 1866. Conformably to custom, he delivered an oration on the assumption of the rectorate, taking as his theme : " Die Universitäten Sonst und Jetzt." He gave an outline of the history and present condition of the European Universities, which I here reproduce. Of course it could not be expected that Doellinger should do justice to the Protestant element in modern intellectual growth ; but, leaving this very natural defect out of the question, his survey is remarkable for conciseness, learning, and a profound appreciation of the advanced state of learning in the present century.

The first great school of any note, combining the main features of the modern university, was the medical college at Salerno, which enjoyed a wide reputation in the eleventh century. After the lapse of a century we hear of the flourishing law school of Bologna. In the thirteenth century, the law school at Padua was founded. But these institutions were surpassed in extent of studies and financial support by the university at Naples, founded by the king of Sicily in 1224, for the education of young men. The laws of the country were so stringent that no young men were permitted to attend any seat of learning in other parts of Europe ; hence it was natural that this institution should grow up devoid of that freedom and breadth peculiar to the real university in its best sense.

The spirit of usurpation exhibited by the popes, long anterior as well as subsequent to this time, found expression in the studies of the Italian universities. The branches that favored the temporal sovereignty of the papacy and humiliated the princes were taught with great assiduity. There was at that day no scientific tendency whatever in Italy, though that was the very country which contained the great treasures of the classic age. Dante made the complaint that " every body was studying the decretals of the popes." Roger Bacon says : " The jurisprudence of the Italians has, for forty years, been destroying the study of philosophy, natural science, and theology, yea, even the Church and all the kingdoms." This ecclesiastical or papal jurisprudence was the sole pursuit of the theological students ; and it was far back in these times that the Roman priesthood assumed that character of political management and trickery which long since took organic shape in the order of the Jesuits. The Italian universities were visited by immense numbers of students. In Roger Bacon's time—taking the year 1262 as an example—there were in Bologna alone 20,000, nearly every one of whom was engaged in the study of papal jurisprudence.

Coming north of the Alps we find the great school of Paris, which was at first devoted to " general studies," but afterward elevated to a University. It was at the outset under the patronage of the popes, but afterward under

the care of the French kings. But the popes still controlled the studies, as, indeed, they controlled every thing
else in Europe. So they prohibited the study of jurisprudence in Paris, fearing, no doubt, that at that distance from
Rome there might be an admixture of independence or
political heresy in the instruction. Theology was the
principal study in Paris ; the students remained generally
fifteen or sixteen years, until they were from thirty to forty
years of age, before they were thought sufficiently indoc-
trinated to become trusty priests. Nearly half of Paris
was converted to the use of the students, who flocked
thither in great multitudes from all parts of Europe, except Italy. A Venetian embassador, living at the end of
the sixteenth century, states that there were then more
students in the universities of Paris than in all the Italian
universities together. He reports the number to have
been 30,000, a statement which is sustained by an account
of the General Procurator of the same period.

It is remarkable that three centuries passed by after the
founding of the first of the Italian universities before the
thought seems to have occurred to any one in Germany to
establish a similar institution. Even England had followed in the wake of Italy, and had endowed Cambridge
and Oxford long before. But in Germany there was no
school of any prominence, much less one bearing any resemblance to the German university of to-day, until 1348,
when the Emperor Charles IV. founded one at Prague
after the model of the University of Paris. In this he
does not seem to have been actuated by any very elevated
motive, but from the mere accident that he had himself

been a student in Paris, and had been fond of student
life. Very soon the University of Prague was visited by
many thousands of students, the Germans taking a
national pride in it. The University of Vienna followed
that of Prague, in 1365.

But two more centuries elapsed before the German university attained that universal and liberal character which
it now possesses in a remarkable degree. Doellinger cannot be expected, Catholic as he is, to do justice to the
Reformation, and to Protestantism in general, in their elevating influence on higher education at this time. But he
does make the confession, that in the sixteenth century a new and better era dawned upon the German universities. This was the time when the Humanists, or
Philologians, first brought the classics of Greek and Roman literature home to the German mind, and when scho-
lasticism was in its death-agony.

The German universities increased rapidly, though now
and then one was compelled to go down with the downfall
of a patron prince, or the decline of a tendency which it
had been established to sustain. But wherever the Reformation gained a firm footing, new universities arose as by
magic ; for example, Marburg, Königsberg, Jena, Helmstædt, and Altdorf. The Thirty Years' War, which laid
all Germany waste and revolutionized the history of
Europe, seems to have had but little power to destroy
these institutions. Yet the decline in scientific learning
and religious spirit in the universities was deplorable.
John Valentine Andreä says : " I have long ago learned
from my own experience that there is nothing made more

profane than our religion; nothing more fatal than our medicine; nothing more unjust than our justice."

As far down as the end of the seventeenth century Latin was the only language in which lectures were delivered. Any man who ventured to use the language of the people was regarded vulgar. But men of any good degree of etymological and rhetorical acuteness could see that the German tongue was eminently adapted to the purposes of higher education. Leibnitz had long ago said that "the German was the best language in existence for the purposes of philosophical and scientific technology." Thomasius, of Halle, and Buddæus, of Jena, made a desperate effort to introduce the German language into the universities. They offended all the professed advocates of good-breeding and culture by lecturing in German, in spite of opposition. The result was, they carried their point. From their day down to the present, the German student has heard the professor lecture in his own vernacular.

From 1690 to 1730 Halle occupied the first rank among the German universities. Each of its faculties possessed men who were representatives of the varied progress of their times. In one respect, however, it was surpassed by Göttingen—we mean in the study of history. The eighteenth century closed and the nineteenth began amid as violent convulsions as have ever occurred in Europe. At this time of general disruption a number of the universities—some of which had previously enjoyed a good share of favor—ceased to exist. We may reckon among the unfortunate number those of Helmstædt, Rinteln, Frankfort-on-the-Oder, Duisburg, Wittenberg, Erfurt,

Mayence, Bamberg, Cologne, Paderborn, Münster, Dillingen, and Salzburg.

The foundation of the University of Berlin, in 1810, was Prussia's offering to the new period of the progress of humanity in art and science. This institution was the first university established in Germany that did not formally embrace in its programme some distinct ecclesiastical confession. For this reason there has always been the largest liberty granted to the theological professors, from the beginning down to the present time. The University of Berlin very soon rose to high honor. In 1815—only five years after its foundation, and when Germany and Europe were settling their long grudge against Napoleon at Waterloo—Berlin had in all fifty-six professors, and as large a number of students as many of the oldest institutions in Europe. In 1860 there were one hundred and seventy-three professors and subordinate lecturers. As far back as 1835 there were two thousand students in attendance.

Turning to the universities of France, we find that there is no real bond of unity connecting the faculties, as there is in Germany. Each faculty is a sort of independency—or rather, a college working on its own account, instead of being an organic part of a university. The greatest university is the College of France, which was established by Francis I., and in 1789 had nineteen professorships.

Dr. Doellinger disclaims for the English universities, as well as for the French, any title to be ranked with those of Germany. He holds that the professors, unlike their

German confrères, "do not place themselves in the middle of a subject," but take their position on one side of it,
and lecture in such a way as " to produce a satisfactory
effect on a mixed audience."

The Scotch universities are of a more liberal cast than
those of Cambridge and Oxford. Still, even here, learning has declined of late. Blackie makes the broad asser-
tion " that Scotland, at the present moment, is in no sense
of the word a learned country ; especially in our universities learning is at the lowest possible ebb." " The American universities," says Dr. Doellinger, " are of a low grade,
occupying a midway position between the German gymnasia and the philosophical faculty of a German university."

In Spain there is no institution that is worthy of the
name of university. For a century her best institutions
of learning have been deserted, the buildings have been
lying in ruins, and the Spanish young men who desired an
education have resorted to Paris or Germany. Russia has
seven universities, all after the German model. The University of Odessa was founded in 1865. Switzerland,
small as she is, boasts three universities—that of Basle
being the largest and strongest. Holland has also three
universities, though they are not supported as they should
be by the Government. Belgium has four universities,
which bear the twofold character of the French and German systems of higher education. Denmark, with its two
universities, has lately enjoyed the advantages of more
than an ordinary class of scholarly divines. We need
only refer to Münter, Guntvig, and Martensen. The two
Swedish universities of Upsala and Lund are not equal

to the demands of the present day, for they are still hampered by the obstructions that have come down from the Middle Ages.

After Doellinger has completed his survey of the European universities, he strikes a balance vastly in favor of those of Germany, and then indirectly attributes their superiority to a rare "capacity of perceiving and appreciating every foreign trait of character, every national peculiarity, or foreign service to universal human growth. . . . As far as this capacity manifests itself in science and literature, it may be called the historical sense of the Germans." We must make due allowance for Doellinger's partiality for his own countrymen; but even then we have to confess that it is a partiality pretty well sustained by the achievements of the Germans themselves in this very sphere. Gladstone, the English statesman, was found one morning with Huber's "History of the English Universities" on his breakfast-table. A visitor calling attention to it, Mr. Gladstone replied that it was an indispensable book, and far better than all which the English themselves had written on the same subject. The works of Gneist on English law, the historical works of Ranke relating to England, Schäfer's History of Portugal, Ranke's French History, Hermann's History of Russia, Hegel's History of the Italian State Constitution, Schäffer's History of French Law, Schack's History of Spanish Dramatic Literature, and the German criticisms on Dante and Shakspeare, are all indubitable proofs of the German power of properly estimating the men and work of other nations.

This historical sense has crystallized itself in four Germans, whose services to mankind have been, and will hereafter be, of inestimable value. The first of these is Niebuhr, who is the founder of a new mode of historical writing, and of a race for the first time capable of reading history aright. He combined the imagination of a true poet with patient and profound research, and was the first to lift the vail which Livy had drawn over Roman history, and which had been undisturbed 'from the Roman period down to Niebuhr's day. The second in the quartet is Alexander von Humboldt, who knew no part of the world except as a member of the great organism—the universal cosmos. His groupings of the results of scientific investigation, and his combinations of them with the great truths of universal history, have thrown all similar efforts into the shade. Ritter, the third in this honor-group, was the creator of the science of the earth. Instead of confining his attention to any particular country or geographical characteristic, he combined geography, ethnography, and history into one mighty force, and showed its varied influence on individual man, and on nations and their history. Jacob Grimm completes the number of these rarely-endowed men. He, more than all others, has penetrated the depths of the German language, and has shown its growth through custom, legend, myth, and law. And this unwearied work of love for Grimm's own tongue is but the pioneer of labors that are to be expended upon all the great languages of man. As a peerless example of reducing language to law, and of reading its mysterious philosophy, Grimm is scarcely inferior to Niebuhr, Humboldt, or

Ritter, in the universal character of his services as a representative of the historical sense of Germany.

Taking leave of Doellinger, I derive from the Budget of the Italian Minister of Public Instruction this account of the present state of the universities of that kingdom.

Italy has no less than twenty universities, fifteen of which are entirely supported by the State, and three of the remaining five receive a fixed annual subsidy. The number of students in attendance at the universities that are supported solely by the State is stated as follows : Bologna, 453 ; Cagliari, 35 ; Catania, 151 ; Genoa, 306 ; Messina, 82 ; Modena, 348 ; Naples, 1,503 ; Padua, 1,488 ; Palermo, 177 ; Parma, 262 ; Pavia, 1,014 ; Pisa, 484 ; Sassari, 63 ; Sienna, 91 ; Turin, 1,144. The five free universities are : Camèrimo, Ferrara, Maccrata, Perugia, and Urbino ; and the amount given by the State for their support, together with that given to the fifteen universities named above, is, in round numbers, $900,000 (gold). The faculties in the fifteen universities exclusively dependent on the State, and entitled to grant degrees, number sixty-one, which are divided as follows : 8 Theological Faculties (one at present suspended) ; 15 Law ; 15 Medicine ; 13 Mathematics and Physics ; 10 Literature and Philosophy. At the six universities of Catania, Genoa, Palermo, Padua, Pisa, and Turin, instruction is imparted by all the five faculties ; at Bologna, Cagliari, Messina, Naples, and Pavia, it is given by only four faculties ; and in the three universities of Modena, Parma, and Sassari by only two, that of Theology being in abeyance.

From this showing, it is very clear that all the universities are dwarfs, and that the nation is suffering seriously from the want of imparting higher instruction in fewer but more favored centers. The number of the Italian universities is out of all proportion to that in other countries where education is far more general. The kingdom of Italy, for instance, with a population of twenty-four millions, has no less than sixty-one faculties ; while France, which has half again as many inhabitants, has but fifty-three faculties. Austria has thirty-four million inhabitants, and yet has only seven universities. Russia has eight, Prussia ten, and all Germany, with double the population of the kingdom of Italy, twenty-six. Belgium. has four universities and Switzerland three ; in Scotland there are four universities, while England furnishes the same number to a population six or seven times greater than Scotland. Spain has ten universities (reduced from thirteen in 1845) ; and Holland, with a population of three and a half millions, has three.

The expense to the Italian Government of supporting this undue number of universities is much greater than would be the case if they were reduced. But a still greater evil would be remedied by supplying a few educational centers with an adequate staff of capable professors ; for each university must, of course, provide teachers for every branch included in the lists of faculties. "Men of talent," says the Budget, " naturally prefer a wider sphere of action, and hence throng to the large university towns, leaving the smaller ones to do as well as they can with second-rate professors; while men of European reputation in the great seats of learning are, by reason of this

8

excessive decentralization, debarred from exercising the influence which legitimately belongs to them, and have to lecture, if not to empty, at least to scantily filled, halls."

A comparison between the number of matriculated students in Italy and elsewhere places in a still clearer light the absurdity of the present arrangement. During the academical year of 1866–67 all the Italian universities presented a total of 7,601 students, against 15,000 in France, 6,490 in Austria, (in seven universities,) 8,611 in Spain, 7,500 in Prussia, and about 20,000 for the whole of Germany, comprising, as said before, twenty-six universities. The five free universities in Italy give a total of something over 300 students, raising the whole number of students to nearly 8,000.

The most richly endowed and important universities are those of Bologna, Naples, Padua, Palermo, Pavia, Pisa, and Turin, with 6,263 students. The eight establishments of the second class are those of Genoa, Modena, Parma, Sienna, Catania, Messina, Cagliari, and Sassari. Those of the first class constitute an annual charge to the State of $650,000, leaving little more than $200,000 for the remaining five. Naples, with an annual endowment of $124,000, stands at the head of the list, and Sassari, with $10,000, at the foot. The average yearly cost of each student at the first-class university is $100, and in the second-class, where the education is very much inferior, his expense to the State is nearly double. It is a noticeable fact, however, that the number of students in the universities has been decreasing every year of late.

CHAPTER XI.

THE UNIVERSITIES.—A WORD ON ATTENDING THEM.

DURING the last few years there has been a great increase in the attendance of Americans at the German universities. In many instances men in middle life have gone to Europe for this purpose, and have spent several *semesters* at more than one university. Some of those men had families, and had the good sense to take them along, thus giving them all the advantages of foreign residence and travel. It would be difficult to enumerate the various measures adopted by Americans after reaching Germany in order to make their stay at a university advantageous and pleasant. That disappointment has sometimes been the result may be occasionally due to mismanagement, but we believe it is more frequently owing to a misconception, before going, of some of the more important practical features of the case.

The most natural questions asked by an American who contemplates a course of study in a German university are these, or similar ones:—What is the expense? Can one depend on earning sufficient money abroad to help him through a university? How much German is it necessary to know in order to hear the lectures to advantage? Which is the best university? How long is it necessary to stay? Should one go directly to a university, or live, preliminarily, in some other place, in order to become better prepared for hearing lectures ? This last question is suggested by the fact that for a number of years Americans have been going to Dresden, Brunswick, and other places to spend some months in private families, and afterward proceeding to a university.

As to expenses at a university, I question whether the average annual outlay of the German student is more than from two to three hundred thalers for attending the lectures, board, fuel, room-rent, books, stationery, and incidentals. Even some Americans have succeeded in spending as low a sum, but the majority go much beyond this figure. Living in some southern university town —Tübingen, for instance—is less expensive than in the north. Still, sometimes cheap rooms and board can be found in the north, and even in Berlin.

In Jena one can get a superior bedroom and study, well-furnished, with first-rate board, including servant's and other fees, for thirty thalers a month. For a single room and a less luxuriant table only about eighteen thalers need be paid. Seventeen years ago I paid at Halle, for a furnished " sky parlor " and bedroom, exclusive of board, five thalers a month. Dinner at a good hotel— the " Stadt Hamburg "—cost me seventeen cents, (gold,) tickets being taken by the month. Breakfast and tea cost from six to ten cents each. Expenses at Halle are higher now, but certainly the increase cannot be over twenty-five per cent.

The amount which a student needs to pay for living in a German university town depends greatly on his tastes.

If he wish to keep up his American luxuriance, he will have to pay for it there as well as at home.

For attendance at the lectures the expenses are about the same in all the universities. The prices range from three thalers to ten, according to the frequency of the lecture. At Jena, for six lectures a week on chemistry and physics, for the term of five months, the cost is ten thalers. For theology, philosophy, mineralogy, history, and a large class of other studies, one pays five thalers each per term. For the use of the chemical laboratory the expense is thirty thalers the term. No text-books are regarded necessary, but it is advisable to have some good one at hand for every course of lectures, to aid in filling out notes at leisure.

Can money be made at a university town? Not much, at least as a rule. The American who proposes to attend a German university had better bring with him enough, or the promise of it, to meet all his expenses. To give English lessons, or any other, would occupy a great amount of valuable time, and bring in return but a meager remuneration at best. Moreover, every town of any size in Germany swarms with people whose business it is to give English lessons, and they will do it for a much less cost than an American could think of accepting. A young American theological student, who spent nearly a year at Halle, obtained, by a mere accident, what seemed at first a very advantageous position as an English teacher to a Polish nobleman, but he gave it up after a while, because, as he said, it took too much of his time, leaving him scarcely any leisure, and only paying moderately. If a young man is ever justified in borrowing money for self-improvement, it is one who is bent on excelling in his profession. His mind can generally be greatly enriched by attending a German university for a while ; and if ever a wealthy man has such a son, nephew, or friend, he should be thankful for the privilege of placing at his disposal a sum sufficient for him to gratify his thirst for truth.

On arriving in Germany the most advisable course is, if one does not design to travel, to go directly to the place where he proposes to attend a university, and begin at once to hear lectures, even if he do not understand one word in ten. The discipline is of itself a valuable German lesson. Private instruction can be taken meanwhile, not only in German, but in Sanscrit, Hebrew, or any other language, dead or modern, one desires to study. Not more than three lectures can be heard a day to advantage.

Berlin excels all other German universities in the extent of its facilities. Tübingen is just as good, and perhaps better, in philology, Göttingen in jurisprudence, Halle in theology, Heidelberg in physics, and Vienna in medicine. Bonn has some fresh young theological blood. But Berlin unquestionably presents the widest scope of study, and, besides, that city furnishes more general advantages for improvement by a foreign residence. The American, in selecting a university, however, should be careful to judge according to the existing, and not past, excellence of the department in which he is interested. For no university continues uniformly superior in any specialty. This is an affair of genius, for it is the men that give excellence and just celebrity. Berlin has never been in Church history what it was in Neander's day, nor Göttingen in law what it was in Sevigny's day, nor will Munich soon find a real successor to Liebig. If one wishes to stay two years abroad, the first one can be well spent in some other university and the last in Berlin. If he has but one year, he will do best to go directly to Berlin ; but if he wish to learn German he should keep clear of Americans and English. Many Americans divide their two years between three universities, spending the latter half of their time in Berlin. And they do not regret this course, for the universities form a sort of republican confederation, and a man can begin in one just where he left off in another.

If an American wish to travel and attend a university besides, he will do well to travel after he has finished his studies, when he can have the advantage of a knowledge of the languages he may have studied in the meantime. The German student, when he travels, does not spend an average of more than three thalers a day ; but not many Americans stop there. Still, one American I knew, who was abroad fourteen months, said to me that for his passage from New York and back again, for eight months, at a university, guide-books, clothing, and traveling through Germany, Italy, Switzerland, France, Holland, Belgium, England, and Scotland, he paid eleven hundred dollars in gold. But while one American can get along in this style, twenty spend three times the amount. There is such a thing as " doing " Europe entirely too cheaply.

The more German one knows before leaving home the better it is for him, for he will need proportionately less time before understanding the lectures. The student would do well to bring with him all his lexicons, a few text-books, and but few books besides. Some knowledge of the character of the German universities is well nigh indispensable before coming. The best information accessible to the American is contained in Dr. Edward Robinson's articles on the subject in the " Biblical Repository," (1831–1834,) in later numbers of the " Bibliotheca Sacra ; " Schaff's " Germany—its Universities, Theology, and Religion ; " Matthew Arnold's " Higher Schools and Universities of Germany ; " and Dwight's " Travels in the North of Germany." Howitt's " Student Life in Germany " has also many good things. Mayhew's reflections, in his book on Germany, are very one-sided, and not worthy of the author of " London Labor and the London Poor."

The academic year at the university begins about the middle of October, and closes about the middle of August. There are recesses at Christmas, Easter, and Whitsuntide. The German Professors are always easy of access, friendly in the extreme, ever ready to give good advice, and do not make the welcome more cordial because of a pocketful of letters of introduction. In the institutions of some countries such letters are a necessity, but not in Germany, where a true love of knowledge hides a multitude of sins. Tholuck lately said to an American student, who apologized to him for calling without presenting a letter of introduction, that he was "glad to see at least one American who had come without one." To literary circles, however, such letters are necessary. I speak only of the American's benefit from them at a German university.

On arriving at the university town, the first thing to be done is the finding of a proper boarding-place. This will need care, and hence it is well to retain lodgings in a hotel until satisfactory apartments are secured elsewhere. A student usually hires two rooms, a study and a bed-chamber. These are likely to be quite small. They are furnished by the landlord, who requires monthly payment for rent and service. He furnishes his boarders with the morning meal—coffee and biscuit, served in each room, when its occupant pulls his bell. The dinner and tea are usually taken at a restaurant or hotel. But the landlord holds himself ready to furnish both these meals, if ordered by his guests. An early opportunity should be seized to report at the police head-quarters one's presence in a university town, and the purpose of residence.

All German students are expected to bring with them certificates of passage through the gymnasium, and fitness in attainment to attend the university. No examination is made. That is supposed to have occurred, and the satisfactory proof to be in the applicant's pocket. The American, however, need not bring any thing in testimony of scholarship. His traditions and usages are so different that the good Germans regard him as a law to himself. On the given day, at the commencement of the *semester*, he should matriculate. He need not designate his lecturers at first, unless he has already determined upon them. The universities vary in expense and usage. Expenses in the south are much lower than in the north. "At Tübingen," so writes Professor C. C. Bragdon, "the matriculation fee is $4; incidentals, fifty cents. For a lect-

8*

ure, coming two or three times per week, the fee is $1 10
for the *semester*, October 19th to March 23d. For one
that comes five or six times per week, $2 to $2 40. In the
medical department the rates are higher. Clinical lectures, with practice in the hospital and about town, from
$6 to $8 for same time as above. After a course has been
in progress for one or two weeks, the professor sends
around a paper which states the number of lectures weekly and their price. All sign who expect to take the
course, and by December 1st the beadle must be paid.
You may attend lectures year after year and no word ever
pass between the professor and you personally. The
teacher enters the room ten minutes after the bell has
struck the hour, begins at once to read or talk, and when
the time is up all rise as he bows and passes out. One
will be surprised at the extensive quotations by the professors of passages and books bearing upon particular points.
This gives an idea of the amount of work a German professor of the right stamp must do. A few lectures are
given on Sundays, not only on theology, but anatomy and
other secular sciences."

III.

BOOKS—WRITING, MAKING, AND SELLING.

Hic mortui vivunt; hic multi loquuntur.

***

Still am I besy bokes assemblynge,
For to have plenty it is a pleasaunt thynge.—BRANDT.

***

Our intercourse with the dead is better than our intercourse with the living.—HAZLITT.

***

" In the corner of my room I have Books, the miracle of all my possessions."— D'AUNOTT.

CHAPTER I.

LITERARY PRODUCTIVENESS.—PECULIARITIES.

THE increase of books in Germany is a permanent marvel to every foreigner. Previously to 1814 the annual issue was only about two thousand volumes, but now it exceeds ten thousand, and each year shows an advance on its predecessor. The stages of growth down to 1834 were as follows : In 1814 there were published 2529 works ; in 1816, 3197 ; in 1822, 4288 ; in 1827, 5108 ; in 1830, 5926 ; in 1831, 5508 ; in 1832, 6122 ; in 1833, 5653 ; in 1834, 6074. Menzel said, many a year ago, that "in Germany alone, according to a moderate calculation, ten millions of volumes are annually printed. As the catalogue of every Leipzig half-yearly book contains the names of more than a thousand German authors, we may compute that at the present moment there are living in Germany about fifty thousand men who have written one or more books. Should that number increase at the same rate that it has hitherto done, the time will soon come when a catalogue of ancient and modern German authors will contain more names than there are living readers."

A wonderful combination of qualities is needed for this great annual supply of literature from the German press. Patience ! I have never seen such patience as that of the real German author. While his volume is in hand it becomes to him his planet, his home. Nothing that can enrich it escapes him. He regards his book with all the fondness of paternal attachment. It is always as the youngest member of his household, and must 'be treated with great consideration by every one. The German author never lets his pen get hasty. Hence it is found, as a rule, that the last page betrays all the provoking coolness and deliberation of the first. There is more directness and real point ; but of impetuosity his Pegasus is never guilty. The way in which he consults large collections of books is a marvel to us unresting Anglo-Saxons. I have seen him go into a library immediately after sipping his morning cup of coffee, and spend the entire day in exam- ining authorities with as much ease and quiet as if the shadow of the sun never changed on the dial. Nor do I believe it does on *his*. Three hundred thousand volumes in sight at once never bewilder his eyes. No Judkins ever walked a steamer's bridge with more composure, as he looked out upon the waste of waters, or knew better what to do, than does the German author as he sits and writes amid the world of books in the libraries of Munich, Berlin, or St. Petersburg. He is content to upturn many a hay- stack for a single needle. Neander's spending an entire day on top of his book-case, feasting on the " Church Fathers," but in delightful ignorance of any post-patristic age, and setting his sister Hänchen more than half crazy as to his whereabouts, is a type of the very habit of those of his fellow-countrymen who ply the pen. They spend more time over the matter that falls into a single foot-note for the darling book than an American would be content to occupy in a whole chapter.

The more one becomes acquainted with the habits of the German author the more decided becomes the conviction of his real and imperturbable honesty. He knows his public, and that it will put up with no nonsense from him ; and, what is better, he knows himself, and that he would not be able, for a disturbed conscience, to calmly pull up his smoke through his cherry-stem or face his publisher any day if he had failed to put into his manuscript the best stuff that his brain and the respectable libraries could furnish. No slovenliness here. Where have I not met the German author, pencil in hand, trying to get the whole truth into his pages ? Delving day after day in the oldest and richest libraries of Germany; sitting on broken columns in the Palace of the Cæsars in Rome trying to decipher the inscriptions of the time of Horace ; working at the Cufic letters on the Tayloon Mosque, in Cairo ; luxuriating, at Karnak and Philæ, in his study of the plans of the marvelous temples ; counting the steps of Mars' Hill, cut out of solid rock, up which the Areopagites and the great teacher, Paul, ascended ; jumping from one housetop to another of Damascus, to note in his own book the celebrated inscription to the triumph of Christianity which even Moslem hate has not dared to erase or deface ; sitting beside Virgil's grave at Naples, testing the verdict of the sweet tradition—and all to tell dear Germany something it never knew or never knew so well.

But what I admire most in German authors is their uncompromising pluck. Talk about Metz, Strasbourg, and Sedan ! Never did Uhlan brave more than do these quiet workers with the quill—I mean the real *goose quill;* for you may as well try to make the German book-writer think that smoking is an impediment to authorship as that any respectable book can be, or ought to be, written with pen of steel or gold. Of course, there are those who have adopted these innovations ; but they are mostly of the younger class, mere *parvenus*, as yet, in the charmed circle. If I should be allowed to wake up from my resting-place five hundred years from this hot July morning, and look over the shoulder of one of the ten Herren Professors of history in Berlin University, as he prepares his manuscript on the German Conquest of France, away back in 1870 and 1871, and writes a letter to his Leipzig publisher, I should likely find him writing with his ink-speckled quill, and, instead of using note-paper and envelope for his letter, employing a great sheet of blue paper, one leaf of which, after the manner of his ancestors, serves the purpose of an envelope, which must be sealed with the bothersome red wax and stamped with the old family seal.

Your German author is never intimidated by the magnitude of his subject. He has his idea, and you may as well tell him that father Rhine ought to belong to the French as to say any thing that could tend to diminish his confidence in his project. He knows what his thought is, and he thinks it is nobody's business but his and his family's. Do not make any reflection on his topic, if you wish to continue on friendly terms. I read a series of brilliant articles, over a year ago, in the Augsburg "Allgemeine Zeitung," on "The Man in the Moon," and I have no doubt they are already matured into a duodecimo. I should not be startled to hear of some one writing on the "Woman

in the Moon." But such odd and plucky subjects stare
you in the face in any German bookstore. The German
will venture on any theme. No Monte Rosa or Matter-
horn dispirits him! He goes diligently to working up a
volume on any science, art, people—dead, living, to be, or
not to be—arming himself with a very arsenal of authorities, sparing neither sweat nor scanty purse, plodding on
with the grand certainty of fate toward the elaboration of
such a thought as would take two generations of authors
with us to summon confidence enough to venture a volume
upon. He knows he has to face a world of critics, men of
every type of savage nature, who furnish the horns, hoofs,
and teeth for the scores of critical serials, and hold themselves ready to masticate any new comer into the domain
of authorship. But do not waste your sympathy on him ;
for not a whit does he care—no more than did old Sam.
Johnson for the carpers at his dictionary. He does not
take the time to read the critiques on him. All he knows
is what the frau or his friends have a mind to reveal. He
is too busy thinking about his next volume. This sublime
indifference to the oracular critics is worthy any body's admiration. If it depended on him, the whole set would be
hanged as high as Haman—that is, if he could appropriate
to those gentry time enough to decide on their destiny.

The German author ventures out early, and the deeper
his soundings the better. Tholuck's maiden effort was in
Latin, and on Sufism—or, as it read in the bibliographies,
" Sufismus sive Theosophia Persarum pantheistica quam e
MSS. bibliotheca Regiæ Berolinensis, Persicis, Arabicis,
Turcicis, eruit et illustravit." And all this from a con-

sumptive stripling of twenty-two ! The fates be praised !
the work never passed into a second edition. Since then
Tholuck has grown into more modest and simple titles, and
a preference for his own tongue. When I see the early
attempts at authorship in Germany, I am reminded of the
efforts of a child to walk. He tumbles down now and
then, and gets bruises numberless ; but is promptly on
his feet again, and in due time can walk and run with
others. The German author tries his legs betimes, for he
knows that he must fall about so often anyhow, whether
he begin soon or late. By and by he wrings his recogni-
tion from the critics, and during the most of his life occupies a position of honor in the guild. He is reckoned a
worthy member, and is pushing out with confidence his
portly octavo every two years, with brochures and duodecimos to give variety to the interval, before his American
brother has blocked out his first undertaking. Luther,
three hundred years ago, published at the rate of a book a
fortnight.

Then he keeps at his oar with astonishing pertinacity.
Goethe working with his pen up into the eighties, and
Humboldt until squarely up to ninety, indicate the rule.
Von Raumer and Boeckh and Ranke are striking proofs
of the freshness, vigor, and confidence of German authors
to the very last. They do not consider their day past, let
happen what will. A more beautiful specimen of literary
life cannot be found than any resident in a university
town may see in the readiness and spirit with which aged
professors, too infirm in body to walk briskly, pass from
a finished work to a new one ; and, like Sir William

Hamilton, who died with a dozen untouched volumes in his head, tell you what book they are next going to begin, what old one they are pledged to enlarge into a new edition, what literary journey they are projecting for the inspection of libraries or the examination of localities. Like Schleiermacher; they declare eternal hostility to old age. And when they die, it is in just the right place, amid plans, some nearly completed, some perhaps just begun. They never commit the mistake of many a sane and capable man with us, no matter about his years, of waiting for death to come. They work, and suffer death to take his own time. And who would question their wisdom ?

CHAPTER II.

SECRETS OF GERMAN AUTHORSHIP.

N O single feature of German authorship is more inexplicable than the causes underlying its fecundity. How do those calm writers contrive to pile up such pyramids of manuscript? By what unheard-of enchantment do they succeed in leaving at death a score or so of octavos, while their American brethren, of equal pluck and health, produce but a tithe of that number? I have often tried in many ways, particularly when enjoying the society, now and then, of a successful German author, to get at his secret, but have invariably given up in despair. The truth is, the Germans do not know themselves how they get so much done. They simply write right on; and, when the volume reaches its conclusion, the head that produced it can give as little account of how the work was done as the printer who puts the manuscript in type. Nevertheless, you can account somewhat for the great fertility of German authorship by looking at the methods of the writers. Their modes of work are so different from those of writers of other nationalities that it may be well to note some of the points of difference. Perhaps a look at Herr Schriftsteller, as he goes to his daily work, and keeps at it withal, will furnish some of his American admirers with valuable hints for the improvement of their own mode of production.

The German knows, as no one else, how to subsidize others into his service, thereby saving a vast amount of time and purely mechanical labor. Almost invariably he has an amanuensis, and frequently more than one, to whom he dictates, or gives in pretty full outline what he proposes to embalm in print. Bunsen—who, despite his long residence in England and identification with English life, never forgot his German method of authorship—used to have half-a-dozen secretaries at work for him. All he did was to give them the general directions, and they thus multiplied his years. Moreover, he had scholars at work for him who lived in various parts of the country. He told them what points he wanted to fortify, what theses they must elaborate ; and they did it gladly—for, poor, half-starved fellows, they knew that Bunsen could pay them well for their toil. Many of the more solid works in German literature are produced by the professors in the universities. These men, almost to a unit, have the services of a promising student (or two) of literary taste, who spends his spare hours in searching up authorities, conducting correspondence, getting the master's own hieroglyphics into shape for the printer, and examining libraries far and near for information to pack into the volume in hand. While the real author is responsible for every word that goes out under his own name, and can justly claim the parentage of the whole idea, and plan, and scope of the work, he is spared much of the drudgery incident to all book-making which is not the immediate fruit of imagination. Where history is to be ransacked, facts to be grouped, and matters of pure detail to be gleaned from various sources, often another could do better service than the author. The real writer is the Powers who furnishes the model, and yet never himself uses the chisel on the block of marble, but takes good care to have the merely muscular part of the execution done by óthers. His eye goes over all carefully, but he saves his physical energies from exhaustion. The late J. Buchanan Read complained, that while in sculpture all the mechanical labor might be turned over to others, in painting, on the other hand, the real artist could allow no one but himself to touch his canvas.

The influence of such discipline on the young men who serve under good direction in these subordinate departments of German authorship is beneficial beyond all calculation. Tholuck has had a great many young theological students working for him during his half century at Halle, and often more than one at a time, as members of his own family. He has had his regular hours for dictation to them ; at other times they have done irregular work at copying, indexing, correcting proofs, and corresponding. This was a discipline of inestimable value to them. It gave them a taste of authorship, a facility in preparing matter for the press, a confidence in their own pen, which all must have who venture to face the grim public. Some of the most successful authors have begun in just this humble way at Tholuck's feet ; for example, Kurtz, the most popular ecclesiastical historian, save Hagenbach, in the German language. The late Professor C. F. Held no sooner ceased writing for Tholuck than he rapidly rose himself as an author and pulpit-orator, and his appointment to a full professorship in Bonn University was ample proof that he belonged in the front rank of the younger group of evangelical theologians. But that same Held did all that could be done by any other than the real author, on Tholuck's " Akademisches Leben des siebenzehnten Jahrhunderts." The work was made up largely of facts which could be gathered only from the university records of the period in question, and Held corresponded with all the librarians of the German and extra-German universities, secured copies of protocols, and put the matter in order. The brain that guided him did little more than suggest the drift, and consummate the generalizations. Jacobi, the author of a Church History, and now Professor of Church History in Halle, was trained in the same way by Neander, who, indeed, lived to see the young man well started, and wrote a commendatory introduction to his first attempt at authorship. Another of Neander's young helpers was the present highest German authority on ecclesiastical art—Professor Piper, of Berlin, really the creator of the science of monumental theology.

Further, the German author takes care to have social refreshment. Without this he would soon fall amid his gigantic literary plans. He cultivates clubbable qualities, and has his circle of friends, with whom he spends his evenings and the afternoons of festive days. He seldom works with his pen at night, and generally not after dinner. He crowds his labors into the morning hours, and where he leaves any thing for the afternoon, it is light matter—the trimming up of the grand trunk he had felled before noon. Reading, comparing authorities, and such easy parts of his labor he can do without weariness after his after-dinner smoke. But for dictation, downright authorship, he commonly takes the forenoon ; and urgent must be your demand if you get a welcome from him then. He often has a placard on his door at this time, exhorting all trespassers on his time not to enter unless their business is very important, and they are willing to leave very soon again. His rule is, to spend all his afternoons and evenings with his family or literary friends. He is a grand diner-out ; knows how to occupy two hours at the table, and four or six hours in digesting what he finds on it. He plays all manner of games with his children, and serves as donkey and what not for them ; goes to the reading-room, and drops asleep over the " Viertcljahrsschrift ; " makes a foot excursion with his wife and children to a neighboring village, and wakes up next morning with fifty brand-new pages at his tongue's end. Thus he goes through his volume, half playing and half working, but always absorbing ; and when he has finished it he does not need a journey to another continent to bring him elasticity, nor does he shiver like a slave beneath the critic's lash. His nerves are strong, his blood far from torpid, his spirits high, his brain ready for any thing. He would begin a cyclopædia on the shortest notice, and fulfill his publisher's best hopes.

What a comment on our spasmodic authorship ! Many an American, when he gets through his work, is actually half dead from the absence of all social relaxation. He became shy of society, and considered every hour among his friends as so much lost time. The result was that he lost flesh, spirits, and the indispensable pluck for new undertakings. The German, on the other hand, knows the high science of compressing as much work as possible into his mornings, and as much play as possible into his afternoons and evenings.

The German author, moreover, owes a large degree of his productiveness to his simple diet and regular hours for sleep and rising. He rises early, and never touches any work until he has taken a cup of coffee and a biscuit. He never puts his brain and eyes into harness, and under spur and whip, without a little food to start with. At ten he takes a light lunch, such as a sandwich of bread and cheese, and goes to work again, and sticks to it until about one o'clock. Then it is all over for that day. He has performed an immense amount of literary work. Six solid hours, and not one minute lost in painful digestion of ham and eggs, beefsteak, hot rolls, and blankety buckwheat cakes. As for hot bread, he never saw any, in all probability ; for all the bread comes from the baker's, and is served cold twice a day. If by any oversight he should eat a couple of steaming soda-biscuits, it would cost him a whole day's work ; for he never could bring himself to the belief that he has the capacity to digest hot bread. He would moan and smoke, and declare, in spite of the papers, that the French are marching straight for Berlin. The dinner is plain but plentiful ; the supper is light, with black bread as the staple. With the fiber and strength from one day's food he does the work of the next ; hence digestion gives him no trouble or thought. He no more

9

thinks of his stomach than of Barbarossa's falcons. Of course, he smokes a good deal ; but even this, I have noticed, he pushes off largely into the play-hours of the afternoon.

The German author, finally, has the great advantage of having his materials at hand for preparing his work. The Fatherland is the paradise of great libraries. The writer can have on his desk the volume which, of all others, he needs in as short a time as it requires us to make out for Scribner or Westermann the order which will require five mortal weeks at least to have filled.   Even the towns have immense libraries, the growth of centuries, which any one can consult at will. What one library does not afford, another, close at hand, does. An American writer has sometimes been compelled to make a voyage to Europe to consult libraries to which the German can have daily access, only a few blocks from his house. The very fact of distance from the necessary facts repels many an American from authorship in his favorite fields. Mr. Motley has found, throughout his historiography, that he could labor with but little satisfaction to himself, or even certainty, away from the dykes and vellum-bound books of Holland. Mr. Bancroft tells us that only through the courtesy of the Spanish Government, and the kind attention of Don Pascual de Gayangos, he was enabled to state with certainty the relations of the English, French, Spanish, German, Dutch, and Russian ministers and kings toward our Revolution ; and that the tenth volume of his " History of the United States" has been delayed through the want of a single document.

What does America not owe to Washington Irving's residence in Spain, Hawthorne's consulate in Liverpool, Mr. Thayer's stay in Vienna and Trieste, and Mr. Perkins' residence in Florence? One needs personal contact with the very localities that are embraced within the scope of his undertaking. Schiller, it must be confessed, could write his "William Tell" without ever seeing any of the glories of Lake Lucerne; but then his imagination was unrivaled. Moreover, he had all the advantage, as Mr. Lewes tells us, of the notes of Goethe, who lazed away many an ambrosial hour within the shadows of the Righi and Mount Pilate.

To give an idea of the wealth of literature at the disposal of the author in Germany we present a

TABLE OF CHIEF GERMAN LIBRARIES.

		Volumes.	Manuscripts.
Royal Library of Munich		800,000	22,000
" " Berlin		600,000	14,000
Imperial Library of Vienna		400,000	16,000
Royal Library of Dresden		300,000	2,800
" " Stuttgart		300,000	3,600
Ducal Library of Darmstadt		200,000	3,000
" " Wolfenbüttel		200,000	6,000
" " Gotha		160,000	2,000
" " Weimar		143,000	2,000
University Library of Göttingen		350,000	5,000
" " Breslau		300,000	2,500
" " Tübingen		200,000	2,000
" " Leipzig		170,000	1,500
" " Heidelberg		150,000	847
" " Erlangen		120,000	1,000
" " Bonn		120,000	1,000

CHAPTER III.

THE MANUFACTURE OF BOOKS.

THE German publishing business, not less than the authorship, differs very materially from that of the United States. The number of publishers is legion. Schulz's Directory for the German Book Trade for 1873 contains the names and addresses of 4,230 firms, 1,068 of whom are publishers. These, instead of being confined to a few large cities, can be found in towns and hamlets throughout the empire. It is not regarded a necessity that a book shall bear the imprint of some great house in order to pass into public favor, but that its contents should be worthy of approval. The question is not asked, Is it a Brockhaus or a Perthes book? but, What is in it? And it is but just to the critical journals to say, that it is very rare for a work to receive either censure or appro- bation because of the house which issues it. The large number of publishers in Germany is due, to some extent, to the fact that a great capital is not necessary in order to publish a number of sterling works. The small dealer finds it necessary, early in his career, to issue a book now and then in order to acquire good standing among his brethren. If he succeed in bringing out a single popular work he is regarded very fortunate, and he takes a place of honor in his guild.

The small expense of manufacturing books in Germany

is due to three causes. First, the cost of printing materials and compositors' work is low. It is now becoming
common for publishers in Great Britain, France, Russia,
other parts of Europe, and sometimes of the United
States, to avail themselves of the cheap German rates for
having such works printed as do not require the author's
inspection of proof-sheets. The Leipzig rates of printing
are from twenty-five to forty per cent. cheaper than those
of Paris or London. But the printing of an English
work in any part of Germany is never advisable. I have
had two experiments in this matter, and each of the books
required the examination of at least five proofs where but
one would have been needed if the compositors had been
English or American. A friend of mine who had placed
a fine work of art in the hands of a Leipzig printer, had
more than one season of shedding tears as he found that
the compositors had made fearful havoc with his copy, and
had then printed all the blunders in a whole edition of
the rich paper that had been manufactured especially for
his work.

Second, the books are not bound, but simply folded and
stitched, with paper covers. The custom of issuing books
unbound is common to all the continental countries, and
is really a great popular advantage ; for many persons are
able to buy an unbound book who, otherwise, could not
have the work at all, and all other purchasers can consult
their own taste as to style. The binding of books not
being done by the publisher, it has become an independent
and important branch of business. The buyer of books
has his own binder as much as his own bookseller. The

binder knows the tastes of his customers individually, and, if his neatness is surpassed in France, England, and the United States, by the countrymen of Hayday, Rivière, Bedford, and Matthews, the firmness of his work is nowhere excelled. The habit of German scholars is to bind only their good books, and to put these simply in substantial stitching, and stiff paper backs. An octavo thus bound costs fifteen or eighteen cents. The same work in half Turkey costs about forty cents. I have had duodecimos bound beautifully by Geffken, in Bremen, for thirty cents gold. My Brockhaus' " Conversations-Lexikon " (a large octavo) cost, in Frankfort, thirty-six kreutzers the volume for binding. The retail dealers keep specimen bound volumes on their shelves, but more for appearance' sake than otherwise. The real German bibliophile does not like to buy a bound volume—just as his English friend dislikes to buy one with the leaves cut—but has a special enjoyment in taking his book to the binder, explaining how he wants it prepared for him, and going occasionally to see how it progresses, and especially how the title is put on. One result of the binding of books not being done by the publisher is the homely appearance of the German private libraries. Books not being loved in Germany for what they appear, but for what they are, many are either not bound at all, or so cheaply as to be very unsightly to the eyes of any Dibdin who might chance to see them. Ninety-nine Germans in a hundred would infinitely prefer to have a volume unbound; and keep the money that the binding would cost, to help them toward another book.

But here an error must be corrected. Whatever be said

of the binding, the book itself is, if it has to pay the author a copyright, dearer in Germany than in America. Schaff's " Church History" is dearer in Leipzig than as Scribner offers it, binding taken into consideration. I believe that the average German prices on all copyright books are, at the lowest calculation, thirty per cent. higher than in America. The publisher unquestionably gets a higher percentage, for the cost of manufacturing a book in Germany is not over two thirds what it is in New York or Boston. ·But then the sales are smaller, and the American publisher makes more in the long run. His risks, however, are greater. The German publisher treads carefully.

Still, no country can equal Germany in the low price of all books on which no copyright is paid. For instance, you can buy Schiller complete now for a thaler, and Goethe for three. I have a superior edition of Goethe in six large octavo volumes, with steel plates and half morocco binding, that cost only twelve florins, or $4 80 gold. Since the copyright of these two German classics has expired, a number of publishers have devised plans for getting the run of the trade. But J. G. Cotta, of Stuttgart—the house which held the exclusive right, and the publisher of the Augsburg " Allgemeine Zeitung"—appears to have underbidden all his rivals, and his several editions of these authors are both the cheapest and best.

The following are the rates, in gold, at which some of the principal *littérateurs* are sold, noted down during occasional loiterings, or gleaned from the profuse advertisements : Schiller's complete works, in one volume, with portrait of the author, seventy-two cents ; in twelve volumes, small octavo, $1 30 ; in two large octavo volumes, with steel engravings, excellent print, moroceo binding, $1 80 ; poems alone, eighteen cents. Goethe's complete works, in thirty-six volumes, small octavo, bound in morocco in eighteen, sell for $6 20 ; in six volumes, large octavo, with steel plates, unbound, $2 80 ; and his poems, in small oetavo, unbound, for twelve cents. Lessing's complete works, in ten volumes, small octavo, bound in five, for $2 40 ; his poetical and dramatic works, with muslin binding, for thirty-six cents ; and his " Nathan the Wise," handsomely bound, for forty-six cents. Chamisso's poetical works, in two volumes, well bound, eost fifty-six cents ; Gellert's works, ten volumes, bound in four, $1 40 ; Uhland's poems and dramas, in muslin, $1 ; Zschokke's complete novels, in twelve volumes, well bound, $3 80 ; Humboldt's " Cosmos," well bound, $1 80 ; Jean Paul's works, in ten volumes, also well bound, $1 40. Sehlosser's " Weltgeschichte," in nineteen volumes, morocco binding, eosts but $8 80 ; Meyer's " Conversations-Lexikon," $15 ; Brockhaus', ditto, (new edition,) $14 ; Pierer's, ditto, (new edition), $20. These last three are unbound.

The third cause of the cheapness of manufacturing a German book lies in the absence of the stereotyping custom. Our own country is the only one in Christendom which possesses the wretched policy of stereotyping well-nigh all the books it publishes. It is, of course, an advantage to the publishers to do so, provided the book has even a fair sale ; but it is fatal to the final literary character of many a book, and to the general interests of authorship.

The ideal first edition, except in fiction, is only a good intention. Every book, to be permanently valuable, should be a growth ; and if the first edition has not vitality to survive its birth, the book deserves to die. But if a thousand copies are sold, it merits again the author's revision, and a re-appearance before the public with all the improvement derived from new studies and the judgment of the critics. It has been to me a matter of interest to place the first edition of a valuable German work beside the last and mark the wonderful development. It is like contrasting the grown man with his little self in baby-frocks. I have beside me a little work—now very rare—Hagenbach's " Uebersicht der Dogmengeschichte," published when its author was a young professor in Basle. But who would recognize, in the present two ponderous volumes, the work of the same hand, the manhood of that of which the thin *brochure* was the infancy ? Had stereotyping been the rule, that work, like hundreds of others possessing great value, would never have ripened into its present golden maturity. Stereotyping precludes the expression of a change of view, embalms errors, frustrates the purposes of criticism by excluding its suggestions, destroys an author's permanent interest in his work, and renders null his new researches in the same department. This can be done if the plates are canceled ; but how many publishers are willing to issue improved editions at the expense of a new set of plates ?

The absence of stereotyping in all the European countries limits each contract between publisher and author to the single edition. For a second edition a new contract is made, and so with each in future.

9*

CHAPTER IV.

USAGES OF THE GERMAN BOOK TRADE.

THE manner of bringing a work in Germany to the knowledge of the public is very different from Anglo-Saxon usages. The publishers have the most thorough methods of communicating with each other concerning their issues, and their alliance is offensive and defensive, to make the public buy as many books as possible. It is regarded dishonorable for one publisher to underrate in any way the issues of any brother in the trade. The reviews, and often the ephemeral periodicals, are very tardy in their notice of new books. I have known years to elapse before a stately work receives the compliment of even a brief notice from some reviews. The sight of a magnificent volume does not disturb the gravity of your German editor. He has seen such things before; lays the work quietly aside; fills his pipe again; and puts off until the next season, or year, the examination of the book. The author does not expect to see his book noticed in the journals of the same month which gave it birth, but is patient, and glad if his white day ever comes.

When a book is issued a certain number of copies are sent out, through commissioners resident in Leipzig, to the booksellers throughout the country. These are not bought by the latter unless they have been positively ordered, but are simply sent to them for the purpose of being brought to the knowledge of the buying public. This result is reached, in great measure, by the following peculiar means. Your bookseller, knowing well your taste, sends you by a messenger every few days, generally Saturdays, one or more books, which you are expected to examine briefly. If you choose to buy one or more of them you simply retain them, but otherwise you cause no offense by returning them. They are not expected to be retained for inspection more than a fortnight. There are two large booksellers in Bremen, Messrs. Müller and Kühtmann, who supplied me every week with valuable new theological books, which I returned in two weeks by the same messengers who had delivered them. Of course, I kept one now and then, checking these on the bills which always came with the books, and which I always sent back. In Frankfort similar kindness was shown by the dealers. This was no special favor to me, but a usage with the booksellers. The clerks always kept a register of all the books thus sent out. Many a time I lost track of a book, thinking I had sent it home. But after a long time the presentation of the bill by the same messenger who brought the books set me to seeking, and finding, and paying. The leaves must not be cut, for this would require you to retain the book. A bookseller has a large circle of customers whom he thus supplies at regular intervals with the latest issues from the press.

If a customer wishes to examine any work in print, and on sale by its publisher, he need only inquire for it at his bookseller's, and, if not on hand, a copy will be ordered "for inspection." In such cases it is generally assumed

that there is some probability of purchase. But if the
work should fail to be just what is desired, the bookseller
receives it back again to return to the publisher, and does
not permit his customer to pay the express charges. It
is clear, therefore, that no one ever need go to another
bookstore than the one he usually patronizes. All his
wants for books can be supplied there. His bookseller is
his friend, knows his habits, and never regards it an intru-
sion to be consulted about books, new or old.

When the Easter Fair at Leipzig occurs, the returns
are made by the retailers to the publishers, and all books
not sold, or not desired to be retained, are returned to the
latter, and settlement made for all copies not accounted for.

The factor or commissioner is an important man to the
book-trade of Germany. He is the mediator between the
retailer and the publisher. The publisher sends his new
work to his commissioner, who fills all orders for it from
every part of the world. At the Easter Fair the commissioner renders his account to his publishers, and the
retailer must account to him. The latter is not expected
to communicate with the publisher, except through the
commissioner of each. If a book is ordered of a bookseller, he does not communicate at all with the publisher,
but sends his order to his commissioner. The order is
communicated on a small slip of paper less than three
inches square, with printed heading, thus: " A. B. desires
of ——." The blank is filled by the publisher's name and
the title of the book. This slip never goes astray. If
the order is filled, it is retained as a voucher, but otherwise,
it goes back again, or the commissioner sends it in other

directions ; and by the time its work is done it is covered with all possible records, illegible to any but such experts as are known only to the counting-room of a German bookstore. I once ordered through a Frankfort dealer a copy of Low's "Annual Catalogue" for a certain year. Of course, the order was not sent to England directly, but first to Leipzig, to the commissioner. It came back in about five weeks, marked, "Can't be fished up."

"These little slips," says Mr. F. Leypoldt, our best American bibliographer, "be they many or few, are sent by mail to the commission house by all its constituents, and are by it deposited in the Booksellers' Exchange post-office, where they are sorted and re-delivered to the commission houses, four times daily. On lively days, from fifty to sixty thousand slips, letters, circulars, or other written or printed communications, pass through this department of the Booksellers' Exchange, and the annual delivery exceeds ten millions of documents. This immense service is done with wonderful accuracy, and absolutely without charge, the expense being borne by the Exchange Association for the benefit of the whole trade. . . . The relation of the commission house to its constituents, in the capacity of banker, is exactly like that of any banker. Interest is allowed or charged on daily balances, as the case may be, the charge being generally one' per cent. per annum more than the allowance. A small banker's commission is also charged, and the extent of credit, if any is allowed, is purely a matter of personal agreement. As a forwarder, the commission house receives an annual (very moderate) fixed salary, gauged by the probable extent of services to be performed, and the share these would represent of the expense account for rent, clerk hire, porterage, etc. This salary ranges all the way from five dollars to one thousand. If the constituent keeps a stock of his publications in Leipzig, he pays rent for storage-room to the commission house, if the stock be kept on its premises. But larger publishers often rent warehouses of their own, placing them in charge of the commission house. The profit of the commission house accrues, however, mainly from the specific charges. The principal source of profit is the item of packing. Constituents are not allowed any price for the embaling material of packages sent to the commission house, while the latter charges at the rate of one dollar per hundred weight for packing the bales it forwards. For boxes the same charge is made by weight, and the price of the box added. There is also a small additional charge for handling the packages between the office and the railroad. For the charge of ·the warehouses and the delivery of ordered books, remuneration is exacted either by a few cents for each package delivered, or by a percentage on the value delivered, which ranges from one per cent. to four per cent. Clearing expenses of the pay-lists are charged according to the number of entries on the pay-lists, in a round sum, ranging from five dollars to fifty. If the payments involve bankers' advances, these come, of course, under the established rules of the banking transactions." *

---

* " Weekly Trade Circular," February, 1872. The two articles in this excellent periodical (Feb., 1872) are the best contributions in our language to the knowledge of the German book-trade.

The relations between the German publisher and his authors are most cordial. London and New York have the advantage over Leipzig in this respect, for while the last city absorbs a large share of the publishing interests of Germany, the authors are scattered all over the country, and often the author and his publisher never meet. The authors' circles cannot be so great, accordingly, as those of London in our day, or even of the time when Byron, in his mock epistle to Dr. Palidori, makes Murray say :—

> " The room's so full of wits and bards,
> Crabbes, Campbells, Crokers, Freres, and Wards,
> And others, neither bards nor wits ;
> My humble tenement admits,
> All persons in the dress of gent,
> From Mr. Hammond to Dog Dent.
> A party dines with me to-day,
> All clever men who make their way ;
> Crabbe, Malcolm, Hamilton, and Chantry,
> Are all partakers of my pantry.
> My room's so full—we've Gifford here,
> Reading MS. with Hookham Frere,
> Pronouncing on the nouns and particles
> Of some of our forthcoming articles."

Of the beautiful friendships existing between German publishers and their authors ample witness is borne by the accounts of the evenings passed at the delightful home of the elder Perthes, to whose wife, the daughter of " The Wandsbeck Messenger," the meetings owed much of their wealth of taste, gentleness, and cheerfulness. No publishers exceed those of Germany in the liberality of their terms, and the pains they take to cultivate intimate social relations with their authors. I have never heard, however, of one going the length of the publisher of M. Edmond About, who, finding he had a destined celebrity on his hands, tore up the original contract, and voluntarily made another, which gave a far greater royalty.

The German booksellers claim that there are seasons when the new books come thickest, and that Easter predominates over all other times ; but you may defy any one not of the guild to notice any difference. The long snowstorm may have its lulls now and then, but they help little if you can barely perceive them, and are all the while fairly blinded by the flaky cloud. Pass a good-sized bookstore window every day, and you may be sure to find a new book or two, if not an armful, among the veteran volumes. And what passes as a new book in Germany must not be measured by the American standard of bibliographical longevity. We call that book new which is really six months old, or it may be even a yearling. But a new book in Germany must be almost as young as the veal you eat in the Continental hotels. It must have seen daylight but a few days ago, and have come from Leipzig or Stuttgart by the last train. Its ink is not firm yet, and its paper is hardly drier than your morning journal.

CHAPTER V.

THE PARADISE OF BOOKS.

LEIPZIG is the center of the world's book trade. All its streets give evidence of the reign of books. It was an easy thing to specify and compliment the book-stores of classic days, but it would require poets of more wisdom and patience than Martial to individualize those of Leipzig as that author could easily deal with those of old Rome:

> " You see a shop with titled posts,
> And read whate'er Parnassus boasts.
> Thence summon me, nor ask the dweller:
> Honest Actretus is the seller.
> From out the first or second nest
> He'll hand me, rais'd in purple vest.
> Five humble tenpences the price,
> A bard so noted and so nice."

Some streets are almost entirely devoted to the business, which is so interwoven with the very life of all the people that to take out of the city all the inhabitants connected in some way with the manufacture of books would amount to a depopulation. But a stranger is disappointed at the comparative absence of books in a city where he expects to see them on every hand. The habit there, as everywhere in Germany, is to do business largely by correspondence, and but little stress is laid upon the exhibition of books. I was amazed, when taking a letter of introduction to a publishing firm, to find the business conducted in a quiet little counting-room, where the members of the firm could hardly be distinguished from the few clerks, and where no books whatever were visible. There was nothing to indicate that I was standing in one of the greatest publishing houses of the world, where valuable books were dispatched, in great numbers, to every continent and the islands of the sea. The books were kept in magazines, quite out of sight of the publishers, and the clerks who did the correspondence had likely never seen a dozen of the many works for which they were constantly receiving orders from all points of the compass. The salesroom of our American bookstores is not considered a requisite in Germany, where the publisher is quite content to do all his business by correspondence alone. The catalogue is made to do all the service of the personal visit. The German bookseller does not like to have his time consumed by literary loungers, nor such of his books as may be visible to be handled by others than his employees. The miserable practice of American publishers making great discounts to clergymen, teachers, and many other classes of buyers, obtains but little in Germany. The German puts his books as low as he can at the start, and then makes every body pay for them. Let American publishers bring down the prices of their books, and then the discounts agreed on at the " Put-in-Bay " Convention.

Leipzig can boast 258 firms of publishers and dealers, and these are connected with some 3,500 firms in various parts of the world. As a publishing center it retains its old supremacy over Berlin. In the year 1789, out of the 2,115 works which appeared in Germany, 355 were published in Leipzig and 261 in Berlin ; in 1859, out of the

perfection of system by which the Germans conduct their trade, we give the following account of the constitution of the exchange, from the pen of Mr. Leypoldt :

" The constitution of the Booksellers' Exchange provides for the common debate on subjects of general interest, and for a common method of settling accounts. Membership is acquired by proof of regular license to do business in any branch of the trade ; by the payment of an initiation fee and annual dues ; by depositing the circular of the firm, personally signed by the members thereof ; and by a written pledge to conform to the rules, and to submit to the judgment of the Committee of Arbitration in cases of dispute with any member of the association or fraternity. The government is vested in a board of directors and standing committees, from whom appeal lies to the General Meeting held each spring. The General Meeting hears the report of the president, elects standing committees, passes upon the budget for the next financial year, and adopts rules to govern the action of the fraternity in their intercourse with one another. The executive functions are committed to the Board of Directors and standing committees, whose members are jointly responsible for any unconstitutional act of such board or committees, and individually responsible for their personal acts in contravention of the constitution or rules of the General Meeting. The standing committees are : On Finance and Accounts ; on the Exchange Building ; on Elections ; and on Arbitration. They are elected for three years, one third of the members going out annually. The functions of the three first committees require no specification.

" The Committee on Arbitration acts as a commercial tribunal between members, who are pledged to obey its *subpœna*, the object being to obviate litigation before courts of law between members. Notice of differences is sent to the chairman in writing, specifying briefly, yet lucidly, the points at issue. The chairman notifics the party accused, orders a meeting of the committee, and cites both parties to appear. The case is then argued, and every member of the committee has the right to propose methods of compromise. Minutes are kept by the secretary, but on demand of either litigant they must be kept by a sworn notary public. The results of the arguments on compromise are kept in " Compromise Minutes," signed by the chairman and secretary, or notary, if one has been employed. Certified copies of the " Compromise Minutes" may be demanded by either party. No charge is made for the services of this committee, except for actual disbursements. The work of this committee has been of great benefit to the fraternity in keeping their quarrels in the family, in deciding all questions by the common-sense views of experts, and in gradually establishing a code of fair dealing which has given a high tone to the morality of the trade, besides saving court costs.

" The official organ of the association is the Börsenblatt, or Exchange Paper, which is published under the superintendence of the Board of Directors, who appoint a managing editor, furnish all official matter for publication, determine the rates to be charged for advertising, and exercise a general control of the financial and editorial management. The Börsenblatt is the recognized Trade

Circular of Germany, through which the trade obtains the first bibliographical notice of new publications, of works in preparation, of changes in price-lists or terms, and whose advertising columns are invariably used by all members of the fraternity in seeking or furnishing trade information. The editorial bibliographical part of this invaluable medium of trade intercommunication is made up from the books actually on the editor's table, never from the mere transcripts of titles, which might be carelessly made by irresponsible clerks. The rule being understood by the trade, that whatever brief mention may have been made of books in preparation or in the press, they will not be officially recorded among new publications until they reach the editor's table, every publisher has a direct interest in sending his new works as early as possible. The editor is thus enabled to prepare absolutely correct lists of new publications, containing complete bibliographical information as to title, size, style, pages of preface and pages of text ; and the result is a thoroughly reliable bibliography, surpassing in merit that of any other country, and exercising a highly beneficent influence on the literary education of the trade, raising it to the dignity of a bibliographical profession.

" The assets of the association consist of the Exchange building and Inventory, the Börsenblatt, investments, and cash on hand. Its income is derived from rents, interest on investments, subscriptions and advertisements in the Börsenblatt, initiation fees, and annual dues. Its financial administration is admirably governed by a perfect system of checks and balances. An archive is kept, in which are deposited all documents concerning the actions of the general meetings of the directors and committees, and the signed circulars and pledges of members, together with every thing connected with the history of the fraternity."*

In connection with the Exchange, and really forming a part of it, are two special institutions. One of them is the school for booksellers' apprentices, where young men propose to pass through a scientific curriculum in preparation for the book business. The three men who have done the greatest service for the school, and whose influence will be felt through it upon the literature of Germany for all time to come, are Friedrich Fleischer, Paul Mobius, and Dr. Bräutigam.

The other feature of the Exchange is the Order Institution, through which all orders to and for the publishers must pass. Every Leipzig publisher commits a certain routine portion of his correspondence to this institution, and receives from it three or four times every day the business papers designed for him. The number of orders passing daily through this institution is about seventy-five thousand. " The immense parcel business," says Mr. Leypoldt, " is done by porters of the commission houses, who deliver and receive several millions of parcels annually, with such accuracy that the loss of a parcel in Leipzig is almost an unheard-of thing. In the event of such an occurrence, the whole machinery of the Exchange Association is set in motion to find the lost article, and it is sure to be found in a very few days. It has generally been demonstrated that the delivery had been correctly made, but

* " Weekly Trade Circular," February, 1872.

that the receiving agent had inadvertently forwarded to one of his constituents what was intended for another. There is, we believe, no case on record that a misdirected parcel was actually lost. This marvelous accuracy bespeaks both intelligence and extreme faithfulness as characteristic of the Leipzig porter." During the year 1867, sixteen millions of parcels of newly issued books passed through the Leipzig commissioners, and in 1868 this quantity was largely increased.

The Exchange is where the booksellers of Germany hold their annual convention, during the Easter fair. It was formerly the custom of the book merchants, when they met at the fair, to compare accounts and receive differences; but these matters are now attended to in advance by the commissioners, and the merchants have little more to do than exchange congratulations and adopt measures for the general interest of the trade. At the fair of 1868, there were present three hundred and twenty booksellers from various parts of Germany, and the payments made through their commissioners amounted to three and a half millions of thalers. The whole amount for the year is reckoned at twice that sum. The booksellers conclude their annual meeting with an elaborate entertainment, where, as is well known, they give ample proof that they are quite as much at home with rich viands and old Rhenish wines as with the spread and perpetuation of literature.

Leipzig is also the great musical center of the world. Its Conservatory of Music takes the lead of all other similar institutions, and one third of all the musical productions of Germany appear there. There are about thirty-five music stores and publishing houses, at the head of which stands the celebrated firm of Breitkopf and Härtel. This house has been in existence one hundred and sixty years. It issues twelve thousand productions in its musical department alone, and employs three hundred men. The music engraving establishment of Röder produces annually, by its one hundred and forty artisans, twenty-four thousand plates of notes, uses thirty-nine thousand pounds of metal, and prints four million sheets of music.

Leipzig being the heart of the book-trade, book-binding likewise forms an important branch of business. It was formerly the habit of the booksellers there to send their books to Berlin for stitching and binding, but so great has been the improvement in the Leipzig binders of late, that the books are now folded and prepared for the retailer before leaving the city. The habit also now is for publishers, in whatever part of Germany they print, to send their entire editions to Leipzig for folding and stitching. In the year 1830 there were in the city thirty-two master binders, and seventy journeymen. In 1867 there were one hundred and twenty-five masters, four hundred journeymen, one hundred and forty-five apprentices, eighty-six women, and forty-seven messengers ; and these numbers are constantly multiplying. Publishers, wherever they live, prefer Leipzig as the place for printing their works. The presses are numerous. In the city and surburban towns there are forty-seven book-printing establishments, where three hundred and sixteen presses are at work, conducted by seventeen hundred and fifty men and

10

women. Many of the journals and reviews of Germany which bear the imprint of various cities are actually printed in Leipzig. The "Bazar" is ostensibly issued in Berlin, but has the Leipzig imprint.

BOOKS PUBLISHED IN GERMANY, IN 1872 AND 1873.

	1872.	1873.
Encyclopædias, Histories of Literature, Bibliography....	321	258
Theology.......	1,234	1,239
Law, Politics, and Statistics.................	1,015	1,051
Medicine and Veterinary Practice.....	485	514
Natural Sciences, Chemistry, and Pharmacy...........	587	600
Philosophy......	180	157
Pedagogical Science, School-Books, Gymnastics.........	1,266	1,314
Juvenile Books.............	296	387
Old Classical and Oriental works; Archæology and Mythology................................	427	438
Modern Languages, Old German Literature............	357	346
History, Biography, Memoirs, Letters.................	735	690
Geography, Travels...................................	267	339
Mathematics, Astronomy...........................	160	162
Military Science, Management of Horses........... ..	318	314
Trade and Commerce.............	488	482
Architecture, Machinery, Railroads, Mining, Navigation.	259	331
Hunting, Culture of Forests.........................	77	90
Agriculture and Horticulture.......	276	310
Belles Lettres, Novels, Poetry, and the Drama.........	998	948
Fine Arts, Painting, Music, Stenography..............	420	391
Popular Pamphlets, Paper Novels, Almanacs...........	209	205
Freemasonry................................,...	6	19
Miscellaneous....................	546	590
Maps...	200	220
	11,127	11,315

The statistics for 1874 show an increase over 1873 of eleven per cent. From 1851 to 1872 about 200,000 new publications were issued in Germany. From 1851 to 1859 the average number per annum was about 8,500. In 1868 the number of 10,000 was reached; in 1869, 11,305, which was the highest during twenty-two years. The lowest was

8,326, in 1851; 1870 produced 10,108; 1871, 10,669; 1872, 11,127. It must not be imagined from these statistics, however, that all works occupying a place in the German bibliographical announcements are so many respectable volumes. The custom is—and it is really the only reliable way of keeping a complete literary record—to announce together all works that are thrown into the market. The pamphlet may stand side by side with the encyclopædia, cover as much space with its little body, and have its price and publishers printed in as large type as Tischendorf's Sinaitic Codex, Sepp's Palestine, or Doré's Bible. So in the classified catalogues, a work that occupied the best five years of its author's life is just as prominent as the brochure that he threw off at a sitting. Down to 1862, Dr. Lange had published forty-one different works—and he has been going on at the same rate ever since, for that matter—and, out of that number, eleven cost less than twenty-five cents each, eight less than eighteen cents, and three but eight cents. The man who worked up a concordance of Tennyson may yet live to produce a Bibliographia Langica. The late Dr. F. W. Krummacher published, down to the same year, sixty-eight works, but the most of them are single sermons, each costing about ten cents. However, among his works and those of Lange there are a good number of octavos, and in some instances several volumes to a single work.

The wisdom with which the Germans conduct the book-trade, and the extent to which they have carried it, will appear all the greater when compared with two neighboring people—the Russians on the east, and the Scandina-

vians on the north. " The Russian book-trade," according
to a critical authority, " is still in a very primitive condition. Credit and mutual confidence are wanting. ' First
the money, and then the goods,' is the Russian publisher's motto. The publisher is also despotic. He will not
deliver three, five, or six copies ; at least ten, twenty, or
twenty-five copies must be drawn at one time. Works
are never sent to the trade on commission ; and the Russian one-sided mode of doing business prevents a development of intellectual life. The Russian publishing
trade is confined almost exclusively to St. Petersburg and
Moscow, and it is an ' event' when a good book is published in Kiew, Charkov, Odessa, or Kasan. The average exportation of books from Russia amounts to about
120,000 silver rubles, and the importation to about 500,000
rubles. In the year 1868 the importation of books
reached the exceptionally large sum of 1,101,000 silver
rubles. Of this sum Germany sent 800,000 rubles' worth
of books, France 260,000 rubles. This sudden increase
of importation was also accompanied by a corresponding
decrease of the sale of Russian works. There are four
hundred and thirteen bookstores in Russia.

"A consequence of the low condition of the Russian
book-trade, and the inactivity of scientific life, is the lack
of an exact bibliography. There have been some bibliographical efforts made in the course of the present century, but they are not to be compared to the thorough
works of Kaisar, Hinrichs, Kirchhoff, Grässe, Engelmann,
and others. From 1820 to 1830, Smirdin and Kraschen-
inikov published really good catalogues of a pretty impor-

tant Russian lending library, which also included scientifie works, and in which nearly all the most important Russian literature is registered. Then eame a long pause until 1860. From this date till 1867 the " Bibliographical Messenger" (*Knischni Westnik*) appeared semi-monthly, edited first by Senkowsky, and later by Rostowzew, in St. Petersburg. It met the most pressing needs of the Russian book-trade, and in a certain degree gave accurate information about new literature. This publication, nevertheless, was discontinued from lack of support in 1867, having only an edition of five hundred eopies." *

The international eopyright movement has been, and still is, resisted by Russia. The "Moseow Gazette," in an article on the subject, gives the following official statistics of the impo'rt and export of books for the last five years, and eoneludes from them that the interests of Russia would not be promoted by an international eopyright law. In 1866, books, maps, and music were exported to the value of 104,097 rubles ; imports amounted to 465,153 rubles ; 1867, exports, 168,813 rubles, imports, 464,765 rubles ; 1868, exports, 128,649, imports, 1,103,380 rubles ; 1869, exports, 106,462, imports, 990,400 rubles ; 1870, exports, 83,714, imports, 1,153,082 rubles.

PUBLISHING STATISTICS OF SCANDINAVIA.

Country.	Area in Square Miles.	Inhabitants.	Cities.	Book-print-ing Houses.	Book-Stores.
Denmark.....	14,000	1,700,000	75	119	623
Norway.......	120,000	1,750,000	46	60	124
Sweden	170,000	4,160,000	82	114	162

* "Magazin des Auslandes." Translated by J. P. Jackson.

The principal cities for the publishing trade are naturally the three capitals—Copenhagen, Stockholm, and Christiana. The university city of Lund is also of importance as a publishing place. There are two book-printing offices in Iceland, one in Reikiavik, and the other in the mercantile city of Akureyri; although the productions of the latter house are confined chiefly to school and devotional works, and two newspapers. There are in the three Scandinavian capitals :—

	Copenhagen.	Christiana.	Stockholm.
Inhabitants......................	180,000	65,000	140,000
Book, art, and paper stores......	128	—	95
Book-printing offices	36	19	19
Lithographic and copperplate engraving establishments.......	31	8	13
Type foundries........	1	1	2
Wood engraving establishments..	10	6	9
Bookbinderies	99	23	57

The book commission business is in the hands of a few houses, of which Copenhagen possesses twenty-one, Christiana twelve, and Stockholm three. The publishing trade is regulated by three unions, all of which are differently organized.*

* From the "Annalen der Typographie."

CHAPTER VI.

THE BROCKHAUS PUBLISHING HOUSE.—PERTHES.

THE celebrated Brockhaus publishing establishment in Leipzig, Germany, was commenced in 1805 by Frederick Arnold Brockhaus. At present it is in possession of Henry Brockhaus and his two sons, Henry Edward and Henry Rudolph. The branches of publishing business conducted by it are so varied, and the energy, system, and foresight exercised in its difficult management from the outset have been so marked, that its reputation is now European, or rather, world-wide.

One morning in the latter part of July, 1868, I made a visit to the Brockhaus establishment. All the accounts which I had heard of the magnitude of its operations and of the management of the business, were far below the real results of personal inspection. The plain sign of " F. A. Brockhaus, 29 Queer-strasse," was all that indicated its locality. Entering through the street doorway, I found that the high and broad buildings were constructed around three large quadrangular courts, each court containing the refreshing contrast of a thick and beautiful growth of flowers and fruit-trees. Each building is devoted to a general branch of the business, while the different floors and sections are used for the respective subdivisions. Every department has its own counting-house, its allotted managers, and its bibliographical head ;

while there is one simple room in which the whole general management is directed. This is the place where the orders are given, and to which all returns are finally made from the most distant workshop and the youngest apprentice. It is the heart, which gives vitality and strength to the whole establishment. I made memoranda of each department—of the number of hands engaged, and much of the machinery used.

The various branches of business conducted in the establishment are as follows :—

1. A book-store, containing an assortment of German and foreign works that are in part issued here, and in part are only on commission. There are several immense store-rooms in which these are placed, each work being assigned its proper place, and forthcoming promptly on receiving an order from any part of the world. It is impossible to compute the number of volumes in all, but they amount to hundreds of thousands. The antiquarian book-store strictly comes under this head, but as it is of so extensive and unique a character, I will speak of it hereafter. The blank paper depository holds fully forty thousand bales of paper ready for use. 2. The press-rooms. These contain thirty-six presses, seventeen of which are lightning presses, driven by steam, and two are hydraulic. This section is undergoing enlargement, and new presses are soon to be introduced. I spoke of the machines in use in some of the large printing-houses in America for distributing type, and also of our machines for setting type. The young man who served as my guide had never heard of them, and says they are not used at all in the

Brockhaus building.   He seemed greatly surprised to hear that such machinery was in existence, and was very much interested in a rough explanation of its operation.   3. A type-foundery.   There are six foundery-furnaces, each requiring four men for its management.   There are twelve machines for casting type.   4. A stereotype-foundery. The stereotyping is conducted according to the systems of Stanhope and Danlé.   Stereotyping by use of paper is also practiced, and extensively applied.   5. A galvano-plastic establishment.   6. An engraving and letter-carving department.   7. A geographical and artistic establishment for printing on stone and copper.   There are thirteen copper and five lithographic presses.   The stone is brought hither in its rough state, and prepared for printing by workmen here.   The only stone in Germany fit for this purpose is transported from an obscure little village in Bavaria.   The Brockhaus maps are celebrated throughout the world, and they, too, are produced here.   Maps are prepared in any language, according to the order.   A magnificent map, ordered by the Chinese government, and containing only Chinese characters, was nearly ready at the time of my visit.   8. A xylographical establishment.   9. A mechanical work-shop.   10. A book-bindery. 11. The antiquarian book-store.

I was on the point of leaving the establishment when an opportune remark of my attendant called attention to this most interesting and attractive department.   It is impossible for even the proprietors to tell how many second-hand books they have on sale without consulting their records, for the number is constantly changing in conse-

10*

quence of new orders and purchases. One hundred thousand is a very low estimate of the present number on the shelves. These works are gathered from all parts of Europe, and combine all branches of science. There are at least ten thousand theological works in store now. Sometimes whole libraries are bought at once. There is one man whose sole business is to travel all over Europe, and make purchases of books that may be for either private or public sale. He had just returned from Venice, whither he had gone to buy Canciani's great library, bringing with him the three hundred and sixty-seven cases, which held from fifty to sixty thousand volumes. One large room contains the folios and rare works alone. Many of them are in excellent condition, and the illuminated missals have been selected with the most critical judgment. I have never seen an antiquarian book-store in which the books are in such excellent condition as are those in the Brockhaus establishment.

In the antiquarian department there is a magnificent collection of both English and American authors. Almost every valuable book issued in the United States for many years may be found here ; I must say, too, that there were some not worth the price of their transportation across the Atlantic. But there is no perfect antiquarian collection ; the Brockhaus is, perhaps, as near it as we can reasonably expect. The young man having the management of this branch of the business is thoroughly acquainted with all its details. His name is Pincus, and he adds to his rare bibliographical attainments the accomplishments of a gentleman. He gets up all the Brockhaus antiquarian cata-

logues, which may be taken as models by all catalogue-
makers. The Bibliotheca Historica (1866) is a completely
classified register, with minute index at the close, of 8,663
historical works offered for sale by this one house. The
catalogue of rare works on America alone, published from
1508 to 1700, occupies seventy-two pages of a closely-
printed octavo volume. Herr Pincus has commenced the
issue of completely classified catalogues of all the second-
hand works now on hand. He had just given to the
printer copy for the Theological Catalogue, which will
constitute the first of the series. Italian literature will be
the second, jurisprudence the third, and philosophy the
fourth ; and so on, until the entire circle is completed.

From this enumeration it will be seen that in this one
establishment there are many subordinate ones combined.
Every thing which a publisher needs, with perhaps the
two exceptions of paper and the heaviest machinery, is
manufactured around those three quadrangles, and under
the personal inspection of those most interested in its use.
If the Messrs. Brockhaus continue to supply their own
wants in the future as rapidly as they have in the past, it
need not occasion any surprise to see their advertisement
for rags, and to learn that they are conducting their own
paper-mill. There is the same diversity in the publications
issued with their imprint as in their antiquarian collection
and in the chemical department. They publish many
theological books in the course of the year, but far more
on other branches. They are as apt to publish a love-
story as a commentary on Romans, and a skeptical as an
orthodox book. There is no specialty, and apparently no

theological preference. Their aim is to publish what has
merit, no matter what it be.   In this, too, they have
made many a miscalculation ; but their general success is
sufficient evidence that they have hit the mark more
frequently than they have missed it. To accomplish this
much in Germany, where there is, if possible, much
greater rivalry among publishers than in any other country, is sufficient evidence of the intelligence and judgment
controlling the establishment.

In proof of the general good character and great diversity of the publications issued during the sixty-two years'
existence of the firm, some of the representative works
may be enumerated. The Conversations-Lexikon is the
most widely circulated work of encyclopædiacal literature in Europe. It is a popular cyclopædia, somewhat
after the style of the British Penny Cyclopædia, but far
more useful and complete. It was completed in 1868.
Three hundred thousand copies have already been sold.
A monthly magazine, Unsere Zeit, has already gained
high favor ; several volumes of the new series have appeared.   A smaller Conversations-Lexikon, for more
practical use, has reached the second edition. Von Rot-
teck and Karl Welcker's Staats-Lexikon is now on its
third edition ; while the Illustrirte Haus-und-Familien-
Lexikon, a work designed to meet the immediate wants of
practical life, has met with great favor. The first volumes
of Wander's Deutsche Sprichwörter Lexikon have appeared, and give promise of a good reception of the entire work.

Of works of art, the Schiller Gallerie and the Goethe

Gallerie, with designs by Pecht and von Ramberg, stand deservedly high. The first half of the Lessing Gallerie is not behind its predecessors of the same class. In addition to these engravings on steel there are many others on copper, stone, and wood. The Illustrirter Handatlas, and the Geographischer Handatlas über alle Theile der Erde, together with many works of travel and adventure, abounding in wood-cuts, are also issued here. One series of German Classics of the Middle Ages, and another of German Poets of the Sixteenth Century, have been already commenced. There are also many works published in the English, Italian, Spanish, Portuguese, Polish, and Russian languages, embracing the most of the representative works in the belles-lettres sphere of the respective nations. There have also been published scientific works in Persian, Turkish, Sanscrit, Syriac, Tamul, Calmuck, ancient Greek, Ethiopic, and Hebrew. In addition to all these publications a daily paper is issued, the Deutsche Allgemeine Zeitung.

There is a bindery in which all the books manufactured by the Messrs. Brockhaus are bound, while they manufacture their own plates for stamping and ornamenting the covers. They take orders from other publishers for printing books. I saw a large English work, an order from a London house, which was passing through their press.

At the beginning of the year 1867 there were five hundred and sixty-two persons in their employ ; they now have six hundred and fifty. There is one respect in which the Tauchnitz house has far surpassed that of

Brockhaus. I mean in the number of republications of British and American works. No other publisher has done a tithe of what Tauchnitz has accomplished toward the dissemination of English literature on the continent. I found Longfellow's Translation of Dante with the " Tauchnitz" imprint, served up in paper covers and mediocre paper almost as soon as Ticknor and Fields had given it to American readers. The English language is now getting to be studied in all the German schools, and almost all intelligent Germans to be met with on the highways of travel can speak English more or less fluently. Tauchnitz has contributed largely toward this favorable result by presenting a good share of our general literature to the Germans in the language in which it has been written.

The Brockhaus establishment is exceptional among German publishing houses for the variety of its publications. Generally, the German publisher has his line of books, and would as little think of diverging from it as a Frankfort banker would go in quest of the northeast passage. One house is confined to theology, another to gymnasial text-books, another to the Greek and Roman classics, another to the German classics, another to social science, and another to agriculture. In Gotha there is a publisher who limits his issues to cartography, geography, and ethnography ; and his catalogue extends to forty-nine compact pages. His name, Justus Perthes, will recall that of Christopher Friedrich Perthes, who alone has been to the publishing interest of Germany what Charles Knight and Robert and William Chambers have been to those of Great Britain. The elder Perthes was born in 1772. His early

years in Leipzig were bitter enough, and no little bookseller's boy was treated worse than "Fritz." But he fought
his way up, became a bookseller in a small way himself,
then a publisher, and, after the overthrow of the Napoleonic supremacy, the representative of the German publishers on all important occasions, and the reorganizer of
their business in its relations to the German government.
His wife seems to have had no less foresight than her husband. The whole story of their checkered life, crowned at
last with abundant success, is told in a number of books,
but best of all in a translation from the German, entitled
" Memoirs of Frederick Perthes."

The son has been for a long time endeavoring to gather
about him the best geographers of Germany, and secure
the very best fruit of their pens. And he has not been
unsuccessful. Both the Berghauses, Petermann, Spruner,
Stieler, Sydow, Barth, Van de Velde, Menke, and many
other geographers and cartographers, appear on his catalogue, and seem to publish solely through him. In the
special department of map-publishing he has no rival.
Booksellers and others—for example, Meyer of Hilburg-
hausen—publish maps on a large scale; but those which
are prepared by the artists of Justus Perthes are the most
carefully and scientifically gotten up, and are the recognized standards in Europe. They are always accepted by
the governments as authority. Petermann's Geographical
Communications, Van de Velde's Map of Palestine,
Menke's Bible Atlas, Spruner's Atlas of the Ancient
World and Historical Atlas, Curtius' Maps of Athens,
Kiepert's Maps, and many others, are among its issues.

CHAPTER VII.

SECOND–HAND BOOKS.—BIBLIOGRAPHY.

NO country can equal Germany in the multitude of old books. The very groceries get their wrapping paper from among the unstitched and unsold sheets of cyclopædias and classics. An old fruit woman in quiet Göttingen gave me a quart of cherries in a cornucopia made of the unfolded leaves of a Greek Hippolytus. Thirty years ago the antiquarian trade of Leipzig was nearly monopolized by one house—T. O. Weigel. But the business has developed very rapidly, and now there are twenty-five important antiquarian book-stores in that city. The six largest of this number have a stock of one million of volumes on hand, whose yearly circulation of money amounts to 140,000 thalers. The auction business is confined to five houses, and these held in 1868 twelve auctions, when fifty-four thousand lots were disposed of, amounting to two hundred thousand volumes. The proceeds therefrom realized 50,000 thalers.

The custom of selling the libraries of distinguished men after their decease, and sometimes before, is much more common in Europe than with us, and more frequent in Germany than in England. The entire fortune of many a fine scholar consists solely in books, and when he is gone they must be boxed up and sent to the Leipzig auctioneer, to keep the wolf from the door of the survivors.

The magnitude of some of these individual libraries is astounding; and when the catalogue is made up and distributed, the number of works proves to be so great, and the books themselves often of such value, that orders are made from all parts of Europe and America. The books of a distinguished man, however, do not sell because of their ownership, but solely because of their intrinsic worth. The average German book-buyer does not care a groat for the hands that once handled a book, or for the rare autograph on the fly-leaf. His only concern is, the book's necessity for him. The library of the late Prussian court preacher, Frederick William Krummacher, was caught up by a Potsdam antiquarian, who issued a catalogue on very poor paper, and sent it around among the trade. The books were priced, and offered at private sale. They were declared on the title-page to have belonged, every one of them, to Krummacher. But the prices at which they were offered were exceptionally low, even below the average. No advantage was taken, and none would have been expected, of the great man who had once possessed them. I bought a number of works from this collection, some of which proved that even in Germany a presentation copy is not always read by the recipient. The leaves of a copy of Lange's "Vermischte Schriften," bearing the author's affectionate autograph, were not even cut; while a presentation copy of Van Oosterzee's "Christ among the Candlesticks" had only been read a little here and there, and a paragraph or two marked by an unsteady pencil. In the early part of 1869 the library of the late Maximilian, of Mexico, was offered for sale in Leipzig by List and Francke.

This was a collection of rare worth, for Maximilian was not only a man of cultivated literary taste, and an author, but spared no pains or money to collate all works relating to Mexico and the western hemisphere. They sold well, but, even in monarchical Germany, not because of their connection with an unfortunate emperor.

The luxury of personal attendance at book auctions is not known in Germany among literary men. Purchases are made by orders to booksellers, who had taken pains to distribute catalogues of the sale among their patrons. I made several attempts to attend an auction, in ignorance of the usages, but found that, not being a bookseller, my presence was not desirable. It is no more expected that a private purchaser attend a book auction in Germany than that he attend the semi-annual trade sales at Leavitt's, in New York. The great stores of second-hand books, like the new books in sheets, are deposited in storehouses. Consequently, when a book is called for at the salesroom the chances are that it is not to be had immediately, but must be brought from the place of deposit. The storehouse is generally in an obscure street, where rents are cheap, and often occupies the whole floor of an immense edifice. My curiosity to see a storehouse, or "magazin," was once satisfied by Herr St. Goar, of Frankfort. He kindly gave me an attendant, who conducted me through labyrinthian alleys to the mysterious place, and showed me his immense collection of second-hand books. These were all beautifully arrayed in appropriate departments, a slip of paper protruding above each work, bearing the catalogue number. Not a work could be called for without an immediate answer being given whether or not it was on sale. I am convinced that the German method of conducting the antiquarian trade is the wisest. In the case of auctions, the catalogues are distributed by the venders to the retail booksellers at home and abroad, who distribute them to those who are in the habit of giving orders.

Then in the regular antiquarian trade there are complete catalogues of the works on hand, so that no time need be lost in delving in a mass of unclassified books, in uncertainty as to whether the desired one can be had. The German dealer can tell you in a moment if he has the book you wish. You can tell yourself, for he will hand you his catalogues. No respectable dealer is without a catalogue of his collection, and, to adapt it to the changes of his assortment, he issues new editions constantly. Unlike our American catalogue makers, he enriches his catalogue but sparingly with enlightening notes, from the Dibdins and Hornes and Lowndes of the Fatherland, on the rare excellence of the particular works ; for he is well aware that those who wish the works know quite as much about them as he does himself, and that praise begets doubt.

Nowhere as in Germany is cataloguing reduced to a complete science. The whole land abounds in Sabins and Ezra Abbots. Some of the catalogues of second-hand book houses are of marvelous size. Lempertz of Cologne issues annually a stout duodecimo, with supplements at frequent intervals. The one for 1868, the sixty-ninth in number, contains 13,710 lots. Brockhaus and Baer issue, in addition to their special catalogues, an alphabetical monthly list, which is afterward brought together in solid shape. Frederick Müller, of Amsterdam, is the only man on the continent who gets up a catalogue equal to Brockhaus. His catalogue of books on America (on early voyages) is an octavo of 288 pages, with specimen frontispieces. Weigel, of Leipzig, has an octavo catalogue of pamphlets of Luther and his Contemporaries, in 262 pages. There are 3,000 lots. Frederick Müller's noted theological catalogue of 1857, on dingy paper, is one of the best ever issued. It is no longer to be had at any price. Some of the second-hand catalogues have little cuts on the cover—portraits or coats of arms, with characteristic mottoes. The device on the theological catalogue of Wagner, of Brunswick, is a lion rampant, with the words, "Nunquam retrorsum;" that of Beck, of Nordlingen, a griffin quiescent, with the words, "In der Arbeit Friede;" that of Kirchhoff and Wigand, of Leipzig, a broad-frilled and skull-capped portrait of calm old Sigismund Feyerabend; and that of Schweizer, of Zürich, a portrait of Christoffel Froschammer, with the words, "Habent sua fata libelli."

The Germans surpass all other people in bibliography. One of the rudiments of the book-trade, which every apprentice is supposed to learn, is a good measure of this science. The second-hand dealers have boxes, in which are slips, alphabetically and topically arranged, containing the exact titles of their entire stock. When a new catalogue is to be issued these are simply passed over to the printer. Petzholdt, the author of the " Bibliotheca Bibliographica," is the prince of living bibliographers now that Brunet is gone. He publishes a bibliographical monthly, and nothing escapes him. Hinrichs, of Leipzig, publishes a semi-annual alphabetical catalogue of all the publications of Germany. He also issues an excellent quarterly catalogue, classified both alphabetically and topically. The last number of the semi-annual is a closely printed duodecimo, in 366 pages, comprising twenty-two rubrics. While these publications, not to mention the many special bibliographies constantly appearing, are intended for the general public as well as for the trade, the booksellers have a class of directories and helps of various kinds which are limited to themselves, and designed to simplify and enlarge their intricate business. The excellent " Directory of Booksellers," by Mr. J. H. Dingman, of New York, may be regarded as an American specimen in the same important line.

CHAPTER VIII.

LITERARY CHARACTERS.—AUERBACH, AND OTHERS.

AN account of two or three of the literary men of Germany may not inappropriately close this survey of the publishing interests. I must premise by saying, that, to the great honor of the country, its own reverence for its language and literature is constantly on the increase. There was a time, and that not long ago, when the German mind was skeptical of its own productive power. This was owing largely to the influence of the court of Frederick the Great, who, himself a skeptic, and more French than German, was never so much at home as when surrounded by Baron d'Holbach, Voltaire, and as many of the destructive Encyclopædist school in general as flattery and gold could entice to Potsdam. The manners, tongue, and literary models of France were held in such repute that any attempt to banish them from the court and the drawing-rooms of the nobility, and the leaders of society, met with severe censure on the part of the Germans themselves. The outside world regarded the Germans as heavy and dull thinkers, good enough in their way, but incapable of great achievements in literature. This can be seen in the entire tone which pervades Madame de Stael's " L'Allemagne." She entered Germany in a spirit similar to that of a boy about to visit a menagerie. She regarded the men whom she hoped to meet as admirable because of their grotesque and clumsy greatness, not because of any many-sided affinities with the great thinking world. What she found at Weimar was a surprise to her; and what she wrote was the first revelation to Europe of the original creative power of the modern German mind. Lessing was the first recent writer to appeal to his countrymen in defense of their own language and letters. He pleaded for total independence from foreign masters. Klopstock and Körner, who were brought into the national struggle for deliverance from the domination of Napoleon, followed in the same strain. Goethe and Schiller were proofs of what the German intellect was capable of producing, and their greatest service lay, not in what they immediately accomplished, but in the confidence and self-poise with which they endowed the national mind. Waterloo proved that the French military power could be broken. The Prusso-Austrian war of 1866, by its happy issue for Prussia, separated the Germans as never before from the Slavic element, and taught them the possibility of taking the initiative with tolerable safety. The Franco-Prussian war of 1870–71 achieved the unity of Germany—far less in politics, however, than in literature; and now, for the first time, the Germans are pursuing a course totally independent of French models. French is still taught in their schools, and always will be, but is receiving no more attention than the English. Throughout the non-German portions of the continent—save in France itself—German is found to be as convenient to travel with as the French, while in Scandinavia and the Orient the English is getting to be more available than either.

I.

BERTHOLD AUERBACH.

THE little village of Nordstetten lies high up in the mountains of the Schwarzwald, or Black Forest. The people of that region, separated from the stir and bustle of the world, maintain themselves by agriculture and the rearing of cattle, after the custom of their ancestors. They are the real Black Foresters, who, scorning all the storms of the times, have remained unchanged for centuries. The general progress of culture has not been able to disturb their traditional customs. Before high-roads and railroads formed the means of communication between the plains and the inhabitants of the mountains, few travelers found their way thither; but now, since the railway has been brought to the town of Zorb, within an hour's journey of Nordstetten, the romantic beauty of this part of the Schwarzwald has become known, and no tourist through that primitive region neglects to visit the village of Nordstetten. Thousands annually make their pilgrimage thither from far and near; for the little spot, so long unknown to the outer world, has now become a place of renown. It is the birthplace of one who is Germany's foremost living literary celebrity in fiction, and almost in poetry. For the basis of the present account of him I am indebted to an essay, in the German, by Emil Danneberg.

Berthold Auerbach was born of Jewish parentage on the 28th of February, 1812. He received his first instruction in the village school of his native place; but later entered the Jewish school which had been established there. The worthy teacher, Bernhard Frankfurter, whom Auerbach honors to this day, put a just estimate on the talents of his scholar, and exercised an important influence on the development of the subsequent master in fiction. As his parents, by the advice of his teacher, intended to devote him to the study of Jewish theology, he studied the Talmud at an early age, and, when thirteen, entered the Talmud School at Hechingen, where he remained two years, and then went to the Jewish Theological School at Carlsruhe, for development as a rabbi. There, among other studies, he undertook that of the Latin language, which he had commenced in Nordstetten. He also spent some hours every day at the gymnasium of that place. He has since given expression to the impressions of this period in his "Ivo, der Hajrle." In the spring of 1830 he returned to his native Würtemberg, and, after a short period of private instruction, entered the gymnasium at Stuttgart. Two years afterward, in 1832, we find him a student of jurisprudence in the University of Tübingen ; but he soon turned from this study to become a pupil of David Frederick Strauss, that ardent disciple of the extreme Hegelian wing, who was soon to launch upon the world his destructive "Life of Jesus." The fame of Schelling attracted young Auerbach the following year to Munich, in order to continue his philosophical studies.

The youth of Germany were at that time full of schemes of progress and free government. The rulers were suspicious of the "young, bold seed," and Auerbach became complicated in some disturbance of students, and was arrested at Munich. He accordingly spent three months

11

in the prison of Hohenasperg, in Würtemberg, which had
been made celebrated as the place where the poet Christian Schubart had spent ten years' imprisonment, from
1777 to 1787. When again at liberty, Auerbach went to
Heidelberg, where he completed his studies during the
years 1834 and 1835. He became a most zealous disciple
of the celebrated historians Schlosser and Gervinus. Both
the scholars manifested especial partiality for the young
and laborious student ; and then was laid the foundation
of that intimate friendship which, at a later period, existed
between the three. During his residence at Heidelberg
Auerbach made his first appearance as a writer by the
publication of a large historical work under the pseudonym
of Th—— Ch——r, the proceeds from which enabled him
to carry on his studies.

The first work under his own name—" The Jews and
the Latest Literature," (Stuttgart, 1836)—appeared in the
strife of that time in which Wolfgang Menzel, like Richard Wagner of to-day, railed at all endeavors for improvement coming from the Jews, and stamped Gutskow,
Laube, Mundt, Winparg, and others, as followers of the
Mosaic legislation. This first experiment was followed,
in the year 1837, by the romance of " Spinoza ; " and, a
short time later, during his residence at Frankfort-on-
the-Main, by that of " Dichter and Kaufmann," Poet and
Tradesman.

In the year 1840, we find Auerbach in Bonn, engaged
in a translation of the complete works of Spinoza from
the Latin, which appeared in five volumes in 1841. From
this period dates that intimate attachment with the poet

Freiligrath, (who at that time lived at Unkel, on the Rhine,) of which Auerbach, in his speech on his friend, delivered on the 7th of September, 1867, gave an eloquent proof. During his residence in Bonn the plan of the "Dorfgeschichten" (Village Stories) was projected. Auerbach himself says concerning it: "When I received the news of the death of my father, (in the summer of 1840,) I wandered for several days alone through the Siebengebirge. Deeply moved by a longing for home, I wrote out the plan of the first twelve 'Village Stories' under the great beeches near Plittersdorf. I went to Freiligrath. I must have related to him very obscurely the plans that were in my head, for they were not distinct in my own mind."

Two years afterward, Freiligrath greeted, from St. Goar, the beautiful edition of these "Village Stories"— which had already appeared in numbers—with a charming poem, of which the following strophes are a specimen :—

> "This is a book! I can indeed not tell
> How it has seized right deep my inmost soul ;
> How by *this* leaf this heart of mine was struck,
> And how by *that* one I was nigh o'erwhelmed ;
> How I, at that, was forced to bite my lips,
> And how, again, I was obliged to smile !
> All these things have in you alone succeeded,
> Because in life you let your labor ripen.
> What freshly hath sprung forth from out of life,
> Will, even as life itself, seize hold of us ;
> And right and left, with pleasure and with pain
> Will take by storm the generous human heart."

Auerbach's village stories disclosed to German narrative poetry a new sphere of national material, and made an epoch

by its form as well as its matter ; for it appeared just when,
in consequence of the continued suppression of public life
in Germany, literature had come to a complete state of
lassitude, so that even the most prominent poets of the
time considered their gift a misfortune.   But "what
freshly hath sprung forth from out of life will, even as
life itself, seize hold of us."   These words verified themselves.   The volume had a complete success, and, in a
short time, made the author the popular favorite.   It introduced the people once more to themselves, and showed
them what had been lost in the preceding period by the
romantic endeavors of " Young Germany."   Auerbach is,
in the molding and description of his forms, more sub-
jective than objective ; but forms, like facts, are capable
of distinct meaning, and stand under his treatment by
themselves, alone in all their freshness and life.   One is
surprised at their great simplicity and artistic finish, as
well as at their profundity and spiritual apprehension.
The thoughts and representations are joined to a work of
art in which we see the mind of a poet who has observed
the world in its depths and grandeur.

The importance of Auerbach does not consist in the
fact that he has created in his " Village Stories " a new
kind of poetry, for in this he had been anticipated ; nor
in the objects which he has created, for in the description
of the people of the provinces and in certain peculiarities of the style he is even outdone by others ; but his
strength lies in the kind and manner of his creations.
For many years he was the only one who held that the
first principle of art is to submerge the artist in his object,

a merit all the more striking, since the very opposite idea had, for a long time, held sway.

Many have tried to imitate Auerbach, but without success. His " Village Stories " are not only translated into almost all living languages, and have thus become the common wealth of all people, but have furnished material for other forms of literature. We may mention here the dramatizing of one of the most beautiful of these poems, the " Frau Professorin," (the Lady Professor,) by Charlotte Birch-Pfeiffer, under the title of " Dorf and Stadt," (Village and Town.) The poet gave utterance to his feelings at this in the " Europa," when he said that the putting of this piece on the stage gave him as much pain as it must give a father to see his favorite child among mountebanks.

From 1840 Auerbach lived a wandering life. We see him in 1842 in Mayence ; in 1843, in Carlsruhe and Baden ; in 1844 and 1845, in Leipsig, Berlin, or Dresden ; and after the winter of 1846–1847, in Breslau. In the latter place he married Auguste Schreiber, daughter of the banker Schreiber. He then settled in Heidelberg. There Auerbach spent many happy days, his affectionate wife sympathizing with the character and retiring ways of her husband. But he was not destined to be so fortunate in his domestic life as in his literary productions, for his wife died in less than a year. Then Auerbach again commenced his wandering life. He first went back to Breslau, and from there, in the autumn of 1848, to Vienna. To his residence in the latter city we owe his " Tagebuch aus Wien," (Journal from Vienna,) which appeared in 1849, and the tragedy, " Andreas Hofer," in 1850. While there he married Nina Landesmann, daughter of the deceased banker Landesmann, and sister of the novelist of the Vienna " Presse," who writes under the pseudonym of Hieronymus Lorm.

Auerbach then settled in Dresden, which he made his permanent residence, and gave himself up entirely to literary labors. There followed in quick succession, " Neues Leben," (New Life,) in 1851 ; two other volumes of " Village Stories " in 1852 ; and, in separate editions, the exquisitely beautiful " Barfüssle," the pearl of the " Village Stories," in 1855. " Deutsche Abende," (German Evenings,) first series, was issued in 1858, " Edelweiss " in 1859, and " Joseph im Schnee " (Joseph in the Snow) in 1860. From the years 1845 to 1848 there had appeared, besides " Schrift und Volk," (Writing and People,) in 1846, a series of people's almanacs, under the title, " Der Gevattersmann," whose contents were particularly designed for the country people, and had much influence. As the poet had, in his " Village Stories," found the right way to make the higher classes acquainted with the humbler ranks of society, so he had now discovered a way of influencing the people in a stricter sense. During the four years of its appearance, the " Gevattersmann " became the household treasure of every rural hearth in Middle and South Germany. The series was, at a later period, collected and issued in a complete form, under the name of " Schatzkästlein des Gevattersmannes," (Treasure-chest of the Gossipman,) first in a separate edition, and then in the author's complete works, which appeared in Stuttgart in 1858, in twenty-two volumes. In 1848 there appeared a counterpart to the

" Gevattersmann," with the title of " Berthold Auerbach's Volkskalender," under the co-operative management of the first scholars and artists of Germany ; but it only reached a second issue.

If the " Village Stories " gave a representation of the life of the people in an artistic form, for the educated, the " Volkskalender " gave a representation, not of the life of the people, but of the entire movement of the time. It was a noteworthy sign of progress that a talented writer like Auerbach should so far depart from the literary traditions of Germany as to stake his name in producing a book for the people, and not teach to-day what had been acquired with difficulty, and only superficially, the day before, but to instruct, to strengthen, the popular heart, to teach independence of mind, and to excite thankfulness for daily blessings.

Since the year 1860 Auerbach has resided in Berlin. During the summer months, however, he generally migrates to his native South Germany. Among his latest publications are "Auf die Höhe," (On the Heights,) new "Deutsche Abende," (German Evenings,) and " Landhaus am Rhein," (Country House on the Rhine.) What qualifies Auerbach for his high position as the most popular German writer of the present time is, his love and esteem for the people, but more especially his honest manner of expressing his opinions and feelings, without prejudice or restraint. It can truly be said of him that he is a poet, a deep thinker, and a well-wishing, true-hearted man, who seeks by his writings to have a good and lasting influence on the people. He belongs to the few writers, the aim of whose lives is the culture and material elevation of the people. Most popular authors strive, first of all, to amuse their readers—few to teach them. In order to do this, the author must not stand on the height of contemplation only, but he must also have the power to portray what he thinks. The German who would be the instructor of his countrymen must have closely observed the period just passed as well as the present, and comprehend the possibilities of his land and people, and the necessity of development. And this height has been reached by Auerbach, who, in prose fiction and in poetry, has already taken his place in the German literary Walhalla as "teacher of the people."

II.

Augustus Petermann.

The real author of all the great German expeditions of discovery for the last twenty years is Dr. Augustus Petermann. Without himself being a practical explorer, he has traversed in thought the unknown regions, searched out the real traveler, inspired him with his own love of research, furnished him with assistants, apparatus, and money, and after sending him off on the great work of exploration, has seen that he was not forgotten when disaster overtook him, has kept the public informed of his movements, and has aided him, on his return, in the final preparation of his reports for the reading world. He was born on the 18th of April, 1822, in the village of Bleicherode, situated in the Golden Meadow, lying between Eichsfeld and the Harz Mountains. The salary of his father, who was an actuary in the place, was so slender as barely to enable him to send the boy to school. Yet the mother, secretly entertaining a desire that her son should become a theologian, did every thing in her power to give him an education. After he had gone through the highest school at Bleicherode, he was sent, when fourteen years of age, to the gymnasium at Nordhausen. Here he soon distinguished himself by his cartographical labors. In the lowest classes it was customary, and still is in such institutions in Germany, to assign this employment to the scholars for their labor at home, and Petermann's work in that department soon attracted the attention of all his instructors. But even later, when he reached the highest classes, he exhibited a preference for geographical studies.

In 1839 Professor Henry Berghaus, the celebrated geographer, established an institution in Potsdam for the education of geographers and cartographers. He called this new institution, with the special advice of Alexander von Humboldt, a School of Geographic Art. Through some agency, young Petermann's mother was persuaded to renounce her preference for his becoming a theologian, and though the father's means were still meager, we yet find the son, on the 1st of August, 1839, an inmate of Berghaus' school. Two of his associates were Henry Lange and Otto Goecke, the former of whom is now in the employ of the Statistical Bureau at Berlin, and the latter died a few years ago. Through the skillful management of the director of the school, all the young men became enthusiastic in geodetical, hydrographical, oro-

11*

graphical, and cartographical studies ; and a number of them were colaborers in the preparation of Berghaus' celebrated "Physical Atlas." This work indirectly led both Lange and Petermann to England, for it had created such attention in Great Britain that A. Keith Johnston, of Edinburgh, having resolved to prepare an English edition, found it necessary to get Germans to work on it; and, in 1844, Petermann and Lange were in his employment in Scotland. In some parts they labored together, and in other parts alone, on Johnston's "Physical Atlas," which, so far as both the maps and the text are concerned, is not simply a translation of Berghaus' work, but in more respects than one is new and independent.

During their stay in Edinburgh the two German friends made many excursions to the Highlands, carrying with them all the necessary apparatus for scientific investigations. In 1847 Lange returned to Germany, leaving Petermann a while longer in Scotland. Six months later Petermann went to London, where, though without employment, he continued his geographical labors in a quiet way. He was full of faith that he would some day be placed in easy circumstances, when he could pursue his chosen studies untrammeled. He soon became acquainted with Baron Bunsen, at that time the Prussian embassador to the Court of St. James. Bunsen received him with great warmth, and during the whole period of Petermann's stay in London was his firm friend. Petermann also became acquainted with the great English geographers, Sir Robert Murchison, president of the Royal Geographical Society, Smyth, Washington, and others,

who had already become aware of the share which he
had taken in the preparation of Johnston's "Atlas," and
who were well pleased with his enthusiasm for geographical studies. Their praise of him was very ardent after
the appearance of his two magnificent maps of the British
Isles, one of them describing the hydrographical relations,
river-plan, and net-work of canals, with all the climatic
information bearing on the country, and the other being a
representation of all the English statistics. In 1850 he
published, in connection with the Rev. Thomas Milner, an
"Atlas of Physical Geography," with explanatory text.
He established in London a Geographical Institute, and
was appointed geographer to the Queen.

He now began to work in that department which has
since done more than any thing else to raise him to the
very front rank of geographers, namely, the organization
of expeditions for research and discovery in the unknown
portions of Africa. In 1849 he was the means of setting
on foot the plan by which the English Government sent
out an expedition, accompanied by German scientific men,
to Central Africa. He owed the success of his ideas in
this affair to his friend Baron Bunsen, who represented
the matter to Lord Palmerston. Palmerston likewise approved of it, and gave orders, with the Queen's consent,
for the fitting out of the expedition. But the great difficulty was to select the proper German geographers to
accompany it, and this part of the undertaking was left
to Petermann. He corresponded immediately with his
friend Lange, who was at that time in Berlin, and requested
him to consult with Carl Ritter, of Berlin, on the subject,

and proposed to him to be one of the expedition. But as Ritter was at that time absent from the city, Lange made the same proposition to Dr. Henry Barth, who had already distinguished himself by his journey to Syria, and by his bold tours along the north coast of Africa, but was now settled as a private tutor in the Berlin University, and could not think of going upon such a long and dangerous expedition. Petermann, fearing that either no Germans, or none sufficiently scientific, would join the enterprise, hastened to Berlin, and had a conversation with Barth and Overweg on the subject. Barth, whose enthusiasm was by this time fully awakened, no more felt easy in his quiet tutor's chair, and promised to be one of the number to join the expedition. Overweg united with him.

The expedition set sail on the 5th of October, 1849, and its celebrated career is well known. Richardson and Overweg died in Africa, and Barth was left alone to pursue the work of research. It was now necessary to send assistance to the solitary traveler, and Petermann, who was well aware of the absolute barrenness of astronomical observations in Africa, resolved to supply Barth with an astronomer. He at once bethought him of Dr. Edward Vogel, who was at that time an assistant in Bishop's Observatory in Regent's Park, and who, he knew, would be perfectly willing to go. Through Bunsen's intervention, supported by Admiral Smith, Colonel Sabine, and Sir W. F. Hooker, Petermann gained the consent of the Minister of Foreign Affairs, Lord John Russell, who sent Vogel to Barth's assistance. The sad fate which Vogel met had a depressing influence upon Petermann, but it was only for a moment, and was really the beginning of that brilliant series of German exploring expeditions which were conceived and organized by Petermann. He did not confine himself to Africa, but was the first who created, by his lectures before the Geographical Society and his numerous treatises and newspaper articles, the popular sentiment in favor of expeditions in search of Sir John Franklin, which have become an integral part of the history of modern discovery.

The year 1854 was the turning-point in Petermann's life. His influential friend, Baron Bunsen, retired from political life, and left London, and Petermann acceded to the repeated call of young Bernhard Perthes, the proprietor of the Perthes Publishing House of Gotha, to settle in Gotha, and take charge of a Geographical Institute, which should prove a center of geographical knowledge for Germany and the world. Perthes believed that Petermann was the proper man for the great undertaking, and therefore secured his consent. But Perthes died in 1857; this, however, did not seem to deflect Petermann in the least from his purpose. In 1855 he had started a new journal, which has long since outstripped its competitors in every language. It is styled, " Mittheilungen," —" Communications," from Justus Perthes' Geographical Institute, on New and Important Researches in the Entire Department of Geography. But he did not give up one of his favorite branches of geographical labor—the organizing of expeditions of discovery. In 1860, he managed to get up one for throwing light upon the fate of the unfortunate Edward Vogel. He worked long in doubt, but succeeded in securing the assistance of his friends, and others who were interested in geographical undertakings, for the organization of the first purely German expedition, and Theodore von Heuglin, Steudner, Munzinger, Kinzelbach, Hansal, and Schubart composed it. The last three of these found their graves in Africa; and though the specific object of the expedition was not reached, the fruits which were reaped by it have been of incalculable service. Petermann, by dint of shrewd management, sent out another African expedition under Moritz von Beurmann, with the design of crossing the desert from the north to Wadai. This expedition, too, notwithstanding its unfortunate termination, has thrown a world of light upon the district traveled by Beurmann, and has already been made use of by subsequent explorers. The brilliant results of the expeditions of Gerhard Rolfs and of Mauch, the former of whom reached the hitherto inaccessible regions of the Sahara, and the latter the almost unknown border lands of the Republic of Transvaal, likewise owe their origin to Petermann. He also organized the German North Pole Expedition of 1868. At present he is in the very midst of great plans and new endeavors.

III.

KARL VOGT.

KARL VOGT, the early friend and colaborer of Agassiz, has attracted more popular attention than any other German scientist of the last three decades. He has great popular talents as a public lecturer, and never fails to draw

large audiences. He is a strong advocate of the Darwin-
ian theory of development; opposition to the Mosaic account of the creation is with him almost a monomania.
His influence is of immense weight in strengthening and
clothing with scientific garb the materialistic tendencies
now, unfortunately, rapidly 'spreading through Germany.
He was born July 5th, 1817, in Giessen, where his father
was professor of medicine in the university, and where
young Vogt afterward attended the gymnasium and university, with the design of becoming a physician. On
the removal of the family to Berne, Switzerland, in consequence of the father's call thither as professor, the son
became enchanted with the study of zoölogy, and, after
his promotion to the doctorate, entered into hearty scientific co-operation with Agassiz and Desor. In company
with these men he undertook the celebrated expedition
of exploration in the higher Alps. He became joint author with Agassiz of the "Natural History of Fresh-
Water Fishes, Fossil Fishes, and Studies on Glaciers."
In addition to these associated literary labors, he published,
while yet young, several independent works, among which
are, "In the Mountains and On the Glaciers," (1843,)
"Text-Book of Geology and Petrifactions," (2 vols. 1846,)
and "Physiological Letters," (1845.) These works have
passed into several new editions. From 1844 to 1846
Vogt lived in Paris, where he continued his scientific
studies with great energy, and united with a number of
his fellow-countrymen in establishing the Society of German Physicians of Paris. This association is still in
existence, and has been of much service in aiding young

medical students from Germany in the successful prose-
cution of their studies. From Paris, Vogt went to Italy,
but receiving a call to the University of Giessen, he re-
paired thither in 1847. Just then the political revolution
was preparing to break over Europe, and he united heart
and soul with the revolutionists, even accepting an official
command of troops in their interest. In due time he
appeared as a member of the Imperial Parliament in
Frankfort-on-the-Main, where he distinguished himself
more for his fearless utterances in behalf of political freedom than for practical political skill. He went to Italy in
1851, and while there wrote one work, and laid the foundation for several which have since been published. In
1852 he went to Geneva, in obedience to a call to a professorship of geology, and, in 1861, took charge of a very
successful scientific expedition to the Norwegian coast
and Iceland.

It has been during this last period of Vogt's life, embracing his residence in Geneva, that he has occupied
most public attention by his strongly pronounced materi-
alism, and by his untiring efforts in giving it currency
among the masses. In his celebrated controversy with
Professor Wagner, of Bonn University, on the relation of
the soul to the body, and on the relation of faith to knowledge, he appeared at the head of the young materialistic
school with Moleschott, Büchner, and others. In his
" Implicit Faith in Science," he says: " He who is a friend
of science cannot recognize the truth of those doctrines
of revelation which enter into conflict with science; natural science should be totally liberated from the influence

of religion and faith." This one sentence is the whole of his barren creed, and, indeed, of the whole school which he represents. No stronger expression was needed to convince every one of Vogt's contempt of revelation ; but his individual views, though carefully elaborated, have been already successfully met by his own countrymen with arguments on the evangelical side.

Vogt, having become greatly embittered by the reception that he has met from his theological opponents, has spared no pains to gain a foothold for his opinions in the public mind. The following is the substance of his views on man's origin, as expressed in the concluding lecture of a course in Leipzig. The extract may be taken as a specimen of the general tenor of the lectures delivered by him to large audiences nearly every winter in the German cities :—

Man, in his pre-historic period, had to defend his existence against other species, but he is the only species that has been brought to civilization and culture by his own labors. With the progress of civilization, the human form has been developed in the symmetry and harmony of its members, but especially in the development of the brain. The skull belonging to an earlier period shows a great similarity to that of the brute, and, as the ages advance, it indicates a higher development, until, at the present day, it is found in the highest state which the world has ever known. In comparing man with the monkey, there is a great difference perceptible in the development of the brain. The young ape and the human child resemble each other in the formation of the skull and brain only relatively, and the older they grow the more unlike they become. With these differences in the formation of the ape and man, there are still gradations: the lower grades extend, as by individual branches, up to the higher, and these again connect with the lower. The gorilla, which is physically most like man, recedes before the orang-outang when compared with the skull and teeth.

The result of Vogt's whole argument is : The present man derives his origin, not from similarly-formed fore-fathers, but equally as little from the present ape. The ape and the man originate from the same stock. Hence, the ape and man, when young, approximate each other in form. Both are derived from a related stock, whose form of brain stands upon a lower scale than that of the present ape. From this uniform stock the ape and man have proceeded in their widely separated paths. This theory of progression, from the imperfect to the per-fect, by individual men and generations, through peculiar power and by the continuous exercise of the intellectual faculties, Vogt holds, is much more feasible than the idea of a degradation of humanity from an ideal and more per-fect state to a more imperfect state.

Vogt claims that between faith and knowledge there is a world-wide and irreconcilable difference on the history of the creation, and that only science can rectify the legends of orthodox theology. He and his school are continually decrying the doctrine of a fall, and hold up their hands in scientific horror at the mention of man's being a sin-ner, which, they say, is degrading to human dignity. Yet these same men declare that man and the brute have the same common origin in nature. The strongest word that Augustine, Calvin, or Wesley ever said on human depravity is not so degrading to the dignity of our race as the fundamental tenet in the materialistic school—the common source of man and brute. The renewed attention lately directed to Vogt, in consequence of his lectures, has subjected him and his school to the wit of the caricaturists. As a result the German comic papers abound in illustrations of his views. In one, for instance, he is represented as being seated in his study, hard at work, when the door is suddenly opened, and Mr. Gorilla walks in, dressed like a man, holding his hat in hand, and making a low bow to his honored friend, thanking him for having given him and the rest of his race their true position in science and before the world. In another caricature a man is represented as going through a menagerie, when a little monkey suddenly sees him, recognizes him as an old friend, and stretches out his paw through the bars of the cage to give him a characteristic welcome.

Vogt cannot complain of any injustice being dealt him, for he and his school are of the same thinking as a certain Berlin materialist, who, in closing a lecture a few years ago, said to his students: "Gentlemen, my next lecture will be devoted to proving to you, beyond a doubt, that monkeys are our first-cousins!"

IV.

Adalbert Stifter.

Although Austria is no longer regarded, since the war of 1866, as a part of Germany, the German tongue is spoken by the great controlling body of her people. The empire is not productive of strong literary characters, and only here and there one appears above the surface. The Austrian who has taken the best position in poetry during the century, and the nearest approach that any part of Germany has furnished to the sweet and quaint Jean Paul, is the late Adalbert Stifter. He was the son of a linen-weaving peasant, and was born in Bohemia on the 23d of October, 1806, just at the time when Austria, and indeed all Europe, was reëchoing with the triumphal songs of Napoleon I. After entering the University of Vienna as a student, he gave up first one and then another department, without having heart for any in particular. In this way he drifted, in turn, from jurisprudence to political economy, philosophy, history, mathematics, and natural science.

When he left the university he was, of course, a proficient in nothing. He became a tutor in the family of Prince Metternich, meanwhile contributing poems to the Vienna " Zeitung." On the appearance of his poetical works his name became at once known to all Germany. The critical journals abounded in his praise, and he was the subject of conversation in all literary circles. But his sudden greatness was as much a surprise to himself as it could have been to any one else. He never seemed for a moment to think there could be merit in his achievements or worth in himself.

Stifter was not at all adapted to society. Heavy, clumsy, and grotesque in form, he was still more unattractive in company. He would never take part in conversation if he could avoid it, and it was indescribably painful to him to be thrown into the society of ladies. He always cut a sorry figure in the parlor. For example, at the time when he was tutor in Prince Metternich's family, and when his praise was in every body's mouth, some ladies who were calling on the princess eulogized his poems in the warmest terms, and expressed a desire to see him. The princess replied to them, that she would give them the opportunity of seeing a poet ; and on the appointed evening her drawing-room was merry enough with their lively conversation. They were all expectation, and scarcely knew how they should conduct themselves best in the presence of the great man whose overpowering presence they were expecting every moment. The door opened, and a tall, heavy, and slowly-moving figure entered. He stood a moment, bowed confusedly right and left, not knowing whether it was to the ladies or to the chairs and statues that he was paying his compliments. He dropped heavily into a convenient chair, and was as silent as the tomb of the Hapsburgs. The ladies took courage and talked to him, but only " yes " and " no " escaped his lips. The princess used every art to make the interview pleasant, but all to no avail. The ladies blushed, looked at each other, started new subjects, talked together, as if to relieve the stranger, and yet could do nothing to make him feel at ease, or engage him in conversation. Suddenly the door opened again, and the poet, as if endowed with new life, sprang from his chair, darted out of the room with the velocity and vigor of a beast of prey, and was seen no more by the laughing eyes that had long looked in vain for a poet.

" Do you call him a poet ? " said the ladies.

" Yes," said Princess Metternich, " that is the poet whom you have praised so highly, and you now see how differently a man looks from his books. I hope you are cured of your fancy to see a poet, and that you will never desire again to see or have one in your society."

The first edition of Stifter's works appeared in six volumes, under the title of " Studien"—Studies, (Pesth, 1845–51,) which was followed by his " Bunte Steine"— Colored Stories, (2 vols., Pesth, 1852,) and subsequently by his " Nach dem Summer"—After Summer, (Pesth, 1857.) Both his poems and tales attracted universal attention, even in the exciting revolutionary years of 1848 and 1849. He is admitted to be by far the best writer of fiction in Austria. His descriptions of natural scenery are the great charm of his works, and in his poems he frequently reminds the English reader of Wordsworth. His main defect is his bringing inanimate nature too much into his characters, making his men sometimes more like a forest than human society.

In 1849 he was appointed a School Counselor in Upper Austria. He resided in the charming city of Linz, on the Danube. He seldom saw either teachers or scholars, and only held his office by name, and by the slender salary it yielded. It was his great joy to sit at his cottage window, overlooking an angle of the river, and spend his hours between watching the picturesque scene before him and recording his thoughts on paper or his pictures on canvas. Stifter had a profound contempt for his own material existence; his heart was in the world around, and his own lips and pen would have been the last to repeat whatever shade of romance may now and then have colored his life. He died at Linz in January, 1868, and his body, covered with flowers and evergreens by kind hands, was followed to his grave overlooking his own beloved and beautiful Danube.

CHAPTER IX.

ODDITIES OF THE NEWSPAPER, HOME, AND GRAVE-YARD.

WHEN the American in Germany becomes sufficiently conversant with the language to read the journals, he is constantly surprised at the curious announcements. At first one is apt to regard them as ridiculous. But after a time, when the simplicity and beauty of the home life, and especially the strength of domestic attachments, are fully comprehended, they assume a more serious character, and the appearance of provincial oddity is found to be due to the primitive habits and traditions of the rural classes. These peculiarities, however, are rapidly passing away; even during my residence in Germany a marked decline was perceptible, and in a few years many of these peculiarities will disappear entirely.

The following may be regarded fair specimens of some of the oddities of the present newspaper, and the house and grave-yard of the olden time.*

The announcements of birth, marriage, and death are made often in large type, at considerable length, and signed by the appropriate persons. The editor seems to regard it proper to insert the notices just as presented.

---

* Compare Braunschweigisches Magazine, (June, 1867,) the Cornhill Magazine, (1873,) and an article in the New York Evening Post (1869) by that best of all authorities on the quaint and grotesque features of German life, John P. Jackson, author of the "Album of the Oberammergau Passion Play," London, 1873.

The following is from the " Riesengcbirge Bote :"—

"After an illness extending over many years, it has pleased God to take up my dearly beloved youngest daughter, Anna, into his heavenly kingdom, where we shall inter her soulless corpse on Thursday next, at 9 o'clock.

" Master carpenter J. Scɪɪ——."

A Leipzig paper contained this singular obituary :—

" To-day death tore away from us for the third time our only child.   L. A. V. and Fʀᴀᴜ."

The " Chemnitz Anzeiger" had the following notice :—

" Last night at half-past three God took to himself, during a visit to the grandparents, our only little daughter Antonie, of teething.   School-teacher S. and Fʀᴀᴜ."

Matrimonial solicitations are not a purely American institution, as will be seen from this proposition in the Vienna " Presse :"   .

" A soldier, forty years old, sound and strong, is tired of living alone, and would like to marry. He wishes a wife, twenty-five years old, affectionate, talented, and finely educated. Since he possesses nothing but his position, a fortune is perfectly necessary. But since he is thoroughly opposed to making love for money, he takes this way of making his wants known."

Such a topic, however, cannot be expected to submit always to the dull method of prose, as these lines from a Danzig paper show :—

Four men, in the best of years, (not aged,)
With gold and land, and never yet engaged,
Who've never fished for any maiden fair,
And whose acquaintance here has been too rare,

Who long to put themselves 'neath love's soft sway,
And seek in this—a very well known way—
Here perfect strangers in this little city,
Four modest, brave, and good young girls, and pretty,
As little wives to carry home from here ;
Therefore we beg our readers not to fear,
But send addresses, as is oft the case,
With portrait, to this paper's printing-place ;
Fortune with them we do not seek possession,
And hereby vow to act with strict discretion.

But such overtures are not confined to one sex, if we may judge from this confessed expression in the Berlin " Intelligenz Blatt," of March, 1869 : " A young lady of good exterior and pleasant appearance wishes to marry a gentleman of just the same way of thinking."

The festivities of the peasantry on matrimonial and funeral occasions generally involve considerable expense. The following statement relates to inhabitants of the lower part of the Valley of the Inn, in the Tyrolese Alps :

" A peasant left a clear fortune of three thousand four hundred florins, and the funeral and the death-feast cost four hundred and thirty florins ; another left three thousand florins, and the costs before and for interment amounted to three hundred and four florins ; another left four thousand one hundred florins, the funeral and feast cost four hundred and twenty-four florins ; a fourth left one thousand and thirty-six florins, and the cost amounted to four hundred and twenty-five florins. It is even worse, comparatively, with those who have to earn their daily bread. For instance, a servant inherited a fortune of one hundred and twenty-five florins, and the cost of the funeral feast in memory of the departed friend amounted to one hundred and eleven florins, leaving but fourteen florins for himself."

The "Rheinische Zeitung" furnished, in 1869, this testimony to the qualifications of an executioner of the eighteenth century :—

"I hereby certify that the executioner of Tecklenburg, Joest Heinrich Stolheust, brother of the executioner Jägermann, some time ago beheaded with skill and to my especial pleasure Heinrich Schuerkamp, who was imprisoned in the Hellenborg ; and immediately after, during the time my brother was syndicus, skillfully hanged a person named Rötter, above the masses ; also, that in similar duties people will be well served by him. Signed the ninth day of June, 1709."

The following scale of fees given to mediæval executioners of Darmstadt and Bessungen has appeared in a number of the German papers :—

	fl.	kr.
To boil a malefactor in oil	24	00
To quarter a living person	15	00
To execute a person with the sword	15	30
To lay the body on the wheel	5	60
To stick the head of the same on a pole	5	00
To rend a man into four parts	18	00
To hang a man or any delinquent	10	00
To bury the body	1	00
To burn a man alive	14	00
To wait upon a torture, if so called	2	00
To place in a Spanish boot	2	00
To place a delinquent in the rack	5	00
To put a person in the iron collar	1	00
To scourge one with rods	3	30
To brand the gallows upon the back or upon the forehead or cheeks.	5	00
To cut off a person's nose or ears	5	00
To lead a person out of the country	1	30

In addition to these charges, the executioner was gratuitously boarded, and usually received some douceurs besides.

The Black Forest, Hartz Mountains, and Tyrolese Alps are the chief districts where the doorways of the houses are superscribed with quaint mottoes. These are generally in a pious vein. Here is one :—

> The Lord this dwelling be about,
> And bless all who go in and out.

Here is another, imploring Mary's help :—

> Mother of God, with gracious arm
> Protect our beasts and us from harm.

This would suit any place as well as a house :—

> The love of God 's the fairest thing,
> The loveliest, this world can bring ;
> Who sets his heart elsewhere, in vain
> Hath lived ; nor may to heaven attain.

And this also :—

> The help of man is small,
> Trust God alone for all.

Here is a common one in northern Tyrol :—

> We build us houses strong and wide,
> Though here we may not long abide ;
> But for the great, eternal rest,
> We take no thought to build a nest.

This is in the same sad strain :—

> This house mine own I may not call,
> Nor is it his who follows me ;
> A third is borne from out its hall—
> O God ! whose may this dwelling be ?

The following is worthy any optimist :—

> The old folks to me they say
> The times grow worse from day to day.
>> But I say no !
>> I put it so :
> The times are just the times we've always had,
> It is the people who have grown so bad !

This is less hopeful :—

> To please all men's a vain endeavor,
> And so it must remain for ever.
>> The reason true
>> I'll tell to you :
> The heads are far too many,
> The brains are far two few.

The following, in two languages, is pithy. One pater-familias betrays a classic taste :—

> Qui ædificaturus est
> On the highway
> Debet stultum dicere
> Let as he may,
> Optat mihi omnis
> What he will, I don't care,
> Opto ei
> Just the same to a hair.

The following has a pardonable smack of egotism : —

> Zum Stainer this house we call;
> He who built it, roof and wall,
> Is Hans Stoffner by name,
> Full-handed, and of worthy fame.

It is difficult to tell whether piety or pelf predominates in this :—

> I love the Lord, and trust his promise true ;
> I make new hats, and dye the old ones too.

One of the inn mottoes runs thus :—

> Come within, and sit thee down :
> Hast no cash ? be off full soon !
> Come within, *dear* guest, I pray,
> If thou hast wherewithal to pay.

An old inscription in Upper Silesia runs thus :—

I have builded as I pleased. Let the envious man enter. If he dislike my style of building, no matter—my house is all the better for what it has cost me.

Another gives a landlord's taste :—

> The kind of guest that I love best
>   Will have a friendly talk ;
> Will eat and drink and pay his score
>   And then away will walk !

This from Lower Saxony has a touch of selfishness :—

> If your purse is filled with gold
>   Blessed be your entrance here ;
> Blessed be your going out
>   If you pay your wine and beer.

Inscriptions, however, are not confined to private dwellings or humble inns, but are met with over fountains and other public places.   In my daily walk around the Anlage, at Frankfort, I used to pass a large pump, surmounted by a huge bust of a laughing Bacchus that bent beneath his burden of grapes, which bore this selfish couplet :—

> Blessed to us may our drinking be—
> The water to you, the wine to me.

The quaint and simple methods of recording on the graves the manner in which the departed had died, are very familiar objects to every pedestrian through the most retired parts of the Tyrol.   For instance, near Meran, the celebrated center of the Tyrolese grape cure, this epitaph is inscribed on a tablet which bears the picture of a man's head peeping out from under an avalanche, and a little Tyrolese scampering off to the left:—

> Here died Martin Kausch:
> The avalanche came and rolled
> Upon his body, and made him cold
> Also, Jörg under it was bound,
> But to-day is lively and sound!

Near by is another grave, over which is a tablet representing the death of a woman by being run over by a heavily-laden wagon, with the words:—

> Here died Marie Wiegl, who
> Was mother and seamstress of children two.

The following is found in the heart of the mountains. A picture, painted in glowing colors on the smooth face of a rock, represents a furious ox running his horns into a man, with this result:—

> By the thrust of ox's horn
> Came I into heaven's bourne;
> All so quickly did I die,
> Wife and children leave must I;
> But in eternity rest I now,
> All through thee, thou wild beast, thou!

Among the newer inscriptions in Austria is the following epitaph over the grave of the common goods-carrier between St. Gilgen and Salzburg. He went by the name of the "St. Gilgen Bote," and died in 1869:—

> Here rests in God,
> The dead St. Gilgen Bote;
> To him be gracious, Lord,
> As he would be
> If he were Thou,
> And Thou St. Gilgen Bote!

The posting of lampoons in public places is always a very hazardous business in monarchical countries. If the perpetrator is discovered, the least punishment is imprisonment. The following example will be of interest to some future Austrian Macaulay. During the reign of the reforming Emperor Joseph II. the following was found on a wall :—

> A friend of arms,
> A foe to priests,
> A hypocrite
> Our Kaiser is !

The Emperor, to catch the author, caused it to be torn down, and this to be put in its place :—

> The first is true,
> The second plain ;
> Of need the third,
> And to the author fifty ducats are due.

But the trap failed, as is shown by this answer, which appeared on the following day :—

> Four are we—
> Pen, ink, paper, and I ;
> Each other we shall not betray,
> So the Kaiser his ducats may keep.

IV.

GERMANY IN FIGHTING MOOD.

12*

A space of near two hundred and ten years—so long has Germany stood at bay with Rome! Not the Samnite, nor the republic of Carthage, nor Spain, nor Gaul, nor even the Parthian, has given such frequent lessons to the Roman people. The power of the Arsacidæ was not so formidable as German liberty. The Germans can recount their triumphs over Carbo, Cassius, Scaurus Aurelius, Servilius Cæpio, and Cnelus Manilus—all defeated or taken prisoners. With them the republic lost five consular armies; and since that time, in the reign of Augustus, Varus perished with his three legions. Caius Marius, it is true, defeated the Germans in Italy; Julius Cæsar made them retreat from Gaul; and Drusus, Tiberius, and Germanicus overpowered them in their own country; but how much blood did those victories cost us! The mighty projects of Caligula ended in a ridiculous farce. From that period an interval of peace succeeded, until, roused at length by the dissensions of Rome, and the civil wars that followed, they stormed our legions in their winter-quarters, and even planned the conquest of Gaul. We did, indeed, force them to repass the Rhine; but from that time what has been our advantage? We have triumphed—but Germany is still unconquered.

TACITUS, DE MORIBUS GERMANORUM.

Es brausst ein Ruf wie Donnerhall,
Wie Schwerdtgeklirr und Wogenprall,
Zum Rhein, zum Rhein, zum deutschen Rhein;
Wer will des Stromes Hüter sein?

Lieb Vaterland magst ruhig sein,
Lieb Vaterland magst ruhig sein,
Fest steht und treu die Wacht, die Wacht am Rhein!
Fest steht und treu die Wacht, die Wacht am Rhein!

SCHNECKENBURGER.

CHAPTER I.

WAR A BUSINESS IN EUROPE.

WAR is the normal state of the continental nations. The total ordinary expenditure of the German empire is about ninety million dollars, and the army gets seventy-two million dollars of this! Germany, Russia, Austria, and France live as if fighting were their only mission. Look, for instance, at the quick, but strictly professional way in which those two mighty peoples, the Germans and French, went to searching for each other's throats in 1870. As I read the papers, I had continually before me the image of two great bears, which threw themselves on their haunches in a trice, and went to hugging each other to death. At the outbreak of hostilities, both countries were as well supplied with all the material of war, requisites for wounded and sick included, as we were after we had been fighting the South two years. As to men, they must have begun pretty much where we left off. There was no feeling the popular pulse, as with Lincoln ; no evidence that either monarch depended alone on the sympathy of the masses for his success. France expected every thing of her historical army, and Prussia looked to hers and those of her noble sister States, to fight and win as surely as she herself had done at König-grätz. On both sides the soldiers had been trained in peace for their work ; the numerous arsenals had not

known what it was to have a hammer idle, or a fire extin-
guished ; and, so soon as the tocsin sounded war, all grades
of railway-cars were thrown into an almost unbroken
train to bring these disciplined foes face to face along the
Rhine.

Notwithstanding the constant pressure of immense
bodies of troops there, and the coloring that standing
armies give to every branch of business, and to all forms
of social life, I never knew before what sort of a thing a
large standing army really is. In whatever country you
find it, it is as one great and thoroughly trained soldier,
fully supplied with every necessity at the nation's cost ; for
whom harvests bend and mills grind, without his taking
his hand from his smooth musket ; obliged to ignore the
rights of household and the high joy of conforming to
his natural tastes, standing with weapon ready to level at
another man in exactly his condition, with only different
uniform or language, each drawing about eighteen cents
for his daily wages, and both representing nations exchang-
ing all the while the most exquisite civilities, visiting in
splendor each other's courts, decorating each other's citizens with all manner of titles of nobility, and each seeing
in the other a giant, and warily waiting to take advantage
of the bruise in the heel, or the unhelmeted spot in the
forehead. The army stands, but the nation staggers.

The speed with which the Prussian army is mobilized
is marvelous. To-night you go to sleep in peace ; to-morrow you are quartered with troops on the way to the front.
In 1866 the whole regular army, and the first levy of the
militia, were on the march to Austria in less than two

weeks, and in the late war with France the German troops were on the Rhine in twelve days. Any fortnight Prussia can have seven hundred thousand troops on the Rhine, the Vistula, or the Adige. The method of mobilizing is thus described by Archibald Forbes :—

The mobilization machine grinds its grinding in this wise. The whole country is divided into districts, in the central city of each of which are the head-quarters of the army corps recruited from that district. Thence is sent forth the edict for mobilization to the towns, the villages, and the quiet country parishes. The authorities there make out individual summonses, appointing day and place for the gathering, and these are left at the "respective places of abode" of the reserve men. Max has married, and children have begun to toddle around his modest table. He is in the midst of his harvest. Carl is to be married next week ; he has bought his humble plenishing, and the priest or the minister has been spoken to. Hans is just entering into partnership ; he has built new premises, and his presence may be essential to make the spoon—his absence will spoil the horn. Heinrich is on the eve of emigrating. His traps are bought, and his ticket is paid for. But the burgomaster's clerk, or the orderly corporal, comes round one pleasant summer evening, and serves on one and all a certain bit of paper. Max, when he reads it, growls "Donner wetter," and actually lets his pipe out in the dismal pause that follows its perusal. Carl walks off with it to his sweetheart, and there is a blubbering match. But when the appointed day arrives, Max and all the rest come to the front—genuine children of the Fatherland. Max leaves the harvest *in statu quo*, kisses his Gretchen, and wishes her well in all her troubles, slobbers the bairns, and strides off to the muster—the wallet on his shoulder, into which Gretchen has crammed a couple of shirts, a lump of *schwarz brod*, a few slices of *schinken*, and a coil of fearfully and wonderfully made sausages—a little unaccustomed water in his eye, and a queer lump in his bare brown throat. Carl puts off his wedding indefinitely, and war becomes his mistress, *vice* the other *fräulein*, superseded for the time being. Heinrich postpones expatriation, perhaps to enrich the soil of France with certain phosphates, the product of the decomposition of bones. Hans leaves the new business and partner (an "exempt" let one hope) to take their course; he for the time has other fish to fry. The contingent of the village, duly called over and found complete, is sent off toward head-quarters. By the way it meets other contingents, till finally, as the rendezvous is reached, the several contingents make quite a procession in traversing the streets. Now, it can be recognized what a pure democracy, in a social sense, is the Prussian army. In the same file walk the laboring man and his master's son, the farmer's boy and the banker's clerk. And if you follow them till they have got their uniform, it is likely enough that you will find the laboring man, who already has his medals on his breast, wearing the gold stripes round his throat, and the petty centurion over his quondam superior, to whom he says, 'Do this, and he doeth it.' *

Of the rapid transition from peace to war I had an unpleasant experience. When the duel of 1870 broke out, my domestic group were at Heyst, a watering place on the Belgian coast, whither we had gone to stay a while before making the up-country English tour. It was only a week since we had left Frankfort, and barely a whisper of war was heard. At Brussels, which is only a little Paris, the people were in feverish excitement over an utter novelty—the candidacy of Prince Leopold for the Spanish throne. Finally, the news came that the candidacy had been withdrawn, and that France had thereby gained a great diplomatic victory over Prussia. With the popular effervescence, every body seemed to think the matter ended. From Brussels we went to Ghent and Bruges, and then to charming little Heyst. After a few days there came news

* "My Experiences of the War between France and Germany," vol. i, pages 15, 16.

of real war, and we hastened homeward, though forewarned of long detentions and all possible inconveniences.

What passed under our observation, on the journey to Frankfort, was in direct contrast with the ordinarily quiet and unobstructed traveling on the continent, and with the peaceful life we had so lately witnessed by all the way-sides, and conclusive withal as to the healthy and universal enthusiasm of Germany in her hour of trial. Every Belgian I talked with, with one exception, sympathized with France. "If you withdraw from your neutrality," I said to one living near the Luxemburg frontier, "what side will you take?"

"Perhaps France, but never Prussia," was his answer.

And it was one that expressed the result of about all my conversations with Belgians, both on the coast and inland. But what wonder? Belgium is really a mere colony of France, speaks the same language, worships the same "Holy Virgin," and has the same traditions.

The cars from Brussels to Cologne were crowded to suffocation. They were filled with Germans hurrying home from Belgium, France, and Great Britain, to take their place in the army as true sons of the Fatherland. They were at first quite reticent, but as we neared the Prussian frontier they became voluble, denounced Napoleon's pretensions, and lauded old Germany to the third heavens. There was not the slightest difficulty in cross-ing the frontier into Prussia. Not a word was said about a passport, and a custom-house officer told me that I need not unlock my satchel. After reaching Cologne, our heavier luggage was dispatched almost as speedily. At

Aix-la-Chapelle, where that old warrior-king Charlemagne sleeps in the historical and venerable cathedral, far beyond the reach of the strife and din of warfare, the self-forgetting and exultant patriotism of the people called to mind similar scenes I had frequently witnessed in New Jersey and New York during our late war. One lady in our car regarded it an honor that nine soldiers had been quartered in her house the night before. She expressed herself ready for every sacrifice, and rejoiced that King William was calling on all classes to unite in repelling the French invaders. The soldiers exhibited by every word a healthy confidence in the triumph of Germany. They spoke intelligently of the points at issue, and felt that if the war did nothing else, it would unite Germany—as, indeed, it did in greater measure than ever before.

A good proportion of the private soldiers were highly intelligent and cultivated. No wonder. Every class was called out, up to forty years of age. No money could buy a substitute ; you would not know where to find one. The substitutes had to go themselves. The learned circles were broken up ; all educational institutions were for the moment forgotten. The professors vied with the students in hurrying under the flag.

We reached Cologne, after many delays, late at night. At first there seemed no prospect of finding a hotel that could accommodate us, so utterly filled was the city with soldiers and officers. I think it was at the fourth one to which we applied that we first gained admittance. A short sofa was all the bed I had in the third-rate inn, but having adjusted myself to it as well as possible, I comforted myself with the hope that I would have better accommodations the next night. A sweet delusion! The next night I was destined to find in Mayence only the floor for my bed! A few nights in that style would have accustomed me to the campaign and all, without standing on the muster-roll or firing a needle-gun. Of course, we could not leave Cologne without visiting the Cathedral again. I had never seen so many worshipers in it before. Soldiers of all grades, the relatives and friends accompanying them, and little school-children, with their book-knapsacks on their backs, were drawn thither in the early morning by the sad partings—yes, the numberless possible sacrifices of the war. The following day I witnessed similar scenes in the Mayence Cathedral, whither I had wandered before breakfast.

As all regular steamboat travel on the Rhine was broken up, we took the only train of cars running from Cologne to Mayence. The time should have been four or five hours, but the delays lengthened these out to ten or eleven. The whole way was literally through a mass of soldiers hurrying to the front. We could not run over a few miles before reaching trains carrying soldiers, guns, and all the requisites for a campaign. Then our train, while it was switching off, or backing, in order to pass them, would be overtaken by other military trains. At one time we became entangled in a perfect network of cars, and it was very clear for some time that nobody knew how to get our train out again. Here and there we passed great piles of broken cars—the wrecks of collisions—and learned that several deaths of soldiers and railway workmen had occurred within a few days, owing to the irregularity of the trains, and the extraordinary draught made upon every body and thing connected with the road. This road—and the same may be said of all the German roads running in the direction of the scene of war, all being government property—was in a moment turned into a great military artery for conveying the country's very life-blood to the needy extremity.

We reached Frankfort the next day, but had to conclude our journey by carriage, as the cars stopped a good long distance from the city. The citizens had become thoroughly Prussian within a short time ; for until the war, nothing had been able to obliterate their grudge against Prussia for absorbing their "Hanse city" during the Prusso-Austrian war of 1866.

I found every department of life transformed. Uncertainty and motion were the new laws. My bills, which should not have come in for settlement before January, 1871, were presented by breakfast time, by special messengers. My coal merchant asked me, on my ordering a winter supply of coal, if I would pay cash on delivery ? It was something so new that I looked at him in surprise, not knowing at first what he meant, when a tinge mounted to his face, and he bungled out, hesitating at first for something to say: "You know—in these war times—one doesn't know what—you know—things are so uncertain." "O! yes, I understand. You are quite right." He felt easy again after a time, but his asking an old customer if the cash would be forthcoming, fairly made the perspiration roll from him. It was to him as great an undertaking as for old Von Moltke to figure out the placing of enough Germans to chew up a French division. Every thing was in motion. People talked faster than I could have believed possible. The blood fairly boiled in the German Michael's veins. People walked twice as quickly on the Zeil as they had done before the Spaniards had blistered their throats trying to pronounce Hohenzollern. Our file of street-sweepers, who so generally threatened to fall asleep over their work, now plied their brush besoms as nervously as if they were sweeping an army of Turcos and Spahis into Lethe.

At the Bürgerverein, our city reading-room, where I dropped in at five every afternoon, the people read the papers with at least double their usual speed. I always expected to find about a dozen familiar corpulent dozers here and there in the easy-chairs, with spectacles and papers dropped beside them on the floor; but I did not see one taking a siesta, to the best of my knowledge, after the fatal words that opened the brazen throats. Those venerable and usually torpid burghers were now galvanized, and flew from one journal to the other, devouring and digesting all as rapidly as a New York merchant will finish his morning paper. Indeed, the whole land seemed to have aroused as from a dream. There was bustle, life, quick perception, just as with us during the first three months of our war. All Germany was now living more, thinking more, doing more in one day than usually in two. The mighty energy that pervaded her victorious army passed into all the people it left behind to watch its steps, mourn its losses and rejoice over its triumphs.

CHAPTER II.

GERMAN LITTERATEURS IN UNIFORM.—THE LANDWEHR.

WHENEVER war breaks out in Germany there is
as much strain made upon the literary class as on
any other. Many a busy pen must give way to sword
and needle-gun. German military law knows little dis-
tinction or class of persons ; and the peasant fights by
the side of the tradesman, author, and prince. Every man
in the land must serve in the regular army from his
twentieth to his twenty-eighth year, and no substitute is
allowed. After having served out in the regular army, he
is enlisted in the Landwehr for five years longer, where
he is subject to call at any moment. When his time is
out in the Landwehr, he is enrolled in the Landsturm
until fifty. Here he is called out only in case of invasion.
The slightest disability exempts from duty—for Germany
is economical as well as military, and wants not a single
expensive incubus in her army. In the late war, however, few questions were asked, for it was a time of great
need. Enlistments came in freely from those whom the
examiners had declared unfit for duty, and they were accepted. None were more eager and patriotic than the
literary men—just as had been the case in the War of
Liberation, as told with peculiar interest by Steffens in
his "Story of my Career." The universities were universally ablaze with patriotic excitement. The doors were

closed, and such students as were not allowed to enter
upon military duty, associated themselves, with their
professors, to go upon the battle fields to serve under the
Red Cross banner of the Sanitary Corps. A professor in
the University of Breslau attached the following notice
to the door of his auditorium just after the war broke
out : " Since the gentleman students have something better to do than to run to lectures, I hereby declare my
lectures closed ! "

Of the pleasant relations of professor and student in
warfare, the following account of a correspondent in the
army gives pleasing witness : " It gave me great pleasure
one evening to meet an old student friend, Dr. Meier, now
Professor of Law in the University of Halle, upon the
suspension bridge between Corney and Novéant. The
Doctor could not bear to see all his students going away,
and he joined them as a recruit. He now marches with
the reserves of an Erfurt regiment toward Paris, and not
long ago arrived in Corney, in advance of his regiment,
in order to procure quarters for it. Along with him was
a tall young lieutenant, who had exercised him in drill.
These two shared their room with me. But how happy
they were ! It was charming ! The best of the whole
story was the good relationship existing between the
young officer and the old recruit. ' No, my dear Professor, now I must carry your cow-foot (needle-gun) a bit for
you ? You can't carry it any longer ! ' ' Excuse me, dear
Lieutenant, that would be against all the rules of subor-
dination.' Notwithstanding this, however, the young
officer persisted in carrying the Professor's needle-gun,

and listened intently to the legal wisdom that flowed from
his old friend's lips.   On the following morning Professor
and Lieutenant helped each other in dressing and buck-
ling on knapsacks and accouterments.   They called every
article by its classic name, and quoted with great gusto
the very appropriate lines from "Wallenstein's Camp:"

> "Mit Tornister und Wehrgehäng
> Schlieszt er sich an eine würdige Meng."

A few names will convey an idea of the authors who
fell during the war.   In Dr. Pabst, who was killed at
Metz, Germany lost one of her most promising historians.
He was still young, but had already accomplished much.
While he was yet a student in the universities of Bonn,
Berlin, and Göttingen, he wrote a "History of the Longo-
bardian Kingdom," which met with the most decided
approval of the critics.   He won his doctorate at Berlin,
having written the treatise "De Ariberto II. Mediolanes
primisque medii devi motibus popularibus."   While there,
he undertook at the same time the editing of Hirsch's
"Jahrbücher Heinrich's IV.," essentially supplementing the
work by his own labors.   After completing his university
studies he devoted his principal labors to the "Monumenta
Germaniæ Historica," and much was expected from him
for this work.   He had a keen historical penetration, and
a thorough philological education.   He undertook the examination of Italian historical sources, and was in Italy,
for the purpose of collecting material for lives of the
Popes, when the war was declared by France.   He had
already visited the Vatican, the principal libraries of

Naples and Florence, and the cloister and city libraries of many other cities in Italy ; fortunately, a part of these labors is preserved, in the author's manuscript, in the Berlin Library. He lost no time in returning to Germany to join his regiment, where he was universally respected for his soldierly bearing and courage. He left Berlin, it is said, with a heavy heart, having forebodings that he would never return.

On the same battle field fell Dr. Julius Brakelmann, formerly a student at Berlin, twenty-six years of age, and a valued writer on French literature and art in the columns of the Augsburg "Allgemeine Zeitung." He went through the Bohemian campaign of 1866, and after that had resided in Paris until the war. A son of the celebrated Oldenburg poet, Julius Mosen, fell in the same engagement. He was a spirited young man, and had entered the army as a volunteer. He left his mother in great distress ; she will be remembered by many for her almost superhuman devotion to her husband during the last painful years of his life.

The battle at Resonville took away a promising young poet of Berlin, Paul Herth, known to many readers by his translation of Longfellow's "Evangeline" into German. His short career gave every promise that he would have become renowned in Germany. He was born in June, 1842, at Golssen, and early devoted himself to the postal service. In his spare hours he engaged in the study of the modern languages, and with such zeal that in his twenty-second year he was master of nearly all the European languages. He studied Sanscrit at the University of Breslau.

He devoted his chief attention to Spanish, Italian, Scandinavian, and English literature, and became a regular contributor to the "Magazin für die Literatur des Auslands," particularly on Swedish and Spanish literature. He made the Danish campaign in 1864, and the Bohemian in 1866, returning from the field of Königgrätz an officer. He belonged, in the German and French war, to the third Regiment of the Guards, in whose ranks he was struck by two bullets, through the head and breast. He wrote numerous war songs, some of which have been published, while others are still in manuscript. His latest, entitled "Roses on the Battle Field," was published shortly before his death.

A well-known Saxon poet, Captain Adolph von Berlepsch, a member of the Dresden Literary Society, was also killed. The Princess Salm, whose heroic husband was likewise killed in the war, conveyed the body of Berlepsch, her nephew, to the hereditary estate of the family near Wesel. Berlepsch was a direct descendant of the knights who captured Luther, and conveyed him to the Wartburg Castle, where he translated the New Testament, and passed by the name of "Squire George."

An accomplished author on various subjects, Lieutenant Hoffman, also fell in the ranks. He was one of the most venturesome and successful of the German literary climbers of the Tyrolese Alps.

These few cases will prove the high social and intellectual standing of the German army. And here is another proof, from a living hussar officer, who sent a report of the battle of Sedan, written in Sanscrit, with citations of the

Rigveda. It is a curiosity. It reads as follows, and is dated Sedan, the 2d of September, 1870 :—

"Hxo mahâyud abhavat. Catravah sarve nirjitâh, sarvâ teshâm senâ mahârâjâ ca soayam, baddhâh. Tvashtâr no vajram soaryan tataksha ; ahaumâ 'him soarvilau çiçriyânam (Rigveda, 1, 32.) Aham sukuçalo 'smi, yuddhe na mahad bhayam gato 'ham, yad etasmin kshetre supârvate padâtaya eva yoddhum çaknuvañti, turanginas 'tu nâ 'rhanti. Mahatyâm seoâyâm bhavatah çishyah."

The following is the translation : " Yesterday was a great battle. The enemy were totally defeated ; their whole army, and the Grand King (Emperor) himself, taken prisoners. Tvashtar (Vulcan) forged for us the flaming thunderbolt. We beat the Ahi, (Python,) who erept away into his hole, (Rigv. 1, 32.) I am well ; in the battle I did not come into great danger, because in this very mountainous neighborhood only the foot soldiers are able to get well into the fight, not the riders." Von Thielemann, the author of this remarkable dispatch, is a doctor of laws, and in time of peace is judge in the Berlin Court of Appeals. He is a graduate of Leipzig, and, while there, was engaged in the study of the literature and language of the ancient Hindus. He made the campaign of 1866. His interesting Sanscrit report, above given, was published in the " Spener Zeitung," of Berlin, and naturally ereated considerable interest.

Besides Dr. Von Thielemann there were at least five other excellent Sanscrit authors in the Prussian army, namely : Drs. Thibaret, Goldschmidt, Goeke, Pischel, and Richard Kiepert.

13

The most of the literary men fought in the Landwehr. The Landwehr was made up largely of heads of families. The French soldier is bred to the business, and never thinks of a home. The German soldier has a home and a group about his table. Some have said that the schoolhouse marked all the difference between the Germans and the French in the late war. I believe this to be a mistake, and that domesticity, and not education, underlay the great issue. Archibald Forbes says :—

We have an impression among us—and I confess I shared it—that he makes the best soldier who is the most of an *enfant perdu.* Cut your soldier off from all civil associations—no matter if from all associations of civilization as well ; make the army his trade, the barrack-room his home, and alternate the canteen with the low public-house as his chosen haunt. Let every douce civilian body wag his head in a half-kindly, half-chiding way over the soldier, regard him as more or less God-forgotten, yet still a fine fellow in his way, and capital food for powder. Let the soldier accept this view of himself, drink his pay, wax his mustache, and swagger about the world in peace time—and in war ? Of course your reckless scapegrace, without a tie in the world, who carries his life in his hand, is just the man to make a dashing charge, to cover himself with glory, to start the bells a-ringing and the park guns a-firing, and—to drink himself to death with the multitudinous pots which a temporarily proud and grateful civilian population press upon his acceptance.   ,

Why ? Wherefore should a man fight any better because he is a disreputable scapegrace ? You talk of a stake in the country having a tendency to stimulate patriotism in civil life. Why should the same cause not have the same effect in military? Whether do the "tears fall and blind" the soldier most, when the band strikes up "The girl I leave behind me," if she be an honest woman, a true wife, and the mother of his children, or some dirty garrison trull hardly troubling to see him off in her anxiety to make the acquaintance of his suc-

cessor? In most of the printsellers' windows in London is an engraving representing a farewell between an officer and his wife, as he
quits for foreign service. I often appreciated the true sentiment of
Millais' picture, yet never more so than during those early days when
the mobilization mill was grinding. The husband, leaning from a carriage window, stretches forth his hand, which the wife clasps in both
of hers, gazing into his face in a speechless, yearning agony of parting. I witnessed the scene, with variations, dozens of times in town
and country, in Rhineland. Now it was a sun-burnt woman with
tanned cheeks, and deeper tanned hands, grim, thin-cheeked, and
angular-featured, who gripped the hand of a slightly greasy, equally
brown man in a blue slop, and boots slightly suggestive of small
boats. But the look out of the eyes was the same as in the picture ;
and the hussar officer had no fuller heart as the bell rang and the
train started, than had the greasy *landmann* as he turned away with
the broken muttered "Gott behüte dich," and pulled his cap over his
eyes for a spell before he re-lit his pipe. Did the *landmann* fight any
the worse, think you, because he had left behind him in the village
the sunburnt *frau* and their young ones, than would your dashing
devil-may-care, who goes jauntily away to the war with a laugh and
a jeer? I venture, for my part, to think not. *

Early in the war the Prussian Government took measures for the temporary support of the families and widows
of the Landwehr ; and the Crown Prince of Prussia issued
a call for the founding of a fund for the support of the
families of the killed and wounded soldiers. To show
what "encumbrances" are attached to the Landwehr, we
may add, that the second Prussian Regiment of the
Guard, which was before Strasburg, left no less than
seven thousand and three children at home ! In the early
weeks of the war it was no unusual thing to see the Land-

---

* "My Experiences of the War between France and Germany," vol. i,
pages 18, 19.

wehr men carrying and fondling their children through
the streets to the front ; though now the Government has
prohibited these scenes to be enacted in the ranks.

There is a poem by Ferdinand Roch, which was set to
music, and was very much sung in Germany during the
war, which gives a true picture of the German Landwehr-
man's taking leave of home.   It is entitled "The Land-
wehrman's Departure : "—

> "And now, dear wife, 'tis time to part ;
>   I hear the bugler's blast outside ;
> Do not despair ; be strong of heart ;
>   He'll guard you well in evil tide !
>
> "Give me once more the youngster here ;
>   My darling boy, one farewell kiss !
> But eight days old—the blow's severe
>   That makes me go from thee like this !
>
> "The little rogue, he's smiling, see !
>   I'll take that as an omen bright ;
> No matter where, his face shall be
>   Before me in the thickest fight !
>
> "The blast again !—well, take him now ;
>   Protect my wife and child, O Lord !
> The lot is hard—but here I vow,
>   On France shall fall my vengeance-sword !
>
> "And if, my child, I come no more,
>   Thy mother thee will often tell,
> Among that noble host I bore
>   A soldier's part for home—and fell !
>
> "O ! when will God bring on the day
>   That we shall lay our standards down ?
> Alas ! we hasten to the fray,
>   But Vict'ry will our banners crown !"

CHAPTER III.

REVIVING THE OLD THEFTS.—GERMANS UNDER VICTORY.

A PECULIAR feature of the war was the reviving of the old grudges of Prussia against France. One careful German went to calculating the expense to which the first Napoleon put Germany during his supremacy east of the Rhine, the levies he made on the towns through which he passed, and what not, and claimed that these, with compound interest, should be reclaimed by Prussia from France. Another move in the same direction was of a more literary character. German librarians busily employed themselves in ascertaining what literary and art treasures of value, that formerly belonged to Germany and were taken to France during the various campaigns, should be claimed back at the conclusion of peace. The Augsburg "Allgemeine Zeitung" called attention to a very remarkable work, dating from the twelfth to the fourteenth centuries, containing the poetical productions of one hundred and forty poets of that period,—kings, counts, knights, and singers without rank,—all known under the name of Minnesingers. The work is a clearly written parchment manuscript, with decorations and miniature paintings, some scenes being of great beauty and vividness of color, and includes the most of the poems of the Minnesingers, among whom are mentioned the Emperor Henry XII., King Conrad the younger, (Conradina,)

King Wenzel of Bohemia, the Margrave of Meissen, Walter von der Vogelweide, Wolfram von Eschenbach, the Tanhuser, Meister Gotfrit of Strasburg, Meister Conrad of Wurzburg, Heinrich von Osterdingen, and many others.

The work is said to have been written by a certain Rüdiger Manesse, "whilom of the Council of Zurich." It surpasses in extent and beauty all similar works transmitted to Germany from its forefathers, and forms a testimony of the ancient German intellect than which, outside of the cathedrals, the land has nothing greater. The history of the famous work is given as follows: It first of all went into possession of the Swiss poet-family Sax, of St. Gall. A certain Johann Philipp von Sax was, in 1580, Doctor and Privy Councilor, as well as General of the Elector of the Palatinate, and from his widow the work reached the Elector's Library at Heidelberg. In 1623 Tilly took away the whole library, the manuscript in question along with it; the collection first went to Rome, and later, Napoleon I. took it to Paris. In 1815 a greater part of the library was returned to Heidelberg. But this portion was retained. It was again brought to light by the Swiss scholar, Bodmer, in 1748; a copy of parts was then taken; in 1758 a pretty complete copy was made, and the work printed. Subsequently, Frederick Henry von der Hagen had correct copies, with many of the pictures, printed, in four large quarto volumes. Hagen spent many years of his life upon the work. In the year 1823, and subsequently, till 1838, he spent several months in Paris, in getting up a fac-simile of the manuscript, and having the pictures faithfully copied.

At the peace settlement between Germany and France, in 1815, King Frederick William III. of Prussia, who took great interest in the work, endeavored to get possession of the manuscript for Germany ; but he was only able to get permission for German scholars to have access to it at all times. The city of Breslau, which claims one of the Minnesingers whose songs are contained in the manuscript in question, (those of Duke Henry of Pressela,) offered to exchange old French works for it ; but this was refused. It has remained in France to this day, and an Augsburg journal thinks it a favorable time now to claim it back again. "The work is for us," it says, "invaluable ; for it is the reflection of the German spirit at the time of its greatest development of power. It is to the German nation what the old family Bible and ancestral paintings are to the family." Not every one will see the force of this argument. If all the European nations were to give up the literary treasures which they have taken from each other by force, there would be no end to reclamations. How much would the Royal Library in every European capital have to part with, no one knows.

Nothing during the war surprised me more than the calm and temperate spirit in which success was received. The first victory or two created no joy whatever, but rather a subdued cheerfulness, with a confidence in the further good behavior of leaders and army. We were coming home from church when the official news of the victory at Woerth had gotten well spread. The satisfaction, suppressed for ten days, was now finding expression, for even the German cannot conceal his gladness when under more than three successive victories, and particularly such as those over France and a Napoleon !

Whole families were out together ; even multitudes of little children, clad in their christening robes and borne in their nurses' arms, had been brought forth to join in the jubilee. The black and white flag of Prussia, and the flag of the North German Confederation, were streaming from all the public buildings and the clumsy market-boats along the quays of the Main. Little knots of young men were devouring King William's last grateful and prayerful dispatch to Queen Augusta. Old men, true children of Barbarossa, had crept out of their easy-chairs and down the crooked stairways, and rested on their canes every now and then to drink of the overflowing gladness. There were no deafening vociferations, not a sound loud or harsh enough to grate upon a child's ear. There was no evidence that beer or a stronger beverage had a hand in the joy. It was just the most quiet, but not less hearty, way of treating victory I had ever seen.

But, of course, the battles terminating with the surrender at Sedan of eighty thousand of the enemy, with army material and commanders to match, brought out the people again. This time the holiday lasted about two days, culminating on the evening of the second. A placard, without signature, stood on all the street-corners on the second day: "All patriotic citizens are expected to illuminate this evening." And the illumination came—not of every house, but of about every third one. Rothschild's house was well ablaze, and people naturally thought of it, and looked at it the longer, because of the many insidious reflections going the rounds of the German papers in relation to his patriotism. He was absent from his place at the extra session of the German Parliament to provide means for carrying on the war; but afterward he and his family paid special attention to the wounded. His daughter provided for a whole hospital. The monuments of Goethe and Schiller, and of the first printers, were centers of rejoicing and pyrotechnics. The fireworks were not of the noisy kind, nothing louder than the smart whiz of a rocket. German ears will not endure any thing like firecrackers, except on the battle field, and then a pandemonium on earth is their very element. Processions of juvenile King Williams and Bismarcks, carrying Chinese lanterns, filed up and down the streets. It was indeed a general jubilee, perhaps unequaled since Waterloo, or even the last of the imperial coronations in Frankfort, so beautifully pictured by Goethe in his "Aus meinem Leben."

What would naturally strike an American most favorably, was the perfect good taste and quiet of the celebration. There was no intoxication or roystering. A New York gentleman, overlooking the busiest square that night, said to me: "Why, if this were Paris, the people would be standing on their heads from sheer delirium of joy." There was really less excitement, but no less real rejoicing, than in an American village on Independence Day. So one can wish his friends of weak nerves no better fortune than to be in Frankfort, or some other German city, the next time the world gets glad over the capture of a live emperor and his whole army.

13*

CHAPTER IV.

HELP FOR THE SOLDIERS.

IN our war the Christian and Sanitary Commissions took shape very slowly. But all Germany, as soon as the late war was declared, fell into two classes: the fighters and their helpers. The professional nursing institutions immediately assumed a military form, and the voluntary enlistments from both sexes increased from day to day. Even boys of fourteen joined the Sanitary corps; lint-picking became the fashion in the thatched cottage and the most luxuriant drawing-room. The reception of the wounded at the stations was always an ovation. The dense masses of enthusiastic spectators interfered often with the regular work of the corps, and the bravos fairly deafened one. German and French received alike friendly treatment here. The railway stations had supplies of bandage-linen, drinks, food, beds—every thing, indeed, a wounded man needed—and so soon as the train arrived with the suffering, you saw physicians and nurses of all ages hurrying to do all that could be done for their relief. Every one engaged in the care of the sick and wounded was distinguished by a little white bandage, with a red cross in the middle of it, around the left arm, above the elbow. Volunteers were received for a longer or shorter time, according to opportunity. In the battle of Wœrth, some noble German women were seen to go right out into the thick of the fight, and drag the wounded into the rear, where death might be retarded or prevented by their timely aid.

The voluntary contributions for the sick and wounded did not amount, in individual cases, to as large sums as occurred in our war, but the number of smaller offerings was much larger. A thaler or half thaler, or even less, was the rule.

All names and contributions were published in the journals, and given the widest publicity. The poor gave as much as they could, and showed where their sympathies lay. All were touched by gifts from abroad, though not one of them went quite so far into their hearts as the million dollars from their countrymen in St. Louis. But all tokens of American sympathy touched them profoundly. The German looks upon the American as his brother, and the future of America as in a great sense his own.

In the German army there is no such an organized and powerful measure for the spiritual care of the troops as corresponded with the Christian Commission in our late war. If the war had lasted as long, or even a fourth as long, as ours did, something of that kind might have been expected; but much opposition would have had to be overcome before making the whole army accessible to practical Christian literature by a great agency of this character. A considerable part of the public press would have opposed it; the prevalent theology was, and is, in conflict with such measures; the mass of the clergy would have stood aloof with indifference, if not with opposition. One of the German papers, a real molder of German opinion, the "Weser Zeitung" of Bremen, contained these words, against tract distribution to the soldiers : " We saw tracts in the hands of some ; these had been slipped into their hands on the way. They contain thoughts on death. Now, this is certainly very foolish, since it is all-important that just these people should be kept alive, and, unques- tionably, more cheerful reading would have a much better effect than such sermons to people who have already faced death."

This effusion found, however, a speedy antidote in the columns of another Bremen paper, the " Courier."

Much was done in an individual way for the spiritual interests of the German soldiers. Religious societies within the State Churches accomplished what their means allowed. The influence of the various denominations out- side the State Churches was most salutary.

The most gigantic religious agency, however, in behalf of the German army, was the British and Foreign Bible Society. No barriers were placed in its way, for does not every German ruler know that his country owes every thing to the Bible ? No sooner had the war broken out than the British and Foreign Bible Society gave orders to its agent in Paris, M. de Pressensé, to put a force of col- porteurs in the field, and supply the French army with Testaments. Similar instructions were given to the So- ciety's agent in Germany, the Rev. G. P. Davies, who divided his time between Frankfort and Berlin, and had these two cities, with Cologne and Breslau, as his centers of operation. It was a great undertaking to supply an army of nearly two millions of men already, or soon to be, under marching orders. But the Bible distributers went to work in good earnest, distributing to the troops on their passage through the cities toward the front. Here are some of the experiences of the colporteurs, in their own words :—

"On Sunday, the Sixty-first Regiment of the line passed through Berlin, and halted for a few hours. With longing hearts they inquired for the Bible-colporteurs, but found none. Just as they were about to leave, one soldier took out a worn, yellow printed leaf from his pocket, and, holding it up high, said to his friends and relatives from whom he was taking leave : ' Look, this is a leaf of an old Bible ; no one has come to give us God's word, and this is the only portion of it with which we march into battle, and perhaps to death.' Since the incident occurred, we have trebled the number of our men, and now, if we can help it, no company of any regiment passing through shall march to battle, perhaps to death, with only a torn leaf of the Bible as their only consolation in the thick of danger.

"The work takes place under the most unfavorable circumstances that can possibly be imagined. The troops have often not a quarter of an hour to stay, and then there is a rush for the meat and drink which they receive for nothing ; and it is in the midst of this hurry and scuffle that we have to ask them to buy God's word ; and yet in one single day, among regiments which I could only address in this way, I sold more than three hundred copies. The principal difficulty is to catch the attention of a few men to begin with ; when this is done, they show the book to the rest, and spread the good news abroad, and then the difficulty is, on my part, to supply their wants. I do not mean to say that I am never rebuffed, but such is my general experience. One night, about eight o'clock, I was walking not far from the Potsdam Railway Station, and observed a gathering of troops. 'It would be a nice thing,' I said to myself, 'to supply these people with God's word.' No sooner was it thought than it was done. I hurriedly fetched my books, which I had left for such surprises in a neighboring house. I was in time to catch some of them before they had got into the carriages. Although they were burdened with heavy knapsacks, and it had become so dark that they could not see what they were buying, I kept selling even after the train was in motion. I heard that other trains were to pass. I hurried to the depot at ten o'clock at night to fetch books, and remained at work till midnight. On this evening I sold two hundred and fifty copies to a single regiment."

The plan found to work best in distributing to the troops was to *sell* to the soldiers in the field, and *give* to the prisoners and wounded. There were at one time in Germany about one hundred and twenty thousand French prisoners, and measures were adopted to supply them all with the Scriptures. The French wounded in Germany were not forgotten. The Turcos were generally glad to read the Gospel, and it was the first time they had ever had the opportunity of doing it. The number of copies of Bibles, Testaments, and parts distributed during the early months of the war, was between two hundred thousand and two hundred and fifty thousand. The binders had to furnish five thousand copies a day. The agents of the Society kept right in the rear of the armies. Nancy, Saarbrücken, and Sedan, were the centers on French territory. The universal testimony of the colporteurs was, that the soldiers were glad to get the Bible. Mr. Davies said at the time : "We are not forcing the books on the men ; they urgently beg for them. Last Sunday, the first thing I saw, on entering a hospital in Frankfort, was a Turco deeply absorbed in his Arabic New Testament, which we had given him a week or more before. Germans, French, and Arabs, are alike in the joy with which they receive God's Holy Word. . . . It may give you an idea of what war brings with it for the agents of the Society, when I tell you that in the last two months I have spent twenty-three nights in railway carriages, or sleeping, covered by my railway wrapper, on loose straw."

The British and Foreign Bible Society also provided for the distribution of the Scriptures throughout the armies of Holland and Belgium, which, although not engaged in the war, were placed on a war footing, and were on the frontiers, guarding their neutrality. The agents at Brussels and Amsterdam were instructed to this effect, and distributed the Bible to the Belgian and Dutch soldiers.

CHAPTER V.

THE PULPIT AND THE PRESS. IN THE WAR.

EUROPEAN Governments hold a tight rein on all the forces entering into warfare. War is decided by cabinets, not by the people. Sometimes the two pull apart, as when the Prussians protested in every possible way against the war of 1866. But the Government has always weighed its case well before the public ear hears a suspicious whisper, and, war being decided on, the next point is to use every available agency to make it a success. This thing of bringing man, brute and block, into play is one of the most perfect pieces of European machinery. " If we are to fight," it seems to be said, " in all the land there must be nothing that shall not shoulder a musket."

The first Sunday after war is declared the pulpit echoes the Government order, and continues to do so until Government says : " Stop ! You've said enough ; the war is over !" But it is easy to see, as you listen to the sermons, whether the hearts of the clergy are with the war—whether their patriotism has been touched. Of course, in the late war there was no doubt on that point. The German clergy woke up one Sunday morning and found a French army threatening to cross the Rhine, and their love of Fatherland gave them unwonted eloquence. A young man said to me : " The minister we have is a good preacher —that is, he preaches good war sermons." According to

all accounts, on the day of fasting and prayer throughout
Prussia, at the outset of the war, there were greater displays of real eloquence, the hearts of the congregation
were more deeply moved, than at any time since Waterloo. In Frankfort the churches were crowded—a strange
sight ; and the people wept like children—a still stranger
sight. The state of things was very threatening, and the
clergy saw it, told the people so, and all felt and wept
together. And so every sermon was on the war. The
bereaved had to be comforted, and the popular spirit kept
in fighting trim. Sometimes a plain text was made to do
odd service. I heard a Reformed minister apply the words,
" Hold that fast which thou hast, that no man take thy
crown," to the necessity of continued German heroism to
prevent the French from invading and destroying Germany. The sermon was excellent, came from a sympathetic
heart, and suited the people. Dr. Goldschmidt, a Jewish
pastor of Leipzig, enlightened his flock and supplemented
Plutarch by a parallel between Balak and Napoleon III.

There was no Schleiermacher in Germany, however, and
no sermons gained a national reputation ; but the congregations in various localities were so pleased with what
they heard that printed sermons soon occupied a prominent place in the bookstore windows.

The press of Germany did noble service in the war.
The old differences that had divided the leading organs
disappeared at once, and the Main no longer served as a
landmark. The editorial department lacked the dash,
elaborateness, originality, and freedom of the American
press in our war, but the tone was fearless and chaste. A

few large papers, such as the Cologne "Zeitung," the Augsburg "Zeitung," and a couple of Berlin journals, supplied points for the world of smaller fry. But even the best journals were poorly served with correspondence from the seat of war. Nearly all the details came through the English papers. As to full and satisfactory descriptions of battles, and that by telegraph, the thing was not known. Neither did they come by post. In fact, they were not written ; or, if they were, they were reserved for printing in quieter times. The best thing I found in a German paper was an account of the battle of Saarbrücken by a soldier who took part in it. The New York papers alone had more news going to them from the seat of war than was written for all the German papers put together. But the Government took pains to let the people get the general news as soon as possible. What transpired under "Our Fritz," and "my own direction," and King William's prayer for "God's further merciful help," were printed on buff paper and posted on bulletin boards, erected in the most public thoroughfares and crossings. The newspaper "extras" had up-hill work against this official measure, but still found a sale—at one kreutzer, or two thirds of a cent. It is but justice to the official bulletins to say, that they never failed to give the *French* losses.

The communication of information by non-official persons took quite another shape. A number of new illustrated periodicals on the war were started, and these sold well. Maps of all sizes of the seat of war were a principal source of revenue to the booksellers at this time. These, with a whole army of books on tactics, care of the

wounded, fortifications, gunnery, military history, King
William, the Crown Prince, Bismarck, Von Moltke, good
Queen Louisa, and others ; volumes great and small of
songs that suited the conflict ; new editions of Arndt,
Klopstock, Körner, Uhland, and Freiligrath ; music of
all degrees of merit, with battle-scenes for frontispieces ;
portraits of all the leading personages of Germany in any
wise connected with the war—these, and similar productions of the hot conflict, were the staple that the booksellers relied on for profit. The dry goods merchants
covered up the beautiful dress-patterns in their great bow-
windows by dazzling displays of black, blue, and gold
bunting. The boys wore uniform, and whipped McMa-
hon, Bazaine, and the rest through the narrowest alleys.

The German lampoons and caricatures multiplied, and
in every case I saw they were directed against the Imperial
family, and not against France generally. The Emperor
was always represented as in some state of perplexity and
suffering. In one colored caricature he was wrapped in
swaddling-clothes, and helpless in the hands of Satan, who
looked down in admiration upon his favorite child. In
another, the whole family were going around, exhibiting a
panorama of the war, the Empress serving as lecturer,
and the Emperor as agent. In another, Napoleon was
sawing wood for his bread. In another, a Prussian, with
spiked helmet, was wheelbarrowing him into the Rhine.
And so on *ad infinitum.* These caricatures, with all manner of squibs, found a good sale. The Turcos almost
always played some part in the picture, as cannibals or
little less.

CHAPTER VI.

A SATURDAY AMONG THE FRENCH PRISONERS.

BY a ride of less than an hour by rail from Frankfort, I reached Mayence one Saturday, for the purpose of spending an hour or two among the French prisoners in that place. Mayence being one of the great fortifications of Germany, and not far from the French frontier withal, it was one of the most important bases of operations, centers of supplies and reënforcements, and dépôts for the wounded and prisoners, during the whole war. In crossing the Main, there was time for only the most hasty glimpse at the beautiful statue of Charlemagne that stands in the middle of the oldest bridge over the river, and stretches out its grasping hand Franceward, as if prophetic of 1870. We were soon enveloped in a forest gay in autumn tints. On emerging, the whole Taunus range, with its complement of mediæval towers, lay off at the right, while in front the valley widened until the yellow Main lost its murky waters in the clear, blue, and ever-cheerful Rhine ; and far in the distance, in front, stood the northernmost outlying spurs of the now anew historical Vosges. The busy peasantry were going over their fields for the last time before their winter rest, and were aided by a good number of French prisoners, who still wore their red trousers and caps, and seemed perfectly at home on their new soil. By a government regulation, the French prisoners were required to till the fields, or engage in any occupation which suited them best, and the hire for them went into the State treasury—a most economical arrangement for Prussia, and one that the French seemed generally glad to submit to.

When our train began to thread its way through the labyrinth of earthworks and all manner of fortifications, and crossed the cropped knoll near Castel, where the old Roman fortifications still stand, it was clear that we were nearing the Rhine. Soon we were over the river, trying to find our path through a world of soldiers, officers, travelers, and artisans, into the winding streets of old Mayence.

The first sight that, at this time, would naturally strike one at all acquainted with the demure aspect of Mayence in time of peace, was the unwonted life that war imparted to it. One would think the whole German army was less than a dozen miles away. French prisoners walked up and down the streets, and loitered on the squares, as if they had been born and brought up in the city. Only when large bodies were together was there any guard over them, and even then there seemed little or no restraint. I stopped and talked with them at will, and they seemed glad to have the opportunity to answer a question or two, and tell the history of their disastrous campaigns. The prisoners were generally engaged in some kind of work for the citizens, and their briskness and mobile faces would have revealed their nationality even if they had not been clad in red cloth. They seemed contented, and some even cheerful, and regarded their military misfortunes as the joint work of poor generalship and treachery. Few were so poor as to do Louis Napoleon reverence. While I was standing for a moment at the corner of one of the broadest and straightest streets, an immense body of new prisoners, fresh from defeat and capture, was marched on one side of the street in one direction, while the other side was as well packed with a moving mass of their brethren, who had suffered the chagrin of captivity a little longer, and were probably on their way for some place farther east.

Outside of Mayence, in one of the suburbs, there was the prisoners' camp. It was on a hill, and overlooked the city and the Rhine and Main valleys. On the day of my visit there were in this camp and other parts of Mayence thirty-two thousand prisoners, or thereabout, as I learned from German officers. No one but the authorities placed over the prisoners was permitted to enter the camp; but on one side of it the railing was down, preparatory to putting up new, and any one who happened to pass at the time could see the camp, and even talk at leisure with the prisoners, without interruption by the guards. The apparent absence of all pressure, the care which seemed to be taken by the authorities that no undue restriction be placed over the prisoners to remind them of their captivity, seemed to pervade the very air. I witnessed several familiar conversations between prisoners and the officers in charge of them, and scarcely a word was uttered that could suggest the difference between prisoner and captor. I should have thought the whole community a family of overgrown boys, clad in blue and red.

The camp consisted chiefly of linen tents, but these

were now giving way to strong board ones, with roofing
of cement cloth. There were many Turcos of all shades,
from white to black. I saw some as black as my hat—
tall, graceful, respectful, and of the most intelligent cast
of face. They courted the sunshine, and, like our Southern Sam in winter, had evidently the full supply of their
wardrobe on their backs. Some of the Turcos were of
less elevated type, but their average was as favorable as
that of their fellows of fairer face. That the prisoners
conducted themselves well, was the universal testimony.

The prisoners from the newly-capitulated fortress of
Schlettstadt had just arrived at the Elizabeth Fortress,
and their reception was naturally a matter of considerable
excitement. I was attracted by an immense crowd of
prisoners in the middle of the court formed by the temporary barracks, and found, on approaching it, that a great
wagon, laden with soup, was the center of interest. The
soup was in big barrels, and it was distributed in great
wooden pails ; but it was most welcome to the weary and
half-famished prisoners, many of whom betrayed, by their
features and general bearing, that they had been used to
more delicate fare and richer service. The higher officers
were very silent, and only conversed with the German
officers when spoken to. They were clearly most unwilling
guests, and one could discover a lurking, profound contempt for the country to which they had been brought, and
for those who had arrested their opposition to Germany.
The German soldiers were very tired of the war. Not
one I saw seemed to wish it continued ; all shook their
heads when reference was made to Paris and a winter

campaign. One fine-looking Prussian, who had charge of a section of the prisoners' camp, told me that he had a brother in " Brukeleen," (Brooklyn,) and that if he had been in Germany, he would have had to fight, too, in the ranks. When I told him of the service the Germans had rendered in our war, and how many of them had fought in our army, and how the sympathy of almost all Americans was with Germany in her war, he had no language for his joy.

I have often thought, from repeated conversations, that about every other young German man or woman of the lower classes is fully expecting to come to America some day, and is saving money for that purpose. Fully nine out of ten have friends here, and a letter from one of them often circulates for months from village to village, until the complete circle of relatives and acquaintances have read it. Some of these missives I have seen, so soiled and worn as to be almost illegible. They all tell the same tale of American freedom, and do their quiet work of turning other eyes toward the great land beyond the sea. When the late German and French war was over, there was a new rush from Germany for our shores. Public security was regarded afresh in Europe as too capricious and uncertain a thing for any one of slender means who can find a country where war and peace do not depend upon an individual, but on the judgment of the nation's representatives.

But, alas! how many a brave fellow now sleeps beneath the daisies of France who never lived to realize his fondest aspirations—the enjoyment of a home in the land three thousand miles westward !

V.

KNAPSACK AND ALPENSTOCK.

14

Wer reisen will,
Der schweige still;
Geh' steten Stritt;
Nehm' nicht viel mit —
So braucht er nicht zu sorgen —
Und gehe recht früh am Morgen.

PHILANDER VON SITTEWALD.

My German jaunts have been a period, the most healthy and active, the most interesting and anxious, and all of them the most joyous of my journeying days. In all parts and from every class, I met with honesty almost throughout, with the homeliest courtesy very often, and with friendship far warmer, I blush to say, than an unknown wandering German would have got in Britain.

I could not help bidding farewell to the hospitable shores and kindly inhabitants of Germany, north and south, east and west, with a multitude of grateful feelings to God and man, and with many reminiscences, in which sincere and affectionate regret were apparent for the time. And, even now, I make it my last sentence, as I trust it is my abiding sentiment, that I am fond of Germany and the Germans; and may health and happiness, peace and plenty, ever be with them all !

THE PEDESTRIAN, "EIGHT WEEKS IN GERMANY."
Frankfort-am-Main, 1843.

CHAPTER I.

TOWARD THE TYROL.

I LEFT Zurich, in eastern Switzerland, one mid-July for the purpose of making a pedestrian tour in western Switzerland and the Tyrol, and was favored with the company of the Rev. Mr. Wortman, of the Reformed Church, Schenectady. We had provided ourselves with the necessary outfit. It consisted of as few articles as possible—nearly all of which, even the stockings, were woolen—packed in knapsacks, and ready to be strapped on the shoulders. Alpenstocks of strong ash, about seven feet long, and pointed with good iron spikes ; broad-brimmed hats ; high laced-shoes, trebly-soled and generously peppered with hob-nails, completed our preparation for a long foot-journey, and gave us a completely Alpine appearance. With our scanty supply of baggage we designed to ascend the most interesting glaciers of the Tyrol, and go southward as far as Lake Como, Italy, and eastward as far as the great highway from Innsbruck to Verona. Our knapsacks became very heavy many times, and often, in ascending a mountain, or following a long and tortuous path to a glacier or a waterfall, we were very willing to intrust them to the most thievish-looking mountaineer to carry them a mile for us. But we seldom had any relief in this respect, and became accustomed to our knapsacks, just as a man gets used to his heavy winter overcoat. There were short sections of the tour over which it was better to ride than to walk, for, by this means, much time could be saved, and no object of interest lost. The road from Zurich to Ragatz presented a varied scene of land and lake, and a very watchful eye was requisite in order to use the prospects to advantage.

Ragatz is chiefly remarkable because of the baths of Pfeffers, which are about an hour's walk up a valley back of the town. The Tamina river runs down the valley, and this is such a beautiful stream that the pedestrian, in admiring its bank, is apt to forget the curious gorge where it takes its origin. Finally, the large building where the baths are situated is reached. There you must take a ticket in order to be led to the gorge and the hot spring. Having gained the board walk, which was well guarded by a strong balustrade, we passed along the contracting Tamina until it was nearly hedged in, and rendered almost invisible in many places, by the towering mountain sides that almost meet above, and only permit a few rays of even the noonday sun to reach down to the troubled surface of the imprisoned river. The passage becomes narrower at almost every step, and one is irresistibly reminded of some of the dark passages which Dante describes in his "Inferno." Wherever there is a little soil on a rocky shelf, a tree of the deepest green has taken root and shoots up its slender form to meet the light. Flowers here and there find room to grow ; but they seem to be somber products of some other world than this. There are times when one wishes to have nothing to say to his guide, no matter how worthy he may be, and this was one of them in my case. He talked very volubly, but observing our silence, after many efforts at conversation, he came closely up to me, and put his arms around me. It was an unexpected evidence of affection ; yet it was also an excellent opportunity for one to pitch the other into the stream, and how did I know but this total stranger had been overtaken by a sudden attack of insanity? After I had gotten rid of his embraces he said :—

"I am a good man ; I am not like common guides ; trust me, and I will tell you all about this wonderful thing."

"Talk on," I replied ; and he did talk with a velocity equal to that of the mad Tamina, on whose dangerous margin we were walking. I suppose he meant well enough, but, like many of his fellow-beings, he had a very queer way of showing it.

From Ragatz we went to Coire, and from there, as far up the Splugen Pass as the Via Mala, which is the Alpine gorge whence the Rhine takes its departure. At the entrance of this most appropriately named defile there rises abruptly a high mountain, crowned with the ruins of a very old castle. But the mountains on either side rise higher as the valley is ascended, and their precipitous sides approach more closely. All vehicles and pedestrians must, in one place, pass through a tunnel. The most interesting part of the Via Mala commences at the first bridge, which crosses the young Rhine so far above its surface that the bridge seems as if poised in the air.

Passing over the unfrequented Schyn Pass, through which the Albula hastens to join the Rhine, we reached Tiefenkasten. Before arriving at this place, however, we were compelled to stop at a most forbidding inn. It was not easy to tell how long the smoke of bad tobacco had been lurking in its dining-room, and when the hostess had made her toilet. The best thing she could think of to offer us was garlicky sausage ; but we suggested boiled eggs, always the best resort when there are any doubts of cleanliness. So, on black bread, a little honey, the execrable sausage, and the eggs, we feasted. Worn out with fatigue, we had scarcely finished our meal before we had fallen asleep on the old clothes amid the trumpery that lay scattered on the rough benches of the miserable room. But there never was sweeter sleep in a palace. How rapidly one's fastidious notions disappear in travel ! We were soon prepared to sleep almost anywhere, and eat food that would be intolerable at home, and not provided for in the cookery-books of any of the Blots in Christendom.

We went through the long valley of the Oberrheinsthal, where we spent the night in an hotel on the bank of a very beautiful waterfall. The next morning we crossed the Julier Pass. Here we first came in contact with snow, and were compelled to wrap our shawls closely about us whenever we rested. On descending, the Engadine Valley, with its deep blue lakes, picturesque villages, and fringe of glaciers, suddenly burst upon us. We spent the Sabbath in the town of Samaden, and the following day on the top of the Bernina Pass, whence we descended into Italy as far as the vile town of Tirano. Turning northward again we reached the Stelvio Pass, and there came in contact with huge snow-drifts. We were in the Tyrol.

CHAPTER II.

THE TYROLESE AND THEIR MOUNTAINS.

THE Tyrol, which is the great Alpine province or crownland of Austria, is one of the most interesting portions of Europe, whether we regard its history, natural scenery, or the customs of the people. This " great natural rock fortress, approached only by narrow defiles or passes," was settled by Etruscans and Rhætians. Afterward it fell into the hands of Rome, and continued under its supremacy four centuries. Subsequently it was for a long time independent, being eontrolled by its own princes. Margaret Maultasch—" Pouting Meg"—was its last native ruler, and, dying childless in 1363, she bequeathed her country to the Duke of Austria, Rudolph IV., of Hapsburg. Singularly enough, the people quietly submitted to this arrangement, and have ever since exhibited a love of their monarchical government quite in contrast with their Swiss neighbors west of them. More than once the Bavarians and French have invaded the Tyrol, and occasionally it has been for a considerable length of time under foreign rule. In 1805 Austria was compelled to cede it .to Bavaria ; but the Congress of Vienna, which attempted to make Europe what it was before Napoleon I. appeared, returned it to Austria.

The Tyrolese still retain the peculiar customs of their forefathers. They are clad in the same odd costumes of

the past centuries, and to all appearance will do so for
many a year to come. The women wear broad-brimmed,
high-crowned, black fur hats. In some instances the hats
are of heavy felt, but generally they are of long, shining
fur. These are worn alike in the markets, the vineyards,
and the hay-fields. With the exception of the odd hat,
there is generally nothing peculiar in the dress of the
women. But the dress of the men is fantastic throughout. There is, first, the high, cone-shaped, black felt hat,
ornamented with a very broad band and a little bunch of
natural or artificial flowers, or a feather of a chicken or
turkey. You seldom see 'a man without the flowers or
feather, or both together, in his hat. The coat is adorned
with an abundant supply of broad binding and bright but-
tons, designed to be as much in contrast as possible with
the color of the cloth. The pantaloons, usually of black
buckskin, are surmounted by the greatest of all the ornaments—a very wide leather girdle, covered with stitched
figures, which must have taxed the time and ingenuity of
the manufacturer to devise. Then the long, closely fitting
stockings reach to the knees, while the shoes are low, and
usually fastened by a buckle. This is the chief dress of
the Tyrolese when engaged in labor through the week;
but on the Sabbath, or festal days, they wear a dress
of the same general peculiarities, though of much finer
material, and of even more brilliant colors and strange
contrasts. -

The Tyrolese are ardently devoted to music and dancing, and whenever a holiday occurs whole towns and villages quit labor and engage in the sports, which have suf-

fered as little change as the costume through the lapse of time. Rifle-shooting and gymnastic exercises are the universal sport of the men—an exercise which the Government takes good care to encourage and surround with as many charms as possible, as it is of great influence in making strong-bodied soldiers. The people are as rigid and blind Catholics as can be found in the Papal States. You are scarcely ever out of sight of a crucifix; it is easy to see a dozen at once peering above the vines and hay. They occur at intervals of only a few rods on the sides of all the roads, in the streets and dwellings of all the villages and towns, flanking the narrowest mountain paths, and crowning the glacier summits of the highest passes. The crucifix is always adorned with a bountiful supply of red paint, which, from its peculiar hue, never failed to remind me of the pokeberry juice of juvenile days. This, of course, is designed to represent the blood profusely flowing from the brow, the hands, the feet, and the side of the Crucified. Little chapels are frequently met with, and generally stand on the hill-top.

We found the glaciers lying around in friendly juxtaposition, like great sleeping polar beasts. The sky was unusually clear. Leaving our knapsacks near the road to take care of themselves for awhile, after my traveling companion and I had passed Ferdinandshöhe—the highest permanent human habitation in Europe—we climbed the high peak to the left. The reward was well worthy of the half-hour of difficult ascent. The really immense glaciers near at hand now appeared to be only a small fragment of the whole glacier system bounding the entire horizon. To the west

14*

and south-west were the ranges we had been wandering over for more than a week, while to the north lay others that we hoped to climb in the weeks to come. Eighteen hundred peaks stood out in marble-like relief before us. It certainly gave us a very small idea of the work we had accomplished, or hoped to accomplish, to see the scene of several weeks' labor brought, to all appearance, almost within gunshot of where we were standing. This could be accounted for in a measure by the rarity of the atmosphere ; but this was not the first time that, after performing a task, however difficult it may have seemed at the time, it appeared very small on looking down upon it long afterward from a higher point than where the brain or hands had wrought.

The great white Ortler peak rose directly opposite where we were standing. It is nearly ten thousand feet above the sea, and nine hundred feet above the line of perpetual snow. It stands as a patriarch in the midst of a large dependent group, all the intervening gaps bearing their burden of glaciers, whose depth and story no man can tell. Until lately the Ortler was regarded as the highest mountain of the Tyrol ; but the recent measurements of the Swiss engineer, Denzler, have proved that there are several others between four and five hundred feet higher. Its peculiar conformation makes its ascent very difficult and dangerous. Until 1804 it was thought inaccessible, when, owing to the large reward offered by Archduke John, of Austria, to the first man who would scale it, Joseph Pichler, a bold Alpine hunter, gained the coveted prize. Since then it has been ascended a number of times, and careful surveys have been made of the Ortler and its snow-clad family.

The winding road by which we had ascended on the Italian side could be seen here and there like an unwound gray thread in the deep distance. Just around a rocky angle was the long, low custom-house, connected with which was the inn of Santa Maria, where we had been treated to an unsavory dinner a couple of hours before, and where the Austrian publicans muttered gruffly through their great beards the first tidings we had of the death of Maximilian in Mexico. Beginning the descent where an obelisk marks the frontier line between Italy and Austria, the steep road, numbering fifty zig-zags, came into full view. New and different scenes were presented every few minutes ; in fact, the succession of them was so rapid that our whole walk from the top of the Bormio Pass to the little inn where we rested at night seemed more like a dream, or some description that I had read, than a living · experience.

We spent the night in the little village of Trafui, a corruption of Tres Fontes, which takes its name from the three icy streams that flow out of the precipitous side of a huge rock further up the valley. The forests, which extend as high up toward the Pass as vegetation can exist, abound in wild deer, while there is a certain plateau near by that goes by the name of the "Bears' Play-ground." The mountain shepherds have had many unpleasant experiences with the bears, which come down on their favorite "play-ground," and make sad havoc of the flocks that dare to intrude upon it. An hour's

walk from Trafui brought us to a humble shed covering statues of the Saviour, the Virgin Mary, and Saint
John ; from the breast of each a stream of clear, fresh,
" holy water" is made to flow. Close at hand is the little
chapel containing a picture of the Madonna. This is
supposed to possess miraculous powers. It is visited
yearly by multitudes of Tyrolese pilgrims, and, for all
the confidence they would place in your words, you
might as well tell them that they are citizens of Pat-
agonia as that that execrable daub can never cure their
diseases.

We started about five o'clock the following morning to
complete the journey down the valley, and then to take
the highway through the Vintschgau to Meran. The air
was very refreshing, but it would be hours before the sun
could penetrate the valley. The shepherds were leading
their herds out to pasture. The milk-women were returning to their huts with their well-laden pails, and now
and then a frightened bird would start up before us,
and dart off to its home in the fir-forest. The road
very frequently crossed the now wide and constantly
enlarging stream ; so on every bridge we dropped our
knapsacks and alpenstocks for a leisurely gaze into the
mad torrent below, and then far up and down the valley
sides, where quiet cottages nestled, like little cages, under
some kindly rocky shelf. Villages multiplied as the valley
grew broader; but they were so filthy and unromantic
when we reached them that we tripped through them as
rapidly as possible, preferring to rest by the roadside,
where the unartistic peasantry had not yet disturbed the

lovely work of nature. In due time the road suddenly emerged into the broad historical Vintschgau ; castles of rare beauty crowned every rocky height within view ; the bells from the chapels of the thickly scattered villages held high carnival as the clock had just struck ten ; the hay-fields near and far were alive with groups of gayly-dressed men and women, who were gathering their harvest by the aid of primitive little sickles ; and the deep-green carpet of numberless vineyards lay unrolled all along the hill-sides, and bounded the horizon at each end of the enchanted valley.

The Vintschgau, so called from its ancient inhabitants, the Vennotes, is the broad valley watered by the Adige. The stage-coach traverses its entire length, an arrangement which proved very convenient to us about the middle of the afternoon. Picturesque castles increased on either side, some of them being no longer tenable because of their ruined state, while others are occupied a part of the year by their titled owners. Almost every village has its reigning saint, and chapels line the way-side throughout the valley. In some instances we observed tufts of barley and Indian corn hanging over the crucifix, half-hiding the crown of thorns. On asking a peasant what it meant, he said, as nearly as I can now recall, " That means that we owe all our blessings to Him who died for us." A beautiful reply, and worthy of a less sensuous system of worship than that of the peasant and his countrymen.

Of the castles on the way, Juval is one of the most extensive and picturesque. Before the invention of gunpowder it was considered impregnable. In the year 1546 its owner, Linkmoser, surrounded it with a large outer building, a fact commemorated by a tablet over the gateway. Its halls are ornamented with frescoes of biblical scenes—all made in the sixteenth century—and its doorposts are of the finest marble. From its windows, through which many generations have looked out upon the beautiful valley, there is a very fine distant view of the mountain range bounded on the west by the Ortler. The Castelbello is another very large ruin. It was occupied until 1842, when its wooden work was destroyed by fire. It stands upon one solid rock, and is again surrounded by a dense growth of ivy.

CHAPTER III.

MERAN AND THE TYROL CASTLE.

ALL the different attractions of the Adige Valley combine as you draw near to Meran. The castles increase in number; the vineyards assume even a tropical luxuriance; the chapels multiply; and waterfalls come in to help the splendor of the scene. Meran is not the enthroned queen of all, but lies low in the valley, as a rustic divinity asleep amid her favorite groves and fountains.

A sudden halt before the broad doorway of an hotel was our signal for rest, and we were once more back again to real life. A huge crucifix stood at the end of the hall where we were assigned rooms; but I fear the symbol had but little influence over the management of the hotel. The proprietor's boast was, that kings and princes had been his guests; but of all the hotels where we stopped in the Tyrol, this was the only one where the waiters were impudent; where, so far as I know, a direct and systematic attempt was made to cheat; where we were compelled to sit at the table next to a man who seemed to be an angry cross between intoxication and insanity; and where we were treated at breakfast to loaves of bread which had lost their crust, and suffered huge excavations by hungry mice on their nocturnal peregrinations. We would not eat the bread, but had to make out a long and crooked case before getting better.

Meran, a town of about three thousand inhabitants, first appears in history A.D. 857, and owes its origin to the destruction of the neighboring Roman town of Maja, in 800, by the fall of a mountain. Fragments of buried houses, Roman coins from Drusus to Justinian, and human bones, are still turned up in the fields and vineyards. Meran lies just at the junction of three valleys ; it was the ancient capital of the country, and its castle of Tyrol was the residence of the rulers. In the Middle Ages it enjoyed great prosperity and power as a commercial center, but numerous wars and the conflicts between the princes and their vassals prostrated it, and it now owes nearly all its thrift to health-seekers, who visit it in large numbers every summer and autumn. It abounds in boarding-houses and fine promenades for their accommodation. The stores are mostly under low, gloomy arcades, which are almost blocked up much of the time by lounging peasantry.

The castle of Tyrol, about an hour's ascending walk from the town, has given its name to the country. It is, in part, a ruin, the massive watch-tower being the principal portion now remaining perfect. The doorway of the little chapel is interesting, because of its very old symbolic sculptures. They evidently date from the early art-period of the Christian era, probably not a whit later than the eleventh century. The authorities have created a little literature of disputation concerning their origin, and to this day there is no certainty arrived at. One authority states that they are taken from the "Heroes' Book" of the exploits of Emperor Ornit and Wolfdietrich, in slaying the dragon's brood on the mountains of Trent, a fable emblematic of the victory of Christianity over paganism. Baron von Hammer has explained them to be Gnostic symbols; this is probably the nearest approach to the truth yet reached.

The castle of Tyrol contains an interesting collection of parchment manuscripts, and some vases and armor from the Middle Ages. It would be easy enough to get lost amid its winding halls, dark stairways, and subterranean passages. Its largest room is ornamented with portraits of the later members of the Hapsburg dynasty, all being distinguished by the unusually heavy under-lip characteristic of the family. From the windows of this room you enjoy the richest luxury which the great old castle, with all its history of cruel power and thrilling romance, can give,—a view of brother-castles that may be counted by the dozen; of villages so close together as almost to form a continuous city; of streams running in all directions, as if engaged in some musical, hide-and-go-seek game of their own; of vineyards whose divisions and ownership seem obliterated by their luxuriant overgrowth; of avenues of chestnut, mulberry, and plum-trees winding with the roads; of glaciers that lie high up on the bleak hills, and look down with the same cold eye as in the long-gone centuries; and of the bold mountains of porphyry and dolomite that bound the eastward view toward Botzen, and tell of the Brenner Pass, over which the Roman legions often went to make conquests in the barbarian north, and of the disturbance of whose hardy people by the victorious Drusus, Horace thus sung :—

" Videre Rhaeti bella sub Alpibus
Drusum gerentem.

Drusus, Germanos implacidum genus
Brennosque veloces, et arces
    Alpibus impositas tremendis
Dejecit acer plus vice simplici."

Plucking a few ivy-leaves that hung in wasteful plenty
over the outer wall of the castle, and emerging through
the gateway where the portcullis used to hang, we reached
the main road leading through villages and vineyards
back to Meran. The street corners were occupied by
smoking, lounging peasants, who, in accordance with
their social custom on seeing strangers, whom they regard
no nearer nobility than themselves, gave a homely but
hearty greeting as we passed. The shop-keepers were
half asleep at their stalls under the arcades, and the promenades were alive with slowly-sauntering invalids from
Northern Europe. The setting sun cast long shadows
across the market-place in front of the Archduke John
Hotel, where we lodged—there, now, I have divulged its
aristocratic name in spite of a benevolent design to the
contrary—and thus closed another of Meran's loveliest
days.

Early the next morning we started on our six hours'
walk for Botzen. The road was attractive beyond all the
descriptions of the guide-books, and I had no regrets at
seeing the stage pass by and leave us to enjoy the scenery
at our leisure. This section was a favorite home of the
southern nobility in the Middle Ages, who displayed great
taste in the selection of sites for residence, for their
castles occupy all the points where good prospects are

presented. There is one bridge on which we stood and counted twenty castles within clear view. The Lowen-burg contains sixty chambers, and is surrounded by ter-races and sloping vineyards. The Schonna has more the appearance of a fortress, and the guide can still show its gates, armory, drawbridge, and dungeons. The Frags-burg—the Roman Trifagium—stands on a high cliff and looks down on the Katzenstein and Neuberg at its feet. It is occupied, and still retains its grim mediæval glory and solidity. On the almost perpendicular cliff rising at the left of the roadside there stands one of the most interesting ruins in the Tyrol. It is the Maultasch Cas-tle, so called because it was a favorite home of the last Tyrolese ruler, Margaret Maultasch, or " Pouting Meg." There are many strange stories connected with its his-tory, and in many of the legends of the Tyrol the Maul-tasch plays a very romantic part.

My companion having taken advantage of a rickety old chaise that was bound for Botzen, I was left alone for a while. So I clambered up the hill to see the Maultasch ruin more closely, and enjoy the fine prospect from its crumbling walls. The desolation was complete. Some of the heavy arches had lost their keystones ; others had entirely fallen ; while still others were so threateningly awry that I hastened from beneath them. Lazy lizards lay sleeping on the shapeless stone fragments, whose almost effaced images had occupied years of artistic labor far back in some unknown mediæval century. The ivy-vines had aided the work of decay by softly penetrating every crevice, and thus gently uplifting and overturning the huge stones that war and time had mercifully spared. Fig-trees grew wild in the courts where once the prince-ly halls had stood. But from those old windows, which are now only misshapen rents, you enjoy a scene of nature which never grows old. It was as beautiful when I saw it as when Pouting Meg looked upon it. I then found what I had not perceived before, that the Mault-asch stands just on the rocky angle commanding a view of two immense valleys. But the ruin was lonely be-yond description, and I was glad enough when I could feel satisfied with the enjoyment of the prospect suffi-ciently to leave it, and all its stories, to themselves. In order to save time I took a nearer way down ; but it was a sore experience, for I lost my way. Half-running and half-falling, meanwhile waking up innumerable lizards that lay as dead on the mossy rocks, I finally reached the hill-side of a vineyard. The heat was intense, and it was nearly an hour before I was fit to leave the shade of a convenient chestnut-tree for the last part of the tramp to Meran.

The Sigmundskrone is the most extensive ruin for many miles around. It rests on the rocky base where the Ro-man castle of Formicaria had stood, and may be seen in all directions. The view from it must be very fine, but my Maultasch experience took away all the spare time for that purpose. In 1475 the Sigmundskrone became the prop-erty of Archduke Sigismund, who had it restored to a condition of great beauty. At present it is the property of Count Sarntheim, and its vaults are used as a powder magazine for the local troops.

Botzen is the great commercial center of the Tyrol. Its population numbers ten thousand, who, in physique, language, and customs, bear a strong resemblance to their Italian neighbors. It lies in the center of a magnificent amphitheater formed by the dolomite and porphyry mountains east and north, and by the castellated hills south and west. It was settled originally by the East Goths. The houses have a decidedly Italian appearance, and the principal business is conducted under dingy arcades, as in Padua. From the early period of the history of Botzen the arcade on one side of the market-place has gone by the name of the Italian, while the opposite one has been called the German, because of the respective nationality of the venders. The parish church was finished in the year 1400, and has lately undergone extensive restorations and improvements. The gardens abound in many rare floral varieties, and are justly regarded as one of the principal attractions of the town. As this was the market-day, I had a good opportunity of seeing the costumes of the peasantry, and the various productions of the country. Oranges, lemons, figs, apricots, and mammoth plums were offered in large masses by as unkempt a set of fruit dames as I have ever seen handle dirty coppers and stained pint-measures. As a pleasant offset to their appearance, all the streets were musical with the refreshing mountain streams that are made to flow through them, and the market-places and street corners are ornamented with ever-flowing grotesque fountains.

CHAPTER IV.

OVER A BACKBONE.—CROSSING A GLACIER.

M Y companion preferred to take the stage line of the
Brenner Pass, while I struck to the left, to cross
one of the great Tyrolese backbones. We were to meet in
five days, and resume our journey. The proper point for
crossing the range of mountains separating the Vintschgau Valley on the south from that of the Inn on the
north, is the filthy little village of Staben. You can take
the stage, and in two and a half full days get around into
the Inn Valley at a point opposite Staben; but if you wish
a five days' walk over one of the wildest parts of the Alps,
and then descend into the charming valley of the Oetzt, so
as to traverse every mile of its course, let the stage attend
to its own legitimate business. You have a richer feast before you than that enjoyed by its sleepy, dusty occupants.
It will take you more time than they will need, but you will
gain many advantages for which they dare not hope.

The road from Staben leads precipitously through vineyards, and in due time the narrow valley of the Schnals
is entered. I had hardly lost sight of Staben before I was
overtaken by a Tyrolese pedestrian, who had a friendly,
open countenance, and told me that he was going to Unser
Frau—Our Lady—the very cluster of houses upon the
Pass where I hoped to spend the night. The path was
not very easy to discover at some places, and Christian—

for that was his name—served the purpose of a trusty guide. The valley became narrow and very deep, and the foot-path wound along the left side. Every step had to be taken with care, but there was no danger to any one who is not subject to giddiness. Hour after hour passed by, and still the valley did not terminate. There were little patches of stunted hay below us; and streams of clear water ran down the sides of the mountain, and were carefully directed into courses most advantageous for irrigating the land. No cart or vehicle of any kind can traverse the Schnals Valley; all the burdens must be carried on the backs of the peasantry or the donkeys. The post-boy ascends it only once a week, but he might almost as well abandon his craft, for his work is commensurate with the profound ignorance and superstition of the peasantry. We soon came to a point, whence, far below, we saw a small cluster of houses, the parish chapel standing on a mountain above them. On asking Christian if the people of the village worshiped in that chapel, which could only be reached by a difficult ascent, he replied, "O yes; they all go to Church at the appointed times. They don't mind climbing a mountain." ·I immediately thought of the many pretexts I had heard in the United States in justification of absence from the house of worship, by people who save all their diseases of the week until Sabbath morning, and whom a little shower, or snow-squall, or a walk of a good healthy distance, never keeps from the place of business from Monday until Sunday. It is difficult to tell what sort of an exclamation such folks would make if they were to see the little chapel of St. Catharine, which has stood ever since the year of grace 1502, high above the dwellings of its prompt congregation. But perhaps if they had to undergo the same difficult ascent for a time, they would manufacture a convenient windlass or a comfortable elevator to hoist them up to their devotions.

About the middle of the afternoon we reached the buildings of the old Carthusian Monastery, which bears the imposing name of "Mountain of all the Angels." The monastery was founded A. D. 1326 by King Henry, who was at the time only Prince of Tyrol, but bore the royal title as Pretender to the Bohemian crown. The institution was abolished in 1782, and the cells are occupied by a squalid population of poor and ignorant persons. There are some old paintings in the St. Anna Church by an unknown hand. Knitting stockings and raising cattle are the principal occupation of the people now occupying the monastery and the lowly huts grouped around it. This is a convenient center for many interesting excursions.

It was near sunset when we arrived at "Unser Frau," the last village of the valley of the Schnals, which is here over five thousand feet above the level of the sea. Christian lay down to sleep on the velvety grass beside the door of the inn, and the homely hostess made liberal promises of a good dinner. Meantime I engaged a guide for the following day's journey over the Pass, and had a pleasant chat with the young priest, who was the junior curate of the village Church. He spoke of an intimate priestly friend of his in Cincinnati, but he no sooner learned that I was an American than a very significant expression clouded his face, as much as to say, "Ah, well;

poor land, your people are only Protestants, and they don't know any better." He told the history of his little chapel, and offered snuff, as if to draw me into sympathy with his story. The original chapel was built in the year 1303, but it went into decay afterward, and was restored to its present state in 1746. In the chapel there is a "Mercy Picture," which is highly revered through a large extent of country, and is the object of many pilgrimages. There is also a beautiful picture representing St. Bruno. It is supposed to be by Helfenrieder. There is an exquisite wooden crucifix in the sacristy.

The dinner was not equal to that of an American hotel, but hunger sweetens the poorest fare. Each room was presided over by one or more pendent crucifixes, some of which reached almost from the ceiling to the floor. Arrangements had to be made for food next day, as I was to eat high up on the Pass, far from any inn whatever. The hostess showed me a long chest, which was partitioned off, and contained sundry uninviting bits of dried fat pork, mutton, and beef. They were savory with garlic, and finely coated with cobwebs. I declined all her propositions for dried meat, and finally determined on hard-boiled eggs. The upper hall, on which my bedroom was situated, was first covered by accumulated dirt, and afterward by many loaves of bread, which seemed to be spread there in order to undergo some further hardening process. How many I trod on while passing up and down stairs I will not engage to say; but it is just as likely that previous guests had trampled well over the hard, thin, blackbread loaves that helped to satisfy my hunger. The bedroom was

15

'the best in the house. I had ample accommodations for Catholic worship, even if I had been thus occupied all night. There were several chief crucifixes looking down upon me from the corners of the room, to say nothing of the ornaments wrought into miniature crucifixes. On searching for matches I found a little object, which was surmounted by a crucifix, hanging high at the door. This appeared more like a match-safe than any thing else, but on feeling for matches there was only ice-cold water. Thus I had the benefit of "holy water" to give such pleasant dreams as may be expected of an American when he sleeps on a worn-out and hilly straw mattress, in keeping with the rocky country around him.

Just at half-past four o'clock the next morning I had the satisfaction of seeing my guide, Joseph Rafeiner, trip off with my knapsack on his back. This was to be the most adventurous day of my Tyrolese journey, and Joseph said that the peaks were in clearer view than usual. In about three hours we took a lunch, before crossing the mountain, in the last human habitation—the only one I was to see before evening. Though I had been gradually ascending all the day before, and also ever since Joseph and I had started that morning, it was only now that we came to the direct and precipitous ascent of the Hoch Joch Ferner. Friendly sheep followed close behind us, and a drove of horses seemed to enjoy our companionship. The air was very cold, and every time I stopped there was immediate need of my heavy shawl. About noon we reached the neighborhood of the Hoch Joch Ferner, when we nestled closely under a rock to spend a half hour over our hard eggs and harder bread. Cold chills ran through me all the time, and I was glad enough to be in motion again. It had snowed a good deal the day before—which was the 8th of July—and there was no path to be seen over either the great patches of snow that stretched down on the sides of the mountain or over the glacier itself. Joseph went ahead, and made tracks for me as well as he could; but he needed a hatchet, which he had neglected to bring along. The snow had here frozen to ice during the night, and it was almost impossible to gain footholds. With the exception of a slight fall, that did no further harm than a half hour's excited nerves and a soon-forgotten bruise, no accident occurred. But Joseph afterward took me by the hand, and held me with the iron grasp of an Alpine athlete.

Having reached the glacier proper, we gradually ascended it untill we stood upon its highest point, which is indicated by a rough wooden cross. The view was not as distant as I had anticipated; I could see almost nothing but snow-clad mountains on all sides. It appeared as if that was all there was of the earth. Between the mountains, glaciers many miles in length trailed down like white serpents, and converged into one, the Hoch Joch, on which we were shivering in the cold. The scene reminded me of a colossal, uplifted human hand, the outstretched fingers representing the separate glaciers, and the wrist the magnificent central one formed by their convergence. The air was as clear as ether itself; the Similan, though twenty miles off, seemed within an hour's walk. The horizon was of a pale green, but the higher we looked toward the zenith the bluer the sky grew, untill it became intensely blue just above us. We had to protect our faces from the powerful reflection from the ice by means of goggles and green vails ; but I relieved myself of mine whenever it became necessary to take advantage of a new view. We passed occasionally a rough wooden cross, which did not mark out the path, but only indicated the spot where some ill-fated hunter or traveler had suffered the penalty of his rashness.

Having begun the descent of the glacier, the valley of the Oetzt broke upon us in all its wild grandeur. We found some chasms that the July sun had already begun to make and widen, and when our feet once more struck the solid ground, or rather rock, a feeling of indescribable relief came over me. Joseph and I took our last lunch together just after finishing our five miles' walk over the glacier. Then we parted; he back to his humble home at "Unser Frau," and I for a fortnight of calmer and less adventurous travel far down below the glaciers and their chill air.

The path was now plain enough for the most of the way, but there were some fearful gorges which it threaded high above the stream, and more than once I wished for Joseph's strong hand again. In a few hours I reached stunted vegetation once more, and herds of sheep, whose shepherds were nowhere to be seen, came up like old acquaintances and rubbed their noses against my blistered hands, as if to kiss me welcome after the completion of the hardest day's work of my life.

CHAPTER V.

FATE OF A TYROLESE GUIDE.

THAT night I found good lodgings in the village of Fend, with the parish priest, Father Franz Senn, for mine host. Fend lies six thousand feet above the sea, and the air is no doubt chilly throughout the summer. I called it "cold" that night, but the priest said, with a smile, as he walked the plateau in front of his house and read his breviary, "O no, it is only fresh." If any member of Father Senn's profession surpasses him in the frigidity of his parish, he is certainly deserving of hearty commiseration, for a good part of it consists of such dangerous glaciers as have defied all efforts to scale and cross them, or have ingulfed, in their unknown depths, many rash intruders upon their slippery and deceptive surface.

Many travelers, coming in from all quarters, stop and spend the night with Father Senn. This proprietor has collected a valuable little library relating to the Tyrolese Mountains, and has been one of the best explorers, and even cartographers, of that intensely interesting section. He has spent his spare days and weeks in scaling hitherto untrodden peaks, making observations, and discovering new paths through the valleys; and his services in Alpine surveys have been duly recognized by many of the writers in this department. All travelers who have been entertained under his roof will remember with pleasure his

pleasant manners, highly intelligent face, and more than
ordinary acquirements.

What Mr. Senn has been in a friendly and scientific
way to travelers in the Tyrol, Cyprian Graubichler was in
a practical way, as a bold and adventurous guide. He was
living when I was in the Tyrol and slept at Fend, but
since then he has fallen a victim to his dangerous calling.
I cannot refrain from giving an account of his last adventure, which closed with his life. His fate will illustrate that
of many a Tyrolese climber. He was endowed by nature
with an ardent love of his native mountains, and soon
rose head and shoulders above the craft of guides, by the
daring character of his undertakings. No boy born on
the sea-shore was ever more fearless on the waves constantly within his hearing, or more ardently longed for
the opportunity of sailing over all seas and of enjoying all their wild humors, than did this plain Tyrolese
peasant hope to traverse untrodden glaciers, look down
from giddy precipices, chop out stairways in the unmelting
ice to fearful acclivities, and to be the first to plant the
crucifix on many of those snow-clad peaks. Mr. Senn,
the Catholic priest, and Cyprian Graubichler, usually
called " Cyper," the peasant guide, were fit companions for
hazardous enterprise, and no wonder that, drawn together
by a peculiar sympathy, their names will be forever associated in the story of Tyrolese adventure, aye, and of
tragedy too. But they have made their last wearisome
tramp together. The priest still reals his breviary and
counts his beads as he walks up and down the greensward
before his quiet inn at Fend, while poor Cyper, who,

though young in years, had achieved the reputation of being one of the most successful of all the guides in the Tyrolese Alps, sleeps amid the towering glaciers that he traversed with staff, and pick, and rope.

Cyper was born at Solden, in the valley of the Oetzt, in March, 1835. When twenty years of age he was required to present himself for military service in the Austrian army, but was declared by the surgeons unfit for duty because of *flat feet*. He was very glad to be released, of course, and thereupon learned the carpenter's trade, a work in which he ever afterward engaged when not employed in traversing the mountains. He commenced guiding travelers over the Tyrolese Alps in the year 1861, and, after four years of minor undertakings, began to scale hitherto unascended peaks, and to attract attention by the daring character of his journeys. Mr. Senn, the Catholic priest, found in him a congenial spirit, and chose him for his companion on his most hazardous undertakings. The last dangerous tour which Cyper made before the fatal one to be recounted presently, was with the Grand Duke Ferdinand Rainer, of Austria, over the Kreutz Joch and Wildspitze and many intervening glaciers. The travelers' registers found in the inns throughout the Tyrol abound in praises of Cyper; and the celebrated mountain-climber, Johann Stuedl, of Prague, says of him, in a late volume of the Annals of the Austrian Alpine Union, the following: " In all his excursions, particularly the dangerous ones, he preserved the greatest composure and foresight, and revealed a remarkable endurance, knowledge, and acuteness of vision."

The account of the final adventure of Mr. Senn and Cyper together, which led to the death of the latter, must be given, to do justice to the truth, substantially as found in " Aus dem Leben Eines Gletcherfuhrers," (Munich, 1869,) in the language of the former:—

" I was in Meran with Cyper from the 26th of October, 1868, to the 5th of November, my object being to restore my broken health, and the aim of us both to recuperate from the extraordinary labors which we had passed through during the summer. We had a most delightful time during our stay in Meran. On Friday, the 6th of November, it was high time for us to leave Meran, in order to reach Unser Frau, in the valley of the Schnals, on the same day. On Sunday I had official duties at home, and, the 7th of November being Saturday, there was only one day left to cross the Hoch Joch. The previous beautiful weather gave us no ground for apprehension of danger ; besides, a man who had just come from Fend, Gregory Klotz, assured us that the glacier was quite free from new snow. We were, therefore, very hopeful when, on Saturday morning, after a walk of two hours, we had reached Kurzras, the last stopping-place in the valley of the Schnals, and had found fresh snow only two inches deep. We thought that this snow, as experience often teaches, did not reach as far up as the glacier. Leaving Kurzras at about half-past eleven, we proceeded confidently on our way to the Hoch Joch. About half-past one o'clock, in the afternoon, we reached the south-west end of the Hoch Joch glacier, without having met with any special difficulties ; we observed, however, that, as we ascended, the snow gradually became deeper, and we at last found it about half a foot deep. Still, this fact, together with the additional one that it still continued snowing, and that the whole atmosphere was filled with very fine snow-flakes, gave us no real ground for alarm; we comforted ourselves, on the other hand, with the thought that we would make good way over the glacier, and then proceed comfortably on our journey to Fend. We were both thoroughly acquainted with the way, and, if it had been summer, we could have gone the whole distance blindfold. But, unfortunately, we were soon to experience a bitter disappointment.

"After tarrying a quarter of an hour at the so-called Boedele, the usual stopping-place of tourists, we both partook of our fat pork, beef, bread, and wine, and about a quarter before two o'clock stepped on the glacier, whose length we hoped to traverse in the course of two hours. Just as soon as our feet touched the glacier, we sank up to our knees in freshly fallen snow. Still, we did not despair, but hoped it would be better. We went on in this way about an hour and a half, sinking all the time in deep snow, and had not reached the so-called Latsch-buechel; therefore had not passed a third of the glacier. Cyper then said to me, ' I think we should return !' I answered him, ' It is Saturday, and consequently my duty to be in Fend ; and since the west wind is blowing, every trace of our way back to Kurzras has probably disappeared ; besides, we have passed over one-half of our way from Unser Frau, and will soon find less snow.' Cyper, without making any reply, immediately went on, merely

15*

complaining occasionally that he found his light summer clothing altogether too cold for him. As I remarked that ' I wished we had taken a man with us from the valley of the Schnals,' he replied, ' Nobody would have gone with us.' We did not reach the Latschbuechel until twilight, both of us being quite tired, the high wind increasing in violence, and the snow growing deeper all the time. ' O, I wish we had returned,' said I, ' but it is too late—therefore, ever onward !' Yes, ' Onward ' was easy enough to say, but very hard to carry out. The wind grew to a perfect hurricane, and the snow came down in heavy masses, and soon the dark night was upon us. I said, ' O, I do wish we were on the other side of the glacier !' But this was not to take place very soon. Sinking at every step to our thighs in the snow, the darkness of the night overtook us but a short distance beyond the Latschbuechel, therefore about in the middle of the glacier ; and as we wished to take the direction of the path used by travelers in the summer, we wished to go to the right. Scarcely had ten minutes passed by before I said, ' Cyper, it seems to me that we are on the way back to the valley of the Schnals, for the wind is now dead ahead of us !' He also was convinced that this was the case, and advised our turning round. We now resolved to bear constantly to the left, to the so-called Hoherberg, and by this means to reach the Steinerne Treppe. This way, it is true, is somewhat further, but it is the one usually traveled, and, by taking it, we were sure of guarding against the danger of getting very far out of the way, for we had the glacier at our right and the Hoherberg at our left. We plodded constantly forward, no change taking place in the weather or in the depth of the snow, and finally reached the Steinerne Treppe about ten o'clock at night.

"We had long been anticipating the joy of reaching this point, hoping there to find pleasanter weather and less snow. But what a delusion! Instead of finding the west wind there which had previously prevailed, we were confronted by a violent hurricane from the north, and the great snow-flakes shut out the little light which we should otherwise have had, and made every step one of the greatest danger. It was almost impossible for us to cross the glacier diagonally to the Kreuzberg and the Neuweg, because of the total darkness and the chasms in the glacier. We had no rope to tie around us, and were therefore compelled to make the dangerous and difficult passage downward to the Erzboedele. We now had to clamber with hands and feet—for neither of us had any longer a stick with us—an effort which first wheeled us to the right and then to the left, so that I now wonder how, under such circumstances, we could ever have reached the neighborhood of the Erzboedele. Scarcely had we gotten a good footing, and gained a few steps, before we were overtaken by a new, and almost greater, difficulty. Cyper regarded it impossible to find either the Hintereis or the Rofenberg shepherd's cottage, and I doubted whether it would be possible to reach the left side of the Hintereis glacier, and, by going along the Rofenberg, and then over the Vernagt glacier, to reach the Neuweg. We therefore resolved to go straight across into the Rofenthal, knowing that there are no chasms in the glacier there, and that the Neuweg was just on the other side of the Kreuzberg.

"We found that the steep smooth ice was covered deep with fresh snow, and it was therefore impossible to obtain a good footing. As we, however, found the Kreuzberg near before us, we did not observe, until too late, an almost perpendicular wall of ice to our right, which was almost perfectly free from snow. Cyper stepped upon it, glided down, and in a moment was lost from my sight. 'How are you?' I exclaimed. 'Too good,' was his response from below. 'Are you injured?' 'No.' 'Then can I slide down to where you are?' 'For God's sake no; for there is an awful mountain chasm, and I have been thrown across it! Go higher up!' So I did as he said, sounding the snow at every step I took. Sometimes I crept along on my knees and hands, and, finally, after considerable circuitous creeping, came down to where Cyper was. My first exclamation was, 'God be praised, now that we have the glacier behind us!' Away down in the depth where we were there was no wind, and I could therefore light a match. I did so, and found it was half-past twelve o'clock at night.

"The glacier was now behind us, and it had taken us eleven hours to cross it, though in summer it is a work easily accomplished in only two. We had long ago given up almost all hope of reaching the end of it alive. I therefore said, as we had thus far been successful, 'Now we will come out all right.' 'O, my God!' was Cyper's response, in a trembling voice. 'Is any thing the matter with you?' 'I have been too much frightened by my fall,' said he. I then noticed, as I came close up to him, that his whole body was in a fearful tremor—and this never left him afterward. Even a few swallows of wine, which he here took, did not help him in the least. I had already repeatedly told him to take a swallow of wine occasionally, but he would not do it. He always said, ' The wine is too cold for me.' We rested here only a few moments, saying, ' We dare not stand here ; we must keep in motion.' For we well knew that, after we had rested a while, if we should fall asleep, we should never wake up.

" The howling of the night wind was awful, and immense masses of snow kept falling all the time. Still, we kept moving forward, sometimes turning to the right, and sometimes to the left. We now found out that we were too high upon the mountain side, and must, therefore, find some way lower down. Now there seemed to be no ground of hope, and our endeavors to progress through the deep snow were utterly fruitless. Still, we often said, ' We must do our best to save our life—therefore, let us go slowly and keep in motion.' Our last drop of wine was exhausted between three and four o'clock in the morning, and we were too weak to chew the bread and frozen fat meat which we had in our pockets. We were expecting death at any moment, and, as soon as the day began to dawn, we found that we were still too high, and that it was almost an indescribably dangerous task to get lower down. Still, our courage was somewhat increased by the daylight, and I said, ' Now come on, we can easily go to Fend.'

It was about six o'clock in the morning, and, therefore,

only a distance, in summer weather, of half an hour's walk
to Rofenberg. 'About ten o'clock,' I said, 'we can be
in Fend.' What a mistake! Scarcely had we gone a few
steps before we were overwhelmed by an avalanche of
freshly fallen snow. I was behind Cyper, and suddenly
drawing back, was hid from him by the avalanche. He
had prostrated himself in a moment, and, after the avalanche had passed over us, rose uninjured. Immediately
there came other avalanches, without any interruption.
Five different ones swept over us, though without carrying
us away with them, for we cast ourselves in the freshly
fallen snow, and fixed our hands and feet as deeply in it
as we could, to prevent being hurled by them far down
into the abyss to the left. Not a single instant were we
safe from avalanches, and we had to be continually looking to the side of the mountain to watch their approach.

"About nine we reached the small, old shepherd's cottage, and, as our strength was now almost totally exhausted,
we entered it to rest for a while, in order to gain strength
for the remainder of our journey. We there found some
wood, with which we made a fire. This hovel was more
fit for beasts than for men, and we found that if we
would reach home we must hurry up as rapidly as possible.
Cyper did not become warm by the fire, but trembled the
whole time we were by it. At last he said, 'It is more
prudent to go. It will help us nothing to stay here. But,'
he added, 'I shall never get to Fend.' About two o'clock
in the afternoon, when we were not far from Rofenberg,
Cyper stood still, and, supporting himself by the snow,
said, 'I can go no further.' It was only about a hundred

and fifty steps to the so-called Rothbach, after crossing which I had good ground for hoping the way would be better. I went on ahead of Cyper now, and tried every way to get him to follow me. He did the best he could, but could not go further. 'Arouse!' I exclaimed. 'Help me, O my God, and give me strength to save his life!'

"He could not move a foot, and I determined to go on to Rofen as soon as possible, hoping, should I find any body there, to send him after Cyper. It was almost impossible for me to advance a single step in the snow. With my feet, hands, knees, and arms thoroughly buried in the snow, I had to roll and twist myself in order to make any sort of a track by which to get my body along. After I had gone a little way Cyper called after me, 'Must I die here alone?' I answered, 'I will go quickly to Rofen, and send people to your help.' I now believed that we should be saved.

"Things now turned out more prosperously. With the exception of a space of about five steps, I could go on my way without hinderance. In the middle of a forest through which I passed, I noticed a man near a bridge. I cried to him with all my might. But he did not see or hear me, and therefore I had to go nearer to him and repeat my cry. He now heard me, and I found that it was that good man Ferdinand Klotz, who was astonished beyond measure to see me under such circumstances. I said to him, 'Cyper is within the Rothbach, and can come no further! Go quickly for him, help him, and let him have no rest, or else he will fall asleep. I will go to Rofen and call more help.' Thus we separated, and Cyper was therefore not more than half an hour's distance from me.

" I cannot tell how happy I now was. I said to myself, 'I shall now get to Rofen easily, and Cyper, too, will be saved.' When I reached Rofen I found it was impossible to go further. It was three o'clock in the afternoon. The only man to be found was Nieodemus Klotz, whom I immediately sent to Cyper. After I had taken some warm milk, and given full directions for the treatment of Cyper, I continued on my way to Fend, which I reached at about four o'clock in the afternoon, after a walk, attended with indescribable dangers, that had lasted thirty hours continuously. My hands and feet were frozen, and I had a peasant man immediately subject them to treatment, for he had a secret remedy for my difficulty. I sent on some more men for Cyper, so that, if alive, he could not be without abundance of aid. Poor Cyper, however, stayed where I had left him, hoping all the time for help. As soon as he saw the first man coming to him, he said, ' Ferdinand, have you no brandy?' After the man had reached him, and given him a little of the contents of his flask, Cyper said, ' I have now drank too much.' Ferdinand Klotz admonished him to come along, and encouraged him by saying that the way was now short. But Cyper now fell into a delirium, and could not stir a foot. He gave two sighs, and there died in the snow. His dead body was borne by the peasants to my house. Heart-rending, indeed, was to me the sight of the stiff, pale form of him who had risked his life for me, and whose spirit was now in another world. May every mountain-climber be blessed with a guide like him !"

CHAPTER VI.

DOWN THE INN VALLEY.—INNSBRUCK.

IT required two more days for me to descend the valley of the Oetzt and reach the great Inn Valley, which is the main thoroughfare of Northern Tyrol. The Oetzt stream gathers strength by frequent tributaries, and after a few hours' walking along its bank it is found to have assumed the dimensions of a little river. The scenery is ever changing, but never dull and unattractive. Sometimes the river almost disappears in a dark gorge, overhung by half-uprooted fir-trees ; then it spreads out like a cheerful mountain lake. The mountains sometimes seem like two immense confronting harps, so numerous and musical are the high, silvery, thread-like cascades. Occasionally one of the cliffs overhangs the road, which often proves to be a narrow footpath, grooved out by hard labor in the past centuries. No vehicles traverse any part of the upper course of the valley.

At Solden the road commences, and when I once more saw wagon-ruts, it appeared to me that I had been some days on another planet. On the east of Umhausen rises the precipice of Angel's Wall, so called from the tradition of " the only child of the lord of the castle of Hirschberg having been carried off in sight of his parents by an enormous vulture, and, while they were wringing their hands in despair, having been rescued from its talons by an

angel." There is a multitude of such legends in the
mouths of the peasantry in the Oetzt Valley. Every
prominent mountain, water-fall, and gorge has its cluster
of them, and the humble people who relate them think
you wickedly incredulous if you do not swallow them as
willingly as they have done. The priests take good care
to foster their superstitious habits, for they thus strength-
en their own hold upon the popular mind.

On reaching the stage-road of the broad and beautiful
Inn Valley I engaged passage for Landeck, which lies at
the eastern end. The scenery, during every minute of the
three hours' ride, was less grand than that which I had
enjoyed for two or three days previously, but it was much
more beautiful and tranquilizing. At Brennbuchl dinner
was served in the hotel where King Frederic Augustus
of Saxony died, on the 9th of August, 1854. He had
been making the tour of Switzerland and the Tyrol, and
was riding through the last valley of his route. By a
sudden turn of the vehicle he fell out, and was mortally
injured by the horses' hoofs. On being taken to the
nearest inn, he died. The blood-stained pillow, the undisturbed bed on which he died, the flowers and beautiful
wreath which he had twined, his little bell, and a number
of other objects of interest, are still to be seen. The room
and furniture remain just as they were twenty years ago,
when its royal occupant breathed his last.

The parish church of Landeck was built in the sixteenth century, though the same site had been occupied
by one erected in 1270. The castle of Landeck is the
most conspicuous object to be seen, and a magnificent

view may be enjoyed from its windows. It was once the home of the founder of the celebrated Schroffenstein dynasty, but is now a deserted and gloomy ruin. Many Roman coins are still found here. I took a second stage from Landeck, late in the afternoon, in order to ascend as far as practicable before dark the upper Inn Valley toward the Finstermunz Pass.

The Pontlaz Bridge, over which the road leads, is a very interesting object, on account of the important part it has played in Tyrolese history. The people have often been compelled to defend it against foreign invaders, and they have never failed to manifest a heroism worthy of a better cause than the support of the Austrian Government. The bridge crosses the Inn just before reaching the village of Prutz, situated on a low, marshy plain at the entrance of the Kaunser Valley. This valley—a sidepiece to the upper Inn Valley, and running off at right angles to it—stretches up to the vast Gebatsch Glacier, · which is estimated at sixty miles long and thirty miles broad. One of the most memorable exploits of the Tyrolese, during the eventful campaign of 1809, took place near the second bridge. I give the account in Sir Walter Scott's words : " The fate of a division of ten thousand men belonging to the French and Bavarian army, which entered the upper Innthal, or valley of the Inn, will explain in part the means by which the victories of the Tyrolese were obtained. The invading troops advanced in a long column up a road bordered on the one side by the river Inn, then a deep and rapid torrent, where cliffs of immense height overhang both road and river. The vanguard was permitted to advance unopposed as far as Prutz, the object of their expedition. The rest of the army were, therefore, induced to trust themselves still deeper in this tremendous pass, where the precipices, becoming more and more narrow as they advanced, seemed about to close over their heads. No sound but of the screaming of the eagles, disturbed from their eyries, and the roar of the river, reached the ears of the soldier, and on the precipices, partly enveloped in a hazy mist, no human forms showed themselves. At length the voice of a man was heard calling across the ravine, 'Shall we begin?' 'No!' was returned in an authoritative voice by one who, like the first speaker, seemed the inhabitant of some upper region. The Bavarian detachment halted, sent to the general for orders, when presently was heard the terrible signal, 'In the name of the Holy Trinity cut all loose!' Huge rocks and trunks of trees, long prepared and laid in heaps for the purpose, began now to descend rapidly in every direction, while the deadly fire of the Tyrolese, who never throw away a shot, opened from every bush, crag, or corner of rock, which could afford the shooter cover. As this dreadful attack was made on the whole line at once, two-thirds of the enemy were instantly destroyed ; while the Tyrolese, rushing from their shelter, with swords, spears, axes, scythes, clubs, and other rustic instruments which could be converted into weapons, beat down and routed the shattered remainder. As the vanguard, which had reached Prutz, was obliged to surrender, very few of the ten thousand invaders extricated themselves from the fatal pass."

I reached the town of Ried about dusk, and there spent the night. Welcome letters from home—the first for nearly three weeks—accompanied with an abundance of American news, were sufficient to obliterate all sense of weariness, and almost to render me indifferent to the superb panoramic view of glaciers which a hill-top near the hotel affords.

Above the town of Stuben the pass of Finstermunz begins. There is a fine carriage road chipped out of the left side of the mountain, and from this the pedestrian can enjoy at his leisure the remarkable scenery which this pass, only inferior in its kind to the Via Mala in Switzerland, presents from base to summit. The rocky eminences overhanging the road are ornamented with life-like images of the wild chamois. I thought one of them living, and the illusion was not dissipated until I found it impossible to frighten him from his cliff. Cascades fall in graceful beauty from the precipitous side of the mountain rising just across the abyss. The infant Inn—whose bed in past ages was hundreds of feet higher, right where the broad, smooth hollows in the rocks are yet clearly visible—is fed and strengthened by many a cheerful tributary; but, without waiting to give thanks for the help it gets, it hastens on to mingle its strain with the harsher notes of the Danube, and afterward to tell its mountain story to the far-off Black Sea.

About ten o'clock in the morning I reached the summit of the pass, and looked far down on the web-like bridge crossing the Inn. The little castle of Sigmundseck, built long ago by Duke Sigmund, cleaves to the rock like a great, beautiful muscle. There is an inn near by, which has a deserted appearance, in perfect harmony with the castle itself. The angle where the two stand forms the boundary between Switzerland and Austria, and off to the right begins the Engadine Valley, which had fairly wearied me with its charms two weeks before. On going a little beyond the Finstermunz, I noticed the dusty volume created by the coming stage ; and from its top could see the waving handkerchief of my genial traveling companion, from whom I had been separated since the first of the week. Unfortunately for me, he had received news which required him to shorten his stay abroad, and I was thus compelled to complete the Tyrolese tour alone.

The traveler who has the good fortune to reach Innsbruck at the close of a bright summer day, when the sun gilds the near cliffs of Martinswand and the distant peaks where the glaciers never melt, receives an impression at once peculiar and permanent—and permanent because of its peculiarity. I had ridden all day, and the most of it on the top of a stage, through the Inn Valley, having started in the early morning at Landeck. The whole road abounds in most picturesque scenery, and no lover of nature can trust himself to sleep a half-hour, lest, when he wakes up, his guide-book tells him that he has lost some hoary, ivied, castellated ruin, or a view of some valley branching off at right-angles to the greater one of the Inn.

The whole of the long road to Innsbruck has a most interesting *known* history, not to mention that which has long since passed into the realm of the legendary. No pen can ever narrate the full story of those lovely

vales, cheerful streams, and scores of castles and rugged
mountains. The castle of Kronburg keeps long in sight,
and commands an excellent view both up and down the
valley. The Petersberg was the birthplace of Margaret
Maultasch, who often held her court here, and made her
palace-castle celebrated for beauty, wit, and statesman-
ship. Her cradle, long preserved as a relic, has now disappeared. The castle proper is a desolate fragment, and,
though the most of the dismal ruins of this once proud
home of princes, with its donjon-keeps, dungeons, and
oubliettes, has passed into a shelter for bats, there are
other parts which are still habitable, being occupied by
the present owner, Count von Wolkenstein.

The village of Stams is remarkable as the seat of a
great Cistercian convent. I counted hundreds of windows as the stage passed by, and caught glimpses of the
beautiful, quiet avenues formed by the old trees in the
convent garden. The convent was founded in 1271 by the
mother of Conradin, the last scion of the house of Hohenstaufen, who perished on the seaffold in Naples. His
mother determined to found an institution where prayer
might be offered for the soul of her murdered son; and
it is said that she even went to Naples and brought his
body to this place for interment. Had she sought all
Europe over, she could not have found a more fitting site
for the location of the institution, for the place was at that
time in the very midst of an immense oak forest, scarcely
ever entered by a whisper from the outside world. The
church and convent were finished in 1284 by Count Meinhard, the second husband of Conradin's mother, who

died in 1273, only one year after the commencement of the enterprise. Her dust reposes here, as also that of the four-children who died before her. Twelve scions of the proud house of Hohenstaufen, who were originally buried in the castle of Tyrol, have been removed hither. Indeed, this is the last resting-place of much royal dust. Meinhard himself lies here, and also Frederick of the Empty Pocket, his two wives, son, and daughter ; Duke Sigismund the Rich, who died in 1495 ; Maria Bianca, second wife of the Emperor Maximilian I.; his son and daughter ; Duke Severin of Saxony, Rudolph, Prince of Anhalt, and many others. They all lie in a crypt beneath the church. It was in the convent that the Emperor Maximilian I. first received, in 1497, "the Turkish embassador of the Sultan Bajazet, who sent to demand the hand of Maximilian's sister, Kunigunde, in marriage, promising to become a convert to Christianity."

The last most remarkable object in the valley of the Inn before reaching Innsbruck is the celebrated Martinswand, or Martin's Wall, whose legends can be counted by the score. Many of them are firmly believed, and as fondly remembered, by the Tyrolese peasants. The face of the rock, or rather mountain, fronts the road, and is an abrupt precipice of one thousand eight hundred and thirty-five feet. It has played an important part in Tyrolese history, the forces occupying its heights almost invariably proving masters of the situation. In the war of 1703, Count Arco, the Bavarian general, was shot at its foot by a Tyrolese rifleman, who had placed himself in ambush to kill the Elector of Bavaria as he passed along the road, but, misled by the greater splendor of the Count's dress, as he rode beside his master, hit him instead.

The known history of the Martinswand is very dry and dull compared with the celebrated adventure of the Emperor Maximilian—a circumstance which may be half fable and half history—to which it owes its celebrity:—"That enthusiastic sportsman, led away on one occasion in pursuit of a chamois among the rocks above, by ill-luck missed his footing, and, rolling headlong to the verge of the precipice, was just able to arrest himself when on the brink of destruction, by clinging, with his head downward, to a ledge of the rock, in a spot where he could neither move up nor down, and where, to all appearance, no one could approach him. He was perceived from below in this perilous position, and, as his death was deemed inevitable, prayers were offered up at the foot of the rock by the Abbot of Wilten, as though for a person *in articulo mortis.* The emperor, finding his strength failing him, had given himself up for lost, when a loud *halloo* near at hand arrested his attention. A bold and intrepid hunter named Zips, who had been driven to the mountains to avoid imprisonment for poaching, had, without knowing what had happened, also been drawn to the spot while clambering after a chamois. Surprised to find a human being thus suspended between earth and sky, he uttered the cry which attracted Maximilian's attention. Finding the perilous nature of the case, he was in a few minutes at the emperor's side, and, binding on his feet his own crampons, and extending to him his sinewy arm, he succeeded with difficulty in guiding him up the face of the precipice along

16

, ledges where, to appearance, even the chamois could not have found footing, and thus rescued him from a situation of such hopeless peril that the common people even now attribute his escape to the miraculous interposition of an angel. The spot where this occurred, now hollowed out into a cave in the face of the rock, is marked by a crucifix, which, though eighteen feet high, is so far above the post-road that it is barely visible from thence. It is now rendered accessible by a steep and rather difficult path, and may be reached in about half an hour's walk from Zirl. The cave is seven hundred and seven feet above the river, and the precipice is nearly vertical from the high-road below. It is traditionally stated that Maximilian rewarded the huntsman with the title of Count Hollauer von Hohenfelsen, in token of his gratitude, and in reference to the exclamation uttered by him—which had sounded so welcome to the emperor's ears—announcing that relief was at hand. From the emperor's pension-list, still in existence, it appears that a sum of sixteen florins was annually paid to one Zips of Zirl."

On reaching Innsbruck I went to the Star Hotel, which stands on the left bank of the Inn, commanding a fine view of the larger portion of the charming city on the other side. Innsbruck has a population of over fourteen thousand. Though it lies really in a valley, it is about two thousand feet above the level of the sea. The mountains, which are several miles distant, rise to a height of six or eight thousand feet above the city, and hence the saying, that "the wolves prowling among the mountain tops look down into the streets." When the Austrian emperor visited Innsbruck in 1838, the people spelled his name in bonfires upon the side of the mountains, extending over a space of four or five miles.

Innsbruck first appears in history in 1027, and in 1234 we find it a walled town, attractive to the traveler because of its natural beauty, and to the marauding princes because of the flourishing trade which had sprung up there. The most imposing building in the city is the Franciscan or Court Church, in which I attended service on Sunday morning. It was a festal occasion, and the large edifice could not contain the multitudes of people who thronged to it. The music was very fine, and was performed by an immense military brass band; but the mummery of the priests and the peculiar devotion of the people were more like the gesticulations of the dancing dervishes than the worship of people in a Christian land. The greatest object of interest in the church is the tomb of the emperor Maximilian I., who ordered by will that a church should be erected here, which should be a sepulcher for himself. It was commenced in 1553, and finished ten years later; but, oddly enough, the emperor does not lie here at all, but at Wiener-Neustadt, in the beautiful Gothic chapel of St. George, with his faithful friend and counselor, Dietrichstein, at his feet. The remarkable sarcophagus in the Court Church of Innsbruck, is thus described in Murray's "Handbook for Southern Germany": "The emperor is represented in a kneeling posture, with his face turned toward the altar, while on each side of the aisles stands a row of tall bronze figures, twenty-eight in number, representing some of the 'worthies' of Europe, but principally the most distinguished personages, male and female, of the House of Austria. There is something imposing in the first sight of these metal effigies of the great of former days ; they are of colossal size, skillfully executed ; and the elaborate workmanship of the armor and dresses gives them an additional interest, as careful types of the costume of the sixteenth century. They were modeled and cast between the years 1510 and 1561, the work, during this period, being frequently interrupted. The principal artists employed were Gregory Löffler and his two sons, Stephen and Melchior, Godl, and Hans Lendenstrauch. . . . The sarcophagus itself is inclosed with an iron railing ; its sides are ornamented with twenty-four bas-reliefs, or, rather, pictures in relief, carved in Carrara marble with a beauty and minuteness of workmanship not surpassed by that of an ancient cameo. They are probably unique of their kind. . . . An ascent of a few steps, on the right as you enter the church, leads to the Silver Chapel, so called from the image of the Virgin, and an altar-piece in bas-relief—both of solid silver—which it contains. It was built by Ferdinand II., Archduke of Austria and Count of Tyrol, as a mausoleum for himself and his wife, the famed Philippina Welser—the most beautiful woman of her time—with whom he lived happily for thirty years. Philippina was the daughter of Franz Welser, one of the wealthy Augsburg patricians. She was born in 1530. Ferdinand first saw her at the Diet held at Augsburg in 1547, and the following year made her his wife. The alliance was regarded by the Emperor Ferdinand, the archduke's father, as degrading, and it was not until twelve years after her marriage that she succeeded in procuring access to her father-in-law, when, throwing herself on her knees, she so moved him by her tears and beauty that he acknowledged her as his daughter, and made her two sons margraves. The armor of the archduke is placed aloft on a bracket, while his effigy, in white marble, reclines upon the tomb; at the back of which are four marble bas-reliefs, masterly productions of art, representing remarkable events in which Ferdinand was present :—1. The capture of the Elector of Saxony by Charles V. at the battle of Mühlberg. 2. Ferdinand appointed Stadtholder of Bohemia. 3. Besieging Szigeth, 1556. 4. Leading the cavalry against the Turkish forces of the Sultan Soliman. Philippina, who died in 1580, has a separate monument, an altar-tomb bearing a recumbent figure in marble, and decorated with allegorical bas-reliefs, said to be by Colin, but probably the work of his son or one of his scholars, representing works of charity and mercy, with Innsbruck in the background. In a recess against the wall, between these two tombs, are arranged twenty-three small bronze statues of saints, all of royal or noble lineage, chiefly allied to the Hapsburg family. These statues properly belong to the tomb of Maximilian; they were executed by Elias and Hans Löffler, and are fine works of art. Under the steps leading to the chapel is the tomb of Philippina's aunt, Katharina von Loxau, who is said to have been almost as beautiful as Philippina herself."

It is astonishing what stories the Tyrolese tell of the beauty of Philippina Welser; but if her beauties and virtues increase as they have done in the last few centuries, and the Tyrol keeps as thoroughly Popish as ever, she probably will yet become a saint. One of the Tyrolese guides in Innsbruck told me that she was so beautiful, and her skin so thin and transparent, that the veins of her neck told the color of the wine as she swallowed it.

In the same church there are monuments to the Tyrolese private soldiers and officers who distinguished themselves by their bravery in opposing the Emperor Napoleon I. The most splendid of these monuments is of white Tyrolese marble, being a statue of Andreas Hofer, who sealed his love to his country by his blood. Hofer was a simple peasant, who gained important victories for Austria, but was afterward hunted by order of Napoleon, betrayed by a peasant, and shot in 1810 at Mantua. He is represented in the fantastic garb of a Tyrolese peasant, holding an Austrian flag in his hand. The inscription is, " For God, Emperor, and Fatherland." The inscription on the great sarcophagus, erected to the memory of the Tyrolese soldiers who died in the same cause with Hofer, is in Latin, " Death is swallowed up in victory."

During my brief stay in Innsbruck I also visited the Parish Church, the Museum, the beautiful promenades along the Inn, and the antiquarian bookstores. Such a mass of Romish trumpery as was to be seen in those bookstores, with a large admixture of Romish pictures, crucifixes, rosaries, and what not, I never care to see again. Unless John Foster had a stronger Catholic tinge in his bibliomania than Ryland attributes to him, he certainly would have been innocent of his customary " temp-

tation to buy books," if he had ever had the ill-fortune to
wander into the antiquarian depositories of Innsbruck.

   After an hour's walk from Innsbruck through the
Princes' Way, in full view of the great snow-clad mountains to the south, I reached the castle of Ambras, having
procured a ticket which guaranteed admission to all the
objects of curiosity to be seen there. The Tummelplatz
is the place where jousts and tilting-matches were held
by the knights in former times. I delayed long in the
old halls, and wearied the great tinseled guard out of all
patience by lingering in the balconies and looking down
on Innsbruck, the beautiful Inn, the bleak Martinswand,
and a multitude of objects which arrested the eye and
chained me to the spot. Soon evening came on. I wandered back to the city by a path leading through fields of
ripe grain, and spent my last twilight in the Tyrol looking
down from the quaint bridge into the restless river Inn,
and fanned by breezes that brought with them a chill,
though in midsummer, from those mountain-tops which
had become familiar by weeks that I had spent within
view of some of them, and by hours, and even days, passed
in the slow but enchanting ascent of others. Who can bid
adieu without regret to the charming valley of the Inn?

CHAPTER VII.

THE HARTZ.—THE BROCKEN.

LEAVING Bremen by a night train, in the summer of 1870, we found ourselves in company with a number of German Americans who had just returned to the fatherland, and had caught the spirit of their adopted country, a fact which they exhibited in more ways than one, but especially by their hearty singing of " Old John Brown," and " Tramp." It was bringing back the old days to hear the familiar notes.

After catching as many snatches of sleep as we could in the stations and in the cars, we reached the picturesque town of Wolfenbüttel, which had once been the residence of the Brunswick dukes, but is now in a state of commercial stagnation. Its old and spacious palace is given over to small tradesmen, and its pillars rise from the mud and green slime of all that is left of its former moat. To us the only interest of a halt lay in its celebrated library, which contains two hundred thousand volumes and six thousand manuscripts. The librarian showed us many mementos of Luther,—his leaden inkstand, one of his omnipresent beer-glasses, his notes on the Psalms, in his own exquisitely neat handwriting, and his revision of his translation of the Bible. It is significant that nearly all his corrections are confined to the prophecies of Isaiah and Ezekiel. The gentlemanly librarian showed us other literary curiosities, among which were manuscript letters of many of the most celebrated German *litterateurs*, and the first edition of Lessing's complete works. It was when Lessing was librarian at Wolfenbüttel that he published his celebrated "Fragments," which produced the rationalistic conflict in Germany that has not yet terminated. The present librarian, Dr. Von Weimann, who has distinguished himself by his contributions to German history, led us through his house and grounds adjoining the library, once the home of his celebrated predecessor. We saw the room in which Lessing wrote his "Nathan," and, across the broad hall, the one where his idolized wife died, and out in the garden the fruit-trees planted by his own hand. I plucked a few leaves from them as mementos of the visit. Fortunately, we had a copy of Miss Frothingham's translation of "Nathan" with us, and we enjoyed our spare time by communing with the trees, with the old Jew, Saladin, the Templar, Recha, and the other characters of one of the greatest, but not least one-sided, of Lessing's productions.

But Wolfenbüttel is only in sight of the Hartz, and a good many up-hill miles lie between it and famous old Brocken. We spent an afternoon at Harzburg, the hill above which is crowned with the ruins of a temple, said to have been dedicated to the worship of Wustan, or Donnar, and destroyed by Charlemagne, who erected a Christian church in its stead. On the same hill is a stately castle, built by the ill-starred Henry IV., and made the repository of his treasures. We then pushed on to Goslar, the most northern fortified residence

16*

of the old German emperors, and by far the most interesting city in the Hartz Mountains. The ancient character of Goslar is still well preserved. One finds himself
in the Middle Ages. The walls are standing, for the
most part, and nearly all the towers preserve their original shape. One of them forms a portion of the hotel in
which we lodged, and from its summit we had an excellent view of the city and of the country for many miles
around. My own bed leaned squarely against the old
town wall, and, thanks to the weariness of foot travel! I
had no disturbed dreams of tramping invaders and destructive sieges. The romance of my room, however,
flew to the winds when I found out that the intense heat
of its atmosphere, inexplicable at first, was produced by
the cooking for the whole hotel, as the kitchen lay directly
under it. I was, therefore, compelled to spend nearly all
my in-door day time for the two days that we were in
Goslar with my traveling companions, the Rev. Dr. A.
Stevens and the Rev. C. S. Eby, who were favored with
cooler, but less romantic, quarters.

Every body who goes to Goslar is expected to visit the
mines of Rammelsburg, about a mile from the city. It is
said that they owe their discovery to the following circumstance:—When the Emperor Otho I., the son of Henry
the Fowler, founder of the city, was on the throne, one of
his horsemen named Ramm was riding over the hill,
and a piece of silver ore was knocked out of the ground
by his horse's hoof. It was picked up by Ramm and carried to the emperor. The emperor rewarded him with a
gold chain and one thousand pieces of gold, and, sending

for Frankish miners, had the mines worked energetically,
and with great success. They were called Rammelsburg,
in honor of the discoverer. After being dressed in as dirty a mining costume as one would wish to see—a Mammoth Cave suit is not to be compared to it,—it would
have required a familiar eye to detect the identity of any
of us, so completely was the propria personæ of each of
us concealed by the outlandish and subterranean blouses,
patched trowsers, and dilapidated pieces of felt in which
the venerable old dame arrayed us. We entered by the old
shaft, down which the miners had passed for nearly nine
centuries, and in due time wound our way through various
descents, on slippery ladders, to the place where the ore
is now extracted. Gold, silver, copper, lead, zinc, sul-
phur, vitriol, and alum are taken from almost contiguous
veins. The water is pumped out and the ore brought to
the surface by the aid of immense wheels, hundreds of
feet below ground. But the whole mining process is
utterly antiquated, and it is not surprising that the mines
do not pay expenses.

The ancient cathedral of Goslar was torn down in
1820, owing to the weakness of its walls. It was built in
the year 916 by the Emperor Conrad II., and, according
to all accounts, was very magnificent. Only the side ves-
tibule is still standing, and bears the inscription : " Propy-
læum æd. Cathedr. tuendis antiq. Germ. monum. instatur.
A. D. 1824." It is now the depository of many articles of
interest which formerly stood in the original cathedral.
Among them is the celebrated " Crodo altar," supposed to
have been used for the worship of the Saxon god Crodo.

It is made of brass, and was once elaborately studded with gems of rare value, but they were taken out by the French, who carried the altar to Paris during the Napoleonic supremacy. There are some curious antiquities in the Town Hall, the most noticeable of which is the "Biting Cat," a cage in which quarrelsome women were imprisoned in by-gone times, before their sex had laid aside the infirmity of using their tongues to bad advantage. The ancient Guildhall of Goslar is now the chief hotel, and its façade is ornamented with statues of eight of. the more celebrated German emperors. As for their mechanical execution, perhaps Heinrich Heine was not far astray when he said that they reminded him of "so many fried university beadles."

From Goslar we went to the village of Ocker, and began the passage through the pleasing valley of the same name. Here we were suddenly overtaken by a thunderstorm, and were compelled to shelter under some projecting rocks, until a change in the wind brought the rain squarely into our faces, and made us search for better protection. This we found, after getting pretty thoroughly wet, in a shed made of fir-bark. We there built a fire, and after resting and getting dry again, spent the remainder of the day in walking to Zellerfeld and Clausthal. The real ascent of the Brocken from the south-western side, where we made it, begins at Oder Teich. There is a fine carriage-road on the northern side, but we were compelled to find our way as best we could through only pathways, and that, too, with a threatening storm above our heads. From sheer weariness, we could say many a time, with

Goethe's ˉgrotesque company, who went much faster
than we :—

> " Is our wizard journey ended?
> Is the Brocken yet ascended?
> Round us every thing seems wheeling,
> Trees are whirling, rocks are reeling—
> All in rapid circles spinning,
> With motion dizzying and dinning.'

However, we reached the Brocken without undue bewilderment and the feared drenching, and enjoyed the
rare fortune of an excellent view. We were not very high
above the sea, only three thousand five hundred and eight
feet, yet in the very center of the old German legendary
world. More witches, and giants, and dwarfs are said to
have lived here than in any other one place in Europe.
There is not a German boy or girl who has not heard many
stories of the haunted height, and the German juvenile
literature of to-day is as abundant as ever in creating new
and reproducing old. At the right are the "Hexen-
altar," (Witches' altar,) and the "Teufelskanzel," (Devil's
pulpit,) on the former of which, as the story goes, human
sacrifices used to be made to Woden, and the witches still
come to it to celebrate their May-day eve. There are a
great many immense boulders near the top of the Brocken,
and nearly all of them have their names and clusters of
legends.

The view is far more extensive than the elevation would
lead one to expect, and is really very beautiful. It is by far
the finest prospect in Northern Germany. The whole
Hartz range stretches right and left, and far off in front
lie cities and towns in abundance. Hoary old castles peer

up above the towns, which bask in the sunshine at their feet like disarmed and sleeping guardsmen. Fields carefully tilled and undivided by fences, extend northward, like unrolled, bright-colored ribbons. Over all this charming landscape were the spent clouds we had been hastening to avoid. Both ends of as perfect a rainbow as I ever saw stood far down in the valley, while the arch rose high in front of us, above all the lesser Hartz peaks and the supreme Brocken.

By the aid of a glass we could descry our route for the morrow. It lay to the right, over a rough path which every body declared would require a guide. The most distant mountain visible was the " Hexentanzplatz," (Witches' Dancing Place,) lying across the chasm through which the sinuous Bode works its way. It is confronted by the Rosstrappe, a spot second only to the Brocken in legendary interest, and a very appropriate point for terminating the Hartz tour. Our descent from the Brocken was over the same winding way through which Goethe leads Faust, Mephistopheles, and the Meteor. But, alas! slow and knapsacked pedestrians can hope for no such easy and swift traveling as they experienced :—

> " Woods—how swift they vanish from us !
> Trees on trees—how fast they fly us !
> And the cliffs, with antic greeting,
> Bending forward and retreating,
> How they mock the midnight meeting !
> Ghastly rocks grin, glaring on us,
> Panting, blowing, as they shun us !"

CHAPTER VIII.

THE WITCHES' DANCING-PLACE.

THE Hartz Mountains are naturally divided into upper and lower, the upper Hartz being that part lying west of the Brocken, and the lower the portion to the east. Having descended from the Brocken, our road lay eastward, at first amid immense forests abounding in deer. We finally reached an open country, where we passed through the squalid villages of Schierke and Elend, (misery.) The latter was no misnomer, for the poverty and miserable appearance of the inhabitants, who were nearly all charcoal-burners, were quite un-German, and, except the begging, worthy of Italy itself. But as the country improved in fertility the appearance of the people improved with it, and by noon, when we reached Elbingerode, we found a thrifty class of people, and comfortable, cosey dwellings.

There was nothing that took us to Elbingerode save its convenience as a stopping-place. Its inhabitants are chiefly miners, if such a term can be applied to people who work in ore that abounds in such large masses as to be quarried in the open air. There is not enough of the old castle now remaining to enable one to identify its original shape. After a brisk morning's walk of a couple of hours we reached a narrow and romantic valley, in which are the Baumannshoehle and Bielshoehle caves—the former of which is noted as the place where bones of the Great Cave bear, now extinct, have been found, while the latter is remarkable for its fine white stalactites. An American, however, who has groped and crawled for over half a day in any of the remarkable caves of his own country, need not throw away his time in visiting those of Europe. Still, that of the celebrated Adelsberg, in Austria, is a notable exception, and no traveler from Vienna to Trieste should lose the opportunity of exploring it. After ascending from the valley we came to a frightful plateau, where we had an excellent view of the Upper and Lower Hartz, and an opportunity of hearing some of the simple Hanoverian peasantry describe their hatred of Prussia and the increase of their taxes, with other burdens, since they had been summarily Prussianized.

In due time we reached Wilhelmsblick, where some ingenious man had drilled a passage, at right angles from the road, about a hundred feet through the solid rock, on the opposite side of which he had made a neat upward path, relieved by little ingeniously devised resting-places, to the very top of the mountain. We had a view, on the right, of a magnificent amphitheater of almost artificial perfection, amid wild, romantic scenery; while on the left, we saw the exquisitely winding and cheerful valley of the Bode. At Treseburg, which lies in a delightful mountain nook, our party were compelled to separate, and I continued the tramp alone.

It was a walk, or rather a difficult climb, of two hours to the Hexentanzplatz, or Witches' Dancing-place. But I had not gone over twenty minutes before regretting my

disregard of the advice of travelers and the guide-books
by taking no guide, for the forest became very thick and
dark. The beaten path had divided into many lesser ones,
the most of which were covered with grass and moss, and
in some places it was difficult to detect any path at all.
It was then after four o'clock in the afternoon, and my object was to reach the Witches' Dancing-place in time for
its sunset view ; but there was now every prospect of being
compelled to return to Treseburg. The maps which I had
gave but little comfort in the extremity. In fact, I must
say, that, for at least that one section of the Hartz tour,
there is no reliable map. I do not speak of the large government maps, that cover the whole walls of the police-
offices. In my perplexity I saw a little rough seat, on
which was sitting a solitary, middle-aged German traveler,
with knapsack and staff.

" Where are you going ? " he said.

" To the Witches' Dancing-place, if I can find it," I
answered.

" You may as well give it up ; here are all the maps and
guide-books, and a compass to boot, and yet I have become
exhausted in trying to discover the right path. Now I
am going to find my way down as I came up, if I can, to
Treseburg again."

. This, to make the best of it, was not a very comforting
testimony. After some deliberation, however, we concluded to put our heads together, and make a desperate trial,
though my new acquaintance was evidently very weary.
We had not gone twenty rods before every thing failed
us, and even my companion's pocket-compass seemed very

untrusty at times ; for when we ought to be going up the
mountain, as we thought, it would incline us down again.
By his taking one course and myself another, always keeping within safe hearing, and sometimes meeting again, we
at last found traces of an old, and now unused, forest-road.
This was, perhaps, after an hour's uncertain walking. But
we forgot the toil, for it gave us a gleam of hope ; and
when we saw a fine bronze statue of a' deceased forester,
mounted on a chaste pedestal of highly polished marble,
and then caught a glimpse of one of the present foresters'
little huts, where we enjoyed some milk and black bread,
and found that we were on the right road after all, and
that, too, without much unnecessary walking, we enjoyed
our adventure with exquisite delight ; and now that it is
all over, but with my companion's pleasant face still like
a picture before me, I would not exchange the memory of
it for any other experience during the tour.

The forester's direction brought us safely to the Witches'
Dancing-place, where we found the best-appointed hotel
I had seen since entering the mountains.

" Shall we not be friends as long as we stay in the
Hartz ? " said my companion.

" Most gladly," I replied, " so long as our tour remains
the same."

" Suppose we take a room together for the night ? "

" Certainly," said I ; and I doubt if either of us ever had
slept more sweetly than that night, when we occupied the
same room, each of us, like the law, assuming the other to
be honest.

Before sunset we had ample opportunity for enjoying

the excellent view, by far the most varied, taking all things together, in the Hartz, not even excepting that from the Brocken. The narrow Bode, apparently more beautiful at the outlet than at its rise, had been working its way through the rocks, leaving the smoothly-worn traces of its current upon the higher ones, and now glistening and murmuring at the foot of a precipice of eight hundred and forty feet, at the top of which we stood. At our left were the mountains, combining beauty and grandeur in such rare harmony as can seldom be seen in a single picture; while directly at our right the mountains terminate, and beginning with the village of Thale, the railroad terminus, you command a view of Halberstadt, Wernigerode, Quendlinburg, Blankenburg, (where Louis XVIII. lived, from 1796 to 1798, under the name of Count de Lille, in perpetual fear of assassination by the French Republicans,) and I know not how many other towns and villages. Directly across the gorge, and rising nearly as high as the Witches' Dancing-place, where we stood, was the Rosstrappe, or Horse's Foot-Print, which takes its name from the tradition of Princess Brunhilde, who, "being pursued by a giant, leaped her horse, which had previously been endowed with supernatural strength, across the gorge to the opposite cliff, where the charger, as he alighted, left the dint of his foot."

The next morning, after parting from my new friend, who desired to visit the Brocken, I went on to Victorshoehe. This point commands a very extensive view of the Lower Hartz and Alexisbad,—a quiet and retired spot, whose neat hotels owe their patronage to the excellent mineral water that flows from the rocks near by. I pushed on as far as Harzgerode, in company with a middle-aged peasant man. The Hartz peasants have many expressions which, though the persons using them be strangers, are frequently heard on the highways. As we met a boy taking bread out to some harvesters, the man with whom I was walking addressed him with these words :—

"A cheerful heart and lively blood."

The boy replied :—

"A full heart and good courage."

The peasant assured me that he had never met the boy before. This calls to mind one of the songs which the watchmen in some of the Hartz towns sing at night. For instance, the night I spent at Zellerfeld the watchman blew a horn at ten o'clock under the hotel window, and sang these words :—

> "Now hear me say, all ye good men,
> The city clock has just struck ten ;
> Take care of fire, put out your light,
> Lest you some danger should invite.
> Praise the Lord, all ye good men !"

At four o'clock in the morning either he or one of his associates returned, and, after blowing his horn, sang :—

> "The day makes gloomy night our town forsake ;
> Come, people dear, be jolly and awake !
> Praise the Lord !"

In the afternoon I took the stage to Nordhausen, a city noted, in a literary way, as the birthplace of Justus Jonas, Luther's friend, and of Gesenius, the Oriental scholar, and, in a spirituous way, for its brandy. In this place, of eighteen thousand five hundred inhabitants, the principal branch of industry is the manufacture of brandy. It distills yearly from forty-two thousand to forty-six thousand casks of brandy, one hundred and eighty quarts being in each cask. This quantity is increased, by the addition of alcohol, to about eighty thousand casks. There are sixty distilleries altogether, and, in 1864, the taxes paid to the Government by their owners amounted to one hundred and sixty-seven thousand three hundred and ninety-one thalers.

CHAPTER IX.

CASSEL.—A BIT OF ITS ROMANCE.

THE most important place lying between the Hartz range and Frankfort is the city of Cassel. It was here that the Elector, Frederic II., hired, or rather sold, his subjects to George III. of England, to help him conquer his revolting American colonies—a traffic which cost twelve thousand Hessian lives, and brought twenty-two million of blood-stained dollars into the ignoble Frederic's treasury. The ruins of an unfinished palace lie in the valley below the city, and near them a magnificent bathhouse, now unused, adorned with allegorical sculptures from pagan mythology. From the streets of the city one can see the celebrated Wilhelmshöhe Forest, where Napoleon III. was a prisoner in the same palace in which his uncle Jerome had lived and reveled as king of Westphalia. The highest elevation in the forest, lying back of the palace, is surmounted by a large edifice. This is crowned by a colossal statue of Hercules. The club which he holds will contain nine men.

No one conversant with one of the most touching books of recent German literature, William von Humboldt's " Letters to a Female Friend," can walk the quaint streets of Cassel without calling to mind the pathetic secret history of that work. I will give it here, though with regret at being unable now to recall the name of my chief German authority.

On the 16th of July, 1846, a lonely old woman died in a wretched house in the Wilhelmshöhe Alley, at Cassel. She was seventy-five years old, and had gained her subsistence by her own hands, at work, indeed, which was only suitable for young persons of her sex. Her aged and trembling fingers had also made delicate artificial flowers, and from the workshop of this lonely, sorrowing old woman went out the most elegant floral adornments for the gay society of the city. Many tears and sighs of recollection may have accompanied this toilsome labor. For the poor creature who was compelled to plait bouquets and wreaths for her daily bread had once been a young girl of perhaps even greater beauty than the wearers of her work. She had also been happy.

The name of the poor old bouquet woman was Charlotte Hildebrand. Her father had been a Hanoverian clergyman in good circumstances, and she had received a careful training and an almost scholarly education. With her nineteenth year she became enthusiastic for "the true, the beautiful, and the good ;" read philosophical writings, composed poetry, and longed for some ideal friendship. Her home was in a lovely part of the mountains rising along the Weser, and the romantic ravines, the green meadows, the towering oaks, and the thatched peasant houses were the familiar, picturesque objects she saw on her excursions. She often wandered to the little hunting seat of Baum, belonging to the Baron of Buckeburg, which lay in calm solitude in the green wilderness. Here Herder had lived. He was the favorite of the general and philosopher William von Schaumburg Lippe, and the friend of

the latter's amiable lady—a princely pair whom the older
Mendelssohn honored, and has described in his writings.
A monument was erected over the united graves of this
couple, who were bound together in a remarkably happy
marriage, and this was a place of pilgrimage in those
times for prominent poetical and enthusiastic natures.

The minister's lovely daughter, too, fed her youthful
imagination with dreams of an ideal marriage, but had not
the least presentiment that they would never be realized.
The memories connected with the hunting castle of Baum,
near Buckeburg, proved to be the pleasantest pictures of
her lonely old age. Other beautiful parts of the mountains fringing the Weser were also visited by the young
girl when she was accompanied by her parents, who, in
accordance with the custom of the times, paid an annual
visit to some of the watering places. It was thus that
Charlotte Hildebrand became acquainted with the neighboring Rehburg; with its incomparable fir-forests and
meadows ; with the lovely Eilsen, which, in the deep
ravine, with its red-tile roofs, looked like the exterior of a
fresh apple amid green leaves ; and, finally, with Pyrmont,
then the most fashionable watering-place.

Under the linden archway of the Pyrmont avenue she
once sat with her father upon a bench near the cool
fountain, when a youth approached and seated himself
beside them. He had a threadbare coat, but gave evidence of good manners ; he was homely, but he had an
intellectual look. People in Germany easily became acquainted with one another in those days at the watering-
places ; they were not so distrustful of each other as they

are now, and in a few minutes the beautiful young girl
had led her neighbor into a deeply philosophical conversation. She listened to his words as if they came from a
better and previously undreamed-of world, and he was
pleased with the lovely being who could listen so intelligently and speak so suggestively. The clergyman, who
was likewise charmed by the youth, whom he took for a
student from Göttingen, invited him to dinner, and they
all entered the dining-hall together. It was there discovered that the enthusiastic speaker was in reality a Göttingen student, but a very eminent one, none other than
William von Humboldt, of Berlin, the brother of Alexander von Humboldt.

It is well known that at that time, and later, William
von Humboldt possessed a very plain-looking exterior; in
his best coat he was still gray, small, and thin; and how
must he have appeared in his dusty and worn traveling
suit? But his young friend had quickly recognized his
mental beauty, and even after the lapse of half a century
spoke of the clear repose of his nature, of the salutary
effect of his entertaining conversation, of her deep and in-
effaceable impressions, and of the sublime emotions that
he then awakened in her.

During three happy days of a free, unemployed life at a
watering-place, the young girl was frequently thrown into
Humboldt's society, and when he took his departure he
wrote, according to the custom then prevalent, a pathetic
sentiment in her album, but did not utter a word expressive of the real feelings of his heart. She herself felt infinitely enriched, mentally, by his conversation, yet she was

17

too modest, too true and feminine, to cherish a hope of a nearer relation with the prominent and intellectually important youth, in whom she already recognized the future celebrity.

This meeting took place on the 16th of June, 1788. Humboldt had expressed his intention of visiting the parsonage in the following August; but he never went, having remained longer than he had expected with Jacobi in Pempelfort, which was then the gathering place of many of the great intellects of the day. Many a time did she stand at the gate of the small manse door-yard, overgrown with rose-trees and shrubs, and look out for Humboldt's visit. She has described somewhere her parental home, and its exquisite situation amid the beauties of nature ; a little brook rippled close by the garden hedge, and a shaky stile led into a meadow surrounded by bushes. It was here that she loved to direct her steps when she wished to be alone with her dreams. The autumn mist would undulate like a vail in the moonlight, and call up Ossianic pictures before the eyes of the dreamer. In the quiet of her own chamber she would read her treasured album leaf :—

"A sense for the true, the beautiful, and the good, ennobles the soul and makes the heart happy; but what is even this feeling without a sympathetic soul with whom we can share it ?   WILLIAM VON HUMBOLDT.

"PYRMONT, 1788."

But the "sympathetic soul" never came. Instead of that there came a Doctor Diede, and he sued urgently for

Charlotte Hildebrand's hand. She would fain have given him a refusal, but her parents found no fault with him, and desired, nay, almost commanded, that she should accept him. It was the mode in earlier days in Germany, and is even now, to marry off the daughters very early.

Charlotte Hildebrand entered into the union without any inclination on her part ; and when she was scarcely twenty years of age she removed to Cassel with her husband, and henceforward lived as Madame Diede. The marriage proved an unfortunate one, and, after five years, the two were divorced. She herself narrates this event with sadness : " I was married in the spring of 1789, lived but five years in this childless union, and never married again." Three years after her own marriage, in 1792, William von Humboldt married a rich heiress, Miss von Dachröden, who charmed many men by her intellectual acquirements. The marriage was perfectly happy and harmonious. They had three sons and three daughters. William von Humboldt always spoke of his wife in terms of the highest esteem and love, and his testimony suffices to refute the slanders, now whispered and now outspoken, which have been made against her.

By her divorce Madame Diede lost her secure position as wife ; and in the troublous years under the Napoleonic supremacy she lost her whole fortune. She then lived some time in Brunswick, where the good-hearted duke promised her compensation for her losses ; but he fell at Waterloo, and could not fulfill his good intentions. Totally without means of support, no longer young, but sickly and forsaken, Madame Diede was nearly driven to despair, and did not see the slightest prospect of securing aid. One day she read in the newspapers an article eulogizing William von Humboldt, who was then engaged as plenipotentiary of the King of Prussia at the Congress of Vienna. The precious recollection of the three happy days in Pyrmont gave her courage, in her great need, to apply to the now celebrated and powerful man. She began, with many misgivings and tears, the following letter :—

"Not to your Excellency, not to the Royal Prussian Minister—no, I write to the still unforgotten and unforgettable friend of my youth, whose image I have cherished in my mind for many, many years ; who never heard again from the young girl whom he once met, with whom he spent three happy days, the memory of which still elevates me and makes me happy. The name upon which the world looks with such great expectations, the position in which you, through your intellectual capacity, have been placed, made it not difficult for me to hear of you frequently, and to accompany you with my thoughts. I have preserved the dear little album-leaf more carefully than any of the little holy relics of youth, as the only joy of life which fate awarded me. This leaf, which I beg of you to return, will call up to your Excellency an acquaintance which the great pictures and events of your life will long ago have erased. In feminine natures such impressions are deeper and less mutable than they can ever be with others, the more so when they — what scruples could withhold me, after twenty-six years, from giving you this proof of veneration ?—were the first unrecognized emotions of awakening intellectual love. For the youth of a woman and the development of her character, the object to which the earliest feelings are attached is of the highest importance. Feelings change with time, but the cherished image once deeply engraved within us never fades away. On this loved image, which appeared my ideal of manliness and greatness, I rested. Here I reposed when I was well-nigh sinking under the weight of my hard life ; here my courage rose when my faith in humanity was shaken. Believe me, ever dear friend, I have ripened amid great tribulation—not dishonored, nor profaned by unworthy feelings."

Thus did the poor soul admit the veneration and love which had made her once happy in beautiful Pyrmont, and which she had concealed for a quarter of a century.

The Prussian Minister replied to her letter on the same day upon which he received it. He was deeply touched and surprised by this recollection of youth, and a certain regret might have passed for a moment through his soul, that the once lovely creature had withered unknown and unthought of by him. He felt at the same time the duty of aiding the unfortunate being who trusted in him so implicitly. He wrote to her a letter full of most heartfelt sympathy and the noblest delicacy ; he persuaded her to rely solely on his care ; and really compelled her to accept a sum of money to alleviate her most pressing necessity. Her pride, however, allowed her this only so long as her sickness continued. At Humboldt's express wish she went to Göttingen, having been previously in Cassel. She followed his advice to take care of her own health, but when she recovered her strength she returned to Cassel, and began her toilsome labor in making bouquets and wreaths.   It was only when Humboldt pleaded urgently that she concluded to accept a small pension from him, which, being paid regularly, greatly assisted in obtaining her daily bread.   But there was another gift of her friend Humboldt which furnished her real comfort and imperishable food for her mind—the letters which he began to write, and continued uninterruptedly for twenty years.   These have since become the property of the educated world, and serve as a book of consolation for many isolated hearts.   Who does not know William von Humboldt's " Letters to a Female Friend ?"   The aged minister wrote with the noblest tenderness of feeling and affecting gallantry, comforting her, inciting her to intellectual activity, and communicating to her all that came within the scope of his feeling and observation.   The negative spirit of the times has often tried to ridicule the noble letter-writer on account of attentions to a poor old woman. The motive is easily explained, when we remember that nothing attaches a man so firmly to another as the consciousness of making a soul happy.   This consciousness Humboldt could have, in the fullest measure, in regard to his friend ; his intellectual relation to her constituted the only ray of light of her otherwise dark life.

Humboldt saw his aged friend twice again in life.   The two hearts enjoyed in sadness together the faded recollections of their youth ; and after this their correspondence was even of a more cordial character than before. Nobody ever thought, until the publication of the " Letters," that Humboldt had ever sought out the lonely, miserable dwelling of the poor, forgotten, and once despised Madame Diede ; and even the few friends whom she possessed in Cassel never heard about the occurrence. She retained the treasured correspondence most sacredly ; and it was not until after Humboldt died that she made it known, believing it to be her duty then to surrender the rich intellectual treasure for the benefit of her contemporaries and posterity, and not selfishly keep all to herself. She entered with zeal into the publication of Humboldt's letters, first overlooking them, almost too anxiously, for fear that a possible indiscretion in judgment should escape. A young literary person of that period, Theresa von Bacharacht, assisted her in this work, and received the letters in return for support she had earlier given to the poor old creature.

Theresa von Bacharacht had made the acquaintance of Madame Diede as teacher, and had become enthusiastic for the intellectual and uncomplaining sufferer, who, in her joy at her young admirer, sent Humboldt a very flattering description of her. Madame Diede lived more than ten years longer than her friend and benefactor, but she had afterward the needed comfort in her old age of receiving from Alexander von Humboldt the pension secured to her by his brother William, and which was punctually paid to the day of her death. Few literary friendships, it must be confessed, have had so romantic a beginning, so faithful a continuance, and so happy a close.

CHAPTER X.

TWO RESTS.—OLDENBURG AND HELIGOLAND.

WE passed a brief Whitsuntide rest during one of our Bremen years in old Oldenburg, the capital of the grand duchy of the same name. It lies north-west of Bremen, and is separated from Holland by a narrow Prussian strip. A ride of an hour and a half by rail, through a level tract of turf country, brought us to the quiet, easygoing city. It has all the characteristics, soldiers included, of an oldtime German capital. The present grand duke, Peter Frederic Augustus, who is very much beloved by his people, does not occupy the palace proper, but a smaller and newer building, which, in point of style and size, is surpassed by many of our better American homes. For generations the fatality of short life and sudden death seems to have attended all the duchesses and their children occupying the real palace, and for this reason the present grand duchess will on no account live in it. It is consequently given over to distinguished visitors and state occasions, the ducal family inhabiting the less pretentious building elsewhere.

The old palace is very large, and many of its rooms are not inferior to those of more celebrated royal residences in the great capitals. When we went through it a large suite was in process of refitting for the widow of Otho, the ex-king of Greece. The Augusteum is a neat building, containing the few masterpieces of painting which the present grand duke has had the good taste and liberality to collect. One of the most celebrated and interesting objects in Oldenburg, however, is the remarkable linden-tree in the cemetery. Its branches have all the general appearance of roots, being gnarled and inclined downward. It is from eight hundred to a thousand years old, and stands on an elevation just inside the cemetery. The legend of this tree is, that a beautiful and good young girl was unjustly accused of crime by a young nobleman who could not win her affections, and, to avenge himself, secured her condemnation to death by false testimony. On the spot of her execution she broke off a switch from a tree, and, inverting it, stuck it into the ground, and said that, as it would finally become a tree, and its roots would grow above ground, so would it be a constant witness to her innocence. Her last words were, " I know that my Redeemer liveth," which are now inscribed in large gilt letters on one side of the gateway of the cemetery. The nobleman, after her death, repented his crime, declared her innocence, and died of remorse. His last words were, " O, eternity is long!" which are inscribed in similar characters on the other side of the gateway. The two inscriptions are very prominent, and meet the eye of every one who enters the cemetery.

During the summer the grand-ducal family occupy a plain and small cottage in Rastede, a little town lying about twenty minutes' ride by rail west of Oldenburg. Though there is a palace of no inconsiderable size at Rastede, the grand duke does not occupy it, but leaves it to his visitors,

17*

friends, and state occasions. The grounds lying around the palace are very large, and abound in game. The stables contain sixty-nine horses, each one having its own harness, with name attached. The ex-queen of Greece, like her brother, the grand duke, is very fond of horses, and, when she makes a visit to Oldenburg, has the reputation of signalizing it by killing several of her brother's horses by fast riding ; and no wonder, for she is said sometimes to keep pace on horseback with a passenger train of cars. On the Saturday morning that we strolled through Rastede the two young princes took a ride at eleven o'clock, when six horses were led up to the front door, and, just as the clock struck, the eldest made his appearance, clad in a suit of light blue. He bowed pleasantly to the few bystanders, and was soon off at a quick pace, leading his five attendants. His younger brother, who is quite delicate, did not ride that morning, but amused himself by boyishly peeping in at the windows and doors as we were guided through his father's humble summer residence. This place is a model of simplicity. The room of the grand duchess abounded simply in familiar books and the photographs of her friends, and neither in her room nor in any other was there the slightest evidence of luxury. Even the grand duke's study had no more books than I have often seen on an American sophomore's bookshelf, and his old quill-pens had been as economically pared as if his land were not celebrated for the best geese in Christendom.

The entire section of flat land around the city of Oldenburg is singularly devoid of interesting ruins. The Hude

Cloister, which is reached by a half hour's walk from a little station between Bremen and Oldenburg bearing the same name, is a notable exception. It is not unlike Kenilworth Castle, and is not less remarkable for historical associations. The chief part of the ruin consists of an immense brick wall, containing many fine windows and graceful archways, the whole perforated here and there by trees, and crowned by ivy of great age and almost fabulous size. The Cistercian Cloister of Hude, according to the most reliable accounts, was founded in the year 1236. Because of its possessing a picture of alleged miraculous power, it became a place of frequent pilgrimage in the Middle Ages. It received many valuable gifts, and in time grew very rich. In the fourteenth century it was greatly enlarged, and had three hundred cells, besides chapel, refectory, dormitory, and many adjoining buildings.

About the middle of the fifteenth century the decline of the cloister began. It was finally destroyed by Francis, the proud bishop of Münster, whose love of fine horses led him to demand of the proprietors of the cloister two excellent ones, and who, on his demand being refused, led an army against the great edifice, and destroyed it, the monks escaping only by a subterranean passage. The ruins lie adjacent to the beautiful grounds of Herr von Witzleben, a nobleman of fine taste. The only place where I happened to see the American sweet-smelling calycanthus floridus on the continent was on these grounds, where there was a number of large bushes.

By walking two hours beyond the ruins, we reached a German primeval forest. While some of the oaks are of late growth, others are of unknown age and extraordinary dimensions. There is one which goes by the name of the " Big Oak." It is not very high, but measures thirty-two German feet in girth. It is a place of frequent resort in fine weather, and the inclosed grounds around it are seldom free from excursion parties from Bremen, Oldenburg, and other places. A plain repast of eggs and black bread, in a peasant's thatched cottage, was a welcome termination to an interesting and laborious Whitsuntide day, and furnished an occasion for learning more of the household and agricultural life of the North-German peasant than could have been gained by a great many books of travel, even including the excellent sketches of Dr. Kohl himself.

I do not recall any excursion we made, during our residence in Germany, of more peculiar interest than the one to Heligoland. It is a little island in the North Sea, reached from Bremerhafen or Hamburg by steamer, after a sail of five hours. It is a triangular chunk of red clay, rising perpendicularly two hundred feet above the water, with its sides hollowed out into fantastic archways and grottoes by the intruding sea. It cannot be measured by miles, but by feet. Its greatest length is six thousand feet, and its greatest breadth is two thousand. I walked around the whole island in twenty minutes. On the southern side a piece of low land makes out into the water, and only here a landing can be effected. The Lowland is covered by a village of one hundred houses, chiefly hotels and lodging-houses. The few shops contain mostly marine curiosities, plain groceries, and articles for bathing. You ascend, by a flight of one hundred and ninety steps, to the Upperland, where the prospect is very fine. We lodged in the " City of London," which stands on the very brink of the precipice. The village on the Upperland contains the church, the governor's residence, the light-house, and an old tower. The governor is generally a retired officer, and England has a plenty of such easy positions for those who have done her good service. The present governor is a genial gentleman, and one of the few out of the " six hundred ". who returned from the charge of the Light Brigade at Balaklava. There are five hundred houses on the Upperland, nearly all of which have flowers· in the windows and little door-yards. On the whole island there is not a single horse or donkey. Every body can walk in the middle of the narrow streets with impunity, and the only sound that you hear is either the occasional salute on the arrival of a steamer, or the town-bell, which rings at three o'clock every afternoon for every body to eat his dinner. There are about five hundred sheep and but two cows on the island. The trees are few and stunted ; but ample compensation for the absence of shade is made by the constant sea breeze which often amounts to a gale. More than once it required more strength than lay in my two arms to open and close our front door, so high was the wind during the ten days we were there.

This little speck upon the map has a most interesting history, though down to the fifteenth century much of it is only legendary. Peter Saxe, a historian of North-Friesland, holds that Heligoland is the " wonderful island " of

Virgil's "Æneid," and that it is mentioned by Tacitus under the name of Hertha. Helgo, after many a love adventure, is said to have given his name to it. According to one legend, St. Ursula came to Heligoland with eleven thousand virgins, but she and her attendants were persecuted, and even killed, by the idolatrous people. As a punishment, the greater part of the island was sunk into the sea. The ancestors of the present inhabitants were unquestionably of Frisian origin, and, like all the Normans, pirates. The castle in which Radbod, one of their greatest chiefs, lived, stands on the old maps as a cloister bearing the name of Radbodsburg. A later prince, Eilbert, was baptized, and afterward established a cloister. Like all the Frisian islands, Heligoland belonged to the Duchy of Schleswig, and passed with the latter into the hands of Denmark in 1714. It remained Danish until the great European disruption caused by Napoleon I., when it was taken from Denmark by England, in 1807. Ever since then it has been an English possession.

The principal occupation of the humble folk is fishing, and their chief markets are Hamburg and Bremen. Wrecking is likewise a very important source of revenue. I have the authority of a German writer for saying, that, down to the present century the Heligoland pastor implored the Lord every Sunday morning to send his people a new supply of shipwrecks. The Heligolanders are of very different physiognomy from the Germans. The women are of graceful carriage, fine form, clear complexion, pleasant and cheerful expression, and regular features. All the early and later writers speak of them as remarkable for beauty. The men are tall and stalwart. For seafaring people, they are the most upright I ever met with. We had a great many conversations with different persons, and found them all intelligent and good-principled. Their good morals are attested by all the writers on the island. If further proof were needed, it is found in the fact that the total police force for the two thousand five hundred inhabitants is only six English marines. During the late American war a number of the people went to the United States, and entered the naval service on the side of the Government. At least one Heligolander was in the army, and had the rank of major. He fell at his post in North Carolina. I noticed a fishing boat which bore the name of " Washington."

During the early part of the present century, there extended from the southern end of the island a long tongue of land, the extremity of which was a high sand-bank. But the sea broke over this strip, and the bank, which is now greatly reduced in size, constitutes an island of itself, and is a mile distant from Heligoland. It is on this little beach, or dunne, that all the sea-bathing takes place, except in very bad weather. The bathers are rowed over in boats every day from Heligoland. The hours for bathing are from eight until two in the afternoon. The American who happens to be there, and witnesses the decorum, and absence of all ostentation and dissipation, will be forced to draw a comparison very unfavorable to his own country-men between the manner in which the German visitors to a watering-place conduct themselves, and such scenes as we often witness in America. I never saw, for example, the first instance of intoxication on the part of either visitor or native. The contrast in expense is even more marked.

The cost of a comfortable bed-room and sitting-room, with breakfast, is ten thalers a week. We dined and took tea in the hotel, or at the fine restaurant down at the landing, or anywhere else we pleased ; but, in either case, dinner cost about half a thaler, and tea a quarter of a thaler. The bath, including the sail to and from it, cost another half-thaler. The daily expense of each person might be safely reckoned at less than three Prussian thalers, or about two dollars in American gold.

Each house is surrounded by a lane or alley, thus constituting a block of itself. The brick church has immensely thick walls, and is of rude architecture. The pulpit is half way up to the ceiling, and the ceiling itself so painted that it resembles gaudy furniture-calico. The long collection-bag, made of velvet, is one hundred and three years old, and has a noisy little bell attached to it. We could see no other purpose for the bell than to wake people up when the bag with which it is connected is handed around for contributions. Whenever any one dropped his offering into the bag the collector bowed his head, as much as to say, "Thank you." At the service we attended, the pastor read the announcement of the engagement of two worthy young Heligolanders, and elaborately exhorted the congregation to pray for them, in view of the important relation into which they had entered. Think of the engagement of young Mr. S——, of Forty-ninth-street, to Miss T——, of Fifth Avenue, which had been concluded only two days before, announced by their respective pastors to a large congregation on Sabbath morning.

I heard a sermon by the celebrated Rev. Dr. Gerok, the chief preacher of Southern Germany, and author of the homiletical portion of one of the volumes of Lange's "Bible Work," and of those exquisite poetical works, "Palm Leaves" and "Pilgrim Bread," now re-published in London. The grave-yard about the church has some very interesting tomb-stones. The names on them are chiefly Danish and Frisian. One poor-box serves for the whole island. It is stationed in a conspicuous place, with this inscription, from the son of Sirach : "Extend your hand to the poor, that you may be richly blessed."

CHAPTER XI.

GERMANY'S ATHENS.

THE first time I visited the Thuringian Forest, a region rich in literary and historical associations, was in the autumn of 1857, in company with the Rev. Dr. William A. Bartlett, of Chicago. We were then students at Halle, and lodged under the roof of good Frau Müller, with Poles, Hungarians, Germans, and Americans as neighbors. Our home was a Babel only in sound, not in heart. Having agreed on our excursion, we spent a few hours in supplying ourselves with every requisite for a week's tramp. Our knapsacks were faultless, and not only then, but many a day afterward, they did us excellent service. Since then the years have passed by—kindly to both of us—and though I have visited the charming Forest several times since, nothing has removed the delightful recollection of the companionship and enjoyment of the first.

Every reader of "L'Allemagne" will recall the enthusiasm with which Madame de Staël speaks of charming little Weimar, the first important point in the Thuringian tour. She could well say, "Weimar, more than any other German principality, makes one feel." It stood alone, then, as the literary center of the continent. Herder had just died ; but Schiller, Goethe, and Wieland were living, and formed the ornament and pride of the little capital and court of Saxe-Weimar. The Grand Duke Charles Augustus had gathered around him the greatest men in Germany ; and his kindness toward his distinguished countrymen is one of the most striking instances of the special honor given by a ruler to the nobility of mind since the days of the Emperor Augustus, of a greater capital. As Horace and a large group of literary celebrities were favorites of the Augustus who lived beside the Tiber, so did Goethe and Schiller receive the attentions of the humbler Augustus, who held his quiet court in the Thuringian Forest.

It was no wonder whatever that Weimar was the place from which the young author first expected a criticism on his maiden production. It was at once the study, the studio, and the sanctum of the German land. Madame de Staël held that the prevailing taste of the place was literary, and, as a proof, said, " The women are devoted disciples of the gifted men, and are constantly employed in literary labors, considering these the most important public interests." But little Weimar is different now from what it was in the closing years of the last century. The sun shines as brightly on the neighboring hill-tops, and the many mountain streams are coursing as cheerfully as ever toward the ocean ; but of the great men who once lived there we can only visit their old homes, stand beside their last resting-places, and pluck from their graves a sprig of myrtle or ivy for the sake of the dead. The very appearance of the people is different from that of the citizens of most German towns. The more intelligent still hold in memory the humble greatness of their home, and the most casual observer can see in their very faces that they are proud of their little city, and of the part it has played in the history of literature. The true Weimarian expects visitors, and is glad to see them. The traveler, then, should visit the place with the spirit of a welcome guest—as much so as if he were going to sit by a friend's fireside. He should not walk about the quiet streets as if he had but two hours to devote to the little city, and must then be off for another place. On the contrary, he must find a lodging-place, set his pilgrim-staff in the corner, take his knapsack from his shoulders, and prepare himself for a friendly visit.

Around Weimar are many beautiful hills and vales. For the purpose of enjoying them we took a random walk, and left the city to our left. After passing through a forest of well-trimmed linden-trees the path grew winding, and led through a passage or stairway cut in the solid rock. A narrow foot-bridge spanned a deep-blue, hasty stream, and then the path divided into two or three more. We were now at the edge of a beautiful meadow-vale. The grass was green and fresh, save in little patches where the morning sun had not yet dried the frost. We knew not which of the paths to choose, for they all seemed to be equally well trodden. A house stood on the opposite hill. The November morning was cool, but no smoke arose from either one of the two little thatched chimneys. There was no quiet farmer walking about the yard and smoking his pipe, as one would see at almost every country residence in that part of Germany. In fact, there was no appearance of life and happiness. The house was exceedingly plain, and the coarse gravel used in rough-casting it gave a very irregular surface to the exterior of the walls.

There was a rustic lattice-work attached to the house, completely surrounding it, and extending from ground to roof. There were many dead vines hanging to the lattice, but in the midst of them was one which was living, although neglected. A narrow window was obstructed by cobwebs, and the door, hung with long, old-fashioned hinges, was held by a very heavy, rusty lock.

This was Goethe's country home. Here he spent his summers in the evening of his life. The first front gate by which we tried to enter the yard was locked, but the other was open, and we went in and explored the grounds. The inclosure to the garden, or rather grove, is a hawthorn hedge. But it is not what the Englishman would call a hedge, and is by no means a fair specimen of the German *hecke*, which is always neatly trimmed. Once this Goethean hedge had been well cared for ; but the branches were afterward permitted to grow in all their wild waywardness. The few acres embraced in the hedge present as many varieties of scenery and appearance as can conceivably be embraced in such a small extent of land. From one end of the house stretches out a little level piece of land, which is used, perhaps, by some neighboring family for a flower garden. Low shelves extend along the inside of the hedge, where, when we visited the premises, many varieties of the chrysanthemum were spread out to dry. At the end of a little bed of flowers is a square block of stone, which serves for the support of a huge stone ball. There is no commemorative inscription on either, but they were placed there to mark one of Goethe's favorite spots. There are several other places in the grove, however, which

claim the same honor ; and none can mistake their meaning, so plainly and unmistakably are they marked. A few
rods distant is a beautiful arbor, where the trees which
encircle a round space are laden with long-neglected vines.
In this rustic nook is a stone table. There is a seat by
the side of it ; and here, too, is another spot where the
great man used to study. By taking a little meandering
grass-grown walk, you come to another table ; but this is
oblong, and a long seat stands beside it. It is half en-
circled by a stone wall, and in the middle of the semi-
circular space is a beautiful block of marble, on which are
engraved some familiar lines from " Faust," composed on
the spot. This is the place where the great poet concluded his " Faust." He did not begin it here, however,
for it must not be forgotten that forty hard-working and
not very happy years lay between the beginning and the
end of the composition of that work. The tables in these
secluded places have undergone changes, too, with every
thing else about the poet's home. They are beginning to
gather moss upon their surface, and are already leaning
awry. As we saw them, they were covered by newly-
fallen leaves, and the frost-nipped flowers in the half-
tilled garden formed a fit accompaniment to the overgrown hedges and the desolate house.

While we were examining the grounds, some one came
running down the hill, through the thick shrubbery, and
wished to know what was the matter. We told him our
errand, and asked permission to be shown the house. He
informed us that it was not allowed under any circumstances, but he finally changed his mind, and showed us,

I believe, every room in the cottage. It was in much the same condition as when Goethe occupied it, and was as fully abandoned inside as were the yard and the garden surrounding it. There are in the house a great many articles of ordinary furniture which had belonged to the poet. There was his little folding iron bedstead in the corner, which seemed scarcely large enough for a school-boy, and was not a whit larger than Napoleon's camp bedstead in the museum at Moscow. On a nail hung the basket in which Goethe used to carry his lunch when going on those charming excursions to Jena, and elsewhere, of which Mr. Lewes has told us in beautiful style and spirit.

Later, on our return to the city, we made diligent search for the poet's house in the heart of the place. It was a long time before we found any one who could show us where it was. A peasant, for example, of whom we inquired, did not seem to know that such a man had ever existed. Just think of it! This Weimar was the place in which the great Goethe had spent the chief part of his working life, had contributed more than any ten grand-dukes together to give it a national reputation, and had, before and after death, attracted thousands to those peaceful, grave-like streets, and yet a couple of strangers found it difficult at first to learn, from casual passers-by in the street, where the wonderful Titan had lived! But this is a common European experience. I once spent nearly an entire afternoon in searching for Swedenborg's house in Stockholm, people living in the same street not knowing even the name of their seer.

Goethe's town home stands in a dull market-place,

where we saw several wagon loads of hay—in charge of peasant drivers clad in very odd costumes—waiting for purchasers. But all efforts to see the interior of the house were unavailing, "for," said the steward, "the two sons of Herr Von Goethe are at home, and will never, on any account, allow any one to enter and inspect the house." This was only a confirmation of what some persons had positively stated; indeed, in making a search in the first instance we had but little hope of seeing more than the exterior of the dwelling. Murray says that visitors may enter on Fridays, but even this was stoutly denied at the door.

Schiller did not have as many of life's comforts as the serene, majestic Goethe. Before going to Weimar he had to work hard for his bread, and the world doled out its comforts with a niggardly hand. The grand duke could not make him rich, for he too was poor, and had to part with many an ancestral jewel to maintain the literary splendor of his court.

Schiller's humble house is in town. It is a plain, small, quaint two-story building, with a diminutive garden or yard in the rear. Over the front door are the simple words, "Hier wohnte Schiller"—Here lived Schiller. The three historical rooms are up stairs—the parlor, the bedchamber, and a small room now used for the sale of literary mementos of the place. One of the first things to strike the eye is a good portrait of President Lincoln. And what more appropriate picture could adorn the house of the grand German minstrel of freedom? Schiller and Lincoln! Let them grow together in human love.

Though an ocean and a century separated them, they both spoke the same sweet language of liberty, had the same sense of man's brotherhood, and entertained the same firm faith in the final triumph of the right.

Schiller's bedroom is smaller than I ever slept in at college, and the couch on which he died is simply a little trundle-bed. Here are the wreaths woven and deposited at the poet's funeral. The walls are covered with a poor green wash, and a faded picture of Macbeth hangs beside a window. There is the same porcelain stove that Schiller used, and also the plain deal table on which he was accustomed to write. The sight of the drawer in this table called to mind Goethe's story to Eckermann. Goethe related that he once went to visit Schiller, and, finding him out, sat for awhile at his table waiting for him. All at once he became faint, and it was some time before he discovered that the odor from decayed apples in his friend's drawer had caused the trouble. Schiller's wife then told him that her husband always kept spoiled apples near him, for they were necessary to his enjoyment and successful composition. I recalled the story to the present proprietor of the premises, as we stood before the writing-table, but he absolutely denied that there was any truth in Schiller's fondness for apples of that character.

A number of fragments of Schiller's manuscripts are to be seen, and a little tuft of his hair and Goethe's at different times of life. On a broad piece of paper is his first draught of the *dramatis personæ* of "Wilhelm Tell." There are scattered here and there, in different parts of the room, a good many objects which Schiller had himself used, such

18

as his quaint, plain inkstand, a candlestick, his seal, little cups and saucers, and letters. The largest of the three rooms is covered with a carpet, embroidered by the Weimar ladies, and presented, as a token of love for the poet, to his home. A Schiller Society has the premises under its care, and in a bookcase one finds the rapidly multiplying works on the poet and his writings. It is a complete Schillerian bibliography. It seemed hardly possible that we were standing in a house where was idolized, and sacredly preserved, each little memento of the man who, in early life, had stood in the middle of the old Frankfort bridge and looked despairingly down into the muddy, rapid Main, only restraining himself by violence from putting an immediate end to his stormy and desperate life.

There is a little yard in the rear of the house. It is half filled with shrubbery, and the sun has little play upon it. At one corner, where the vines are densest, there is the chair in which Schiller used to sit and study when he grew tired of his room. In another is a fine, large bust of him. The only relief we saw to the miniature autumn scene was a single green stalk of Indian corn, which, in Northern Germany, is regarded tropical, and frequently occupies an honored place among the plants of the elegant home.

There is a fine bronze statue of Herder in front of the city church. The inscription upon the base is plain, but more touching on account of its simplicity:—

JOHN GOTTFRIED HERDER.

Born at Morungen, August 25, 1744.

Died at Weimar, March 18, 1803.

ERECTED BY THE GERMANS OF EVERY LAND.

The grand duke's big heart had room enough for Herder too, and he had a slab placed over his grave inscribed, " Licht, Liebe, Leben "—Light, Love, Life. The dust of the theologian, philosopher, poet, and historian lies beneath the slab. Wieland, at his own request, was buried in Osmanstadt, in the same grave with his wife. His old home in Weimar is still preserved with scrupulous care. Schiller and Goethe lie in the grand-ducal mausoleum, in the city cemetery, which is very beautifully situated on a gentle hill-side, and abounds in tasteful monuments. It is well-cared for, and a great many of the graves are beautified with fresh wreaths and bouquets. The grand duke, keeping up until the end his affection for the two great poets, provided that after death they should be buried beside him—one at his right, and the other at his left. But royal etiquette has since banished them to a plebeian distance, though not without the thick walls of the mausoleum. Among other celebrated men interred in the cemetery are Hummel, the composer, and John Falk, the children's friend, whose life has been touchingly portrayed by Stevenson in his " Praying and Working." In the cemetery of the city church is the tomb of Lucas Cranach. The mason who carved his epitaph, inscribed, *Pictor celerrimus*, instead of *celeberrimus*—not so much of a mistake, after all.

CHAPTER XII.

THREE MECCAS.

WITTENBERG is not within the Thuringian Forest, but is a place generally visited at the same time with the latter because of its historical associations. Some time before one reaches the city its extensive grass-covered fortifications, still kept in excellent condition, are clearly seen. A pleasant walk skirts a grove, and leads past the " Luther Tree" to the chief city gate. This oak tree is very large, and is strong and thriving. It is carefully inclosed, and protected by police regulations against all damage,—and all because it is the immediate successor of the very one under which Luther burned the Pope's Bull, in the presence of the students and others, on December 10, 1520. After passing through the city gate you find yourself in a town where one street—and that paved with cobble-stones, and sadly in want of a street commissioner—almost monopolizes the trade.

The house in which Luther lived is on the left, and is soon reached. It is part of the old building connected with the university. When I last walked through the streets I found that the Crown Prince and Princess of Prussia had just paid a visit to the city, to attend an industrial exhibition.. Luther's house was literally covered with festoons and wreaths of oak and ivy, in acknowledgment of the royal honor. All the halls and stairways were a mass of wreaths. The principal room in the house still contains some of the furniture used by Luther. The great porcelain stove, designed according to his own direction. is covered on all four sides by reliefs illustrating events in sacred history. There are several old books, and in some of them annotations in the neat and clear chirography of Luther himself. The windows are of little, round, thick panes, and these none the clearest. In one of the rooms is a plain pine chair, or, rather, a short bench, in which Luther and his wife used to sit together in the evening, and enjoy the fresh air and busy street scenes. Among other objects of interest are the table on which the Reformer wrote, a drinking-jug, his chair, Cranach's portrait of him, a cast of his face taken after death, and Peter the Great's chalk autograph over the door.

Not far distant is Melanchthon's house. A teacher lives in it now, but, as he was not in, his servant showed us the premises. There is but little furniture in the large room on the second floor, where Melanchthon used to spend the most of his time. This room has, clearly, undergone almost no change since the death of its great occupant. But its neglect and destitution, and the entire absence of all effort to make it attractive, give it a peculiar charm. The garden is overgrown with shrubbery. On one side is a thick, time-worn stone table, now quite out of its horizontal, and almost obscured by overhanging trees. This was Melanchthon's table, on which he wrote whenever the weather permitted. On going further along the main street, the same old woman who had conducted me over the place fourteen years before, and who, with her hus-

band, has been taking strangers to Luther's house and
the Castle Church these thirty years, pointed out the identical house, with gable-ends fronting the public square, in
which Hamlet used to live.   Shakspeare has told us that
he studied in Wittenberg, but the old woman's story of
his exact residence was a little too much for my credulity,
though this might not have been the case if I had not
been trudging along in a drenching rain, in the middle of
a very muddy street.

The Castle Church, where Luther nailed the ninety-five
theses to the door, is at the further end of the town.   It
is very large, but is not attractive, if we except its important connection with the Reformation.   In the floor are
the graves of Luther and Melanchthon.   There is no
elaborate inscription over them, and their dust is covered
by two simple, heavy bronze plates, which are protected
by a wooden trap-door.   During the celebrated triumphal
visit of the Emperor Charles V. to this church, as he stood
at these graves the cruel Alva advised him to take out
the dust and burn it publicly.   " No," replied Charles V.,
"we make war on the living, not on the dead ! "   In the
same edifice are the tombs of Frederic the Wise and John
the Steadfast, Electors of Saxony, and Luther's stanch
friends.   Frederic's monument is by Peter Vischer.

In visiting Erfurt we fell in with a party, all intent upon
the same object—a visit to Luther's cell.   After engaging
rooms we hurried off in search of the cloister where the Reformer had been a monk.   Several persons whom we met
in the streets could give no satisfactory answer to our inquiries as to the locality.   One would suppose that Luther

had never lived. "Don't know any thing about it," was the actual response we had from as many as four or five people. At last we seemed to be on the right track, and finally passed under the archway of what proved to be a large court, surrounded by a cloistered building. On being told where the place of admission was, we went to it, rang the bell, and soon heard hasty footsteps along the hall. The door was opened by a nun, clad in black, with the usual broad linen collar and black gown. We were as deferential as we knew how to be, in asking to see the cell where Luther had been a monk. The " sister " gave a very porcine grunt as the only answer, and then slammed the heavy door in our faces and bolted it, and left us no wiser than we were before.

We were knocking at the wrong door, for it was the entrance to a Roman Catholic nunnery, where Luther's memory was not very tenderly treasured. It took us a good quarter of an hour to find the Protestant Martinsstift, or Orphan House, lying in another part of the city, where Luther's cell really is. We were here received in a friendly manner, and ample time given to inspect the stiff old portraits adorning the walls the entire length of the building. The cell is very small, probably not larger than eight feet by ten. Several old missals, which Luther used, are still shown the visitor ; and there are a number of books containing elaborate notes in his own handwriting. The walls are adorned with passages derived, in part, from his works, and in part descriptive of his life. Our guide was not impatient, but allowed us all the time we wished, in spite of the twilight, to examine every little object of inter-

est as leisurely as one could desire.   Besides, she had the
excellence, so rare in her craft, of not bewildering and disgusting you, in the midst of your reflections, by some
monotonous set speech on the glories of the spot.   It was
enough for us to be told that we were where Luther found
the light ; the rest belongs to history.

The road from Erfurt to Eisenach is very beautiful.
We kept to the fine old country roads, and though we
were often inclined to throw aside our knapsacks and take
the cars, we nevertheless adhered to the pedestrian part
of our tour.   We ascended one of the Drei Gleichen,—
three great castellated ruins covering lofty eminences,—
and could overlook a great part of the Thuringian Forest.
We spent a night in beautiful, peaceful Gotha.   On our way
up the Wartburg, at Eisenach, we passed the new and
stately mansion of the celebrated Low German poet and
novelist, Fritz Reuter.   In less than an hour afterward we
were in the small, plain room where Luther worked with
prodigious energy from May 4, 1521, to March 6, 1522, on
his translation of the Bible.   The guides have become
ashamed of inking over the place where he threw the inkstand at the devil's head.   Indeed, it would now consume a
good sized bottle of ink to carry out the practice, for the
spot has grown into an immense patch, covering a large
section of one of the walls.   The relic-hunters have not
been idle of late years, for, shortly before our visit, the plas-
ter had been pulled from a spot about a foot square !   The
low bedstead has suffered some additional kniving, but the
Reformer's table is so heavily bound in iron that its proportions will probably suffer but little diminution in future.

On the table there is a good supply of photographic views and of pocket Testaments—Luther's translation ; and after making a selection from them, and viewing Cranach's picture of the Reformer's parents, we left the memorable little room. Other interesting parts of the castle—if there is any thing interesting after seeing Luther's room—are the hall where the Minnesingers met in 1207 for a trial of their skill, the curious armor, and the tasteful chapel, of interest alike to Catholic and Protestant. To the latter it is interesting because Luther used to preach in it ; and to the former, because of its association with Saint Elizabeth, the apostle to Thuringia.

The Grand Duke of Eisenach has lately subjected the entire castle to a thorough renovation. The breaches that time had made in its storm-beaten walls had been widening for centuries, and now every room in the majestic pile, save only Luther's, has been so restored and beautified that any visitor who saw it a few years ago would hardly recognize any thing more than the usual outline of the great structure, and the magnificent hill on which it stands. On leaving the castle our guide took us to an outer corner of a bastion, remarking that, as we were no doubt glad to meet a fellow-American at any time, he would introduce us to one. He thereupon pulled a little chain, when out walked a little black bear, wagging his tail and smelling about our feet in the most amiable manner possible. He had lately been presented to some one connected with the Wartburg, and made the journey all the way from his home in the Rocky Mountains.

18*

CHAPTER XIII.

MARBACH : SCHILLER'S BIRTHPLACE.

THE quaint Suabian village of Marbach is the birth-place of Schiller. It is far in the south, in liberty-loving Würtemburg. I left the cars at Stuttgart, where, indeed, one begins to see very decided reminders of the great poet. The powers in that capital once rejected and hunted him as a revolutionist and wild-pate, because of his triumphant " Robbers ;" but the present occupants of the great palace look out from their windows upon Thor-waldsen's statue of him in the square in front. The man whom Würtemberg would have been glad to hang three quarters of a century ago, is now the one she looks upon as her greatest son ; to whose button-hole, if he were living, she would tie all her ribbons of nobility, and for whose slender form and pale face she would rear palaces from her richest quarries and her choicest forests.

I visited the court chapel in the old palace, the Stifts-kirche, the second-hand bookstores, the Royal Park, and some of the most picturesque of the oldest streets of the Suabian city. At the railway station I had the oppor-tunity of seeing how a royal visitor, who, in this case, was the Queen of Holland, was received. There were some three or four hundred towns-people gathered, through curiosity, in front of the depot, while as many as a half-dozen special drivers and lackeys in livery were waiting

for the guest. All the court carriages were highly polished, and were designated by the crown, with the national escutcheon painted on each side. One carriage, however, was drawn by white horses, and I soon saw that this
was the one intended for the queen. At a given signal
there was a general flutter, the carriages fell into line,
and the white horses were made to feel the presence of
the whip, with an air which seemed to say, " Now, know
that royal blood is near, and that you are to be on your
best behavior."

The queen—who, with a lady at each side, now came
quickly from the rear of the station to the front, seemed
intent on communicating as much as possible to her attendants in a short time—graciously inclined her head to
the uncovered bystanders, stepped quickly into the carriage, and was driven off at a rapid pace. Her attendants
took the other carriages, and soon there was no other
person in her train to be seen except a sergeant, who,
in his Dutch bewilderment, could hardly tell where to begin to get his royal mistress's baggage in order. The
queen was pale, apparently about forty-five years of age,
had light hair, a thin, but ruddy face, and high cheek-
bones. She wore a black cloth dress and mantle, embroidered sparingly with silk of various colors. There
was not a cheer to welcome her to the Suabian Court—
but these are not always given nowadays in the presence
of royalty. I have never yet heard a dozen, though I
have been present on several occasions when the people
and royalty have come within greeting sight of each other.
I was much less favorably impressed with her appearance

on this occasion than at a later time, when I had a much better opportunity to see her while visiting her House in the Wood—her country home in the grand park at the Hague.

Proceeding to Ludwigsburg, one of Schiller's several Suabian homes, I found that, in order to reach Marbach the same evening, I had to take a post-coach. It proved to be one of the olden time. The driver, Gottfried, (God's peace,) seemed to be a general pet, but no amount of trinkgelds appeared to expedite his movements. I wondered why he was not more industrious, why he did not make use of his big whip; but was told that it was through no fault of his that he did not make his horses start. And I soon saw for myself that Gottfried was as innocent as the stars of what had seemed to be an endeavor to make us keep late hours, whether or not. He, poor fellow, could not move an inch without the orders of the officer in charge of the post-office, who, when he was ready, came tumbling out, and in as authoritative a manner as if Barbarossa himself had spoken, gave Gottfried the following orders, in the hearing of us all: "See that you depart and arrive in due time at your destination!"

Surely the Neckar never reflected the moonlight more beautifully than on that clear October evening. The road lay along the elevated bank of the river, and much of the way under branches of trees. Like the Suabian roads in general, this, too, was fringed on both sides by fruit-trees; but the wayfarer is not allowed to pluck the fruit from them. I know the case of a child whose father wa compelled to pay a gulden because a single apple was plucked on the roadside, near Heidelberg, by the little offender. Along the road that Gottfried was taking us there had often passed armies, from the Roman times almost down to our own ; but especially in the age of the Hohenstaufens—the glory of Suabia, and one of the greatest royal race ever given to Germany's imperial throne.

To me, however, it was of as much interest because of its connection with Schiller's name as for any other reason. Many a time, when a boy, he had wandered along this pleasing section of the Neckar, and as he lingered by the water's edge and gathered flowers, and played his ungainly harp beneath the overhanging trees, he dreamed of his future, wondering what sort of fate was going to be meted out to him. Many a time, after the family had removed to Ludwigsburg, he went along the road with his mother to visit his aged grandparents in Marbach. Christophine, Schiller's sister, has prepared for us a sweet little record of one of these juvenile journeys, though this one was not along the Neckar, but by the mountain road. "Once," says she, "when we children were accompanying our mother to our dear grandparents, we took the road from Ludwigsburg to Marbach over the mountain. It was a beautiful Easter Monday, and in the way our mother related to us the history of the two disciples whom Jesus walked with on the way to Emmaus. Her narrative became more earnest the further we went, and, as we came to the top of the mountain, we were all so affected that we kneeled down there and prayed. This mountain was our Tabor."

I reached Marbach about nine o'clock at night, and was

directed to my lodgings by several kind villagers, to whom the arrival of the stage was the principal event of the day, and who crowded around every traveler, as if anxious to bid him welcome. As by the aid of lanterns, borne by these friendly hands, I picked my way along the filthy streets of the town, then through the old gateway of the grim, gray tower, then past an old church ruin, how could I forget the history which lies back of all this unassuming, prostrate, but contented present?

It is the old story of war and pestilence. As long ago as the Roman supremacy in Germany, Marbach was a thriving town. Ruins, still in existence, prove it to have been an important Roman colony, which served as a meeting-point for several important country roads. In the year 978 it appears in history as a part of the Rhenish Franconian diocese of Speyer, and in the possession of the bishop resident there. After the end of the thirteenth century it was the property of the Count of Würtemberg. It was plundered by the Spanish troops of Charles V. in the Smalkaldian War, and the French allies of the Germans, under Turenne and Bernard of Weimar, were quartered there in the Thirty Years' War, from 1642 to 1646. Notwithstanding all the drawbacks, however, the little city managed to live. In the fifteenth century it had grown so much, on one side, that the Alexander Church was built to satisfy the increased religious wants of the community. But the third war of conquest, under Louis XIV., brought destruction to the town, and in July, 1693, the inhabitants of Marbach were driven out by the French, the city was set on fire, and in a few hours it was a mass of ruins. It had taken seven hundred years for the little town to grow to the height of its prosperity, and now it fell in as many hours. In the eighteenth century it began to be rebuilt ; but it had many difficulties to contend with, and was compelled, amid the convulsions of the former half of that century, to quarter the troops of the French, Russian, and Austrian armies.

The connection of Marbach with the Schiller family dates from the 14th of March, 1749, when a young man, in military costume, rode along the Neekar.to this little town. He came directly from the Netherlands, the winter quarters of his regiment, and had taken this opportunity to pay a visit to his native country. His birthplace was Bittenfeld, near Waiblingen. His father had been dead sixteen years, his mother had wandered to the village of Marbach, and his brothers and sisters had become scattered to Ludwigsburg, Bittenfeld, Neckerems, and Marbach. The soldier came to Marbach because it was now the home of the sister, whom he was especially anxious to see. The young officer went to the hotel of the place, the "Golden Lion," which belonged to George Frederic Bodweis, who was a baker, and who passed for a man in good circumstances. This man had a daughter who was seventeen years of age, Elizabeth Dorothea, and in five months from the time when the officer first put foot on the door-step of the Golden Lion, he and the proprietor's daughter were man and wife. They became the father and mother of the poet Schiller, and Marbach was henceforth their permanent home.

Early the next morning after my arrival in Marbach I

went in search of the house where Schiller was born. It is small, one story and a half high, and, like the most of the houses in the town, and throughout Suabia, is so built as to render all the timbers constituting its frame-work visible. There is no door-yard whatever. You step directly into the house from the unswept street. The house bears the following inscription: "The birth-place of Schiller, who was born November the 11th, 1759, and died May the 9th, 1805."

In the middle of the plate containing the inscription there is a medallion bust of the poet.

Over the door there is a metallic plate, showing that the house is insured in the Phœnix German Insurance Society. An old-fashioned bell-knob hangs at the door. A young man bade me enter. The room in which Schil-ler was born is at the left, and is not more than eight feet wide and twelve feet long. There, in one corner, is his mother's old spinning-wheel; some of its smoothness, no doubt, dates back to the boyhood of little Fritz. The wheel is worm-eaten, but the principal parts are still there, and I had no difficulty in making it revolve as much as I pleased. The chief articles of furniture in the room are a secretary, in perfect preservation, and a stove of the olden time. There is a letter, framed, which Schiller's mother wrote to a friend about a servant she was trying to get along with. Every line betrayed the fact that good house-wives had trouble with their domestics over a century ago, and in what we regard the paradise of good servants, the Fatherland. The pictures of the poet's father and mother are well preserved.

The stairway is very narrow, dark, and angular. The front upper room, the largest in the house, is a museum of relics of the poet and tributes to his memory. In a glass case there is an old leathern hat, ten times more romantic than the old broken felt hat of Napoleon, at the Louvre, which he wore at St. Helena. One of the pictures is a pencil sketch of Schiller when a young man, clad in peasant costume, and sitting sidewise on a sleepy old donkey, and smoking a long pipe. The picture was sketched by a friend, and taken from life, as Schiller appeared one day at Wildbad. There is in another frame something that looks like a little cheap bow-knot of various colors. This, on close inspection, proves to be hair, and the knot is really the hair of Schiller and his family, his own being the *red* threads. In the table are magnificent copies of illustrations to Schiller's works, presented by authors and publishers. The list of strangers shows many arrivals every day. One large book contains selections from the principal printed testimonials to the poet's greatness, on the occasion, in Marbach, of the hundredth anniversary of his birth. Among them are many of English authorship, Carlyle's figuring prominently. There is a large book-case containing copies of Schiller's works, which are for sale to visitors. There are also pictures of the house; some large portraits; crayons of various rooms; and famous illustrations to scenes in his works. There is in one corner an exact copy of Dannecker's bust of the poet, the best in existence. It is crowned with a laurel wreath.

Every year, on the 11th of November, the old wreath is

taken away and replaced by a new one. As it was in October when I happened to visit the house, and the old wreath was soon to give way to a new one, the man in charge gave me a number of the laurel leaves, which I found much more fragrant than the faded roses. To me one of the most interesting objects was a copy of the first play-bill announcing in Mannheim the performance of Schiller's " Robbers." In it there is not only the enumeration of the *dramatis personæ*, but also an account, by the poet himself, of the principal points of the play. The public are invited to come early, as the play is long, and cannot be concluded until quite late in the evening. I concluded my visit by purchasing some little mementos of the place. ·

The greatest season of rejoicing Marbach has ever had was on the 9th, 10th, and 11th of November, 1859, at the time of the centennial celebration of Schiller's birth, already referred to. Strangers from all quarters streamed into the town. Presents from all parts of Europe came day after day. The far-off city of Moscow, for instance, testified to its love of Schiller by sending an immense bell, which now hangs in the desolate Alexander Church. On one side of it there is a medallion head of Schiller, in relief. Over it is the word " Concordia ;" beneath it the words, " Gather the loving congregation for worship, for hearty union." Around the bell there is a garland of oak and laurel. On the side opposite the bust of Schiller you read in an open book the words, " I call the living, and I lament the dead ;" and under these words, further, " To the home of Schiller from his lovers in Moscow, November 10th, 1859." The tribute, with its inscription, will naturally call to the reader's mind Schiller's celebrated " Song of the Bell," which suggested the gift.

Schiller's house belongs to the town of Marbach, and the association having charge of it are endeavoring to beautify it, and place it on a good financial foundation. The most elevated point in the neighborhood of Marbach is called the Schiller Height. It affords a fine view of the country for miles around, and the Schiller Association, when it can collect funds enough, proposes to erect there a suitable monument to the memory of little Marbach's greatest son.

CHAPTER XIV.

DOWN THE NECKAR IN VINTAGE-TIME.

IN order to go down the Neckar in vintage-time, I left Marbach in the early morning. The picture presented at the quaint old post-house was one of the olden time— just such as might have been seen about a hundred and fifteen years before, when, in all likelihood, that very post-house, and the inn near by, served the same purpose as on the crisp October morning of 1869, when I threw my knapsack on top of the old coach that was to draw me down through the grape region of Würtemberg. How did I know but that Schiller's mother, unquestionably a belle of the place, had often looked through the identical panes of glass, in the second story of the inn, through which a couple of boys were now peeping, with laughing eyes, at the stranger below, half hidden in an old American shawl? Our coach was as much one of the olden time as you could well find in the imperial collection of carriages in St. Petersburg, or in the immense carriage-house in Windsor Castle. As for the horses and the general outfit of the post-coach, they would have been as much at home in the fifteenth century as in the present. This contact with the remote past, which one experiences everywhere in Suabia, always gave me a singular pleasure, and has taken a place among my most delightful recollections.

The villagers collected around us as we took our places

in the stage, and the postmaster came out at last and delivered elaborate orders to the driver. A band of musicians, that had been doing hornpipe service at a village wedding in the small hours of the night before, took possession of a supplementary coach, and we were all soon clattering away over the rough cobble-stones of honest, simple, memorable Marbach. As we passed the house where Schiller was born, the man having charge of it put his head out of a side window—how often had boy Schiller done the same thing!—to watch the departing stage, and, recognizing me as one of his visitors and a customer of his little memorials, bowed until we turned a corner. We saw him and his shrine no more.

It was only after leaving Marbach that I could form an idea of its former importance, and fully realize its actual history. The place had once been surrounded by immense walls, and these, now extending far beyond the present dimensions, are more than half-covered with ivy and grape vines. It is the old warrior grown too thin and lean for the neat armor of his strong manhood. You see broad gashes here and there in the massive fortifications, as if some quavers from a South American earthquake had reached them ; and, by the aid of a little fancy, you can detect the scars from balls hurled during the war of the Austrian succession. The walls are still high, but have long ago forgotten their perpendicular, and the vines are doing their best, in their slow but efficacious way, to complete the task of their demolition.

The road lay through continuous vineyards all the way to Heilbronn. Not long after leaving Marbach we left also the Neckar, and when I had sight of it again, it was as if grasping the hand of a friend. I had the comfort, on the following day, to see it again at Heilbronn, when it was no longer the little babbling brook, but the vigorous young river, boasting broader hillsides for its vineyards, prouder knolls for grander castles, dashing furiously against the Heilbronn piers, and even claiming a place with the great family of navigable streams.

The vineyards through which we passed had no inclosure whatever, and yet the rich clusters hanging by the road side were fully ripe—a testimonial to the proverbial honesty of the Suabian peasants; or shall I call it a respect for law? The villagers along the road were alive with vintage glee. The coopers were actually at work in the street, getting ready wooden vessels of all sizes for the new wine. In some of the vineyards there were throngs of gleaners, and people were passing to and from these with tubs of grapes, which were deposited in receptacles by the road side. The very air was filled with the perfume of the vintage, and man and beast seemed to rejoice together that now the reaping-time had come, after a year of tender and ceaseless nurture of the vines.

At Beilstein I ascended a high hill to an old castle, celebrated for its still unscathed tower and the strong walls inclosing it. It bears the name of "Der Lange Hans"— Long Jack—and is so prominently situated that you can see from its top a vast landscape of quiet but exquisite beauty. The upward road lay through vineyards. The depression surrounding the massive outer wall marks the exact outline of the ancient moat, and the bridge crossing it and leading into the castle is so out of its original position, and such a prey to wild-flowers, vines, and weeds, as to make it a perfect gem for the landscapist's pencil. A part of the structure within the inclosure betrays Roman workmanship. The whole ruin is a rare treasure.

On our return to the village we stopped to take a look at the now dilapidated church of the knights of Beilstein, the former lords of the whole district. The old stone pulpit is still standing, and the tombstones of the Beilsteins, notwithstanding the numerous fractures and losses, are still distinguishable, but only by the aid of the stone escutcheons of the family. The coat of arms was three battle-axes, in the form of a triangle. Hence the name of the Beilstein knights—*Beil* meaning *ax*, and *stein*, stone.

At Heilbronn I found the Suabian vintage in its grand climax. It was no more the quiet thing I had been viewing for twenty miles, but the real hilarious and crowning glory of the year. The streets and roads were thronged with people, going to and from the vineyards. All classes, both sexes, and horse, donkey, and dog, were willing followers in the train of Bacchus. Those who were not taking any part as laborers in the vineyard came as guests or overseers. I found it, or so it seemed, the grand time for renewing acquaintances and settling differences. The very road sides were thronged with people merely looking at the gleaners. Horses and donkeys drew small carts, and carried the must, or impressed grapes, to the different places of ownership. Peasant women bore on their shoulders long wooden tubs, filled with grapes, to the press, or to the donkey-wagon at the road-side. *Press*, did I say?

Yes, in some cases, but not in all. The press was a little machine, something like a fan, and turned by a crank. But this was not the real Suabian way of getting at the juice of the grape. The principal press was the human feet, with jack boots on. The grape-treaders were, in every case I saw, young men, who were tramping in terrible earnest, as if determined to take vengeance on the grapes for all the labor they had caused.

"What sort of boots are those you have on?" I asked one of the treaders of the grapes when on my way to a tower called the Wartburg.

"O, they are old," replied the fellow, good-humoredly.

"I suppose you cleaned them well before you got into this tub of grapes?"

"Of course."

"But your feet cannot be comfortable, as the grape-juice is certainly quite cold."

"They are cold enough, and wet too."

If my temperance principles had not been pretty strong already, this would have had some effect in strengthening them. What would the American devotee to imported wines think, as he empties his overflowing decanters, if he could for a moment see these unkempt rustic peasants treading out grapes with their dirty feet?

Heilbronn, or Health Fountain, takes its name from a spring near St. Kilian's Church, of alleged healing property, and flowing out of seven pipes. This fountain is the source of a host of old legends; but only the most important one, because connected with the introduction of Christianity into that region, I will here give.

Far back in the early period of the Christian era, when a vast wilderness overspread nearly all Germany, the apostles of peace entered this dense forest from a far-off country, in order to extend the doctrines of Christianity. Among the number was the pious Kilian, whose holy calling led him to the inhospitable regions of the Main and the Neckar. Here, where Heilbronn now stands, but where no friendly dwellings were then found, he gradually collected his followers beside the fresh fountain. He preached with great zeal the word of life, and extended to his hearers the boon of Christian baptism. It was not long before he fell, a martyr to his faith, at the hands of the barbarians ; and, although one of his disciples continued the good work, the pure light was nevertheless overcome by the prevailing darkness, and the consecrated fountain was visited less and less by eager seekers of the truth. Many years passed by, and the Lord sent one of his greatest servants, Charlemagne, the strong pillar of Christianity in his times, to this neighborhood. One day the mighty ruler was hunting deer and wild boar in the primeval Scheuerberg Forest. In the middle of the day he and his attendants became very thirsty, and gathered about the beautiful little fountain, or brook, which they fortunately discovered. This was the fountain of the devoted Kilian, and the crystal water slaked the thirst of the weary hunters. By and by the hunting-horns sounded again for the chase, and the emperor was about to start, when a preacher, whose look betrayed deep sorrow, made his appearance from amid a dark thicket. He was at first overcome by the grand appearance of the hunters ; yet the

19

emperor encouraged him to speak, and tell the secret of his grief. The old man then related the story of the pious Kilian, and added these words : " Great ruler, only a few come here now to receive holy baptism, for the men of this wild country have grown worse in time, and are so set against the pure doctrine of Christianity, that I and my spiritual brethren can gain only a few followers."

Charlemagne replied : " Be of good courage ! I give you my imperial word that, as I and my followers have found refreshment at this fountain, so shall it become a fountain of heavenly blessing again to others." Soon after this the emperor sent a great number of ministers to this region, and had a church built over the fountain. Then, in process of time, the vast forests were felled, and beautiful fields and a peaceful population took their place. Charlemagne called the fountain the " Healing Fountain," and in a little while he had one of his imperial residences built very near it. The example of the ruler worked powerfully on the inhabitants of the country. The doctrines of the Gospel again reached many hearts, and around the palace and church there gathered a multitude of believers.

The historical foundation for this touching legend was found in a German manuscript, which was taken to Rome during the Thirty Years' War ; then found its way to Paris in 1796, and in 1816 was restored to Germany, and placed in the ducal library of Heidelberg.

The old parts of the city of Heilbronn present all the interesting features that characterize the Suabian architecture. The projecting gable fronts, the quaint bay-windows, the stone carvings, the winding stairs, and the enormous and almost unwieldy old pumps, tell of a very old past. The present St. Kilian's Church is a renaissance treasure from the thirteenth century, though the foundation was laid in 1037. The great bell, cast by Bernhard Bachmann, the father of the famous theologian who won Heilbronn over to Protestantism, is tolled every day at noon.

The most interesting object in Heilbronn, to an antiquarian, is Goetz's Tower, so called because it is the alleged scene of the imprisonment of Goetz von Berlichingen. This Goetz of the Iron Hand, an odd fellow withal, was one of the best knights of his time, and, with Ulrich von Hutten and Franz von Sickingen, was the last representative of the real knighthood of the Middle Ages. His whole spirit was full of honorable strife ; and no sooner did war break out anywhere in Germany, than he offered his broadsword to one or another of the contending parties, and was always to be relied upon at the risk of life and every human interest. In 1522, while aiding Ulrich of Würtemberg to crush the Suabian Confederation, he was betrayed, captured, and imprisoned in Heilbronn. He was also a participant in the "Peasants' War," and suffered imprisonment in consequence. He left behind one of the most entertaining autobiographies of the period, as it contains a faithful and minute picture of the social and moral state of his times. Goethe made much use of it in his maiden drama, "Goetz von Berlichingen ;" but so far deviated from it as to make Goetz die in the tall red tower in Heilbronn, by the Neckar bank ; while the Knight of the Iron Hand really spent only one night in it, and

survived that night thirty-seven years, dying in peace and
freedom in his own castle of Hornberg, lower down the
Neckar, when over eighty years of age. He lost his right-
hand in one of the battles, but succeeded in having an iron
one so skillfully made that he was able to use the sword
with it, and to box the ears of any knight of less sincerity
and valor than himself who ventured into his presence.

From the top of the tower I enjoyed a charming view
of Heilbronn and the surrounding country. The premises
are poorly kept, and I felt like employing a force of scrub-
bers and sweepers to put them in presentable condition.
There is one little room containing the rickety chair in
which Goetz is said to have sat when a prisoner. On the
stair-way there is a full coat-of-mail, standing as a knight
prepared for war, representing him of the Iron Hand.

The last sounds I heard that night were those of laborers returning from distant vineyards, or some place of
amusement; and early in the morning I was awakened by
the not unwelcome salutations of the same joyous notes
of young men and women going out to glean.

The next day I went down the river as far as Heidelberg. The whole journey was one of enchanting interest.
Old castles fringe the river banks, and in some places there
are immense beech-forests. These latter form the dark
green meeting-place of the Odenwald and the Scharzwald.
The most picturesque castles are Mittelberg, Zwingenberg,
Hornberg, and Ehrenberg, each redolent of tales of love
and hate, troubled and eventful life, and hasty death.
Who shall tell the history of those gray stones? The
kindly ivy is ever laboring to prevent your fancy from

delving into the hoary and bloody past, as much as to say, "Judge the past as I do, and cover the misdeeds of your fellows as charitably as I cover these rough gray stones."

The chief town is Wimpfen, one-half of which lies in the valley and the other on the hill. Wimpfen on the hill stands on the site of the Roman Cornelia, named after the wife of Julius Cæsar. Attila, at the head of his unsparing Huns, sacked and destroyed the castle. The whole Neckar region felt the full blast of the Thirty Years' War, and near Wimpfen the imperial army, under Tilly, defeated the Margrave George Frederick, of Baden, in 1622.

Near the village of Bottingen is a chapel of unknown age, celebrated for the following legend:—

When all this region was still pagan, a bold and strong young man became betrothed to a beautiful girl. They loved each other devotedly ; but she was a Christian and he still a heathen. He adhered tenaciously to his idols ; and when the girl strove in vain to direct him to the pure Gospel, her sorrow at his course drove her from her peaceful home into the thick forest, where she secluded herself in a rocky chasm, and prayed day and night for the salvation of her lover. Even the wild animals took compassion on the sorrowing one, and daily carried nourishment to her. After some years, she was released from the bonds of her sorrowful earthly life, and the angel of death bore her spirit to the realms of the blessed. Often, after she had gone, did her lover wander through the forest in search of her, but all in vain. One day, as he was hunting, a deer sprang out before him, and remained a moment standing in his presence, and looking at him with a supernatural sadness. The animal seemed to beckon him to follow, and the man followed it to a rocky cell, which he immediately knew had been that of his loved one, for there was an inscription at its entrance, made by the girl herself; besides, the occupants of the valley confirmed his belief. He threw himself down beside the cell, and wept bitter tears of sorrow. Just then the image of the departed one came, as an angel from heaven, into his presence. The soft, sweet spirit of Christianity settled upon him. He resolved to be a Christian; and immediately afterward went to the city of Worms, where he was baptized by the bishop. Having returned to his native place he built a cottage near the former secluded home of his departed loved one, and lived a hermit, in the retirement of his holy thoughts. He taught the doctrines of Christianity to all who surrounded him, refreshed the weary traveler with food and drink, and showed him the right way through the forest. The fame of his good deeds soon spread far and wide, and pilgrims came from distant places to his lonely cell, and sought from him comfort and strength for the sorrows of their life. Finally, after many long years had passed by, and the pious hermit had reached a hoary old age, he one night heard a rap at the door, while a fearful storm was raging without. He immediately arose and opened his door, and stood face to face with a beautiful form and sweet visage. This wanderer was clad in snow-white garments, and in his eyes there glowed a heavenly peace. The hermit immediately kindled a fire for him to warm himself by, and placed food before him; then kneeling, he offered his evening prayer with trembling voice.

Arising from his knees, and looking at his guest, he found that the head of the stranger was surrounded with a halo of unearthly splendor. It was the angel of death, who said to him: "God has heard your prayer; go, now, to your rest, and inherit eternal joy!" Then the stranger kissed the old hermit softly on the forehead, and he sank back—his soul was in the better world. The next morning the old man was found as if in sweet sleep, and he was buried amid the lamentations of the multitude. The visitor in the white robe was the archangel Michael. A church was built by the people, and dedicated to St. Michael.

Such is the explanation given for the name of the St. Michael's Church in Bottingen, and the height on which it stands is called Michaelsberg, or St. Michael's Mountain.

At Neckarsteinach I found myself on familiar ground again. Fourteen years before, I had wandered up there, when a student at Heidelberg, in company with some other young Americans, and had spent the night in the neighborhood near the old castle. The next day we threaded the dense forest and visited the four old castles, now in ruins, which belonged to the family that went by the name of the "Landeschaden," or Land's Bane. From the highest one of them we enjoyed a magnificent view of the Neckar Valley for many miles. After resting under some trees of immense size and great age, and getting a humble repast of black bread and poor butter, we took *raft* for Heidelberg in the afternoon. Our sail, or rather float, was exciting, and the only injury we suffered was to get wet feet, and, before reaching port, an appetite that our friendly peasant raftsman had no means to satiate.

CHAPTER XV.

CASTLE WEIBERTREUE.—WOMAN'S FIDELITY.

ONE of my most interesting excursions was to Weinsberg, in Würtemberg. It lies at the base of the
Castle of Weibertreue, or Woman's Fidelity. The cars,
on entering a tunnel, slackened pace very perceptibly. I
saw that the tunnel was lighted in some places, and that
its arching was supported by an immense number of
beams and pillars. On asking why this was, I was told,
in the most complacent manner, that the tunnel had been
looked upon for some time with great suspicion, and that
a caving-in would not be a surprise at any time.

On emerging from it into daylight again, we entered
upon a valley of rare beauty. The town of Weinsberg
was at our left, and rising above it in queenly glory was a
magnificent vine-clad hill, which is crowned with the still
wall-girt ruins of the Weibertreue Castle. We were received at the station by a good Suabian of the town, who
was expecting us. We threaded street after street of the
curious place, and finally reached his home in a quaint old
dwelling. Soon a lunch was spread for us, and as we sat
and regaled ourselves, our host entertained us with the
story of the historical town and of its still more historical
castle. I have since found his narrative substantially
confirmed by the most reliable authorities on Suabian
history.

The history of the castle is really that of the town itself, for in the former lived the ruler (or his representative) of the latter, and his fate, of course, decided that of the men, women, and children in the humble dwellings below his castle. The town was originally a Roman colony, and there is evidence, though doubted by some, that it dates from the Roman Emperor Probus, A. D. 282. It is said that after the Allemanni, whose land had been incorporated with that of the Franks, were conquered by the French king Chlodwig, near the end of the fifth century— the year 496—much land in private hands was declared imperial property, and was given away by the Frank kings to Frankish or Allemannish grandees. From this time forth the Christian religion made great headway, and the more progress it made the more did the inhabitants acquire security of home. The castle on the Weinsberg was built either during the Frankish. occupancy, from 536 to 748, or soon afterward, under the dominion of the Carlovingians, from 748 to 917. It must have been in the possession of a baronial family, judging from the Book of Privileges of the city of Weinsberg of the year 1468. According to other sources, the city of Weinsberg is said to have become a part of the see of the Bishop of Würtzburg, and was the head of the chapter in the ninth century.

From the year 945 the Knights of Weinsberg took an important part in the German and Swedish wars, and in the great continental tournaments. They were prominent figures for several centuries. On the fields around Weinsberg, now clad with vineyards, occurred that great conflict

19*

between Count Guelph of Altorf—the guardian of Henry
the Lion of Brunswick—and Conrad III., of Hohenstaufen. The prize at stake was the possession of the estate
of Weinsberg, and the Hohenstaufen was successful. The
contest was bitter, hand-to-hand, and hung long in the
balance. All at once the shouts burst forth from the contending forces, "Strike for the Guelphs!" "Strike for
the Ghibellines!"—two war-cries which resounded through
all Italy and Germany, and were heard for full four hundred
years, until the two great parties, self-exhausted, disappeared before a current of greater interest. The whole
of Europe was drawn into the vortex, and divided into
friends and foes, the question of partisanship with one or
the other often changing the fate of nations. Rienzi, of
Rome, around whose strange life Bulwer weaves one of his
best romances, was a stout warrior of the Guelphs, and did
much to revive their prestige. Every-where the Guelphs
represented public liberty, while the Ghibellines were the
exponents of personal power. In Germany the Guelphs
were the advocates of the rights of the minor princes and
knights against the despotism of the emperors, who were
upheld by the Ghibellines. George IV., the late King of
Hanover, whose kingdom was absorbed by Prussia in the
war of 1866, is a Guelph, and boasts proudly of his pedi-
gree. Queen Victoria, of England, through her connection with the House of Brunswick, traces her ancestry
back to Queen Kunegunde, a Guelphic princess.

After a hearty lunch at our Suabian host's board, we
started for the ruined castle overlooking the town of
Weinsberg and the broad and charming vale. On our

way we came to a beautiful house with back-lying grounds, and, across the street from it, a monumental bust of its former proprietor, Andreas Justinus Kerner, the cele- brated Suabian poet and prose writer. To him, more than any one else, the castle on the hill, at whose foot he lived and wrote, owes the great labor that has of late years been taken to beautify the grounds, and endear it and its story to all Germans. Kerner wrote several ex- cellent poetical works, was a friend and fellow-laborer with Uhland, and, by his earnest songs and hymns, touched many a chord in the German heart. His taste and edu- cation as a physician led him to study closely the human organism, while his strongly poetical temperament induced him to give a fanciful interpretation to many of its dis- tinctive features. He was a firm believer in demonology in our days, as is plainly proved by his " History of two Somnambulists," " History of the Possession of Devils in Modern Times," and especially his masterpiece, " The Prophetess of Prevorst." I can find in no sketch of his life a confirmation of the account given by his fellow- townsman, our host and friend in Weinsberg, that he professed to have communion with spirits, *à la Sweden- borg*, and that the picturesque old tower in the rear of his house was the scene of his preternatural conferences.

By a narrow way, with a Norman hedge on either side, we ascended the hill on which the Weibertreue Castle stands. Passing through the portal we saw another way at our right, leading downward. This was the original road to the castle ; and, as we stood beside it and looked down the vista into the town below, we listened to the story of the castle for the first time, and how it came to be called Weibertreue.

I have already said that Conrad III. defeated Count Guelph, of Altorf, in the plain below. The disaster brought with it some hard conditions, one of which was that all the men of Weinsberg should be put to death, but that the women might march off unmolested ; and, to make the imperial grace more splendid, they were promised that they could take with them whatever was nearest their hearts. But what was nearest the hearts of the daughters of Weinsberg ? We shall see. A messenger hastened to Conrad with some terrible news. No new enemy was marching with flying banners from the bold hill shutting in the valley. It was nothing but a woman's trick. All the women of Weinsberg were standing at the castle gate, bearing upon their shoulders their husbands and lovers— all the men of the town, to the number of eleven hundred ! Duke Frederic protested against this female ruse, that such a thing was an abuse of imperial grace, and that the thing was not to be thought of. But it was not Duke Frederic's part to speak the decisive word. Conrad, worthiest of the Hohenstaufens, replied : " *Non decet verbum regium immutari*"—The royal word shall be kept. Never spoke emperor a nobler sentiment.

Down the walk, at the head of which we were now standing, those noble women passed with their precious burdens on their shoulders. The town was burned and razed, and a few inhabitants who were left were put to death. But the deed of the women, giving the name of Woman's Fidelity to the castle, passed into song, and story, and German hearts, for all time to come.

Many German minstrels have made it the burden of elaborate poems. Peter Nichthanius has written a drama on it, and relates the story in a poetical prologue. Bürger, a Suabian poet of the last century, has also paid a fitting tribute to the memory of the noble deed of his country-women. Addison, likewise, relates it in Number 469 of the "Spectator."

The old castle is one of the most interesting ruins, even leaving out its history, that I have ever seen in Würtemberg, which is a paradise of mediæval recollections. The very cap of the hill seems to have been scraped off somewhat for building upon, and all around the outmost verge runs a massive wall, which has here and there suffered a breach by powder and ball, or, which is more powerful because more persistent, by the tooth of time. The whole wall still preserves the holes where the soldiers used to shoot through. The perforations are smooth and round, and the views through them are charming. The old tower still stands in solitary glory, and from its base—its top is dismantled—the view on either side, up and down the valley, is beautiful in the extreme. The whole valley where Guelph and Ghibelline first raised their party watch-word is spread out before you as a picture. Off to the right, just around an intervening hill laden with ripe grapes, was charming, historical Heilbronn. On the Weibertreue there was much shrubbery, and a few gnarled, venerable trees grew out from the very foundations of the old walls. In a little stone *jalousie* I saw, written in black paint, in one corner, some words in verse by Kerner, in his own hand, of which the following is the import : " My wife never bore me on her shoulders, but has *borne with* me ; and that has been a heavier burden than my tongue has power to express."

We lingered a long time about the old ruins, first climbing on the wall, then swinging in boyish glee from the trees, then gathering a few mementos from the spot for some lady friends far away. We went down the hill rapidly, and only halted before the quaint town church. To pass it by without a visit would have been to do an injustice to its history, and especially to the memory of one of its pastors, the great Oetinger, who, with all his tinge of mysticism, was one of the noblest men and devoutest Christians of Germany in the eighteenth century. He and Bengel were the two great theological lights of South Germany in their time. The side of the church is ornamented with some curious sepulchral sculptures. The faces of some of the statues are very expressive, but all of them quite odd-looking and stiff. The church itself is very plain. The only thing worth noticing is a curious picture painted by Keller, the Alsacian, in 1650, in which an old document in the town archives faithfully followed. It represents the women of Weinsberg carrying off their husbands and lovers in triumph. Some have the men on their shoulders, others have them hanging to their backs, and still others are dragging them by the heels. Above the picture is the following citation from Proverbs : " The heart of her husband doth safely trust in her, so that he shall have no need of spoil."

Weinsberg and its memorable castle have passed through many fearful ordeals since Guelph and Ghibelline fought around it. In 1237 the emperor, Conrad IV., granted the town all the rights of a free imperial city. In the Peasants' War both the town and the castle were delivered, through treachery, to the peasants. The captors showed no mercy ; they killed many of the citizens in cold blood, and hurled some, as Dietrich von Weiler, from the church-tower. The houses of the rich were sacked, and the gold and silver plate became cheap in new hands. By and by came the Thirty Years' War, when poor Weinsberg and its devoted castle suffered by famine, pestilence, and the whole train of horrors that Mars never fails to leave behind him. Weinsberg, it should be remembered, gave to the Reformation one of its stanchest friends and defenders, Œcolampadius, who, besides doing all he could for the good cause of Germany, was the first to preach the doctrines of Protestantism in Basle, Switzerland, now one of the most thoroughly Protestant cities on the Continent.

We spent the remainder of the day at Weinsberg, among the happy gleaners in the vineyard across the valley. Their hospitality knew no bounds. When we had eaten all the grapes we wished, they spread us a rustic table, with the branches and trunks of old trees for our seats. The meal was interrupted by the young men firing the vintage guns around the crowd of laughing and singing gleaners.

INDEX.